WHEN ONLY MEMORIES REMAIN

ALISTAIR DUNLOP

1

Wilma had been standing staring out of the window for 10 minutes, her irritation increasing with each passing minute. If Sandy did not arrive soon they would be late for the meeting of the Young Farmers' Club. He would then probably decide that he should drive because he would get there quicker than she could.

The house was one of several substantial Victorian villas in the crescent. The villas had been built by some of the wealthy merchants from the nearby town of Dalcairn. They had regarded Burnbrae as a pleasant place to live, away from the hustle and bustle, the dirt and the grime of their places of work. Wilma's home was almost in the middle of the crescent and from the bay window in the lounge she could see to where one end of the crescent joined the main road. Still there was no sign of Sandy.

Wilma was home from university for the Easter break. The previous summer, before her studies began, she had sat and passed her driving test. Since then she had had little time to do any actual driving. Tonight Sandy had decided that she should be the driver. On the return journey she would be able to get in some night-time driving and, of course, he could enjoy a pint or two at the meeting. Wilma knew the road well but mostly as a passenger in her dad's car or on the school bus. Being behind the wheel was still something of a novelty, and a bit daunting, especially in Sandy's car with him sitting beside her.

Fortunately, before this train of thought made her lose her nerve completely, she saw Sandy's car approach. She hurried out into the hallway.

'I'm off,' she called to her mum and dad. She was almost out the front door before she heard her mum's reply, 'Be careful' and her dad's, 'Hope your meeting is more interesting than mine will be.'

Sandy was already out of the car when she closed the garden gate behind her.

'Sorry I'm a bit late. Bit of a problem with that calving this afternoon.' He gave Wilma a quick peck on the cheek as he handed her the car keys. 'Never mind, still plenty of time, if you put your foot down. By the way, we have some passengers.'

Wilma had already noticed the youngsters in the back seat and was about to ask what was going on. She recognised Sandy's sister Kirsty and her friend Sally. She had no idea who the boy was.

'They have a dance at the school tonight. End of term and all that. Sally asked Kirsty if we could give Brian a lift. He lives across the road from her.'

So, now I have to drop them off at the school before we go to the hotel for our meeting. We'll never get there in time, Wilma thought.

'Better get going then,' she said, keeping her thoughts to herself but making it clear to Sandy, by her look and the tone of her voice, that she was not amused.

As she got into the car she smiled to the backseat passengers. 'Hi, how are you?'

There were two replies of 'fine' from the girls and a mumbled 'OK' from the boy. Still no one introduced him to her.

Once she was settled in the driving seat, Wilma adjusted the rear-view mirror, took a deep breath, composed herself and turned the key in the ignition. The Ford Cortina responded immediately. The car was three years old, a 1972 model, and despite being kept on a farm, still in remarkably good condition inside and out. Wilma checked her mirrors, pulled out from the kerb and drove off.

As she passed the manse, one of the other Victorian villas in the crescent, the minister, the Rev. Paul Johnson, was stepping out from his garden. He waved as the car passed him and Sandy and Wilma waved back. The minister was off to a church meeting, the same meeting that Mr Watson, Wilma's dad, was attending. He was the local bank manager and also the church treasurer.

Wilma was cautious as she drove through the town. Once out in the country the road was almost free of traffic and her confidence began to return. Judging by the grunts and sighs coming from Sandy, she was clearly not driving as quickly as he would like, but so far he had made no comment. Her speed on the straight stretches was increasing, gradually creeping up towards the national speed limit. As they rounded a bend Sandy commented, 'You know the sharp bends where this is fast enough, but ones like this aren't sharp. Forty is a bit too careful.'

'It's all right for you. You've been driving for years. I'll take my time. And the chatter from the back seat isn't helping either.' Wilma's eyes never left the road as she spoke. Her grip on the wheel tightened.

The passengers in the back were paying no attention to what Sandy and Wilma were saying. Their chatter grew even louder.

Sandy gave a half-hearted apology. 'You're the driver. Sorry. I'll sit back and enjoy the ride. And you lot in the back, behave yourselves.'

The young ones were quieter for a bit, but gradually the noise level rose again. Wilma tried not to be distracted. It wasn't easy and Sandy constantly looking at his watch was not helping. She reduced her speed as she approached another bend. Sandy sighed. As she came out of the bend and straightened up, she turned and glanced in his direction.

'Look, I don't have your experience. And I wasn't the one who was late.' She looked back at the road. It was straight and empty of traffic. She turned her head slightly again and added, 'If you want to drive, just say so, or shut up.'

She turned to look at the road ahead. There was a movement in the verge to her left. She was accelerating as the rabbit hopped out into the road in front of her. Her reaction was automatic. She pulled the wheel hard to the left and, at the same time, pushed her right foot hard down on the pedal. The rabbit continued safely on its way.

The car lurched to the left, mounted the verge and crashed through the hedge, gaining speed as it went. The ground sloped gently downwards. The youngsters screamed. Sandy shouted at her to brake. Wilma was unable to do anything, and her foot was still pressed down on the pedal, the accelerator pedal. The ground in front of the car became steeper.

The car gained momentum. Now there were boulders ahead. The

car smashed into one of them.

Paul's route to the church took him onto the main road, where he turned right. A short walk brought him to the other end of the crescent. As so often happened, he met Mr Watson coming out from his end of the crescent. They exchanged a friendly greeting. They had agreed years ago not to discuss anything to do with the business of the meeting as they walked along to the church, a further 10 minutes away. That had been attended to after the church service the previous Sunday.

'I gave Wilma a wave as she drove past the manse. Not often Sandy lets her drive,' Paul commented.

'No, but this time he said she needed more experience. I think the real reason was that he will probably have a few pints before the night is out.'

'I suppose he will,' agreed Paul. 'It's Young Farmers tonight, isn't it? They need to relax from time to time.'

The two men walked on, comparing their jobs to that of farmers and others.

'They say the grass is always greener on the other side of the fence,' Paul concluded as they approached the church, 'but I think I will continue with the job I have. I really enjoy it, most of the time.'

'And so do I. I know being a bank manager doesn't seem like fun to most folk, but I like it, most of the time,' agreed his companion.

By half past seven, the time for the meeting to begin, everyone was present. The congregation was a long-established one and the business of the church, both spiritual and secular, was in the hands of the Kirk Session, an all-male group. Paul was officially the teaching elder, the others the ruling elders. The decision to appoint female elders had been made recently by the General Assembly of the Church of Scotland, but so far none had been appointed in the parish of Burnbrae.

Paul had made it very clear to all from the start of his ministry

6

in Burnbrae that the advertised time of services, and of any other meetings, was the time they would begin. Very quickly the members of the congregation realised that he meant what he said.

Much of the business of tonight's meeting was routine and moved along swiftly until the property convenor gave his report. For years there had been a problem with rainwater finding its way into the old church building. It seemed that as soon as one problem was dealt with the water found another way in and further repairs were needed. The problem was not so much what to do, but how to find the money required to carry out a thorough repair of the whole roof. Various suggestions had been made but no idea had gained overall support.

Paul had listened to the various options, not sure himself what was the best way forward. Mr Watson had advised the meeting that there was some money available, but it fell far short of the sum being talked about. Several ideas had been put forward to raise more money. One would simply not work, the others had merit, but whatever was decided by the Kirk Session, it would have to be put to the members of the congregation for their approval and support.

Paul could see another meeting looming, preconceived ideas being promoted by some and other members' suggestions dismissed out of hand: not a happy thought. He decided that any further discussion at this meeting would get them no nearer to a solution. There were a few non-contentious items yet to be addressed. It was time to move on. He stood up.

'Gentlemen, I think we have taken this as far as we can tonight. I suggest that we leave it there, think about what has been said and agree to make a final decision at our next meeting. With a bit of luck, it might not rain before then.'

His last remark caused some laughter and lightened the mood. He was about to introduce the next item on the agenda when the door at the back of the hall opened. The local police sergeant took one step into the room, stopped and beckoned to him.

'Excuse me, gentlemen,' Paul said as he made his way to where the police officer was waiting.

There was some scraping of chairs on the wooden floor as the elders turned to see who had interrupted the meeting. Paul and Sergeant Anderson left the room, closing the door behind them. Even then Paul could hear the scraping of chairs and raised voices from the other side of the door. Whatever had happened, everyone would expect him to tell them what was so important that the police had to interrupt the meeting.

'I'm sorry, Minister, but I had no option,' Sergeant Anderson explained, his voice, pale face and furrowed brow showing that he had come on serious business. 'There has been an accident. A bad one, I'm afraid.'

Paul's mind was working overtime as he heard these words. Had something happened at the manse, or to one of their children?

'Sandy Meikle's car has gone off the main road to Dalcairn. There are serious casualties and possibly fatalities. How many or how bad the injuries, I don't know. And we don't yet know the identity of all those in the car either.'

'The car passed me as I was leaving the manse. I waved to them. Sandy was in the passenger seat. Wilma Watson was driving. I didn't really see who was in the back,' Paul replied. He felt the colour drain from his face.

Sergeant Anderson put his hand on Paul's arm before speaking. 'Right. Thanks. I had assumed that Sandy would be driving. The situation at the moment is that Constable MacDonald and I went straight to the Meikles' farm to break the news to them. Only Mrs Meikle was at home. I understand her husband is here at the meeting.'

'Yes, I'll ask Bob to come out.'

'Not yet, let me explain. I don't have all the details. Dalcairn are dealing with the matter. It could be that all the young folk have been killed.'

'Oh no!' Paul gasped.

'It's not confirmed, but it's very, very bad. We haven't said anything to Mrs Meikle, only that there has been an accident. Constable MacDonald is with her. I came to ask Mr Meikle to return to the farm.'

'I understand. I think I should also ask William, Wilma's dad, to make his way home.'

'That might be a good idea. We'll have to call on him after we've been to the farm.'

'William walked here tonight. I'll ask someone to run him home.'

'And I'll take Mr Meikle back with me. We can arrange to get his car collected for him later. Sorry to land this on you without any warning, Minister, but it's important we let the families know what has happened as soon as possible.'

'Of course. I'd be involved anyway, Sergeant. Unfortunately the others present are going to leave here knowing something has happened.'

'That can't be helped, but perhaps you could skim over the details, such as they are.'

'I understand. We'll no doubt speak later. I'll go and fetch Bob and William.'

As soon as Paul re-entered the room the talking stopped. The silence was absolute: all eyes were on him as he made his way to where Bob Meikle was sitting. He whispered to him, and then as Bob stood up, Paul approached William Watson and whispered to him. All three then left the room.

Sergeant Anderson very quickly told the two men what had happened. Paul watched them closely. Their faces were white with the shock. Neither of them said a word as they listened to the grim news.

Bob Meikle broke the silence. 'I better get back to the farm.'

'I'll give you a lift,' Sergeant Anderson replied.

'No, I think we'll need the car. We'll have to go to the hospital. We'll have to see how Sandy and Kirsty are. She was in the car too.'

Obviously the sergeant knew better than to argue. 'Fine, if you're sure. I'll follow you. Just take it easy. What about you, Mr

Watson? I could drop you off before I make my way out to the farm.'

'Thank you, Officer, but I will walk. It'll give me time to work out what I'm going to say to Mary. And if she happens to see a police car stopping outside, well, that might make matters worse. If that's possible,' William added with a sigh.

'Off you go, William,' Paul said quietly. 'Once I've closed the meeting and gathered up your papers, I'll call in to see you.'

Paul watched the three men leave the building, wondering what the news would be when he next saw them. He re-entered the room and solemnly took his place behind the table. All eyes were upon him. Again there was not a sound.

'I regret that what I have to say is not good. But first, may I remind you that this meeting is conducted in private. I know we are not very good at observing that rule unless we actually agree to keep a particular topic or decision private.'

He looked at the men sitting in front of him. 'There is no way that what I am about to tell you can be kept quiet, but please, I implore you, do not elaborate or speculate on what may or may not have happened. There has been an accident.'

Several of the elders gasped at the news. Someone asked, 'Is it serious?' Another said, 'A road accident?'

'All I can say at this point is that Sandy Meikle's car has gone off the road. Those in the car are being taken to hospital.'

'How bad are they?' one or two voices asked.

'Gentlemen, that is all I can say at this time. I propose that we close the meeting now.'

There was some tapping of feet, some quiet mutterings of 'yes' and 'agreed'. Paul offered a prayer for those involved in the accident and their families before pronouncing the Benediction.

Despite his plea, Paul knew that even on the way out of the building some of the elders were already speculating on what had happened and who was involved. He heard one voice, louder than the rest. 'Must have been really serious when the police stopped the meeting.'

It was with a heavy heart and a sense of foreboding that he gathered up his own papers and those of his treasurer before making his way back to the manse. It was going to be a long night.

2

Driving away from the church, Bob was tempted to ignore his promise to take his time. He wanted to get home as soon as possible. He needed to know what had really happened. He needed to be with Jessie.

Bob had no idea what he would say to Jessie when he saw her. What could he say? And what would the police have to tell him? He would soon find out, but he feared the worst.

He pulled into the farmyard. The police car was right behind him. He stepped out of the car and waited for Sergeant Anderson to catch up with him. The formality of the earlier meeting was forgotten. Donnie had been in Burnbrae for a number of years and Bob knew him well enough to be on first-name terms with him.

'I'm sorry, Bob,' Donnie said, with a shake of his head. 'I'm afraid it doesn't look good.'

'Can you tell me anything?'

'Not really. I mean, not in any detail. I'm still waiting for more information from Dalcairn. Let's get inside and I'll speak to you and Jessie together. And I promise, as soon as I have any more news, you'll be the first to know.'

Jessie flung the door open, rushed out and threw herself into her husband's arms. Constable MacDonald stood watching, as if unsure what to do.

'What's happened? Tell me they're all right!'

Bob held her tightly. He wanted to tell her everything would be fine, but he was afraid that it was going to be anything but.

'There now, I'm here. Let's just hear what Donnie has to say.'

Gently he led her back into the kitchen of the farmhouse, to the old sofa against the far wall. Donnie and Constable MacDonald followed. Bob pulled out a couple of dining chairs for them to sit on before joining Jessie on the sofa. He was doing his best to remain calm as he held her close. He could feel her shaking, and he saw the tears in her eyes.

'I'm sorry,' Donnie began, 'but there's no easy way to say this. Sandy's car has gone off the Dalcairn road and careered down a steep slope, finally stopping at the bottom.'

'Are Sandy and Kirsty all right?' Jessie blurted out.

'I'm afraid all those in the car have been injured, some quite badly. At present I have no more news. All the occupants are being taken to the hospital in Dalcairn.'

Jessie turned to Bob. 'We have to go. I need to see them. To know how they are.'

'I understand that, Jessie, and I don't want to hold you up,' Donnie assured her, 'but I have to ask if you can confirm who else was in the car. You mentioned Kirsty, so I assume she was one of the others.'

'Yes. And her pal Sally. And Wilma, Sandy's girlfriend. He said he was going to let her do the driving tonight,' Bob added.

'So, Wilma, Wilma Watson, she would be the driver, you think? Who's Sally, and what about the other passenger?' Donnie asked.

'Yes, Wilma Watson, and Sally MacCallum.' Bob was puzzled. 'That should be everyone. Sandy and Kirsty never mentioned anyone else.'

'We'll sort that out later. I think there's a great deal of confusion at the moment. I hoped I might have had an update by now, but there has been nothing so far. Is Sally the daughter of Tom MacCallum, the ironmonger?' Donnie asked.

'Yes, that's her.'

Donnie was shaking his head as he spoke. 'I'm sorry. I have children of my own. I feel for you, but I can't give you any real details. You have to prepare yourselves for some bad news. From what I've been told, some of the injuries sustained are serious.'

'Oh no!' sobbed Jessie. 'Please, God, they will all be all right.'

Bob held her tight. 'We have to be strong, Jessie. Maybe it will not be too bad.' He turned his head and looked straight at Donnie.

'Can we go to the hospital now?'

'Of course, and I hope that things are not as bad as we think,' Donnie replied.

'What about your mum and dad?' Jessie asked Bob. 'Should we not let them know? And Iain, he's still over at Jim's place. He'll come home to an empty house.'

'Of course, we have to let them know. I'll go over to the bungalow before we set off. We can leave a note on the table to tell Iain to go over there too when he gets back from his pal's house.'

'What will you say?'

'As little as possible,' Bob replied. 'No need to have everyone in a panic.'

'I think the less said the better at this stage,' Donnie agreed. 'I'm very sorry I can't put your minds at rest.'

'That's not your fault, Donnie. You're doing the best you can. It's not an easy job you have at the best of times, and there's no easy way to break bad news.' Bob held out his hand.

Donnie took it in both of his. 'Take care, both of you,' he said as he turned and looked kindly towards Jessie.

Bob's parents, Helen and Alec, were watching TV. Bob knew right away that they were unaware of the police visit.

'Mum, Dad,' he said, his voice quivering.

'Has something happened?' his mum asked.

'I don't know what to say,' he replied.

'It can't be that bad,' his dad said as he switched off the TV. 'Is it one of the beasts?'

'No, it's Sandy and Kirsty. And Wilma too,' he added. 'They've been in an accident. The car went off the road.'

'Are they hurt?' Helen asked.

'Yes. They are on their way to hospital. Jessie and I are going there now. We won't know how badly injured they are until we see them. Will you look after Iain till we get back? He's out, but we'll leave him a note to come over here. I'm sorry, I have to go.'

'Yes, of course. We'll see to Iain,' his mum replied before adding, 'Take care.'

Shortly afterwards the two of them set off for the hospital.

Walking home, William Watson was going over in his head how he would tell Mary what had happened and how much he would tell her. He was so focused on this and worried by how bad the injuries to Wilma, and the others, might be that he failed to notice one of the bank's customers coming in the opposite direction. Even when the man said, 'Good evening,' he made no reply.

He kept his feelings very much to himself. Some of the bank's customers were convinced that he was hard-hearted, cold, unfeeling and lacking any vestige of compassion. These were the customers who had been refused an overdraft, an increase in their existing overdraft or extra time to make a repayment. Even some of the customers who had no problem with their account still found him rather stand-offish, but he knew every customer and never failed to acknowledge them when they met outside the bank.

There were very few in the village who knew that in his younger days he had been a very good footballer at amateur level. He was naturally left-handed and had made a name for himself as a speedy and dangerous left-winger. That was in another place at another time. Now he was their bank manager, and one not to be messed with, strict but fair.

William opened the front door to his home, stepped inside and made his way to the sitting room. The television was on. Mary was so engrossed in her programme that she was only aware of his presence when he said, 'I'm back,' and leaned over to give her a peck on the cheek. What he really wanted to do was pull her off her chair and hold her tight. He was not without feeling as some of his customers thought; that was work. At home, and with his close friends, he was quite the opposite, and whatever decision he made at work, it was always with the customer's best interests in mind.

'You're back early. Everything go well?' Mary asked, her eyes still fixed on the screen as the drama unfolded before her eyes.

'Oh Mary, I don't know how to tell you this, but Wilma has been in an accident. She may be badly hurt.'

Mary turned to face him. He could feel the tears running down his cheeks. He sat down in his chair and put his head in his hands.

We have to go to the hospital. We have to find out how she is. To see her, to support her,' Mary said after a long silence. They were now sitting together on the small sofa. William's arm was round her shoulder.

'Of course, but Sergeant Anderson said he would call in and give us more information.'

'How long will he be?' Mary asked. 'He could be ages up there. We have to go now.'

'I'm sure Sergeant Anderson will be with us just as soon as he can. He's a good man and does a good job by all accounts. And there were others in the car, not just Wilma and Sandy.'

'Who?'

Before William could answer, the doorbell rang. It was Sergeant Anderson and Constable MacDonald.

'Come in, Officers,' William said, holding the door open. 'Have you any more news?'

'I'm afraid not,' Sergeant Anderson answered.

William ushered them into the sitting room.

'Good evening, Mrs Watson,' Sergeant Anderson said. Constable MacDonald nodded.

Mary looked at the two men. 'How is she? Tell me she is OK.'

William saw the fear in Mary's face. Very quickly Sergeant

Anderson explained the situation. William knew that despite his calm, professional tone, Mary was not reassured.

'We have to go to the hospital, William. We can't just sit here. I have to see her. To hold her.'

'I know. Being here isn't helping anyone, least of all Wilma. We need to be with her.'

Sergeant Anderson's radio beeped.

'Excuse me. I'll take this outside,' he said as he left the room.

There was absolute silence at first. William stood beside Mary, who was sitting motionless, her head in her hands. William had regained his composure to some extent. He put a hand on her shoulder to reassure her. Mary began to sob quietly. He and the constable exchanged a look. William realised that the young man did not know what to say, how to help or comfort them.

'I hope it's good news,' the constable muttered.

William nodded.

Footsteps sounded in the hall. The serious look on the sergeant's face as he re-entered the room said it all.

'It's serious, very serious, I'm afraid. Do you happen to know what Wilma was wearing?'

Mary looked at him. 'Why do you need to know that? Is she unable to speak, to give her name? She can't be.' Mary lost control and let out a terrible scream.

William had sat down beside Mary and was holding her tightly as she spoke. 'She was wearing denim jeans, a white top, blue jumper and I think she would have a jacket on. Not sure what colour.'

'That's OK. I'll pass the information on.' He left the room again.

'Try not to think the worst, Mary,' William said in a whisper.

Sergeant Anderson was back in the room in minutes.

'Mr Watson, could I have a word, please?'

William stood up.

'Don't leave me. I want to hear what he has to say,' Mary pleaded.

William sat back down.

Sergeant Anderson looked straight at them both and in a very quiet, formal voice he said, 'Wilma was dead on arrival at the hospital. The ambulancemen did their best, but to no avail. I'm very sorry.'

3

Alan Maxwell, the Session Clerk, had given Paul a lift back to the manse after the sudden end to the meeting. Paul had thought it best not to stop off at the Watsons' house with William's papers. He would deliver them later. First he would go out to the farm and find out if the Meikles had heard anything more about the accident and the condition of the casualties.

'You take care of yourself,' Alan advised as Paul got out of the car. 'It might be a long night. And you have the Easter services to think about.'

'I will. I'm still hoping and praying that I will discover that things are not as bad as all that.'

'Let's hope so. If I can be of any help, don't hesitate to give me a call.'

'Thanks, I will.'

With that Paul closed the car door, waved to Alan and walked up to his front door. Ruth was surprised by his unexpected return. Paul explained what had happened and how serious it might be. He made no attempt to hide his worst fears. Ruth's only comment when he finished was, 'Oh no! How awful!'

She had switched off the TV while he was speaking. Now she rose from her chair, took the two steps that separated them and put her arms around him. Paul responded by hugging her. He relaxed his hold a little and looked into Ruth's eyes. 'I'll have to go out. Will you be OK?'

'I can't say I'll be OK, but don't worry about me. You have to do what you think best. Will you go to the hospital?'

'No, not at first anyway. I also promised Bob that I would go over to Fauldshead and see how they were. After that I better look in on the Watsons. If I am going on to the hospital I'll come home first and let you know what's what.'

'Just drive carefully.' She kissed him. 'Give my love to the families.'

As Paul drove into the yard at the farm he realised he was too late. Bob always parked his car in the yard. It wasn't there. He tried the back door, the one that family and friends always used. It was unlocked. He shouted a 'Hello, anyone in?' but got no reply. He made his way over to the bungalow.

Alec, Bob's father, answered the door. As soon as he saw Paul he blurted out, 'Have you more news? Are they all right?'

'No. I mean, I don't know. I came here to ask if Bob had more news, but there's no one in at the farmhouse.'

'No, they've gone to the hospital.'

'Who is it, Alec?' Helen, his wife, called out as she made her way to the door.

'It's the minister.'

'For goodness' sake, Alec, ask him in. Don't keep him standing on the doorstep.'

'Sorry, Minister. I wasn't thinking. We're just so anxious about the young ones. Come in.'

Paul declined the offer of a cup of tea from Helen.

'Maybe you would prefer something a bit stronger,' Alec suggested.

'No, not tonight,' Paul replied, and before he could say anything further, Helen added. 'We need to keep a clear head. At least until we hear from Bob, and that applies to you too, Alec.'

'A very good idea,' agreed Paul. 'I want to call in on the Watsons before I get back to the manse. The police said there were several passengers in the car. Do you happen to know who they were? I would also like to visit their parents.'

'Kirsty was in the car,' Helen said as she burst into tears.

Paul wished he had not been quite so blunt with his question. What more was there to learn?

Helen wiped at her eyes with her hand and took a deep breath. 'Sally MacCallum, Tom's daughter. She and Kirsty are great friends.'

'Please God they're not hurt.' Alec shook his head. 'Terrible, just terrible,' he muttered.

Helen appeared deep in thought. Paul could see the dread in her eyes.

After what Sergeant Anderson had said earlier, Paul knew that he dared not give the older couple false hope. Instead he said, 'Perhaps Bob will be in touch soon. He must be near the hospital by now.'

'Aye, I suppose so,' Alec agreed. 'He said he would drive carefully, but he was anxious to get there as soon as he could. Maybe you could wait till he calls.'

'I would, but the Watsons know I'm coming. I don't want to keep them hanging on too long.'

'No, of course not, we mustn't be selfish. It was good of you to call. Next time we see you things might be much better.'

Paul managed to leave the bungalow soon afterwards, hoping that he had not given the impression that all would be well. He had a feeling that he might yet end up visiting the hospital.

As soon as William opened the door, Paul could tell by the look on his face that there had been more news, and that it had not been good.

'Come in,' was all William said, and led the way to the sitting room. Mary was sitting on the sofa. She looked towards Paul as he entered the room. He saw the utter despair in her eyes. Paul went forward to shake her hand, but her hands remained clasped in her lap. Her head had gone down. When still neither of them spoke, he was forced to say something. He turned to William. 'Has someone been in touch?'

'Yes, Sergeant Anderson was here. He got a call from someone at Dalcairn. He asked us what Wilma was wearing. She's dead,

Paul.'

Paul's instinct was to put his arms around the poor man, but he didn't feel that he could. William was not that kind of a man.

'I'm sorry, so sorry,' he said. 'Is there anything I can do?'

Mary looked up. 'What can anyone do? We've lost our daughter. She's gone. No one can help us now.'

'Mary,' her husband said softly, 'Paul is only trying to help.'

'It's all right, William. I understand.'

'Do you?' Mary's despair had suddenly turned to anger. 'How could you possibly understand?'

William moved over to where Mary was sitting. He placed his hands on hers. 'Please, Mary, Paul is here as a friend. It's not his fault. He wants to help and we'll need his help.'

Mary looked up, her anger cooling somewhat after her outburst. 'I'm sorry,' she mumbled.

'Mary, I don't understand how you feel, of course I don't,' Paul replied. 'I just can't take in what has happened, but I promise that I am here for you. Whatever you need, whenever you need it, I will be here.'

'Thanks, Paul.' William said. 'Have you seen the Meikles?'

'I called at the farm as promised, but Bob and Jessie had already left for the hospital. Bob's parents are very worried, but they have had no more news.'

Paul was relieved that he had not known of Wilma's death before visiting the farm. It might have been possible to keep the news to himself, but Alec and Helen weren't stupid. They would probably have guessed that he wasn't telling them everything he knew.

'Would you promise me one thing, Paul?' William asked. 'If you hear anything, no matter what, will you let me know?'

'Of course I will.' Paul dreaded to think what the news would be and how William and Mary would cope if anyone else had been killed.

He sat with the desolate couple. There was very little said. Paul was remembering the very wise words of an older colleague. 'Sitting quietly, saying nothing, is better than uttering meaningless words. Simply being there is what matters. The time for talking will come later.'

Eventually he took his leave. On the doorstep, William shook hands with him. He put into words what he and Paul, and no doubt Mary had been thinking. 'Wilma was driving. What on earth happened? What has she done?'

This time Paul did put an arm around his neighbour's shoulder. 'We'll find out in due course. Until then, the only thing you can do is look after one another. I'll be back tomorrow.'

Paul soon covered the short distance to the MacCallums' home. They lived in a large flat above the shop in the centre of the town. He was able to park outside the shop as the parking restrictions didn't apply in the evening. He made his way to the door of the house with a sense of foreboding, certain that after what he had already discovered, there could only be more bad news. He tried to convince himself that he had already heard the worst as he rang the doorbell.

4

Bob and Jessie arrived at the hospital, parked the car as near to the entrance of the A & E unit as they could and hurried up to the reception desk.

'Can I help you?' asked the nurse behind the desk.

'Our son and daughter are here. They were in a car accident. Can we see them?' Bob blurted out.

The welcoming smile disappeared from the nurse's face. 'Can I have your son and daughter's names?'

'Sandy and Kirsty Meikle.'

'Thank you.' The nurse looked briefly at the book on his desk. He picked up the phone.

'Hello, I have a Mr and Mrs Meikle at reception. Their son and daughter were involved in the car accident.' There was a short silence before the nurse said, 'Thank you,' and ended the call. He rose from his seat. 'Would you come this way, please,' he said.

He led Bob and Jessie along a corridor and ushered them into a small room. 'Please take a seat. Someone will be with you as soon as possible. Would you like tea or coffee?'

Bob and Jessie declined the offer. 'We just want to find out how Sandy and Kirsty are,' Bob said.

'Someone is on his way now. He will be able to answer your questions.' He closed the door quietly behind him.

Bob found himself wondering why the nurse had said 'someone'. Surely it would be a doctor, or another nurse? The signs were not good. He did his best to hide his thoughts from Jessie as they sat holding hands.

Very soon the door opened. It was not a medical person. It was a police sergeant.

'Mr and Mrs Meikle? I'm Sergeant Campbell.'

Bob and Jessie had stood up when he entered the room. They shook hands with the officer.

'Please be seated.' They sat down again. Sergeant Campbell remained standing.

'I'm afraid your son and daughter have been involved in a very serious accident. I understand from the information Sergeant Anderson obtained that it wasn't your son driving, although it was his vehicle. It was a Miss Wilma Watson.'

'Yes,' Bob replied. 'It was.'

'And your daughter and her friend were also in the car?'

'Yes. Kirsty and Sally,' Bob confirmed.

'Could you tell me what Kirsty was wearing?'

Bob's worst fears were being confirmed. They must be so badly injured that they could not answer questions. He tried to push the other possibility away.

Through her tears, Jessie managed to give the officer the information he had requested.

'Thank you. I know it's not easy. I'll pass that on to the doctor. He'll be with you shortly.'

When they were alone, Jessie and Bob turned to each other.

'Oh, Bob, what do you think has really happened? Are they going to be all right? Will we be able to see them?'

'Jessie, I am as much in the dark as you are. I want to reassure you, but I can't. We'll have to wait till the doctor comes.'

'But–' Jessie began.

'I don't know any more than you,' Bob said. He pulled her towards him, hoping she wouldn't see the tears beginning to trickle down his cheeks. He needed to be strong, but it wasn't possible. He was as afraid as Jessie.

After what seemed an eternity, but in reality was no more than seven or eight minutes, the door opened again. It was a doctor.

'Good evening, I'm Dr Millar.' He shook hands with Jessie and Bob. All three sat down, Dr Millar facing Jessie and Bob.

'There's no easy way to say this,' Dr Millar began. 'It was a very bad accident. Somehow or other your son was thrown clear, but he has sustained serious head injuries. We're arranging for him to be transferred to Glasgow.'

'Oh no!' Jessie sobbed. 'Will he be all right?'

'At this stage I can't make any promises. We're doing our best and he'll be in very good hands at the Southern General Hospital.'

'And what about Kirsty?' Bob asked. 'Is she badly injured?'

The doctor looked at Bob, then at Jessie. His face said it all. Even before he spoke they knew what he was going to say.

'I'm so sorry. Your daughter had severe internal injuries. There was nothing we could do.'

Jessie wept uncontrollably. Bob held her tight, his heart breaking too.

Dr Millar sat and watched them as they tried to take in the grim news.

Bob relaxed his hold on Jessie. Slowly he turned his head towards the doctor. 'Can we see her?'

Dr Millar shook his head slightly. 'I'm afraid not. Not tonight. Tomorrow you will be asked to make a formal identification. I'm sorry, I had assumed the police would have already explained the situation.'

Bob sensed that what the doctor was saying was only part of the truth. He wondered if his dear, beautiful daughter had been badly maimed in the accident.

'I understand. We'll be back tomorrow.' He turned to Jessie. 'Come on, dear, we better go home. There's no more we can do here tonight. I'll phone the Southern and find out about Sandy as soon as we get home.'

'I'm afraid his head injuries appear to be very serious. How serious we will probably not know for certain for several days. But he is in the best place,' the doctor emphasised again as he bade them goodbye.

If his words were meant to bring some kind of comfort to them, they failed miserably.

Standing outside the entrance to the MacCallums' home, Paul heard footsteps from inside as someone hurried down the stairs in response to his knocking. The door was opened by Tom, Sally's father.

'Come in, Minister, good of you to call.' His voice was a whisper. He held out his hand and they shook hands.

The MacCallums were members of the congregation but not by any means the most regular attenders at Sunday worship. Mrs MacCallum was usually present at Christmas and Easter and attended a service every so often in between. Her husband seldom accompanied her, and the children too had more or less opted out. Paul's dealings with Tom were usually conducted over the counter of the shop, and as Paul was not the greatest DIY person in the world, his visits to the shop were not at all frequent.

'We can't take it in, Minister. You always think things like this happen to other people. Now it has happened to us, I don't know how we will manage.'

Tom kept hold of Paul's hand as he spoke. Paul's mind was racing. Was the distraught man talking about serious injuries or had Sally also been killed?

'Come up to the house,' Tom said. 'Nan and Gary are there. Maybe you can help us, say something that will comfort us, but I doubt it. No one can.' He shook his head. 'Not Sally, she didn't deserve this.' He broke down, great rasping sobs.

Paul held him until the sobbing stopped. Gary had appeared at the top of the stairs, seen his distressed father and promptly hurried back to wherever he had come from.

'How bad is she?' Paul asked, although he was now certain he knew.

'She's dead. Our lovely daughter is dead.'

The sobbing began again. Paul did his best to support the desolate father until he regained some measure of control.

When he had, Paul spoke softly. 'Let's go upstairs and join the others,'

Tom looked at him, the pain he was feeling written all over his face. 'I'm sorry, I need to be strong, but I don't know if I can.'

'You will be, you'll manage, but you also have to let it out.'

'Aye, you're right. I feel a bit better now. Thanks.'

He led Paul up the stairs, along a wide hallway and into a large lounge. Nan MacCallum was sitting in an armchair, her eyes red from crying. She was clutching a handkerchief. Gary was sitting near her. He turned as his dad and Paul entered the room. It was clear that he was trying very hard not to show any emotion, to be strong. Paul thought he understood, but Gary too would need to find a way to express his feelings.

Paul offered his sympathy to the grieving parents and to Gary. Loving words were said about Sally but at each remembrance of some aspect of their much-loved daughter, clearly Tom or Nan, and often both, found it difficult to say what they really felt. The words stuck in their throats and they were constantly wiping the tears away. Soon there was silence, the parents deep in thought. Gary looked as if he did not know what to say.

Later Paul and Tom talked quietly about the little they knew of the accident. The only fact they knew was that the car had left the road. Why it had done so was still a mystery. Whatever the reason, they knew Sally, Kirsty and Wilma had died, that Sandy was seriously injured and the boy in the car was also badly hurt. No one had any idea who he was.

'I wonder if it was young Brian Thomson from across the road,' Tom suggested. 'I sometimes saw Sally talking to him when they got off the school bus. Do you think it could be him, Gary?'

'I don't know,' Gary mumbled. 'No one said anything to me.'

'Were Sally and Brian friends?' Paul asked.

'No. Well, not special friends. At least I don't think so,' Tom replied. 'Sally never said anything to me that suggested they were anything more than classmates and neighbours.'

'Brian's mum doesn't have a car,' Gary muttered. 'Sally probably offered him a lift. You know what she's like, always helping someone.' He paused. 'What she was like.'

The dam burst and Gary left the room in a flood of tears. His mum got up and went to console him.

'He was trying to be brave,' Tom said to Paul, 'but that will help him. What happened to me downstairs has helped me.'

'I know,' Paul said, seeing that Tom was close to tears again as he spoke, 'and it will happen many times in the days ahead. I just hope I can be of some use to you and to all those who like you are devastated by what has happened.'

'You are already, and although I don't know you very well, from what I hear in the shop, I'm sure we'll all be glad that you're our minister.'

'I'll do my best,' was all Paul could say in response.

'Do you think I should go over and ask Brian's mother if he was the other person in the car?' Tom asked Paul shortly afterwards.

'I was wondering if I should do it. I don't know her personally, though I've probably seen her around.'

'Maybe not,' Tom said. 'She works in one of the factories in Dalcairn and most of the time she keeps herself to herself. I think she and her husband are separated. Poor woman, if it is her son who was in the car.' He paused for a moment then added, 'If it wasn't Brian, then who *was* the other passenger?'

Paul considered his words before replying. 'You know, I think we should leave it to the police.'

'Aye, you're right. Brian might have got a lift from someone else. Best let the police sort it out. Maybe we can help her later, if it is her Brian.'

Nan entered the room before Paul could reply. He was amazed

that Tom could even think of offering someone else help in the midst of his own tragedy.

'How is he?' Tom asked.

'He's not bad. I think he was embarrassed, especially with the minister here.'

'Tell him not to worry about me. I may manage to hide my feelings when I'm working, but that doesn't mean I don't cry,' Paul replied.

Soon after, he took his leave of the distressed couple, making it very clear that he was always available should they need him, no matter what time of the day or night. As he stepped out onto the pavement, he looked up at the windows in the flats opposite, wondering which one was Brian's, asking himself if there was a mother waiting to hear the door opening and the sound of her son returning from the school dance. Poor woman, he thought, and if not her, then some other mother somewhere in the parish.

Paul was tired and physically and emotionally drained when he returned to the manse. As he entered the family room, Ruth rose to welcome him. 'How are you? You look shattered.'

Paul gave her a kiss, holding the embrace for longer than usual before he stepped back.

'I think you already know the answer.' He shook his head as he sighed, but said nothing.

'Was it that bad?'

'Worse than that.'

While he spoke, Ruth sat motionless.

'Are you going to cope?' Ruth asked when finally he stopped speaking. 'How can you help each family, and at the same time? That's impossible. And you need to look after yourself, or you will be no use to anyone.'

'I have to. Some of these people are good friends, and I'm the parish minister. It's my duty to care for them, all of them.'

'I know, but are you forgetting it's Easter? You have a service on Friday, as well as Sunday.'

'Yes, but Easter is easier. I don't have to be clever. It's all there in Scripture. In fact, I could probably get away with simply reading the gospel accounts and leaving it at that.'

'Well, maybe, but I know you. You will manage to say something, you always do. And you have a wedding on Saturday, don't forget that.'

'I know, and I am remembering. Some mistakes can be forgiven, but not forgetting a wedding.' He was going to add, 'Or a funeral,' but managed to stop himself, just in time.

5

After a night of tossing and turning and very little sleep, Paul and Ruth eventually decided that it would be better to get up. Breakfast was a slice of toast and a mug of tea.

'What do I do?' Paul asked Ruth as he drained his mug.

'What do you mean?'

'I have an Easter service at the primary school. Do I make some calls before I go to the school, or do I wait till after the service?'

'You have to do what you think is best. Do you have to be at the school?'

'Of course I do, I'm the chaplain.'

'The teachers are quite capable of conducting the assembly if you feel you have to visit the parents again. You have nearly two hours to think about it before the school opens. By then you may have more news. And it's far too early to be thinking about house calls.'

Paul decided to stay where he was. Rushing here, there and everywhere, not sure what he was doing, was unlikely to help anyone.

The Meikle family were also up early, but they always were. Life on the farm was a round–the-clock business, especially in the spring. Iain helped Bob with the normal chores that morning: feeding the cattle, checking the lambing shed and generally making sure that all was well.

'Will you be OK staying here and helping Granddad?' Bob asked Iain as they returned to the house.

'Yes, I would much rather be here than at school today.'

Bob put an arm round his son's shoulder. 'It's going to be a hard day for all of us,' he managed to say. He turned his head away as he felt his eyes fill.

He had phoned the hospital as soon as he was awake, only to be informed that there was no change in Sandy's condition. He was still in a coma, and likely to remain that way for some time. Bob satisfied himself that he had done all he needed to do on the farm, and that his dad and Iain would cope until he got back.

'What do we do first?' he asked Jessie as they sat at the kitchen table. 'Do we go to Dalcairn or Glasgow?'

'I don't know,' Jessie replied with a shake of her head. 'I want to see Sandy as soon as possible, but I can't get the thought of Kirsty lying in a cold mortuary out of my head. I think I want to go to her first. Sandy is in the best place. He's being looked after.'

'I was thinking the same, so that's what we'll do.'

'But will you be all right to drive after seeing Kirsty?' Jessie's eyes brimmed with tears.

'We have no choice. We have to say goodbye to Kirsty, and we have to visit Sandy. I wish yesterday had never happened, but it has. We'll manage. I'm not sure how, but we will.' Bob gulped down the rest of his tea. 'I'll phone the police at Dalcairn and make the arrangements. Sitting here talking isn't helping. We have to get this done.'

William and Mary, after a sleepless night, were having breakfast. They had said all they had to say during the night. Silently they supped the porridge Mary had insisted on making. William had refused to have his usual bacon and eggs and only just managed to eat a slice of toast after forcing himself to swallow the porridge. Mary made do with a cup of tea after her bowl of porridge.

William looked at his watch. 'As soon as the bank opens I'll call my area manager and explain what has happened, but first I'd better let Kevin know I won't be in today.'

He made the call. There was no easy way to say what he had to say. 'Kevin, it's William here. I'm afraid I will not be in today. Wilma died last night. In an accident.'

There was silence on the line. 'I, I'm sorry,' Kevin finally blurted out. 'I don't know what to say.'

'You don't have to say anything, Kevin. Just make sure that the rest of the staff know I can't be in today for personal reasons, a family bereavement, and leave it at that. Make sure the bank runs as normal as far as the customers are concerned. And if any of them ask questions, just say the same to them.'

'I will make sure everything is as it should be. I still can't believe it. Take care.'

'Thanks, Kevin, I will. Oh, and tell any customer who was hoping to see me the same thing. No doubt there will be all sorts of stories going around, but I have every confidence in you. It will not be an easy day for you. You will manage.'

'Thanks, I will do my best. And we will all be thinking of you and Mrs Watson,' Kevin added.

Tom MacCallum was unsure whether or not to open the shop. He too had to make the journey to Dalcairn Hospital: to identify Sally. His two shop assistants were very capable but he wondered if it was fair to ask them to work under the circumstances. As news of the accident and the death of the young people spread round the town, customers were bound to ask questions. No doubt some of the customers who entered the shop would have no intention of making a purchase, but hoping to find out as much as possible about the accident: who was involved, how it had happened, every little detail.

Tom was also very much aware that many of his regular customers would be carrying out DIY projects during the Easter holiday period and would be relying on getting tools and materials at the shop. They had been loyal to him over the years and he had a corresponding loyalty to them. Most of them would understand if he kept the shop closed, but he felt he had a duty to remain open.

When the staff arrived for work he explained what had happened. Although Mairi and Sadie understood that it would be a difficult day, they both agreed that they would keep the shop open. Tom thanked them and went back up to the flat to prepare for the journey to Dalcairn. Nan had made it very clear that she wanted to remember Sally as she had been. Tom would have to go alone.

Across the road from Tom's shop, Brian's mother, Doreen, had slept soundly until the shrill trill of the alarm clock warned her that it was time to face the new day. The previous night she had intended to stay up until Brian's return from the dance, but had nodded off in front of the television. A loud burst of music from the TV had roused her. She had looked around, noticed the time and decided to go to bed, assuming that she would hear him when eventually he came home. Now, not quite fully awake, she realised that she must have been sleeping so soundly during the night that she hadn't heard anything when Brian returned.

She went to waken him. She was surprised to find his bedroom door open. Usually he shut it tight when he was in the room, a sign to her to keep out, or at least to knock and wait until he invited her to enter. She hoped he hadn't been drinking. So far she had no reason to suspect that he had been doing what so many who were not much older than him did regularly at weekends. No doubt before much longer he too would be persuaded to try. She hoped last night had not been the night. She had to go to work and he had to go to school.

'Brian,' she shouted as she approached the open door. 'It's time to get up.'

Doreen didn't expect to get a reply. Most days she had to give him a shake before there was any response. Nor did she expect to find that the bed had never been slept in.

'Surely not again,' she exclaimed to the empty room. Brian had once stayed over at a friend's house and hadn't let her know where he was until his return the next day. He had been well warned not to do that again. If he had to, and he would have to have a very good reason for even thinking about it, he was to at least give her a phone call to let her know he was safe and where he was staying. It had happened once since that warning and he had phoned, explaining that he had missed the last bus. His pal James had taken him home and James's parents had allowed him to stay the night with them.

Last night Brian was getting a lift to the school dance and, she had assumed, a lift home, although she was now not sure that he had actually told her that. Her mind was working overtime. Had he fallen out with the folk who gave him the lift? Had he been with his friends and missed his lift? Was there a girl, or alcohol, or both involved?

Doreen was both angry and worried. She was also thinking back to a time in her own life when she had been not much older than Brian was now, a time that had resulted in a sudden, dramatic change in her life. She and Ed had been careless and Doreen had become pregnant. They had married in haste and Brian had been born. For a time they had been happy despite a constant worry over money. Now she and Ed were more or less leading separate lives and Brian, while not neglected, didn't have the kind of home life Doreen had planned for him all those years ago.

She worked in the clothing factory in Dalcairn, a job that she found both tedious and tiring. In the evening she often fell asleep after doing any household chores that had to be done, and at the weekend she seemed to spend her waking hours washing, ironing and cleaning. If Ed did appear, and that was happening less and less often now, he spent much of the time out drinking. In recent months when he came off the North Sea oil rig where he worked, he stayed in Aberdeen more than he did in Dalcairn. Who he was with and what he did, Doreen had no idea, and she had now reached that stage where she didn't care.

Ed took care of the rent, sent Doreen an allowance and tended to be rather generous towards Brian. She knew that her husband loved their son as much as any father could, but she was also aware that Brian would far rather his dad spent his weeks off at Burnbrae. Doreen had a feeling that each time he did appear, the money he gave Brian a couple of days later as he said goodbye was not seen as a loving gift but an attempt to buy Brian's affection and ease his own guilty conscience.

She made her way to the kitchen. There was nothing she could do until Brian came home. No doubt by then he would have worked out a plausible reason for his non-appearance last night.

Teenagers, she said to herself with a sigh.

It would soon be time for Paul to make his way to the primary school for the short Easter service. One minute he had decided that visiting the bereaved families was more important, the next he changed his mind and decided that he should attend the service. A few minutes later and he told himself that that was merely delaying the inevitable. He had to make the visits. He had no idea what he would say, but he had to be with those who had lost so much.

He picked up the phone, began to dial the school's number, stopped and replaced the handset. Ruth had been right, the school service could go ahead without him, but he was the chaplain. It was part of his duty as parish minister to take part in that service. He was almost certain that no one at the school, staff or pupils, had any direct connection with the victims of the accident and their families, but what had they heard? There were no further details yet on the news bulletins. No names had been broadcast, but what, he wondered, was being said on the streets and in the shops. People were beginning to move about; daily life was following the normal pattern for most people. For some it would never be the same again.

As soon as Paul entered the school staffroom he realised that word of the accident was indeed spreading fast. Immediately, after the usual 'Good mornings' had been exchanged, Mrs Duthie, one of the teachers, asked Paul if he knew how the people in the car were.

Of course, Paul thought, her father is one of the senior elders. So much for not spreading the news. How many others have been on the phone? he wondered.

'I was at Mum's last night when Dad came home early from the meeting,' she explained.

Paul realised he was being unfair to her father. 'I really can't say,' he replied. 'I know it's bad, but how bad I'm still waiting to hear.' There was no way he could tell her what he knew. This was neither the time nor the place, and it was certainly not for the minister to go around telling all and sundry what had happened.

It was agreed that a general word of prayer for the sick and the anxious would be all that was said during the service. Paul would have done that as routine in any case, so only those who knew of the accident would be thinking of the families concerned.

After the service Paul politely declined the offer of coffee and a hot cross bun. He made his way back to the manse, fully expecting that there would be further news about the accident, particularly regarding the identity of the fifth occupant of the car. There was no news, but within minutes of his return the doorbell rang. Paul was surprised to find Sergeant Anderson, out of uniform, standing on the doorstep.

'Good Morning, Donnie. Come through to the study.'

Once they were seated, Donnie explained the reason for his visit.

'As you can see, Mr Johnson, I'm not on duty. I would like to give you some advice, if you don't mind.'

'Of course I don't mind. In fact I would very much appreciate it. And there's no need to stand on ceremony, Paul will be fine.'

'Right, Paul. I don't go on duty till later, but I got in touch with the office in Dalcairn. As I think you already know, things are very bad, four dead and one in a coma, and not very likely to survive.'

'Yes, that's what I've heard. Do you know yet who the young lad is?'

'No, not officially, but it could turn out to be the boy Thomson. He hasn't turned up at school this morning.'

'Tom MacCallum said that was who it might be, but he wasn't sure.'

'Problem is, quite a few of the older pupils have decided not to bother with school today. Someone is making contact with the mother. We should know if it is him before much longer.'

'I don't really know that family. They haven't been all that long in the parish. I did call to welcome them but there was no one at home. I left my card, but that's as far as I got.'

'Looks as though you may be seeing a lot more of the mother and father soon. However, that's not really why I'm here. Could I ask you a question?'

'Of course, fire away,' Paul replied, wondering what was

coming next.

'Have you had many dealings with the press in your line of work?'

'Not with something like this. It's been simply handing in reports of church activities to the local paper, that kind of thing. In fact, I've never been involved in something as tragic as this. Better rephrase that. I've had to deal with a few families who have suffered a tragic loss, but never several families in the same incident.'

'That's what I suspected. The thing is, road accidents happen every day and most of the serious ones get a mention somewhere in the media. This one will almost certainly get a bit more than that. That will mean reporters looking for information from the relatives.'

'Oh, I see,' Paul said. 'I've been trying to work out the best way for me to deal with things, but I never thought it would involve the press.'

'It will probably all be over quickly as far as they're concerned and then they'll move on to the next disaster or scandal. What I would like you to do, if a few reporters do appear, is to suggest to the families that they co-operate. I'll advise them to do so too, of course.'

'Would it not be better to keep them away from the families?'

'That's just not possible, I'm afraid. They know how far they can go. They'll push the boundaries as far as they can if they have to, but it's better if they don't have to go that far. A little co-operation on both sides is so much easier for the bereaved.'

Paul was deep in thought, wondering how he could really help.

Donnie had a wry smile on his face as he continued. 'One of the requests the papers will make is to ask for a photo of each of the young people in the car. As recent a photo as possible.'

'Surely they can't demand that.'

'They can't demand, but they will ask, and they will keep on asking until they get it. The editors insist because the readers expect to see it. That's how it works. If it gets to that stage, I hope you might be able to help, to gently suggest to the parents that the sooner the request is granted, the sooner the press will fade away and leave us all to get on as best we can.'

'Just something else to deal with,' Paul said with a sigh.

'And you might also find that they want to interview the parish minister, especially the television people if they decide to run the story.' Paul must have looked shocked as Donnie went on, 'Don't worry, it will be for background information to fill in any gaps in what they already know. If it's any more than that, let me know and I'll remind them of the boundaries.'

'Thanks, I might just hold you to that. And if I can be of any help to you, moral support, I mean, you are always welcome.'

'Thanks, it's all part of the job, but some parts take some getting over. I'm not exactly sure how my next shift will go, but one thing is certain, it won't be easy.'

After Sergeant Anderson left, Paul made a quick phone call to the church organist and explained, without going into too much detail, that he was unlikely to be able to have time to choose hymns for the upcoming Easter services before the choir practice later that evening. As it was Easter the hymns more or less chose themselves. The organist would have the final say and Paul would think about other parts of the services after he had visited the families once again.

6

William Watson had tried to persuade Mary that she should stay at home while he went to the mortuary to formally identify Wilma. She was having none of it.

'Wilma is my daughter too. I have to see her. I have to say goodbye.'

William's real concern was that Wilma might have terrible injuries, especially to her face. He wanted to spare Mary that. He would rather she remembered their daughter as she had been: her pretty face and her happy smile. He hoped with all his heart that Wilma had not been disfigured, but that seemed very unlikely; a shiver went through his body at the thought.

'If you're sure, but remember, you can always change your mind.'

'I won't, but if you have doubts about how you'll feel, I'll make the identification on my own. I brought her into the world and I will see her at the end.'

William knew that Mary would not change her mind, nor would he let her do it on her own. They would be together as they almost always had been.

They said very little during the journey. William slowed down as they approached the spot where Sandy's car had left the road. Mary looked towards the verge. She knew William was doing the same. There was nothing to see, other than the gap the car had made as it ploughed through the hedge. If the car was still where it had finally come to rest, it could not be seen from the road.

'I think the car is still there,' William said. 'If they had recovered it there would be more damage.'

'Never mind the car. Just get us safely to the hospital.'

As she locked eyes with William she knew that even if the hedge regrew, every time she passed this spot, she would always remember Wilma and wonder what might have been if her life had not been so dramatically cut short.

A police officer from Dalcairn met them outside the hospital mortuary. After explaining the procedure, he took them inside the building. Mary clasped William's hand as they entered the room where Wilma lay. William gave her hand a squeeze of encouragement, at the same time preparing himself for the ordeal ahead of them. A mortuary attendant stood at the head of the table.

The attendant nodded to Mary and William. 'Please take your time,' he said. 'Just let me know when you are ready.'

William spoke quietly. 'We're ready.'

The attendant slowly and reverently folded down the top of the sheet so that Wilma's face was uncovered. William was taken by surprise. She looked so peaceful, and her face was unmarked. Mary showed no outward sign of emotion as she looked lovingly at her daughter.

'This is my daughter Wilma,' William said softly. 'Our daughter.'

He put his arm around Mary and together they stood gazing down. The attendant and the police officer stood quietly in the background. William and Mary stood there silently for some time until eventually the police officer took a step towards them.

'Thank you, sir, madam. When you are ready, would you please follow me.'

The attendant moved to where Wilma lay. Before he could replace the sheet over Wilma's face, Mary stepped quickly forward and gently kissed her daughter's forehead. As she lifted her head, her hand caressed Wilma's hair for the last time. William too kissed Wilma before taking Mary's hand. Hand in hand they followed the officer. Soon the formalities were completed.

On the drive back to Burnbrae not a word was spoken. William concentrated on his driving. Occasionally he stole a glance at Mary. She was deep in thought. Were her thoughts the same as his? he wondered. How much would Wilma have achieved, if only her life had been spared?

Bob and Jessie were approaching the Southern General Hospital on the south side of Glasgow. Their emotions were all over the place. They had steeled themselves for what they had to do at the mortuary. It had been agreed that Bob would make the formal identification of Kirsty and if her head injury wasn't too bad, he would accompany Jessie as she said her goodbyes. Bob was the most upset he had ever been after making the identification, but despite this when he came out of the room, he insisted that he would go back in with Jessie.

'She has a bruise and a cut,' he said, 'but she's still our Kirsty. We will do this together, it's the least we can do. It's all we can do,' he added. It took him a moment or two to regain his composure.

'Come on, lass,' he said as he took Jessie by the arm. Together they walked into the room. Together they said their farewells. The tears flowed, for Kirsty and for Sandy.

The drive from Dalcairn to Glasgow seemed to take forever. When eventually they arrived at the intensive care unit where Sandy was being cared for, they were shown into the relatives' room and told that a doctor would be along to see them as soon as possible. They were offered a cup of tea and gladly accepted it. It had been a long and harrowing day already, and it was not yet midday. It could be many hours before they were back at the farm.

They did not have to wait too long before a consultant entered the room and introduced himself. His manner and tone of voice suggested that what he was about to tell them was not good news.

'I'm sorry,' he began, 'your son has suffered a massive trauma to the head. He is in a coma, and it may be some time before he regains consciousness, if he does.'

Jessie was crying softly. Bob was doing his best to comfort her and steeling himself for what else the consultant had to say. What he said was almost as bad as what he had already told them.

'There is every possibility that if your son does regain consciousness, he will have suffered brain damage. How much is impossible to know at present, but it could be substantial. We are doing all we can.' He paused before adding, 'I think you have to prepare yourselves for the worst.'

He stayed with them for some time, answering the many questions they put to him. As he left them he assured them that he and his team would do all they could to help Sandy.

A nurse accompanied them to the ward. Sandy's head was swathed in bandages and there were huge bruises on his face; he was barely recognisable. There were tubes and cables connecting him to the machines monitoring his condition. They stayed with him until the nurse caring for him asked them to return to the relatives' room or perhaps find something to eat, as she had to attend to Sandy. They found a restaurant in another part of the hospital but struggled to eat the sandwiches they ordered. Back at ICU they sat at Sandy's bedside until, with great reluctance, they decided that they would have to return to Burnbrae. There was nothing they could do here, except watch and pray.

Back in Burnbrae Paul was having a frustrating late morning. He had called at the Watsons' house, but there was no one at home. He then drove out to the Meikles' farm and spent some time with Helen, Bob's mother. Her husband and grandson were somewhere on the farm repairing a damaged fence. Paul had hoped that they might return to the farmhouse or bungalow before he left, but they did not. Helen was clearly suffering from the tragic news she had received the previous evening, but putting as brave a face on it as she could manage. She was also keeping close to the telephone in the hope that there might be some better news about Sandy.

After a cup of tea and a home-baked scone, made by Helen that morning because, as she said, 'I had to do something', Paul reluctantly took his leave of her. It seemed terrible leaving her on her own, but he was hoping to find that the Watsons had returned home, and Alec and Iain would be looking for some lunch when they got back from mending the fence.

Driving along the high street on his way back to the manse, Paul noted that there was a police car parked opposite the ironmonger's shop. He had been going to call in and see how the MacCallums were coping, but he did not want to intrude. As he passed the parked car he realised that it was more likely that the police were calling at Brian Thomson's home. Paul drove back to the manse, expecting that Ruth might have had a call to confirm that the fifth occupant in the car was indeed young Brian, but there had been no further news.

Doreen Thomson had been working in the pressing room of the clothing factory in Dalcairn, preparing the garments for packaging. It was not a job she particularly liked, but it was the only one that had been available when her marriage ran into trouble and, although Ed had paid the basic costs of running the home, he had not been overgenerous, despite the money he was making working offshore in the North Sea. Fortunately Brian was of an age where he could get himself out to school in the morning. Her shift finished shortly after the school day ended so she was usually home within 30 minutes of Brian's return, thanks to the lift she got from an employee who worked in another section of the factory.

Doreen looked up when one of the office staff entered the room, but as it would almost certainly be a message for the supervisor, she continued with what she was doing. The next thing she knew, the supervisor was standing beside her.

'Doreen, you're wanted in the office.'

'Me?' she gasped in surprise. The supervisor nodded and led her to the secretary, who was waiting for her. Doreen did not know the young lady and she was not introduced to her. She became worried as she followed the secretary, and it was made worse because no explanation as to why she was being called to the office was forthcoming.

Perhaps she had made a mistake with some of her work, but the nearer she got to the office, the more she thought about Ed, or even Brian. Had there been an accident? When she entered the office and saw the two uniformed police officers her knees buckled. The manager was quickly at her side.

'Here, sit here, Mrs Thomson,' he said, guiding her to a chair.

'Is it Ed?' she asked. 'What has happened? Is he all right?'

The police officer shook his head. 'It's Brian.'

Doreen thought she was going to faint. What had he done? Had he got drunk? Been in a fight? Was he in hospital? In a cell at the police station? Someone handed her a glass of water. She took a gulp and immediately began coughing and spluttering. Now a hand was patting her on the back and a voice was saying, 'Just take it easy. Take your time,' but no one was telling her what had happened, where Brian was, nothing.

She took another deep breath, straightened herself up and looked straight ahead. She was seated towards the back of the office. There was a semicircle of people in front of her: the factory manager, his secretary and the two police officers, one female, the other male. She looked from one to the other. It was obviously bad news and no one appeared to want to be the one to break it to her. Finally, the male police officer spoke.

'Mrs Thomson, I am Inspector Shanks. This is Constable Morton.'

The officers displayed their warrant cards as the inspector spoke. Doreen nodded.

'Can you tell us where your son was last night, Mrs Thomson?' Inspector Shanks asked.

'He was at the school dance.' Doreen waited for the bad news. 'What has he done?'

The inspector did not answer her question; instead he asked one of his own. 'How did he travel to the school?'

'By car. He got a lift from friends. Sally MacCallum arranged it.'

The policewoman moved closer to Doreen before Inspector Shanks continued. 'Could you tell me what your son was wearing?'

'Jeans, a tee shirt and a jumper.'

Doreen was beginning to think that Brian was in real trouble.

Constable Morton said in a whisper. 'Do you know what colour?'

'Eh, yes, of course. Denim jeans, blue ones, a white tee shirt with some kind of logo on it and a blue jumper.'

'Mrs Thomson, I'm afraid the car your son was travelling in was involved in an accident.'

'Is he hurt? Is he in hospital?'

Doreen saw the anxious look the constable gave the inspector as he took a step towards her. She began to shake.

'Mrs Thomson, I'm very sorry. Brian was killed in the accident.'

She must have fainted. The next thing she knew she was in the first-aid room. The factory first-aider was checking her pulse. The police constable and the manager's secretary were also present. From somewhere, a cup of hot, sweet tea was produced and Doreen was told to drink it. She was sure she would be sick. Somehow she managed to keep it down.

'Where is Brian?' she asked Constable Morton.

'He's in the mortuary at Dalcairn Hospital. I'm afraid I have to ask you if you, or another family member, would be able to identify him later today.'

'There's no one else. My husband is on an oil rig. I will have to do it. I want to do it. I have to see him. Maybe that will help me realise what has happened.'

Doreen was talking faster than normal, the words pouring out. 'What happened? Did someone crash into them? Did he suffer? Did they try to help him?'

'Mrs Thomson, we don't yet know what really happened, but I can assure you that Brian received the best possible care. There was nothing anyone could do to save him, and no, he didn't suffer.'

Shortly afterwards the police officers escorted Doreen to the mortuary where she identified Brian. She was numb, acting instinctively; it didn't seem real. In a moment she would awaken and discover that it had all been a dream, a nightmare.

Inspector Shanks and Constable Morton left Doreen in the care of the mortuary attendant as she spent time with Brian.

'Will she cope?' Constable Morton asked her senior officer.

'I don't know, but I am worried about her being on her own at home. I have already contacted the surgery at Burnbrae and alerted the local doctor.'

'And did Brian really not suffer?'

'Constable, I know about as much as you at this moment, and that is practically nothing. It would be all over in a very short time. There would be panic in the vehicle, the occupants would be thrown about, there would be fear, and pain, and when the vehicle came to a halt, all, but one, were dead, or dying. Better just to say they would not have suffered.'

'I suppose so.' Constable Morton's reply was almost inaudible.

'It goes with the job, I'm afraid, and you never get used to it. If you do, you should not be in the job. Now, when we leave here, you will drop me off at the Dalcairn police office and then take Mrs Thomson straight home and make sure that she is being looked after by someone before you leave her and return to Dalcairn.'

'Yes, sir,' Constable Morton replied.

The practice nurse, Nancy Fraser, was waiting outside Doreen's flat as Constable Morton helped Doreen up the stairs to her front door. Gently Doreen was led into the house.

'She hasn't said a word on the journey, nurse,' the constable said as Doreen was made comfortable on the sofa.

'It's all right, Constable, I'll take over now,' Nancy replied. 'I can stay with her for a bit longer. Dr Wilkie is coming to see her as soon as surgery is finished. There were only a couple of patients still to be seen when I left.'

When Dr Wilkie arrived, Doreen was able to tell him that her husband was working offshore and her parents had gone on holiday to Spain. It would be another week before they were back home. They lived in Dalcairn where most of her friends lived. The few friends she had made in Burnbrae would be at work. Dr Wilkie prescribed a mild sedative.

'Is there anyone who could keep you company for the afternoon, or at least keep an eye on you?' the doctor asked.

'Old Mrs Melville in the flat opposite is very good to Brian and me.'

The mention of her son seemed to have set her off as Doreen broke down again. Nurse Fraser comforted her until she was able to continue.

'Could Mrs Melville stay with you, do you think?' Dr Wilkie was sure Mrs Melville would be an ideal person to keep an eye on Doreen.

'I don't know. We speak to one another if we meet on the stair, and she sometimes hands in some baking, but we're just neighbours, not really friends.'

Doreen became agitated as she tried to explain.

'It's all right, I'm sure Mrs Melville will do all she can to be of assistance. I know her quite well. I'll pop across and have a word with her.'

Dr Wilkie was soon back, bringing Mrs Melville with him.

'Oh, Doreen, this is terrible, I don't know what to say, really I don't,' she said as she rushed over and clasped Doreen's hand in both of hers. 'I'm not going anywhere today, so I can stay with you as long as you like.'

'I don't want to bother you,' Doreen mumbled.

'Don't be daft, lassie, it's the least I can do. That's what neighbours are for.'

'Now, Doreen, you sit there and rest,' Dr Wilkie said. 'I will have to get on with my visits, but I am sure Mrs Melville will make you a nice cup of tea while Nurse Fraser goes to collect the medication I have prescribed. It will help you to sleep at night. I'll be back in a day or two to see how you are. If you need me before then, let me know.'

'Thanks, Doctor.'

He scarcely heard Doreen's reply as he nodded to nurse Fraser and Mrs Melville. 'Thanks for your help. I'll see myself out.'

7

Paul made his second round of visits in the afternoon. He noticed that there were more groups of people than usual standing talking on the main street. He was aware that not everyone in Burnbrae knew everyone else. That may have been true in days gone by, but in recent times the population had grown considerably. The two new housing estates, one at either end of the town, had seen more than a few people from Dalcairn move out to the semi-rural attractions of Burnbrae. They had brought with them a welcome boost to trade and the local activities. Today, sooner or later, everyone would be talking about what had happened the previous evening.

Presumably, Paul thought, most of what was being said would be speculation, an accident involving members of the MacCallum, Meikle and Watson families, with no one able to confirm the details. At lunchtime everything changed.

The police issued a statement, broadcast on TV and radio, concerning the accident, stating that there had been fatalities and one person was in hospital, critically ill. No names were announced, but what had been said was enough to confirm that the rumour was more than a rumour; it was true.

The fact that the police had spoken to Mr Watson and Mr Meikle at the Kirk Session meeting and they immediately left added further fuel to the fire. It wasn't clear who had actually been in the car, but the suspicion was that it had been younger members of the families. Many knew about the school dance and some were aware of the Young Farmers' meeting.

Paul did his best to be of some comfort to the bereaved, but he too was struggling to make sense of it all. He had no answer to the question, 'Why did this happen?' Even worse was Tom MacCallum's angry comment, 'If God loves us, why did he let this happen to my Sally?' Paul tried to say a word or two to calm the distraught father, but nothing he could say was of any help. Perhaps later, much later, he would be able to discuss what had happened with Tom and the other parents in a calm and rational matter, but today was not that day; everyone was hurting too much.

After visiting the MacCallums, Paul crossed the road to visit Brian's parents. Sergeant Anderson had phoned at lunchtime to inform him that Brian had indeed been the fifth occupant of the car. Paul was surprised when the door of the flat was opened by Mrs Melville, one of the most loyal members of his congregation.

'Mrs Melville,' he began, 'I was…'

Mrs Melville quickly stepped out onto the landing, pulling the door closed behind her. 'Doreen's asleep,' she explained. 'The poor lass is in a terrible state. Dr Wilkie asked me to keep an eye on her.'

'Oh, right,' Paul answered. 'I was just wondering how she was, and if I could be of any help to her.'

'I'm sure you will be a great help to her, Minister, but I think it would be best to let her sleep for a wee while longer.'

'Of course, I will look in again later. Are you all right?'

'Well, I wouldn't say all right, but I'll manage. Doreen has had a hard time of it lately. She and her husband seem to be more or less living separate lives, not that I know very much. She keeps things to herself. But she's a good mum to Brian. And now this. Poor lass! It's just terrible, terrible!'

Paul agreed and repeated his promise to call back later and to do all he could to support Doreen. Mrs Melville assured him that she would let Doreen know he had called.

'I won't let her sleep too long,' she added. 'It will be bad enough for her during the night, without lying awake because she slept all day.' Mrs Melville shook her head as she spoke.

Paul had always known that Mrs Melville had a kind, caring manner. Doreen was very fortunate to have her as a neighbour.

He thought about going back out to the Meikles' farm but decided against it. Bob and Jessie were unlikely to be back from Glasgow. It would be better to wait until the evening. If he was needed urgently he was sure that Alec or Helen would get in touch.

He made his way back to the crescent. Mary and William Watson were holding up well. There was a post-mortem being carried out on Wilma, probably as they spoke, William had informed Paul.

'I don't know why they have to do that!' Mary exclaimed as soon as she heard the word. 'Wilma was fit and healthy. They don't need to cut her up,' she blurted out through her sobs. William tried to comfort her.

'I've tried to explain why they have to do it,' William said to Paul as Mary began to calm down.

'I understand how you feel, Mary, but William is right,' Paul said. 'They have to look at every possible reason for the accident, and that sometimes means finding out if the driver became unwell.'

'I understand that,' Mary admitted, 'but I still don't like to think about it. I know what they do, are doing, at this very moment to my beautiful daughter.'

William and Paul did their best to convince her that everything that had to be done would be carried out with respect. It made little difference to Mary. Paul offered up a prayer before he left and reminded them yet again that he was only a couple of doors away if they needed him.

Ruth was about to serve the evening meal when the doorbell sounded.

'Why does it always have to be at mealtimes?' she muttered under her breath as Paul made his way to the front door.

'Reverend Johnson?' asked the stranger standing on the step.

'Yes, I'm Mr Johnson,' replied Paul, who much preferred the traditional Scottish way of addressing ministers of the Kirk.

'Stewart, *Daily News*, can I ask you a few questions?' The reporter held out his hand.

Paul wasn't a reader of the *Daily News* and he had no idea if Stewart was the man's first name or surname.

'It's not the most convenient time,' he replied. 'I'm about to have my dinner.'

'We'll only be a few minutes, sir. Just one or two questions about the terrible tragedy.'

It was only then that Paul realised there was another man hovering about outside the garden gate, clearly a photographer. He was tempted to ask them to come back later but, remembering Sergeant Anderson's advice, he decided it might be best to invite the two men in.

The few minutes stretched to more than 20. At first all went well, a few questions about how well Paul knew those affected by the accident and what he was doing to help them. Early in the conversation the reporter had informed Paul that his first name was Robert, adding, 'Rab to my friends.' It seemed that Paul was now one of his friends.

'What was the driver like? A speed merchant, perhaps?' Rab suddenly asked.

'Wilma was a very level-headed young woman. She was certainly not a speed merchant.'

'Oh, she was driving? We assumed it would be the owner of the car.'

Paul realised he would have to be much more guarded in his answers.

'No, it was Wilma, and she was a good driver. She was very careful in everything she did.'

'So what do you think caused the accident?'

'I have no idea. You will have to ask the police about that.'

'Something must have happened,' Rab responded. 'Cars don't just leave the road and career down a steep slope. Was it an old banger, not maintained properly, something like that?'

'It was well maintained, Sandy saw to that. Look, there is nothing more I can, or want to, say on the matter. They were normal, decent young people. This has been a difficult time for me. I think you should leave now.'

'Just one final question, Paul, a photo, and then you can get back to your dinner.' Rab was all smiles. 'Will you be holding a special service on Sunday?'

Paul could feel the anger rising. This was nothing to smile about.

'Of course I will. Sunday is Easter Day. It's the most important day in the Christian calendar.'

Rab clearly failed to notice the sarcasm. 'But will you be doing something for the victims?'

'As always there will be prayers for the sick and the bereaved, and the families of the young people will be very much in our thoughts this Sunday. And, of course, there will unfortunately be four, perhaps five, funerals taking place in the next few days.'

That more or less brought the questioning to an end. The photographer took a couple of photos of a reluctant Paul before the two men thanked him, assured him that if they could be of any assistance in the days ahead he only had to ask, and left the manse.

What was all that about?' asked a disgruntled Ruth as Paul entered the kitchen.

'The press,' Paul answered.

'What did they want? I hope you didn't say anything you shouldn't have!'

'I don't know any more than anyone else. They were looking for some kind of scandal, something that would suggest a crash was inevitable. They even wanted a photo of me.'

'I hope you didn't let them take one.'

'I did. I had to. It was the only way I could make them leave.'

'Oh, for goodness' sake, Paul. When will you realise you don't have to do everything everyone asks you to do?'

Paul could think of a reply Ruth placed a bowl of soup in front of him. 'Get that inside you and let's try to relax while we eat.'

By the time the meal was over, Paul realised that if he was going to visit the Meikle family he had better get on his way.

At the farm Paul was shown into the kitchen where it was obvious that Bob and Jessie had just finished eating. Iain, Helen and Alec were also present.

'It's been a long day for you,' Paul said as he took a seat at the large kitchen table.

'Yes, but it had to be done,' Bob said, 'and there will be more like it too.'

Paul looked from Bob to Jessie, who had said very little so far. Jessie lifted the handkerchief she had been holding and wiped her eyes. Still she did not look at him.

'I can't begin to understand what you are going through,' Paul said. 'What was the news of Sandy?'

Jessie was sobbing quietly.

'About as bad as it could be,' Bob replied, his voice breaking. 'The consultant says it is a case of waiting. If they begin to see signs of recovery, then they may be able to do something to help, but the way he sees it, it looks unlikely. And if he does recover, there is no way of telling if any of the damage will be permanent, including brain damage.'

'You mustn't give up hope, Bob,' Paul said softly. 'Sandy has youth on his side, and he is fit and healthy.'

'You wouldn't think that if you saw him now,' Bob blurted out. 'I don't see how he can win this battle.'

Iain rushed from the room without saying anything.

Paul and Helen did their best to console Jessie and Bob. Gradually they calmed down. They spoke of Kirsty, the attractive, loving, outgoing daughter who had been so cruelly taken from them. She had had everything to live for; now they would have to plan her funeral. Paul suggested that they took their time, knowing full well that due to the Easter holiday period nothing could be arranged until the following Tuesday, at the earliest.

'I don't know how I will cope,' Bob suddenly said, anger in his tone. 'This is just not fair. I feel so helpless.'

To Paul's surprise he heard Jessie say through her sobs, 'Bob, we mustn't give up. Paul, would you say a prayer, for Sandy, for all of us. And the other families too.'

There was silence after the prayer. Paul always found this a difficult moment. Did he slip away quietly? In the circumstances, would he, or someone else, make a completely inappropriate comment? He was glad when Helen was the one who broke the silence.

'Thank you, Paul. That was lovely. Now, you are welcome to stay as long as you like, but you too need to have some time when you can sit back and relax, if that is possible.'

Goodbyes were soon said, hands clasped and loving looks shared.

It was with a heavy heart that Paul drove away from the farm. He hoped that his visit had been a help, but how could he help? He stopped before he turned onto the main road, his mind in turmoil. It had been an accident and, as far as he was aware, no one had any idea how or why it had happened. It had nothing to do with God; it had been mechanical failure or human error. There had to be a simple explanation, no matter how hurtful it proved to be. What on earth was he going to say on Sunday? Death and resurrection, of course; it was easy when it was simply the retelling of the Gospel story, but when confronted with the tragic deaths of ordinary people, and especially young people just about to take their place in the world, it was anything but simple. People wanted answers. And many looked to him to provide them.

He offered up a silent prayer for guidance before continuing his homeward journey.

8

'Here he is,' shouted Lenny to his pals as Jackie Brown entered The Brae, officially the Burnbrae Inn, but in reality the town's public bar. 'He'll tell us what really happened.'

Jackie looked puzzled. 'What the hell are you talkin' about now?'

'The accident. Last night. You were there. Probably you were involved, the way you drive.'

Jackie raised his fist and took two steps towards Lenny. 'Shut your mouth or ah'll shut it for ye.'

'Gentlemen, behave yourselves,' called Maurice, the owner of the inn.

Billy, one of Jackie's pals, stepped in front of Jackie. 'Come on, sit down. Ignore him. You know what he's like. Big mouth, tiny brain, and he can't stop trying to prove it,' he added, with a smirk to Lenny.

Lenny was on his feet, but before he could say anything, Maurice called out again, 'Lenny, one more word from you and you're out, and you won't be back for some time.'

Lenny glowered at Jackie and Billy, looked over at Maurice, who was watching him closely from behind the bar, was about to say something, thought better of it, and sat back down again.

'I heard you were first on the scene, Jackie. Is that true?' asked Cammy, another regular and a friend of Jackie.

Lenny muttered, 'See, I knew he was involved.'

Billy gave him a warning look.

'Aye, it's true, Cammy,' Jackie replied quietly, 'and I wish to God I hadn't been. It was horrible.' There was complete silence. Even Lenny was anxious to hear what Jackie had to say.

'I must have arrived at the scene not long after it happened. The road was quiet. I had seen no one in front of me. A few had passed heading for Dalcairn. Most of them I recognised, and no one was acting like an idiot. I still can't understand what happened.'

'What do you mean?' asked Scott, another of the group.

'Well, there was no reason for anyone to go off the road. The car had come round the corner, was on the straight and then veered left, went through the hedge and must have kept going. It was at the bottom of the hill. Why did it not stop before it came to the steep bit? The driver must have passed out or something.'

'Who was driving? Did you see?' Cammy asked.

Lenny was now all ears. This was what everyone was asking. Soon he would be able to pass on the name.

'The police have asked me not to say anything and anyway, the car was in such a mess, bodies in a heap inside the car. There was nothing I could do, not even for the one who had been flung out.'

'Who was it?' Lenny asked loudly.

Jackie looked at him. 'You'll find out soon enough, but it won't be from me.'

'What did you do?' asked Scott.

'I went back up to my van and drove to the nearest cottage, old Mrs White's place, and used her phone to call for help. She could see the state I was in. She insisted on making me a cup of tea while I phoned 999. Think she always has a kettle on the stove, but I really couldn't drink it. I took a few gulps and then went back to wait for the emergency crews. Once I had given the police a statement I drove home. Very slowly.'

'That'll be a first!' exclaimed Lenny. The others glowered at him again. He shrugged his shoulders, gave a look as if to say, 'Well, it would be' but kept his mouth shut.

'Are you OK now?' asked Cammy.

'Aye, just about, but I don't think I will ever forget what I saw. Poor things, I just can't believe it.'

The group fell silent, alone with their thoughts. Even the drinks were left untouched. Lenny was wondering if, like him, the others were trying to picture what Jackie had seen and imagining how they would have reacted in his shoes. Maybe he had been a bit hard on Jackie. He shrugged his shoulders. He'll get over it, he said to himself.

In the church hall, a short distance along the road from the Burnbrae Inn, the Thursday night choir practice was in progress, except that not much progress had been made. Harry Yardley, organist and choirmaster, had informed the choristers that due to the terrible accident and the number of visits that Paul was making to support the families, he had asked him to choose the Easter praise.

'Perhaps you could help me,' he in turn asked the choir members. 'Normally, it would not be a problem, but I wonder how you feel about singing some of the usual hymns.'

'But Easter is about hope and victory, surely,' stated Mark, one of the tenors. 'That should be a help, and anyway, I don't think any of the family members will be in a fit state to attend the services, poor things.'

'It's all right for you, Mark. You have a strong faith, but not everyone has. Some people, myself included, are finding it hard to come to terms with what has happened,' replied Marjory. 'I'm friends with the MacCallums. I'm dreading visiting them, but I'll have to do it soon. I think we should maybe not be too joyful, show some respect.'

Marjory brushed away the tear that ran down her cheek. Most of the choir members seemed to agree with her and eventually the hymns were chosen for both services and the practice began. There were times when the singing was not quite up to the usual standard but Harry said nothing.

'That only leaves your solo, Matt. How do you feel?' asked Harry when the final hymn had been sung.

The previous year Matt had sung 'God so loved the world' from Stainer's *Crucifixion* at the Good Friday service. His beautiful tenor voice had held the small congregation spellbound.

'I've been thinking about that quite a bit, Harry. The Meikles aren't only neighbours of ours, they're close friends. And I feel a bit like Mark. If we change too much, it might give the wrong impression. I'll do it, it's a statement of our faith, my faith, but the rest of you better be ready to join in if I get a lump in my throat.'

'Thanks, Matt, I appreciate that. I have a feeling we might all have lumps in our throats. Right folks, I think we should call it a night. I'll see you tomorrow evening. Thank you, and goodnight.'

Normally some of the choir would have waited behind for a chat, a catch-up with those they did not meet outside of the choir, but this night they all seemed to be in agreement; it was not a night for idle gossip or silly stories. In minutes the hall was in darkness and the door locked.

Bob Meikle had always been an early riser; he had to be. There was always something to do on the farm and no matter what was going on in his personal life, the beasts and the sheep had to be attended to. He was up before sunrise, glad to get back to some kind of normality, if only for a couple of hours. Before long he was joined by his dad, and Iain appeared soon after without having to be wakened. Neither of them had had a sound sleep.

For Paul, Good Friday was always a different sort of a day, and this one was going to be no exception. As soon as he was awake, he looked at the time and remembered what had happened in Jerusalem all those years ago. He could see the crowds following Jesus as he carried his cross to the place of execution. He stumbled and fell; a stranger was ordered to carry it for him. At nine o'clock, Jesus of Nazareth would be nailed to that cross.

Whatever Paul was doing, wherever he was as nine o'clock approached, he would stop briefly, his thoughts back in Calvary, and give thanks for this day and what it meant to him and to millions of others. Until three o'clock his thoughts would often return to that place outside the city walls of ancient Jerusalem, so far away, yet so close in his mind.

He had discussed with Ruth what he should do regarding the bereaved families. Both were of the opinion that perhaps a brief visit would be sufficient, unless it became obvious that something more was required. Paul went into his study after breakfast and tried yet again to gather his thoughts and prepare his sermons for the two services. In the end he gave up. No matter how he started, he found himself returning to the accident and its terrible outcome. He normally had no difficulty thinking of death and resurrection in the tranquillity of the study, but how could he talk about new life when these young lives had been so cruelly cut short? Whatever he wrote, it ended up like 'pie in the sky when you die', and he hated that kind of preaching. He would leave his preparation until after he had made another visit to each of the homes. Perhaps when he had spoken with the grieving parents he would know what to say and how to say it.

When Paul arrived at the home of his neighbours, Mary and William, he found that their concern was more about the other parents. They had informed Paul that they were coping and beginning to make plans for Wilma's funeral towards the end of the following week. Paul assured them that whatever was arranged would be convenient for him.

'Funerals always have priority. It's not fair to the families to put anything in the way, no matter how important something else might seem.'

'I understand, but I sometimes think you forget that you have a family, Paul.'

Paul was not sure if William was simply giving him some friendly advice. There was no sense of bitterness in William's voice, but what he had said underlined their differing situations. Paul chose his words carefully.

'I hear what you are saying, William, but at this moment you and Mary, and the other parents, are first in my thoughts and prayers. Everything else takes second place.'

Paul sensed that William was unable to reply as he struggled to keep his feelings under control.

'There's nothing more I can say, William,' Paul said quietly.

William took a deep breath. 'I understand. I'm all right. Well, I have my moments, but we'll manage. We have one another.' He looked at Mary as he spoke, and Paul was reassured. They were a strong couple. He had always known that. They would cope.

'Paul, there is one thing,' William said, once more in full control of his emotions. 'I have to know why the accident happened. Did Wilma do something stupid? Did something happen and she wasn't experienced enough to deal with it? Did she take ill? There has to be an explanation. I need to know. Have the police told you anything?'

'Not so far,' Paul replied. 'I would think you'll be the first to know. I presume they're making sure they arrive at the right conclusion before they say anything. I have been wondering myself and, if I know anything about Wilma, she wouldn't do anything stupid. There has to be a rational answer.'

'Yes, but what?' asked her father.

Paul shook his head. 'I have no idea, but I'm sure that when all the facts have been ascertained, we'll have the answer. Until then all I can do is once again assure you of my concern for you both, and for everyone else. If there is anything I can do, and I mean anything, you only have to ask.'

'We know you are always there for us, Paul,' Mary said quietly, 'and we appreciate that. I think we are managing. We have one another.'

'Yes,' agreed her husband. 'We're coping, most of the time. You take care of yourself. It's a very busy weekend for you.'

As Paul took his leave of Mary and William he was yet again amazed at how well they were dealing with the tragedy that had struck them. He hoped they were not bottling up their feelings and storing up trouble for the future. He had seen others do that, with devastating effect.

The MacCallums were his next port of call. He found Tom in the shop, stacking a shelf as his two assistants served the customers. Tom admitted that he was finding it hard to deal with the sympathy expressed by those who came into the shop.

'I think most of them are genuine. They did need the items they bought, but one or two simply bought a light bulb, then wanted to know all the details: how we were feeling, what happened, that sort of thing. Human nature, I suppose, but not at all helpful.'

Would you not be better staying in the house with Nan?' Paul asked.

'That's another problem,' Tom replied, shaking his head. 'She just sits there, looking out the window, saying nothing, eating next to nothing. I think she's hoping Sally will suddenly appear, walking down the street towards the house and everything will be back to normal. I don't know what to do.'

'Not much you can do, except be there for her,' Paul replied, his voice full of sympathy for the man standing in front of him. 'And when she's ready, she'll talk and you'll be there to listen, and to help.'

'Aye, but when? And I'm not always there for her. I keep coming down here out of the way.' Tom shook his head again. 'Come on, I'll take you up. Maybe you can get through to her.'

'I can't promise, but I'll do my best,' Paul answered as he followed Tom out of the shop and up the stair to the flat.

'Here's the minister come to see you, Nan,' Tom announced in a cheery tone.

'Good morning, Mrs MacCallum. 'I'm calling to see how you are, and to ask if I can help in any way.'

Nan continued to stare out of the window. It was almost as though she was unaware that anyone else was in the room.

Tom made to approach her. Paul held up his hand to stop him. Very quietly he said, 'Leave her. We can sit here and chat. Perhaps she'll join in.'

They sat down, but neither seemed quite sure what to say. In the end it was Tom who broke the silence.

'I've been in touch with the undertaker,' he began.

Paul was horrified. It was the last thing he thought they should be talking about in front of the suffering mother. 'Of course, I'm afraid it is better to do that as soon as possible, but perhaps we should discuss that later.' Paul signalled that he was worried about Nan.

Tom got the message. 'Of course, that might be better.'

'Have you been eating and sleeping all right?' Not perhaps the best question to ask, Paul thought, but at least it was better than talking about the funeral arrangements. Or was it? he wondered.

'I slept a bit better last night,' Tom answered, 'but then I wakened early and could not get back to sleep. Dozed off a bit before eventually getting up and making a cup of tea. The sleeping pills the doctor gave Nan seem to knock her out. Could be tempted to try one myself,' he added.

'Not without asking the doctor first, I hope?' There was a note of alarm in Paul's voice.

'Don't worry, Minister, I'm not that stupid, and one of us has to be alert. There's a lot to do. Just wish I was a better cook.'

That seemed to answer the other part of Paul's original question. He wondered if there was some way he could help. Food was as important as sleep at a time like this. His concern must have shown in his face.

'Don't worry about my lack of skill in the kitchen, Minister. We're fine. My sister, Isa, is a great cook. She has been providing us with our main meal. I manage to heat it up without ruining it. So far anyway.' He gave a rueful smile.

'I'm sure she's pleased to be able to help. Maybe Nan will be more like herself soon. It takes time, and we all react differently.'

Paul was aware that he was talking for the sake of talking. Yet again he found himself wondering how he would feel if this were happening to him and his loved ones. He quickly switched the conversation back to safer ground. 'I presume Dr Wilkie will be keeping an eye on Nan?'

'Yes, he has been very good.'

At no point during the rather forced conversation had Nan shown any reaction, not even when her name was mentioned.

Paul asked after Gary and was informed that he had been rather quiet, but appeared to be coping. Some of his pals had called round and that had helped. He spent most of his time in his room listening to music. Once again Paul heard himself tell Tom that he would do his best to help, but it was entirely up to Gary.

'There may well be someone else he would rather confide in, a teacher or another family member, or of course you,' Paul suggested.

'Not sure I'll be much use at the moment, but we've always got on well, and I'm keeping an eye on him,' Tom assured him.

Soon after, Paul left the MacCallums' house and crossed the road to visit Doreen Thomson.

Mrs Melville opened the door to Paul.

'She's awake and in a foul mood,' the elderly neighbour informed Paul before he could utter a word. 'Are you sure you want to see her? Might be better if you come back later. I'll try to calm her down, poor soul.'

'No, I think I should stay. Might make her even worse if you tell her I didn't want to see her.'

'I wouldn't put it quite like that, Minister, but if you insist, I'll show you in and then go back to my own house. Let me know when you leave and I'll come back and sit with her. And I'll bring her a bite to eat.'

Paul was shown into the living room and introduced to Doreen. She looked towards him but remained seated. He approached the chair where she was sitting, his right hand extended in greeting.

Doreen simply stared at him. He could see the rage seething in her by the look she   gave him.

'I'm sorry,' he began, 'I'm just dropping in to see how you are and to ask if I can be of any assistance.'

That opened the floodgates. Doreen was beside herself as she gave vent to her feelings.

'Who was this girl who killed my son? Was she qualified to drive? Did she flash a bit of leg, or show a bit up top to the driving test man? Was that how she passed her driving test?'

Paul tried to get a word in, to calm her down, but it was no use. Doreen couldn't be stopped.

'And where is my so-called husband? Says he can't get off the rig. Probably shacked up in Aberdeen with one of his floozies. Good luck to her. She can have him. But just at the minute I need him here. After that she can have him for good. And good riddance.'

Doreen ended her outburst in a flood of tears. Paul turned to Mrs Melville for support, but she had crept quietly back to her own flat as promised. Paul was in a bit of a quandary. Normally he would offer comfort to anyone as upset as Doreen by placing an arm around their shoulder, even giving them a hug, but this was the very first time they had met. What if she got the wrong idea and began shouting at him, accusing him of goodness knows what?

The sobbing continued and Paul's heart went out to the grief-stricken mother. He stood by her side, a hand on her shoulder, patting her gently and said, 'That's good. Let it all out, and when you're ready, we can talk.'

Gradually Doreen's sobbing subsided. Paul kept his hand on her shoulder until the crying stopped completely. He gave her a final pat before moving to sit in the chair opposite.

Doreen looked up, then began to wipe her eyes with a handkerchief which was already soaked. She must have been crying earlier. She began to apologise for her outburst. 'I'm sorry, I just don't understand.'

Paul interrupted her. 'It's all right. Better to get it out of your system. Keeping it in only makes matters worse. And I can assure you that Wilma, the driver of the car, was a very competent young lady. There will be a reason for what has happened.'

Paul wanted to say more, but until the police worked out why the accident had happened he thought it better not to speculate. There would be an explanation in time and if Wilma had been at fault, it would be the kind of mistake anyone could have made, he hoped.

Doreen apologised for her remarks about Wilma but made no apology for what she had said about her husband. She explained that things between them had not been good for some time and it was obvious to her that the marriage was over. It was only a matter of time before it would be legally ended.

'But he is Brian's dad,' she added. 'I just hope we can act in a civil manner to each other until after his funeral.' Her words brought on more tears, but without the sobbing. Paul noticed a box of tissues on the table. He took out a handful and handed them to Doreen, who took them, nodding her thanks before wiping her face. She was desperate to find a reason for the accident. There was nothing he could tell her. He was as much in the dark as she was.

There was an uneasy silence, broken only when one of them thought of something to say to break it. Finally, Paul took his leave, promising Doreen that he was available at any time if she wanted to talk. He called in briefly at Mrs Melville's home. He assured her that Doreen was a bit calmer and thanked her for the comfort she had given to her young neighbour.

'If we can't help one another the world would be in an even worse state than it already is,' she said, somewhat philosophically.

As Paul made his way back to the manse, he had to agree with her and that brought his thoughts back to Good Friday. He knew now what he would say to those who would gather in the evening to remember and give thanks for this special day.

9

The grandfather clock in the hall, a family heirloom that had belonged to Ruth's grandparents, was striking midday as Paul entered the manse. He stopped, listening to the deep, measured chimes as he remembered that at noon on that first Good Friday the skies had suddenly turned dark, day had become night, as Jesus hung on the cross.

'Everything all right?' Ruth shouted from the kitchen.

Paul brought his mind back to the present. 'Yes, well, at least as good as it can be in the circumstances,' he replied, making his way towards the kitchen. 'I'm OK, but I wonder if I'm really helping those who are suffering so much. Words seem so inadequate. And I seem to end every visit by saying that I'm always available if I can be of any help.'

'Well, you are, and I'm sure you're a great help,' Ruth reassured him as she planted a kiss on his cheek and gave him a hug. 'Just make sure you look after yourself. I presume you're taking it easy this afternoon.'

'Well, eh, yes. More or less, but I think I should go out and see how the Meikles are coping and find out if Sandy is showing any signs of improvement.'

'His mum and dad will be at the hospital, surely.'

'Yes, but the old folks will be there. They'll be able to give me the latest update. I've been round the others. I would hate the Meikles to think that I'd forgotten them.'

'Darling, you know they'll never think that of you. And I also know that nothing I say will make you change your mind, so, go and sit down. Lunch will be ready soon.'

Paul did as he was told. His body was still as he sat, but his mind was very much alert. He was going over what he thought he would say at the evening service, and how he would say it. When he got back from the Meikles' place he would put his thoughts on paper, some headings only; this was no time for a fully crafted sermon.

He would be speaking from the heart to the hearts of those present, and thinking very much about those sitting at home, their hearts broken.

He joined Ruth at the table for the light lunch. She did her best to take his mind off those matters that were weighing so heavily on him by changing the subject.

'It will be good to have both Malcolm and Jennifer home with us over the weekend.'

'Yes, I'm looking forward to it,' Paul replied, bringing his mind back to focus on his own family for a welcome change.

Malcolm had been home from university for the best part of a week, but he was often out with some of his old school friends or making an attempt to prepare for the important exams he would have next term. Paul was aware from an earlier talk he had had with Malcolm that his son was having doubts about his original plan to proceed to teacher training after gaining his degree in modern languages. So far he had not heard if Malcolm had come to a final decision about this. Jennifer would be home too but only for the weekend. From previous conversations he knew that she was finding it tough: studying and doing practical work in the wards. Paul had assured her that she would cope, that it would all be worth it, and that she would be an excellent nurse.

Paul had a bit of a rest after lunch before making his way out to Fauldshead. At the farm he was met by Helen, who was working in the farmhouse. Alec and Iain were attending to a ewe giving birth in the barn. Bob and Jessie had been at the hospital since mid-morning where, as far as Helen understood, nothing had changed.

'I sometimes wonder,' she said quietly to Paul, as they drank the tea she had made, 'if they aren't telling us everything. I think they think they're being kind, but it only makes it worse. Alec and I know Sandy is very ill. If we knew what they know, we could help one another. Instead we're all walking on eggshells, afraid to say the wrong thing.'

'I know what you mean. When people ask me if I've heard how Sandy is, I say something like 'no change' or 'holding his own' then wonder how true that is. I just wish I could visit him, but…'

'Minister, you have plenty to do at this time,' Helen interjected. 'There isn't anything you can do for Sandy by visiting him in the hospital. Much better that you look after those who are here and need your comfort and support.'

'That may well be true, but what about Bob and Jessie? I should be supporting them.'

'But you are. You're here making sure that we're OK.'

Paul realised that she was probably right. Just then he heard a clock strike three.

It is finished, he thought. The words Jesus had spoken as he died. Not words of failure but words of confirmation. Jesus had done what was required of him. Paul hoped he would be able to do what was required of him, but it would be many days, weeks and months probably, before this particular part of his ministry would be finished; for him at least, but for the people he was visiting it would take much longer. They would move on, life would continue, but every so often they would find themselves thinking of what it might have been like had it not been for the accident with its terrible consequences. Their lives had changed forever.

Helen was looking at him. She seemed to be waiting on him to say something. Quickly he gathered his thoughts. 'Sorry, I heard a clock chiming and remembered that it was at three o'clock that Jesus died on that first Good Friday.'

'Aye, so it was. I have my faith, and I know why it happened, all part of his father's great plan, but I wish I could understand why this accident happened. I know things that we don't like, don't want, sometimes happen, but if there's a reason, it helps us to accept it. At least that's what I find.'

'Helen, I think you and I are in agreement there. We can't change what has happened. Perhaps when we do find out the cause, it will be of some help to us.'

As they talked, Paul was reminded yet again that the country folk saw nature in all its moods: the changing seasons, life and death, the expected and the unexpected, and they took it all in their stride. What had happened to Helen's grandchildren was terrible, but she wasn't complaining. It would take her, and all the family, time to come to terms with it but she would, and so would the others.

Paul tried to free his mind as he drove home from the farm, but it wasn't easy. There were people who were looking to him for support, while others, people of faith who were not closely related to the victims and their families, were hoping for some kind of explanation of how such occurrences fitted into the grand scheme of things, and one or two of no religious persuasion who had met Paul as he went about his business were asking where God had been. Paul always did his best to give answers, but with some in that last group of people it was more often than not simply mischief-making; they had no interest in Paul's answer and whatever he said was unlikely to change their way of thinking.

Back home, Paul tried to relax. Before the Good Friday service he had to be at the church for the wedding rehearsal. He would try to keep it as short as possible, but he was amazed at how these rehearsals sometimes took longer than the actual ceremony. Perhaps it was nerves: his, as well as those of the bridal party. There always seemed to be yet another question about procedure or who stood where. Paul's stock reply was, 'Just try to relax. I'll tell you what to do and when to do it. If anyone makes a mistake, it will probably be me. Just get here in time, and before you know it you'll be back outside the church having your photo taken as husband and wife.'

Paul had prepared for the Good Friday service as best he could and the small congregation would be aware of the pressure he had been under as he carried out his pastoral duties. He expected that Jennifer would be there by the time he returned home, relaxing for probably the first time in days. The family would be together, a rare event these days, enjoying a meal and catching up with who had been doing what. There would be a shadow hanging over them; the tragedy and its victims would not be forgotten. Indeed, if anything, what had happened would make their time together more precious than ever.

William and Mary had never missed the Good Friday service, and this year they intended to be present as usual. William had suggested to Mary that perhaps she would prefer to stay at home while he attended. Her reply did not really come as a surprise.

'I'll be there with you,' she stated firmly. 'What I believe is part of my being. It's not something to pick up and cast aside whenever I feel like it. I suppose some people will be surprised to see us, but you and I believe the Gospel. Today we remember that Easter was God's plan for us, for all people. If we stay away, does it mean that we don't really believe?'

William thought he knew Mary, but this was quite a statement. 'I don't think anyone will think we don't believe, and what other people think is their own business. We know what we believe.'

'Exactly, and that's why I'll be with you.'

'And to be honest, I'm glad you'll be with me. We've a lot to get through in the days ahead, and we'll do it together, as we always do.'

It had been close, but the wedding rehearsal had been completed with 10 minutes to spare. The Good Friday service was held in the smaller of the two halls at the rear of the church. Even then the hall was never more than half-full, so it came as quite a surprise to Paul when he entered to discover that there were only a few empty seats. Standing on the small platform and looking around the congregation, he soon understood the reason for the increase in numbers.

There were quite a few present who hardly ever entered the church on a Sunday, far less a Friday evening. Indeed one or two he was sure had never been at a service in his time as minister of the congregation. Some of the people looking intently in his direction were obviously expecting to hear something about the accident, anything, no matter how unimportant it might seem. They would be sorely disappointed; he had no intention of saying anything about that particular incident, though he hoped his message would give some comfort, some assurance, to all present.

They sang the usual Good Friday hymns; Paul led in prayer, remembering at one point all who were in mourning, especially those of their congregation and parish. St Mark's account of the first Good Friday was read between the hymns. Matt's rendering of 'God So Loved the World' was very moving, so moving that by the time he reached the final words, there were many in the congregation, men and women, wiping a tear from their eyes. After the final notes died away, there was a moment of complete silence before Paul rose to deliver his sermon.

The message was simple. 'From time to time I am asked a question, and I am sure some of you have been asked the same question. Perhaps we have also asked the question. The question is, "If Jesus was the Son of God, why do you call today Good Friday? Should it not be Bad Friday?"

'There are two ways to answer such a question: a long way and a short way. The long way would take us through the Old Testament, explaining the relationship between God and his people, the Children of Israel. It would talk about rules and obedience to the rules, about disobedience and punishment for failing to obey God's law. It would talk about sacrifice and the need to make amends.

'The short answer is simply to say that in Jesus Christ we were shown a new way, the way of love. A love that forgives and asks for love in return. Today we remember that by his death Jesus made the ultimate sacrifice, and by his death we are assured of God's forgiveness for our wrongdoing and our disobedience. All that is required of us is to acknowledge Jesus as our Saviour and Lord and to follow him. To love God, and to love our neighbour. It is as simple as that. It does not, as some would have you believe, promise that we will not have difficult times in our lives, but we will always have God's love and his Spirit to help us deal with the hard times. This is why it is Good Friday, and that is why we are here tonight.'

There seemed to be a special atmosphere of reverence as the singing of Isaac Watt's great hymn, 'When I survey the wondrous Cross' brought the service to an end. Paul had to admit that he too had felt a deeper sense of the presence of God as he sang. Shaking hands with the worshippers as they left the building, he was certain, not so much by what they said, but how they said it, that many of them had had a similar experience. Mary and William Watson simply said 'Thank you' and 'Good evening' as they took Paul's hand in both of theirs, but the pressure of those hands and the look in their eyes told Paul how much the service and his short address had meant to them more than any words could have done.

Later, having dinner with Ruth, Jennifer and Malcolm, Paul could feel some of the tension of the last two days ebbing out of him. Sleep came earlier that night, a sleep that refreshed him for the days ahead.

10

About 15 years earlier, Alison Munro, a member of the Burnbrae Scottish Women's Rural Institute, had been so moved by yet another tragic lifeboat disaster that she persuaded some of her friends in the Institute to raise funds to help the Royal National Lifeboat Institute. The event had been a great success, leading to the formation of a fundraising branch in the town. Easter Saturday was traditionally the day the group held its annual coffee afternoon and craft fair. Helen Meikle, a friend of Alison since childhood, had been a member of the group from the beginning and had roped Jessie in as a member. William Watson audited the group's accounts each year, just one of the many organisations he helped in this way. He would have known when taking up his post as manager of the Burnbrae branch of the bank that voluntary groups would expect him to help out in such a manner, and head office also expected it of their managers.

When news of the accident involving Jessie's family reached Alison on the Thursday morning, her first thought was that she would have to cancel the coffee afternoon. As the news spread to other members of the group she received a number of phone calls from members who felt the same. Alison called an emergency meeting at her home that very afternoon. Not all the members could attend at such short notice, but those who did, and those who had expressed a view when apologising for being unable to be present, were not all in agreement that the event should be cancelled. One or two suggested that postponement for a month might be appropriate, showing sympathy to the bereaved, but not depriving the RNLI of much-needed income.

The last thing Alison had wanted to do was to put the matter to a vote. If the committee were divided, that division might spread out into the community where the RNLI had great support. 'So, Ladies,' she asked, 'should we postpone the coffee afternoon for a month?'

'Before we decide, could I just say something?' Ella Purdie did not normally say much at meetings of the group, but her comments, when she did speak, were always well-thought-out and concisely presented.

'Of course, Ella, please do,' responded a somewhat relieved Alison.

'This group came into being through a terrible tragedy. What happened last night was also a terrible tragedy, a tragedy that directly affects two of our members, our auditor and their families. Cancelling the event will not help their suffering, and I also think it might not be what they would want us to do. It will be up to the public to decide for themselves if they want to come along, but it is just possible that having something that brings us together will be a part of the healing process for all of us.'

There was silence as the others appeared to ponder Ella's statement. Alison waited before commenting quietly, 'I was going to ask if we should go ahead as usual, but it won't be like usual. However, I think Ella is right. We should go ahead.'

'Hear, hear,' responded the group.

Soon after the members began to leave, and as she said goodbye to the final two, Alison found herself wondering if they had made the correct decision. While she was wrestling with her doubts, the telephone rang.

'Hello, Alison Munro's home.'

'Hello, Alison. William Watson here.'

Alison froze. Surely he had not already heard about the decision? Was he about to tear a strip off her and the committee for not cancelling? These thoughts flashed through her mind, then she realised what Mr Watson was actually saying.

'Alison, someone from the bank will bring you the floats for the various stalls in plenty of time for the opening. Sorry not to be with you this time, but I'm sure you'll manage fine.'

'Of course we will. I was so sorry to hear what happened. Give Mary my love. Take care. And thank you for thinking about us at such a time.'

As Alison put the receiver down, she marvelled at how normal William had sounded. Much more composed than she would have been she was sure.

On Saturday morning Alison was gratified, but also surprised, to find the community centre a hive of industry as the committee and their helpers got ready for the coffee afternoon. People arrived in droves with donations for the various stalls. From some of the remarks that were made to her she understood that many were glad to be doing something practical instead of sitting at home thinking about the accident and the effect it was having on so many in the area. There was such a large crowd waiting outside the community centre that when the doors were opened and they poured in there was scarcely room to move, but despite that, or more likely because of it, the baking stall sold out in record time and the takings exceeded all previous sales. There was a buzz about the hall all afternoon, but every so often one could see two people, or a small group, talking quietly, concerned expressions on their faces; the terrible happening on Wednesday evening was never far from everyone's mind, nor would it be for many days to come.

Soon it was all over, the community centre was tidied up and the stallholders chatted over a cup of tea or coffee while the cash was counted. The final total was beyond all expectations. There was a burst of applause before Alison thanked everyone for their support. Burnbrae was not a place where crime was a problem, but Alison was glad her husband was with her as they walked to the bank night safe. Apart from the safety angle, the bag containing the cash was very heavy.

Normally Paul would have been present at the coffee afternoon to lend his support, but that was not possible on this occasion; he was conducting the wedding service. He arrived at the church 30 minutes before the appointed time for the ceremony, 10 minutes before the bridegroom and his best man arrived.

'Right on time, well done,' Paul said as he greeted the two nervous young men when the church officer showed them into the vestry. 'Remember you have nothing to worry about. Just follow my lead, and don't look so miserable,' he joked. 'This is the happiest day of your life! Now, who's got the ring?'

'Me,' replied the best man. 'It's in my pocket.'

'And do you remember which pocket?' Paul joked.

'Aye.'

'So, when I am putting the vows to the bride and groom, make sure you put your hand in that pocket and get hold of the ring. It's amazing how often there is a frantic search for it because it has got into a corner. And do not slip it onto your finger. Getting it back off could be a problem we don't need.'

Paul turned to the bridegroom. 'And when you go to place the ring on the bride's finger, you will find that she is already holding out her hand, ring finger clearly displayed. No problems there.'

Paul's attempt to ease their tension before the photographer arrived and took them to the front of the church for photographs was not particularly successful, and when they returned after the photography session, the bridegroom was more nervous than ever. Despite Paul's best efforts, he was much the same when the church officer came into the vestry to tell them that the bride had arrived.

'Here we go then. Good luck,' Paul announced cheerily and led them into the church.

Everything went according to plan, well almost. At one point the bride had done her best to prevent a sneeze, but, of course, that only made matters worse. A loud sneeze echoed around the building. Someone laughed. The poor girl was left looking for a handkerchief. She didn't have one, nor did her attendants, and if either of the men had one, they were oblivious to her plight. Quickly Paul reached into his cassock pocket and produced his. The bride took it, a look of relief on her face, used it and handed it back. As Paul put it in his pocket he wondered how long it had been since he had last put a clean handkerchief in that pocket. It might have been weeks, more likely months. The only saving grace was that as far as he was aware, he had not had a cold for ages.

At the beginning of his ministry, Paul had resolved to treat everyone equally. If he and Ruth were friends of the family, they would be invited to the wedding and would both attend the ceremony and the reception. On all other occasions, he would go on to the reception but leave once the newlyweds had led off the dancing. Despite all that he was involved with, Paul was attending the reception as usual. The photographer was now in charge at the hotel, and just when it seemed that the final pose had been captured on film, there was yet another photo to take. Family members used the time to catch up with relatives they had not seen for some time. Before long, Paul found himself thinking of those other families who would be meeting up, not to celebrate, but to mourn.

'Aye, Minister,' said a familiar voice, 'ye'll be havin' a busy time, one way an' anither.'

It was one of the local worthies, old Jock Black, a great-uncle of the bride. Jock was a retired farm labourer who seldom missed a Sunday service. Paul enjoyed calling on Jock and listening to his stories of the 'old days'. There was probably a fair amount of exaggeration in the stories, but they were also a reminder of how hard life had been not so very long ago, and yet, despite that, or perhaps because of it, many an amusing tale was told.

'Yes,' Paul agreed. 'It's busy, but it's all part of the job. I just hope I'm up to it.'

'No fear o' that, Minister. Just be yourself and ye'll dae fine.'

'I hope so, Jock. Thanks.'

'Ladies and Gentlemen, the final photograph has been taken,' announced the hotel owner, adding in a loud whisper, 'Thank goodness!' before continuing in his formal voice, 'Will you please come forward and meet the bridal party before making your way into the dining room. You will find the seating plan as you enter. Thank you.'

Paul hung back. At this point in the proceedings he was part of the bridal party. The only reason he was with them was that he would be seated at the top table and act as Master of Ceremonies. Why he had to line up and shake hands with every guest, most of whom he would never see again, he did not know. Finally, once everyone was seated, he awaited the signal to indicate that the meal was about to be served. After a short grace the guests were soon tucking into the delicious fare, then it was time for the formal speeches.

The normal custom was for the minister to act as Master of Ceremonies and to begin by offering a toast to the bride and groom. Paul had a number of jokes that he had been telling for some years, not that they improved with age, but they were the best he had. It was always easier when he knew the young couple and their parents, or at least the bride and her family. On this occasion Paul knew very little. Both families were local but never came near the church except for special family occasions. He did his best, tried not to embarrass anyone too much and got a bit of a laugh at his jokes, even though some of the guests had clearly heard a couple of them at previous weddings celebrated by him.

'To the bride and groom,' he toasted, as he concluded his remarks. The guests joined in. There was even some applause. Paul could never decide if it was for his speech, or for the young couple. Now it was the turn of the bridegroom. He did exactly as Paul had advised. He kept it short, read from his script, told one joke, not very well, but it was acceptable, and toasted the bridesmaids.

Then it was the turn of the best man, and he lived up to all expectations. He thanked his pal on behalf of the bridesmaids, managing to have them blushing in the process, before moving on to the 'main man' as he called the groom. How much was true, Paul had no idea, but not for the first time he wondered why such a charming young lady had fallen for such a rogue. He assumed, and hoped he was right, that there was considerable exaggeration and even some downright untruths in the stories from the groom's earlier years.

After a short speech from the two fathers, the formal part was over. The tables were cleared away, the band struck up and the new Mr and Mrs Tait took to the floor to much cheering. At the end of the dance Paul wished the young couple every blessing once again, said goodbye to both families and made his way home to his comfortable chair and a quiet evening.

'So much for a family get-together,' Paul said to Ruth once he was settled in his favourite armchair. 'I thought we might spend some quality time with Jennifer and Malcolm this weekend, but no, they're off out, and we're left on our own. Malcolm I think only came back to get his washing done, his meals cooked and to spend the rest of his break with his old pals.' He took a sip of his whisky.

'Come on. Be fair,' Ruth replied. 'Jennifer's only home for a couple of nights. She doesn't have much time and there are quite a few friends she wants to see. And it doesn't help when we were out much of the day, you at the wedding and me involved with the coffee afternoon. And Malcolm is doing what he has always done on a visit home. Here, there and everywhere, anywhere but here. Just hope if I'm asleep when they get in they don't waken me.'

Paul knew better than to continue his moan. 'I suppose so, but it would have been nice. Never mind, tomorrow is another day, and after the service I have no intention of doing anything else, workwise at least.'

'I hope you're not tempting providence with that remark,' Ruth commented. 'You know as well as I do that if the phone rings, or there's a knock at the door, you'll answer it. And you won't say no, no matter what the reason for the call.'

'Well, it is my job. Despite what some folk think...'

'I know, you're on call no matter what the time is, or what you're doing, so sit back, enjoy your dram and I'll do likewise.' Ruth picked up her G and T, raised it in a mock toast and turned her attention back to the television.

He never did hear Malcolm and Jennifer return.

11

The Easter Service was well attended as always; the singing was better than Paul had expected, the music and words uplifting. Some members of the congregation, male and female, struggled at times. His sermon was delivered in a silence that could almost be felt.

He spoke of Mary's meeting with her Risen Lord beside the empty tomb on Easter morning, reminding the congregation that in her grief she did not recognise the man who had given her back her dignity. She thought he was a gardener until he softly called her name, 'Mary'. She recognised the voice instantly. Her grief turned to joy.

Paul moved forward a week to the Upper Room where the disciples were meeting behind a locked door, fearful that they too might be arrested and punished. Suddenly Jesus was there with them as he had been the previous week. Thomas had not been present seven days earlier and would not believe what the others had told him until he touched the wounds inflicted on Jesus.

'"Stretch out your hand, Thomas, and touch." But Thomas had no need to touch, he saw, he recognised the voice. "My Lord and my God!" he exclaimed.' Paul's sermon was one of the shortest he had preached as he made it clear that the Gospels spoke of love, a love that Jesus revealed in his life and especially in his death.

'Throughout his life,' Paul concluded, 'Jesus was there, helping others, turning no one away. At the grave of his friend Lazarus, he wept. Today we remember that God raised him from the dead. He is alive, and he is with us wherever we are, in times of joy and in times of despair. Softly he calls us by our name, gently he holds us and his love surrounds us. Amen.'

Back at the manse the family relaxed over Sunday lunch. Jennifer would have to return to her flat later in the afternoon but there would be time for a walk in the local park.

'Will we be rolling our eggs?' Malcolm joked.

'There are eggs in the pantry and if you want to roll one, all you have to do is boil it,' his mother replied. 'And decorate it, of course.'

Malcolm seemed to be about to make a cheeky reply, but thought better of it. 'Perhaps I'm a bit old for that.'

'What you mean is, you can't even boil an egg,' Jennifer quipped.

Malcolm could, but he clearly realised when he was outnumbered. 'OK, so it's just a walk then.'

Paul and his family enjoyed the walk, laughing and joking as they recalled the many happy times they had spent together on a Sunday afternoon when Jennifer and Malcolm were children. All too soon it was time for Jennifer to leave. Malcolm had decided that he really better do some reading to prepare for his return to university.

'Well, it was nice while it lasted,' Paul remarked, as once again he and Ruth sat in front of the television, just the two of them. 'But it seems as though Jennifer was no sooner here when she had to leave. How time flies.'

'Yes, and the years too,' Ruth added. 'Never mind, before much longer we may be taking the grandchildren for a walk in the park.'

Paul looked startled. 'Do you know something I don't?'

'Don't be silly, of course I don't. I just mean that our children will soon be making their own way in the world, and that way looks as though it means settling down and, hopefully, not only having a career, but having a soulmate and children too.'

'Well, yes, and if a career means Mum and Dad being the childminders, we better make the most of the time we have now.'

'I'm sure we have a few years before we reach that stage,' Ruth reassured him. 'It's something to look forward to though. Only problem is, they'll probably not stay in Burnbrae, or wherever we happen to be.'

'Probably not. Oh, and by the way, I have no intention of leaving Burnbrae, well, not in the near future, though we can never be certain what the future holds for us.'

As soon as Paul said these words, he found himself thinking of the accident and of those whose lives had changed so irrevocably. He would stay where he was for as long as these folk needed him, no matter how long that was.

At that moment the front doorbell rang.

'Who can this be?' Ruth asked, clearly not amused. 'You're not expecting anyone, are you?'

'No, I'm not. What I was expecting was a quiet evening.'

Paul opened the door to find a worried-looking Bob Meikle standing on the step.

'I'm sorry to bother you, Minister,' Bob blurted out before Paul had a chance to say anything by way of a greeting. 'Especially on a Sunday, and this Sunday in particular, but I have to speak to someone. I don't know what to do.'

Bob stopped for breath and Paul managed to get some words out, at the same time gesturing to Bob to enter the house. 'Never mind what day it is. If you need to see me, you need to see me, and I did say you could get in touch at any time. Come on into the study and I'll do my best to help you.'

As they sat down in armchairs facing one another, Paul assumed that Bob would want to speak about the accident and the consequences, but exactly what? Kirsty was dead, Sandy was on life support and what the parents were suffering he could not even begin to imagine. He hoped that whatever it was he would be able to give Bob the help or advice he so obviously needed.

'Would you like tea, or coffee? Maybe a dram?' Paul suggested, playing for time and allowing his visitor to perhaps calm down a bit.

'No, no, it's OK. To be honest, I had a small whisky after my dinner, but it made no difference. Usually I have no problem knowing what to do, even when something out of the ordinary happens on the farm. Might take a bit of time to get the right answer, but this, this is beyond me.'

'I'm not surprised. Take your time and when you're ready, tell me what the problem is,' Paul replied.

'I can tell you what the problem is, that's the easy bit. It's what the answer is that's the difficult part. Maybe even the impossible part. I really do hope you can give me the answer.'

'I can listen, I can advise, but the answer has to come from you, and be assured, that whatever you decide, I'll support you all I can.'

Paul now had several scenarios running around in his head. All he could do was wait for Bob to enlighten him and hope that he could point him in the right direction.

'It's Sandy, Minister. We have to meet with the consultant on Tuesday. I know it's not immediately, but Jessie and I are going round and round in circles, wondering if we should do this or that, or if there is even something we haven't thought of yet. Sometimes we agree, then one of us changes our mind, and off we go again. And we have Kirsty's funeral to think about too.'

'Bob, slow down. What do you think the consultant wants to see you about?' Paul had a fair idea what it might be about, but he didn't want to jump in, in case he was wrong. He had learned that lesson early in his ministry.

'Sorry, give me a minute to sort myself out.'

'Take all the time you need,' Paul replied. 'I'll just pop next door and let Ruth know you're here.'

'I should have waited till tomorrow…'

Paul interrupted him. 'You've done the right thing. I'm not saying we'll resolve the problem, but talking it over can only help. Anyway, Ruth is going to be watching a drama on TV that, quite honestly, bores me stupid.'

He smiled as he said the final words. They were a bit of an exaggeration, but to Paul's amazement, Bob also managed the glimmer of a smile.

Paul quickly let Ruth know who his caller was and immediately returned to find his visitor slightly calmer, but the look on his face suggested that perhaps his problem had no solution.

Bob sighed and then began to speak. 'We were at the hospital earlier today, in fact for most of the day. Sometimes we think we see the flicker of an eyelid, but we're just imagining it. Wishful thinking even. Anyway, there's no change in Sandy's condition. He's still critical. The machines are keeping him alive. The ward sister told us the consultant would like to meet with us and discuss the options. She didn't say what they are, but we can imagine.'

'It's not going to be an easy meeting,' Paul agreed. 'Do you want me to be with you?'

'No, you have enough to do here. The meeting is the easy bit, it's what our decision will be that's the hard bit.'

Paul waited.

'On the farm,' Bob continued, 'the vet gives us a choice. Continue with the treatment, or put the beast out of its misery. The answer is usually obvious. But this is Sandy we're talking about, not a beast.' Bob's voice cracked and his eyes filled.

'But you don't know that's what the consultant is going to say, Bob. He may want to suggest an operation and to talk over the procedure with you. And Sandy can't give his consent, so you'll need to give it.'

'Aye, maybe, but I don't think that's what it's about. And if Sandy does survive an operation, he might well be helpless for the rest of his life. That won't be our Sandy.'

Paul held back from commenting. He sensed that Bob had more to say. He was right.

Bob took a deep breath before continuing, 'There's something else. We need to arrange Kirsty's funeral. Jessie wants to wait and see if Sandy will get better, but if he dies, she wants them to be buried together, to have a joint funeral. Sandy is still alive, but for how long? Do we agree now to switch off the machines so that we can bury them on the same day, then spend the rest of our lives wondering if we murdered our son?' Bob was too upset to continue.

Paul chose his words carefully. 'Bob, I began by saying that I can't make the decision for you, but I'm certain that after this meeting with the consultant you'll have a much better understanding of the situation. The decision may be made for you, once you've weighed up all the options. And sometimes preparing for the worst possible outcome means that if that's not what happens, then whatever does happen is that much better. Sorry, that doesn't seem to have come out the way I meant it to,' Paul added.

'No, it's all right. I understand,' Bob replied, 'and it has helped. I was going round in circles and getting more and more anxious all the time. You're right. You usually are.' Bob even managed the faintest of smiles. Paul could feel his face flushing at the compliment. 'I mean it, you have the ability to get alongside folk in trouble and share their burden. Some people try to help but only make matters worse, but not you. And you have helped. I don't know what the consultant will have to say, and I don't know how Jessie and I will react if it is bad news, but there's no point in going on and on about it tonight. I'll get off home now and leave you in peace for what's left of your evening.'

In fact it was 10 or 15 minutes before Bob departed. He was visibly much calmer than when he had arrived. Paul reckoned that neither he, Bob nor Jessie would sleep soundly that night. As they shook hands on the doorstep. Paul wondered if Bob was thinking the same as him – what will tomorrow bring.

12

'What time do you think we should go round to see Paul?' asked William the following morning as he cleared the kitchen table after breakfast. Mary was washing up the dishes while he put away the butter, milk and marmalade.

'I don't really know. We don't want to go too soon, but then again, we have to make sure that what we're proposing to do is convenient for him.'

'I'm sure it will be. He said that whatever we arranged would be all right as far as he was concerned.'

'Yes, I know he did, but we're not the only ones planning a funeral this week, and today is a holiday for most people,' Mary reminded him.

Planning Wilma's funeral was never going to be an easy task for them. The previous evening they had spent some time, and shed a few tears, deciding what they thought would be appropriate. It would be a simple service, the kind that most folk had. Family and friends would gather at the house and Paul would conduct the service. Space would be a problem but, as was the custom, those who were not family or close friends would stand outside in the garden. The familiar words would be spoken so even if they didn't hear everything, those outside would still feel a part of it.

They had been uncertain as to whether Wilma should be cremated or laid to rest in the local cemetery. More and more families in the cities were opting for the former but in rural areas burial was still very much the custom, partly because local families already had a family lair. Wilma had never, so far as they could remember, expressed a preference. How many young people had?

Their dilemma had been more that they had not yet decided where they would settle when William retired. There had been talk of a bungalow in one of the West Coast seaside towns, but that was about as far as they had got. Now they were being forced to make a decision. If they chose cremation there was no problem, but how could they move away if Wilma's final resting place was the cemetery in Burnbrae? Mary settled the matter when, almost without thinking, she said, 'The cemetery here is so peaceful and well looked-after. I think I would like Wilma to be buried there. She will always remain in our hearts, but if she's there we could visit her grave and remain close, even if we decide to settle by the seaside.'

There was no way he was going to argue with that.

That settled, William had phoned the local joiner and undertaker, Lachlan Mitchell, known to all as Lachie. It was expected that Wilma's body would be released at the beginning of the week, soon after the holiday was over, and the funeral could take place on Friday.

William closed the fridge door. 'Mary, we only contacted Lachie Mitchell yesterday evening to explain what we wanted and to ask him to begin making the arrangements. He said he would be in touch with Paul. I expected him to wait until this morning before he made the call to Paul. Anyway, we can't finalise things until the procurator fiscal gives permission and I had hoped that our nearest relatives would have let us know by now if they had any unbreakable appointments over the coming days. My brother Graham, as usual, has not yet replied. I think he assumes that if he does not immediately reply no, then the answer is yes.'

'We can sort Graham out later. Let's not fall out about when we meet with Paul, dear,' Mary replied, perhaps sensing that William was having difficulty maintaining his normal cool, collected, businesslike manner. 'I think it only polite to get in touch with him ourselves. And I think half past ten would be early enough. Why not phone first?'

'Probably that would be best,' agreed William, as he wiped some crumbs from the table.

It was just after 11 a.m. when Paul showed his friends and neighbours into his study. He had offered to call on them but William had insisted that he would do no such thing.

'You stay where you are, Paul. Once we have talked over what has to be decided, we'll be on our way and leave Ruth and yourself to get on with what you were planning to do.'

Ruth had prepared tea and coffee for the Watsons and served it as soon as they were settled. Paul would be fully responsible for the Scripture readings and prayers. As they talked about Wilma, Paul made notes in order to be able to pay a full and fitting tribute to her achievements and personality. Paul was not really surprised at how much she had done, and done well, in her too short life. Much of it he already knew, but from the little personal stories that her loving parents recounted, often with a tear, the high regard he already had for Wilma was confirmed. His tribute would be full and honest and more than a little emotional.

Paul put his notebook aside before raising the problem that had been troubling him for some time. 'I'm just a little worried that there will be far more people in attendance than your house can hold. Have you considered holding the service in Lachie's new funeral parlour?'

'Not really,' William replied. 'I mean, we're aware of it, and by all accounts it's very nice, but it's not for us. Wilma left her home last Wednesday and never returned. As soon as possible she'll be brought back home, and it's from her home that she'll make her final journey.'

William's manner and tone made it very clear to Paul that the decision was final. Mary was nodding her head as he spoke, and holding a handkerchief to her eyes.

'I understand,' Paul said softly.

Some memories of Wilma were shared as the four of them remembered her, memories that would hopefully bring comfort.

'Just one other thing,' Ruth said to Mary as she was about to leave. 'If you need any help, baking, that kind of thing, just ask.'

'Thanks, but I think everything is under control,' Mary replied. 'If it's not, you might regret your offer.'

That eased the tension, but only a little.

'I don't know how they manage,' Ruth said to Paul, slipping her arm round his waist as they watched their neighbours shut the garden gate.

'Neither do I. Nor any of the other families for that matter. To be honest, there are one or two individuals I'm worried about. I don't think they're coping.'

'Meaning?' Ruth asked.

'I know it's a holiday, but I really do think I have to visit the parents again this afternoon. Do you mind?'

'Would it matter if I did? Of course I don't. I wish someone had warned me that when I married a minister I would have to share him with hundreds of others.'

Before Paul could comment, Ruth got in first. 'Sorry, that was uncalled for, in the circumstances.'

'Perhaps it was, but it's also true.' Paul gave her a quick kiss and a longer hug. How fortunate he was to have Ruth's support.

Mrs Melville had spent most of the morning trying to help Doreen, but it seemed that no matter what she said or did, it made no difference. As had become her custom every morning since learning of Brian's death, she had done whatever had to be done in her own home before popping across the landing to check on how Doreen was coping. If anything, the situation was even more distressing.

'Hello, Doreen. It's only me, Effie,' she called out as she opened the front door to her neighbour's home. 'All right for me to come in?'

There was no reply. She knew that Doreen had been given compassionate leave from the factory for as long as she needed it. It was unlikely that she would have gone out. Effie made her way to the living room. Doreen was sitting in her usual chair. She looked up, saw her neighbour and began to shout. 'If he's not home by teatime tonight, I will not be responsible for my actions. I need him here now and he knows it.'

'What is it? What has happened?'

'It's Ed. He phoned to say he doesn't know if he'll make the lunchtime train. Something about a problem with the helicopter. He might not be home, if this is still his home, until tomorrow.'

'Now, now, dear, I'm sure he's doing his best. These things happen.'

'And that's another thing, my mum and dad won't be back until Sunday! Don't know how they could have been so stupid.'

'What do you mean? I thought they would be here by now.'

'Do you see them?' Doreen shouted. 'Of course you can't. They're still in Spain. Probably having a drink by the pool at their bloody hotel.' Her face was scarlet. 'Sorry, I shouldn't have said that. It's not your fault.'

Effie was really confused. 'I thought they were getting an earlier plane.'

'So did I, but they can't. Guess what they did? They didn't get travel insurance.'

Effie, like most people she knew, had never been abroad. She didn't understand the problem. 'Could they not just get another plane?' she asked.

Doreen took a breath as if to calm herself. 'That was what I thought, but these holidays are special flights. You go out on one day and you come back a week or a fortnight later. That's the deal. Anything else and you have to pay extra. And it's not one plane, it's three, and the cost is huge.'

'Three planes?'

'Three planes. One to Madrid, one to London, and finally one to Glasgow. And no cheap deals. Oh, and probably a hotel in London overnight.'

'Oh dear,' was all Effie could manage.

Doreen took several deep breaths. There was an awkward silence. Effie waited.

'I'm sorry, Effie, I shouldn't have taken it out on you.'

'It's all right, dear. You needed to let it out. Now, I think a cup of tea is called for. I'll put the kettle on,' suggested Effie, as she rose from her chair. Doreen managed a half-hearted smile.

When Paul arrived at Doreen's flat in the early afternoon, she was on her own. She explained why there were no other family members with her. She seemed as if she was keeping her feelings in check but he wasn't fooled. She was hurting. He would have to choose his words carefully. He tried to convince her that Ed would be with her as soon as possible, but that failed.

'I want to believe you,' Doreen replied, 'but I know him. Why should he rush home this time? He has friends in Aberdeen he would rather visit nowadays.'

'He's Brian's father. I think that is why.' Before Doreen had a chance to counter that suggestion, Paul moved on quickly. 'Your parents have learned a valuable lesson about the need to have insurance when going on a foreign holiday. They must be devastated. Far from home, and not able to be with you.'

'That doesn't help me.'

'Of course it doesn't,' Paul agreed. 'Until your husband makes it back, Mrs Melville will always be around to support you. She might be getting on a bit, but she has seen trouble in her own life. She knows what it's like to lose someone close.'

'I've lost my son, my sixteen-year-old son. She lost her husband. He was old and he was ill.'

'I'm sorry. I know it's not the same.'

'And it's not fair. Nothing is. Not for me it isn't.'

The floodgates opened and before Paul could make any reply to her outburst, Doreen was sobbing her heart out. Paul sat on the arm of her chair and put his arm around her shoulder. Gradually she calmed down. He remained where he was for a moment longer.

'I'm not going to pretend that I understand how you feel, I don't and to be honest, I hope I never do, but if talking helps, I'll listen. If you want to scream, that's OK too.'

Doreen looked surprised.

'I mean it. Whatever helps, even screaming.'

'Thanks, eh, Min–'

'Paul will do fine.'

'Thanks, Paul. I don't even go to church.'

'But you live in my parish and I'm here for anyone who needs me, and at the moment that's you.'

In the end, Paul stayed with Doreen far longer than he had intended. When he did leave, she was much calmer and he had a very clear understanding of the problems facing the young woman. He would like to think that the arrival of her husband, hopefully sooner rather than later, would help resolve some of the issues worrying her, but he was not at all convinced that it would. It appeared that the marriage was beyond saving. There might be a truce until sometime after the funeral, but he didn't hold out much hope for a reconciliation. Sometimes he had to reluctantly admit that a clean break was the only way forward for some couples. Before he left it was agreed that once Ed got back, Doreen would let him know and he would return, unless of course he could be of any further help before that.

Paul stepped back out onto the pavement and looked across at the ironmonger's shop opposite. Like all the other businesses in the town, except the bank and the post office, it was open for business as usual. As far as Paul understood, this was a custom peculiar to Scotland. Each city and town decided on the date of its local holidays. New Year's Day and the second of January had traditionally been the only national holidays. Christmas Day had recently been added. This arrangement meant that the inhabitants of one place could spend their time, and their money, in a neighbouring burgh that was open for business as usual. The larger areas of local government about to come into being in a few weeks might be the beginning of the end for this way of doing things.

Paul had more to worry about than the end of an age-old custom. Rather than make his way to the MacCallums' house, he decided to try the shop first. He did not want to disturb Mrs MacCallum. That was what he told himself, but what he was thinking was that he had no idea how to help her if she was as she had been on his previous visit.

Tom was behind the counter. There were no customers.

'Come away in, Minister,' Tom called out as soon as he saw him. 'I was just going to make a brew. Come through the back and take the weight off your feet.'

Tom seemed cheerful, too cheerful, Paul thought. He was about to reply that he had just had a cup of tea, but decided that accepting Tom's offer might lead on to something more important.

Tom lifted the flap in the counter that gave access to the back shop. 'I gave the staff the day off. Never really busy on Easter Monday. Just the odd customer who has miscalculated what he needs for the work he is doing in the house or garden.'

If Nan, Tom's wife, was saying little, Tom was the opposite. Paul couldn't get a word in. As the kettle boiled, Tom continued to talk. He asked Paul how the services had gone, he mentioned the weather, anything but what both knew was the one thing uppermost in his mind. Paul nodded and made the appropriate response, but before he could ask how his host was coping, Tom was off again. It was only when they were both sipping their piping hot tea that Paul got his chance.

'And how are you all doing?' he asked softly.

Tom looked directly at him. He said nothing. Paul held his gaze and waited. Eventually Tom shook his head. 'We're not.' Quickly he pulled out a handkerchief and held it to his eyes.

Paul reached over and put his hand on the grief-stricken man's shoulder. 'Let it out. Don't try to stop it.'

When Tom had recovered the two men began to talk. Tom held nothing back. Nan was still locked up in her grief; Gary was putting on a brave face most of the time, but Tom had heard sobs coming from his bedroom late at night and he himself was faring no better. Paul tried to offer some advice but what could he say? Even a prayer might be ill received.

The tinkling of the bell on the shop door announced the arrival of a customer. Tom stood up, gave his eyes another wipe, blew his nose and said, 'Excuse me.'

'No, on you go. I'll rinse out the mugs before I leave.'

Tom was already greeting the customer. Paul hung back until he heard Tom say goodbye. Quickly he made his way through to the shop. He didn't want to rush out, but he didn't know what else he could say.

'Thanks for coming, Minister. You've been a great help.'

The surprise must have registered on Paul's face.

'I'm glad you didn't make comments like a lot of other folk. I know they mean well, but it doesn't really help. Not at the moment anyway. You sat and listened. I know you have something I don't have, something that gives you a hope that I don't have. I would love to have that hope, that faith, and perhaps someday I will have it, but today isn't that day. When I'm ready, you and I will talk about this again. Who knows, you might get me in the kirk yet.'

With that he took Paul's hand and shook it firmly. Paul was convinced that he saw something in Tom's eyes that had not been there before. Despite what he had just said, Paul wondered if Tom was sending out a message: asking for not just answers but a reason to keep on going.

13

The previous evening, Bob had told Jessie that the car was low on fuel. It was only when he passed the crescent on the way to the filling station that he had decided to call in at the manse. Jessie was surprised as he explained the reason for his long absence when he eventually returned home.

'You could have said you might do that before you left. I was getting really worried that something had happened.'

Bob knew he had been selfish, thinking only of his need to talk to someone other than family members. He would have been worried if Jessie had done the same.

'It was a spur-of-the-moment decision. I should have thought about you. I'm so sorry. I won't do anything like that again.'

'It's all right. I understand. I might even have done the same thing myself. We are both struggling and you thought talking to someone else would be better than adding to my woes.'

'Aye, something like that,' Bob replied. He gave Jessie a brief account of his conversation with Paul. It led on to a discussion about their plans for the following day. Eventually they agreed that if there was no change in Sandy's condition they would stay at home. There were things around the farm that Bob felt he had to check on, and Jessie was struggling to hold it together as she sat by Sandy's bedside. A day at home might help them get a bit of rest and regain their strength for all that lay ahead of them.

Bob knew that his dad and young Iain were perfectly capable of looking after everything in his absence and as he walked around the outbuildings, then rode round the fields in the quad bike, he was reassured; all was well, at least as far as the farm was concerned.

Back in the farmhouse he found Jessie busy baking.

'I thought you were taking it easy,' he said as he gave her a peck on the cheek. 'You look as though you're preparing to feed the five thousand.'

'It's not easy to do nothing. Not that I can forget, whatever I am doing. And I wouldn't want that.'

'No, I was the same. All the time I was out looking at the beasts and the sheep, I was more concerned about Sandy, wondering when he would show signs of improving. And Kirsty was always there as well.'

'Same here.' As she spoke, Jessie threw her arms round Bob, covering his back in flour as she did so. Then the phone rang. Reluctantly Bob released his hold of Jessie and went through to the office to answer it, all the time dreading that it was more bad news.

'You better get on with these scones,' Bob advised her when he returned. 'That was Dan. How many times has he phoned now? Asking how we are and offering help, and this time he says Jean will be round later. And no doubt she'll pass the word around that we're at home today.'

'Jean's not a gossip.'

'I never said she was, but she's bound to tell someone else and then it spreads quickly. You know what it's like.'

And so it proved to be. First Jean and then before they realised it, there were another three of her friends sitting at the large kitchen table, and all of them had brought baking. There was even a large bowl of soup standing on the worktop. Bob had made himself scarce. He was back outside with Iain and Alec. By the time the visitors left, Helen and Alec had joined Jessie, Bob and Iain for lunch.

'That was a great bowl of soup,' Alec announced as he placed his spoon in the empty dish.

'And when was the last time you said that about my soup, or Jessie's?' asked Helen.

'Yours is good. And Jessie's.'

'And it was very good of whoever brought it. And there is all that baking too,' Jessie added. 'Sometimes actions speak louder than words.'

After lunch, retired farmer and good friend Stan and his wife Isobel paid a visit. Jessie and Bob were pleased to see them, but hoped not too many others from the farming community would be behind them. Early in the conversation it became clear that Stan and Isobel were bringing the thoughts of many of their friends.

'We all want you to know that you're very much in all our minds at this terrible time, but at the same time we don't want to impose on you,' Isobel said.

'No, it's fine, but we're not likely to be around much,' Bob began to reply, then saw Jessie's warning look.

Jessie cut him off. 'Please tell everyone we appreciate their concern very much and reassure them that if we need help, we won't hesitate to ask.'

'And that goes for help on the farm, Bob. I might not be as fit as I once was, but I can still have a go at most things,' Stan added.

There was some more general conversation and the visitors enjoyed Jessie's scones along with a cup of tea before taking their leave.

'Everyone is so kind,' Jessie commented as they watched their visitors drive out of the yard.

'Yes, they are, but none of them really knows what to say. Their visit helps to remind us that we're not forgotten, but while they're here I want them to go, and when no one is here, I think everyone else is getting on with life and just glad that what has happened to us didn't happen to them.'

'Don't be silly! Of course they care, they all do. And they do no doubt feel glad that it hasn't happened to them, and then they feel guilty for even thinking that.'

'Never thought of it like that. I suppose you're right, as usual.' Bob tried a smile and yet again failed miserably. 'I'll away out and check the beasts.'

'Off you go then. At least you know all about farming.'

'That's not…'

'What?' Jessie asked.

'Nothing. It's nothing,' he said as he hurried out before Jessie saw the tears streaming down his face. He had been about to add that wasn't what Sandy thought about his farming abilities.

Later that evening Bob contacted the ward to ask about Sandy. There was no change. The nurse looking after Sandy confirmed that the anaesthetist and surgeon would meet them at noon the following day. Bob had hoped that the nurse might have given him an idea of what they might be told at the meeting but, as gently as she could, she made it quite clear that was not her role. Her duty was to look after Sandy, to monitor him and to make sure that he was not suffering unduly, and that was exactly what she was doing.

'Sandy is comfortable, his condition seems to be stable and tomorrow you can ask the doctors as many questions as you like. They will answer truthfully,' she assured him. 'Tonight, try to get some rest.'

Bob thanked her once again for everything she was doing for Sandy. He went back to the room where Jessie was sitting watching a television soap, but probably not hearing a word that was spoken. He certainly wasn't taking in anything. His own troubles were real, not the imaginings of some unknown scriptwriter. Jessie listened to his account of the conversation with the nurse.

'Are you sure you're telling me everything?' she asked.

'Yes, that was what she said.'

'So, why the anxious look?'

'It's just the way she said I should get some rest. Do you think she knows something she didn't tell me?'

'She probably knows about as much as the doctors, and if Sandy had improved, or got worse, she would have said. She was being sensible. We need to get as much rest as we can. We have a long way still to go and no way of knowing what the final outcome will be. A dram and an early night for you. I might even have a wee gin myself. The glasses are over there.'

Bob stood up and went to pour the drinks. As usual Jessie was right. What would he do without her?

Back at the manse, Paul couldn't settle. He kept remembering Bob's final words as he was leaving the previous evening.

'Now, remember, Minister, there's no need for you to be visiting us every day. You have to look after yourself too, you know. The last thing we need is you running yourself into the ground.'

'Yes, but...'

'No "yes buts". I'm serious. We have things to do around the farm when we're not at the hospital. We have our moments, but we're looking out for one another. It's not easy, but so far we're just about managing.'

'If you're sure,' Paul replied, knowing full well that he wouldn't keep away for more than a couple of days, if that.

'I'm sure. Goodnight, Minister. And thanks again for all you're doing for everyone at this terrible time.'

How well had they coped since that conversation? What was the news of Sandy? Were they even thinking about making arrangements for Kirsty's funeral? He had heard nothing more from Lachie. And his mind didn't stop there. Had Ed Thomson arrived home? Was Nan MacCallum still refusing to speak?

'Are you watching this drama?' Ruth said, interrupting his thoughts.

'Eh, yes,' Paul managed to mutter, realising that he might be looking at the TV but his mind had been somewhere else for the last five or six minutes.

'Well, who is this guy who has suddenly appeared, and what has he got to do with anything?'

'Eh, I'm not quite sure either.'

'No, I know you're not. And I'm not really all that bothered. I've seen better. But I am worried about you. You can't spend your every waking moment thinking about these poor folk. If you're going to be of use to them, and you're helping them, you have to relax. Think of something else for a change. Read a book, actually watch TV, don't just stare in that direction. You could even talk to me.'

Paul wasn't quite certain if the last remark was a rebuke or a joke, but he knew that what Ruth was saying was true. Even Bob had said much the same the previous evening.

'OK, you're right. What shall we talk about then?'

And so they chatted about this and that, glanced at the television, had a nightcap, but no matter what they said or did, Paul could not forget the Watsons, the Meikles, the MacCallums and Doreen.

The following morning Effie Melville phoned Paul to let him know that Doreen's husband, Ed, had returned home late the previous evening. Paul promised that he would call in that afternoon, giving Ed a chance to recover from the journey and to be brought up to date with what had happened and with what needed to be done. Whether or not it would restore relations between the two, only time would tell. Paul tried not to jump to conclusions but before he knew it, he was imagining several possible scenarios of his meeting with the couple. He knew it was silly, but it was something he often did, only to discover that what actually took place was something very different.

This time he was not too far off the mark. His first impression of Ed wasn't good. He found him surly, uncommunicative and more than a little threatening. He was probably a little less than average height, but he was broad and clearly very fit. His rugged, weather-beaten face and dark, close-cropped hair did nothing to lessen that first impression. Paul was also worried that Doreen seemed somewhat cowed in his presence.

The conversation didn't flow, and no matter what Paul said, Ed's reply was not much more than aye or no. It was clear that he wanted Brian's funeral to take place as soon as possible, even if it meant that Doreen's mother and father might not be home in time to attend. Eventually it was agreed that the service would take place at Dalcairn Crematorium.

'When will it be?' Ed asked.

'That depends on the crematorium,' Paul answered. 'More and more families are choosing cremation nowadays, and with the Easter holiday, it will probably be next week.'

'This is Tuesday. That's ridiculous.'

'I'm sorry, but I already have a funeral planned for Friday, and the crematorium isn't open on Saturdays.'

'Maybe they could fit us in on Thursday.'

'I doubt it very much,' Paul replied. It was highly unlikely that it would be possible, but for the sake of Doreen and her parents he would make sure that it didn't happen until Tuesday at the earliest, even if it meant asking the undertaker to back him up.

Ed gave a sigh, accompanied by a look of anger that was quite frightening to Paul and appeared even more so to Doreen. Paul was worried for her safety. There was little he could say without making the atmosphere more tense than it already was.

'Would you like a cup of tea?' Doreen asked quietly.

'Eh, no, I'm afraid I have other calls to make. Perhaps next time. Once you have the date of the funeral I'll be back to talk over the service. If you have anything you want to discuss before then, anything at all, please don't hesitate to get in touch.'

As he was talking he took one of his business cards out of his pocket. He handed it to Doreen. 'Anything, no matter how unimportant it might seem. If it is adding to your worries, it's best to sort it out sooner rather than later.'

He was waiting for some comment from Ed, but to his great relief, he just sat still, not even rising as Paul shook his hand before moving towards the door. Doreen rose and preceded him to the outside door of the flat.

'Thank you so much,' she said.

'I'm just sorry I can't do more, but remember, anything, and I mean *anything* that troubles you, don't keep it to yourself. I'm always here to help.'

Doreen was near to tears as she muttered, 'Thanks.'

14

By the time Bob and Jessie returned home from their meeting with the medical team looking after Sandy, it was late in the afternoon. What they had heard was not encouraging. There had been no change in his condition.

Jessie and Bob had held hands while they listened to the consultant neurologist, Mr Fleming. As he talked about Sandy's injuries and the effect they had had on his brain and other organs, it became clear that the words they didn't want to hear were about to be uttered.

'And so, I'm afraid there's nothing more we can do,' Mr Fleming concluded. 'Any attempt to operate on the damaged parts of his brain would almost certainly do more harm. The body is not able to repair the damage. The life support machines are keeping him alive, but after this length of time, it's time to consider switching them off.'

Jessie sobbed. Bob tightened his grip on her hand, took a deep breath and exhaled before looking from Jessie to the surgeon. 'When will that happen?'

Before Mr Fleming could answer, Jessie spoke up. 'Are you sure you've done all you can? Can you not wait a bit longer, just in case? He's a fit young man.'

'I'm sorry, Mrs Meikle, our only hope, and it was always a very remote possibility, was that Sandy's body would itself begin the recovery process. That hasn't happened. To be honest, without the support of the machines you see, Sandy could not have survived as long as he has. Now it's time to let him go.'

After a long silence, Bob asked again, 'When will you turn off the machines?'

'That's up to you. You're his next of kin and you, and only you, can make that decision. There's no rush. We'll do our best to answer all your questions to enable you to understand the severity of your son's injuries and to help you reach your decision.'

For the next 10 minutes they listened as Mr Fleming, backed up by the anaesthetist, spoke in great detail about the damage already done to Sandy. He had head and abdominal injuries which even if they could be operated on, there was no guarantee that the operation would be a success and the most likely outcome was that Sandy would die during the operation.

Jessie and Bob knew there was no more to be said. Mr Fleming understood that they had made their decision. 'I'm sorry,' he said softly. 'We did all we could.'

'We know, and we appreciate it,' Bob managed to say. Jessie was sobbing quietly. 'We have to let him go,' Bob added, his voice no more than a whisper.

'One other thing, you will also have to decide if you wish to be present,' Mr Fleming said gently.

Jessie raised her head and looked at him. Hesitantly she asked, 'Will he die right away?'

'No, not right away, but it will be fairly quick,' the anaesthetist replied.

'I know we have no choice,' Bob said quietly, 'but I'd like to go back home and let the rest of the family hear what you've told us. If it is all right with you can I confirm later that we agree that we have to let Sandy go, and at the same time let you know if we will be present?'

'Of course you can. We'll leave you now. You can stay as long as you like, I'm sorry. We did all we could,' Mr Fleming repeated. 'Take care.'

The two men shook hands with Jessie and Bob before leaving.

'Would you like a cup of tea?' the sister asked.

'Yes, please,' Jessie and Bob replied.

They sat by Sandy's bedside, saying very little, until Bob suggested gently that they should leave. The family at home would be wondering what had happened, and there was no way he could tell them over the phone.

For William and Mary it was in some respects like a normal day, but it was far from that. William was back in his office at the bank. Business was busier than usual for a Tuesday, but that was always what happened after a bank holiday. The customers who had a meeting with him, however, were not at ease in his presence, even those whose accounts were well in credit. He understood that they were concerned that they might accidentally upset him. Some offered their condolences immediately they entered his office, others clearly did not know what to say regarding Wilma's tragic death and there was an unusual tension in the conversations that took place. William did his best to ease it, but he could sense that most would breathe a sigh of relief as soon as they were back out in the street. It was the same with some of the staff. The initial shock felt the previous Thursday had worn off. Now they had to deal with the reality, but how? William felt for them and did his best to act normally, but what would normal be like without Wilma?

Mary had been tidying up Wilma's bedroom. Wilma would be brought home the following day and her coffin would be placed in her room. The bedroom was not untidy as Wilma had always taken pride in her appearance and in her surroundings. The one big problem she had was the bedding. It seemed ridiculous, but she simply could not bring herself to change it, for if she then put the sheets in the wash, she felt that she would be removing all trace of her beloved daughter. It was silly she knew, but that was how she felt. She left the bed as it was. As she was closing the door behind her, she turned and looked at everything once more. If only, she thought, a thought that would not go away.

That evening Mary and William said very little. They were content to sit in one another's presence knowing that the other was thinking exactly the same. The realisation of what had happened was sinking in. Life would never be the same again but Wilma would never be forgotten; she would live on in them.

Jessie and Bob had returned home to find a hot meal ready and waiting for them. Helen had been busy in the farmhouse kitchen, glad to have something to occupy her. She did not like being alone in the empty house; it held far too many memories, memories both happy and sad, but the sad ones were uppermost in her mind at present.

'Come away in,' she called to Jessie and Bob as soon as she heard them enter the house. 'You'll be hungry. You've had a long day. Your dinner's ready.'

Helen saw Jessie give what seemed like a warning look to Bob.

Bob turned to face Helen. 'OK, Mum. Just let us have a wash and we'll be right with you.'

Helen was desperate to hear what the consultant had told them and, at the same time, dreading what it might be. Bob had been very non-committal when phoning to let her know they were on their way back home. No news was good news, but she knew her son. If he had had good news he would have told her. That, and these memories, had been quite a downer. She was doing her best to stay positive for the others, but it wasn't easy.

Alec and Iain joined Jessie and Bob at the kitchen table. Before they ate Bob simply said that there was no change in Sandy's condition. He and Jessie had agreed before leaving the hospital that they would wait until everyone had eaten before going into details of what might or might not happen. The meal was good and Jessie and Bob managed to eat most of it. There was little conversation. Bob could not speak. His thoughts were all about Sandy and Kirsty. Were the others thinking the same? he wondered. The previous evening he and Jessie had agreed that once they had talked over all the information they had been given at the hospital, they would then decide if they were in agreement with the decision to switch off the life support. Then, and only then, would they inform the others how bleak the outlook was for Sandy.

Listening to Mr Fleming they had had to admit that there was nothing more that could be done for Sandy. He was not going to recover. He could not survive without the machines and no one could convince them that he was not in pain. How could anyone know what he was feeling? Now they had to find a way to tell the others. The decision had already been made; they had no option but to agree.

Iain had wondered why so little had been said during the meal. He was beginning to think that he was about to hear what he had been dreading. His granddad had warned him not to build up his hopes. Sandy was very badly injured. If he did recover he might not be his old self, not even able to work on the farm. Before the accident Iain had often thought about his own future. He wanted to be a farmer but the farm would go to Sandy. Could it support them both and would Sandy want him to be a partner? They usually worked well together but Sandy would always be the boss. That problem seemed to be about to be resolved, but in a way he had never considered, nor would ever have wanted. He hoped he was wrong.

'There is no easy way to say this,' he heard his dad say. Iain realised everyone, like him, was now looking at his dad.

'Jessie and I met with the consultant, as you know. There is no change in Sandy's condition. There is nothing they can do to help.' Bob took a deep breath. He looked towards Jessie and just managed to blurt out, 'We have agreed to let Sandy go, tomorrow' before he broke down.

Iain pushed back his seat and rushed out of the room. He did not want the others to see how upset he was.

Helen and Alec had heard Bob announce the decision he and Jessie had made in silence. Alec looked at Jessie. 'I'm so sorry, lass,' was all he said before he turned to Bob. 'There's nothing I can say, son, except this. I hoped I would never have to say it, but you are right. The only way we can help Sandy is by letting him go. And each one of us has to look out for the others. We will never get over what has happened, but we will get through it. We have to.'

'I better go and see to Iain,' Jessie said to Bob as she placed a hand on his shoulder before leaving the room. The next thing Bob knew he was standing in the middle of the room, hugging his mum and dad. He had nothing left to say.

The following morning Bob spoke by phone to the nurse looking after Sandy. She was professional as she talked but he could sense the compassion in her voice. She would be on duty when Jessie and he visited Sandy in the afternoon. She would answer any further questions they might have and a time would be agreed. They would be reluctant to leave Sandy, but no matter how long they sat by his bedside it would not change anything. Tomorrow evening they would return, and at 9 p.m. the machines would be switched off.

Jessie's sister, Alice, and her family lived in Glasgow. They had already told Jessie that there was always a bed for them whenever they needed it. Now they needed it. Jessie and Bob would make their way to her home after their afternoon visit to Sandy. There they would have a bit of a rest if possible, and something to eat, before returning to the hospital. When it was all over they would make their way back to Alice's home. Bob had been reluctant at first, but eventually he was persuaded to see sense.

'You're not going to drive home in the middle of the night,' Jessie insisted.

'But I won't sleep. Might as well get home.'

'Bob, neither of us are likely to get much sleep, but we have no idea when Sandy will actually die. It could take an hour. It could be...' She broke down, unable to speak.

Bob held her tight, struggling to get his words out. 'You're right. It would be stupid. We'll stay, of course we will.'

Finally in bed, they held one another, each seeking strength from the other for the ordeal that awaited them the next day.

15

Paul's intention that Wednesday had been to spend as much time as possible preparing for Wilma's funeral. At exactly 9 a.m. the telephone rang.

'Hello, the manse.' Before he got the words out his caller was already speaking.

'Good morning, Minister. It's Lachie.'

Paul listened as the undertaker informed him that it looked as though the MacCallums were hoping to have their daughter's funeral the following Tuesday. That was what Paul had expected, but Lachie wasn't finished.

'And the Thomsons would like their son's cremation the same day.'

It was not altogether unexpected, but Paul had been hoping that the funerals would be on separate days. Two, even three, funerals were possible on the same day but it meant running from one to the next and risking giving offence to at least one of the families. No matter how meticulous the minister was about timing, inevitably one of the services would take longer than the other, or others, and offence was taken. Apologising or explaining simply made matters worse.

'Not what I would have chosen, but I am at their service, so Tuesday it will be. Will you manage?'

'Yes. The cremation will be in the morning at half past ten, and the burial at two o'clock as usual. I don't think the young boy's service will be as well attended as Sally's. He was fairly new to the town. His classmates might turn up in numbers but most of them will live in Dalcairn anyway. I tried to persuade his folks to wait until Wednesday, but his dad was having none of it.'

'I've already met him. Not an easy man to deal with.'

'No. The mother seems nice. Makes you wonder what she saw in him.'

'If you don't mind, Lachie, I've got enough to be going on with at the moment without trying to answer a question like that.'

'Aye, and so have I. I'll keep in touch. We might even bump into one another as we make the rounds. Hope your car insurance is up to date.'

'It is. Thanks for calling. Speak soon.'

Paul was always amazed at how easily undertakers could be serious one moment and the next be ready to crack a joke. Probably it was their way of coping with the strain of the job.

Almost as soon as he had ended that call, the phone rang again. It was Bob Meikle to tell him of their decision. Paul said he would visit immediately. Bob was adamant that there was no need, they were coping. Paul asked after the other members of the family, offered his sympathy and reminded Bob yet again that he was always available whenever they needed him. Within minutes of the call ending, Paul was on his way to the farm.

A wide-eyed Jessie opened the door before his feet hit the ground.

'What are you doing here? Bob said he told you we were managing. We are. You have enough on your plate at the moment without visiting us.'

Her words came out in a rush, convincing Paul that he had made the correct decision. She might be coping as Bob had said, but it was clearly not easy. How would she and the rest of the family be as they watched Sandy's life ebb away?

Bob soon joined Jessie and Paul in the kitchen. Paul's offer to be with them at the hospital was firmly but kindly refused. If they changed their minds they only had to let him know and he would be there.

He knew that the prayer he offered before leaving had been very much appreciated. Paul could feel the lump in his throat as he spoke the words softly. He heard a sob from Jessie during the prayer and saw the tears in Bob's eyes when he finished. He hoped with all his heart that the peace Jesus had promised would be felt by the Meikles, indeed by all the families who were mourning, and by himself as he sought to comfort them.

As the day progressed the details for the funerals of the other victims began to fall into place. Brian's cremation would take place next Tuesday morning with Sally's service that afternoon. Sandy and Kirsty would be laid to rest after a joint service on the Thursday or Friday. Paul struggled to concentrate on his preparation for Wilma's service. As he made notes on what would be appropriate to say, he was reminded of something that he ought to say about Sandy or Kirsty, but Sally he did not know very well and Brian he had never met as far as he was aware. He must not give people the impression that they were somehow not as important. They were all loved and precious to those who loved them. He would make sure that what he said about them did not in any way suggest that one would be missed more than any of the others.

To complicate matters further, there was still no explanation for why the accident had happened. The police were as baffled as everyone else. Their examination of the scene had given no clues; the car had been mechanically sound and the post-mortem had not revealed any medical problem affecting Wilma.

What had caused the car to swerve off the road and to keep travelling at speed? Her mother and father accepted their daughter's involvement. Her limited experience of driving since passing her driving test might have been a contributory factor, but what had actually caused the accident? There had to be an explanation but none had been found. Theories were put forward by the experts and others, and one of them might be correct, but which one? Paul would have to mention the accident and its dreadful outcome but he would also have to be very careful in his choice of words.

He went to the kitchen and made himself another cup of coffee. Before he had drunk it, Lachie phoned him. 'Minister, I'm sorry, but you have another funeral.'

'Another one?'

'Aye. Old Miss Henderson in the home in Dalcairn has died. Don't worry, there will be very few folk present and it will all take place at the graveside. On Wednesday. Would that be OK?'

'Yes, of course it will. If you can manage, so can I.'

He replaced the receiver soon afterwards. It may be small, but it is still a funeral, another one, he said to himself with a sigh.

Paul spent Thursday morning in his study. His mind was all over the place. One minute he was rereading what he intended to say about Wilma, then his thoughts were of Sandy and that reminded him that Jessie and Bob would be making their way to Glasgow, to sit by Sandy as the machines that were keeping him alive were switched off.

I should not be sitting here, he thought. Perhaps I should go and see how Helen and Alec are coping.

Eventually he talked things over with Ruth. She listened, but said nothing until finally he ran out of words.

'Paul, I understand your problem, but from what you have said, Sandy's parents and grandparents have made it clear that they want to be on their own. You have spoken to them, prayed with them. Now let them be, as they have requested. If you go to the farm or the hospital, there will be talk. This is not a time for talk. It is a time for silence.'

Paul reluctantly agreed, but still wondered if he had made the correct decision.

Alec, with the help of Iain, had just finished checking that everything at the farm was as it should be before it got dark when he realised that two cars were turning into the yard.

Surely not visitors? he thought as he walked over to meet whoever it was. He recognised one or two of the young farmers who were now getting out of the vehicles.

'Good evening, Mr Meikle,' said one of the group as he extended a hand to Alec. 'We're from Dalcairn Young Farmers' Club, friends of Sandy. We were wondering how he was doing and if we can be of any help to you and his dad while Sandy is in hospital.'

'Good evening,' Alec replied, trying hard to avoid giving the impression that he would rather tell them to get back in the cars and leave him to his own thoughts. 'Good of you to call. Come away into the house.'

The young men were soon seated round the kitchen table or on one of the other chairs, even the old sofa, scattered round the room. They had refused a dram or a beer, but accepted Helen's offer of a cup of tea. The conversation was difficult. Alec had told them that there was no improvement in Sandy's condition, that Bob and Jessie were staying overnight in Glasgow. The visitors had said little other than that they hoped things would change for the better soon.

'Let's be positive. Sandy's in good hands,' one of the young men said. 'He's young and fit. He'll soon be back and all this will be forgotten.'

Alec could take no more. He saw the warning look Helen was giving him, but he ignored it. 'Sandy is about to die. The machines are being switched off anytime now. He is not going to get better. He is going to die and we will never forget what has happened.'

The young man apologised as best he could. The others were trying to offer some comfort. Alec apologised for his outburst.

'No, you have nothing to apologise for,' Fred, another of the group, replied. 'We cannot even imagine what you have already gone through, and now this. If we can be of help in the days and months ahead, don't hesitate to get in touch. I am sorry we have only made matters worse. I think the best thing we can do now is leave you in peace, if that is not again the wrong thing to say.'

Alec had regained control of himself. 'It's OK, son. I was out of order too. You came to help, and Helen and I appreciate that. And if we need any help, you will be the first to know.'

As Alec came back into the kitchen after seeing the young men off, he began to apologise to Helen for not being able to do as Bob had asked.

'It's all right. By this time tomorrow every farming family for miles around will know what has happened.'

Alec held her close. He might be trying to comfort her, but he knew that he was also seeking comfort and strength from her. It would be a long time before any of them were back to some kind of normality following this terrible, terrible tragedy.

That evening Lenny and some of the others were in the Brae. They were laughing and joking, talking about this and that, making the odd uncomplimentary remark about one of the group or anyone else whose name had crept into the conversation. Most of it was without malice and would be forgotten before they left the bar. That was until a few young farmers entered.

Lenny was the first to realise who they were. He wondered why they were there. The bar was not a very large room and he caught the odd word.

'Evening, gents. Not seen you around here very often. Missing your friend?'

'Shut up, Lenny,' hissed Billy.

Lenny, as usual, paid no heed to Billy. 'How is he by the way? Heard he's pretty bad.'

The young farmers looked from one to the other, as if not sure if the question was a genuine enquiry or simply one of the local busybodies poking his nose in where it wasn't welcome.

'Sandy's very ill,' Fred replied. 'He's not in a good way. We've been to see his parents and to offer our support. Thank you for asking.'

'Aye, that was what ah heard. If it wis one o' the ferm beasts, ye could get the vet tae pit it oot o' its misery. Pity we cannae dae the same fur humans.'

Fred glowered at him. 'You have no idea how inappropriate that remark is.' He was now on his feet. Stuart, one of the other young farmers, was trying to hold him back.

'Oh, inappropriate, is it?' replied Lenny in as posh a voice as he could manage. 'Are you wan o' the landed gentry then? Slummin' it wi' the common folk,' he added with a sneer.

Lenny could tell that the farmer who had replied to him was becoming angry. As if sensing trouble, Maurice had moved from his usual place at the end of the bar. He was listening and watching, ready to intervene.

'We're simply here to have a quiet pint and to decide how best we can help our friends in their time of need,' Fred informed Lenny and his friends.

Lenny still had more to say. 'Aye, it's a terrible business. Don't know why Sandy let that young lass drive his motor. She had no experience, no' o' the drivin' kind, onywey.' Lenny finished with a sneer and a wink to make sure Fred got the message.

That was too much for Fred. He moved towards Lenny.

Lenny shouted, 'Aye, that's right. Forget the fancy talk. Let's see who's the big man.' He raised his fist.

'That's it, Lenny. I've heard enough,' Maurice shouted. 'Get out! And don't come back. I've had more than enough from you recently.'

Fred stepped back. Lenny turned to face Maurice. 'Ye cannae bar me. Ah'm wan o' yer best customers.'

'You're my worst customer, and I've had it. You're barred. Now, get out before I throw you out.'

Lenny's bravado had gone. Maurice had often threatened him with a ban in the past but he had never followed through with the threat. This time he might just.

'How long will ah be oot?' he asked.

'Until I tell you to come back. Now go!'

By the look on Maurice's face Lenny could tell that this time it was no idle threat. He was about to argue, but before he could get the words out, Maurice pointed to the door. 'Go, now, before I make it *sine die*.'

Lenny had no idea what the strange phrase meant, but Maurice was clearly not in the mood for a discussion on the matter. He turned and, in an attempt to save some face with his mates, he muttered, 'Ah'll be back afore ye know it.'

Clearly Maurice heard him. 'That's for me to decide. Goodnight, Mr Shaw, and shut the door behind you.'

This time Lenny went, making sure the door didn't bang shut, although he was sorely tempted.

'I'm sorry about that,' Maurice said to the young farmers, 'and I'm very sorry that such a terrible occasion has brought you to the Brae. Drinks are on the house.'

The lads thanked him. They ordered another pint. They were not completely silent as they drank their beer; not quite. Maurice understood that coming to terms with the possibility that their friend might die was difficult. They had so much to look forward to. It only took a moment for everything to change. By the look on their faces, whatever they had been told at the farm, it had not been good news.

16

Friday, the day of Wilma's funeral.

If strangers had walked down the main street in Burnbrae that morning, Paul thought they would very soon have realised that something was not quite right. The people passing were somewhat subdued, almost trying not to be noticed, and certainly not wanting to be engaged in conversation. They wanted to do whatever it was they had to do and then get quickly back to wherever they had come from. If they met a neighbour there was a brief muttering of 'terrible day' or something similar, and for once it was not a reference to the weather. And when the news that he had received from Bob Meikle at breakfast time began to get out, there would be even more shaking of heads.

The call had been brief. Bob clearly didn't want to go into details. All he said was, 'Sandy died at five minutes after midnight. Jessie and I were by his bedside.'

'I'm so sorry, Bob. Give Jessie my love and I'll see you when you get home.'

Wilma's funeral, the first involving one of the five victims of the fatal accident, was at 2 p.m. The whole community was in mourning. Even those who had no connection to any of the families, and in the small town that was probably not that many, were aware of what had happened and were saddened by it. The news that Sandy had also died was slowly being passed from person to person, first within the farming community and then among others in the wider community. That only served to intensify the sombre mood. As if to highlight how young the deceased were, before the day was out, news came through that one of the oldest of the town's inhabitants had died peacefully in her sleep at the Eventide Home in Dalcairn.

A great many mourners, family, friends, colleagues and neighbours, had gathered at Wilma's home. They spilled out of the house, spread over the garden and out into the crescent. The front door was open, the windows of the lounge were open and Paul did his best to make sure that his voice carried to those in the street. He was not convinced that it would because, as usual, the spot where he was shown to was in front of the fire. To his relief it had not been lit.

It was not usual for ladies to attend the graveside part of the service. As the cortège entered the cemetery it was joined by the large crowd who had gathered there. A number of Wilma's fellow students, male and female, had joined the large number of townsfolk, quite a few of whom were also women. Paul felt that he had to repeat some of what he had already said at the house for the benefit of those who had not been present there.

At the conclusion of the interment so many accepted the invitation to join Mary and William at The Rowans for light refreshments that at times the staff struggled to cope. Paul observed that this gathering did not follow the usual pattern. The talk was subdued, remembering all that was good about Wilma, but everyone seemed reluctant to tell the kind of stories that would end in laughter. Of course there were shared memories of happier times, but the grief was too new, too raw, for most. It was not yet time to move on; Wilma had been taken too soon.

Paul had also noticed that Alec Meikle had been present at the graveside. He had no idea how difficult a decision that had been, but he was full of admiration for him. He managed to have a word with Alec after the service.

'Bob had hoped to be back in time for the service,' he informed Paul, 'but by the time they did what had to be done at the hospital it would have been too much of a rush. He will visit the Watsons over the weekend. And I don't think I will go back to The Rowans. Give them my apologies.'

'I will. I am sure they will understand. Take care, and give my love to the family. I will visit soon.'

Quite a number of those Paul spoke to at the hotel expressed their appreciation of how appropriate his words had been at both the house and the graveside, commenting that it could not have been easy for him.

Back at the manse in the late afternoon Paul sat at his desk. He should have been preparing for the Sunday service, but he could not get the comments that had been made to him out of his mind. It was something that had concerned him throughout his ministry. Being thanked and complimented on how well he had done was always appreciated. It was his response that was the problem. Several times after a funeral, but not today, he had had to stop himself from replying, 'Not at all, it was my pleasure.' That was fine after a baptism or a wedding, when people were celebrating, but not after a funeral.

A funeral was so often the celebration of a good life, a life well lived, when the deceased was elderly. There was a sense of relief when someone had endured a great deal of suffering in the last days, but always there was that sense of loss for other family members. Life would never be quite the same; the circle was broken and it could not be repaired. The acute sorrow would pass, life would continue, but every so often that sense of loss would rise to the surface. Paul sometimes replied to the expression of thanks after one of these occasions by saying, 'It was my privilege to have been invited to conduct the service. He/she was a lovely person' or something very similar.

When it was a young person, a child, an infant who had died, no matter what the cause of death, sometimes, like today, there were no words. A hug, a handshake was all he could manage.

Paul dragged his mind back to the task in hand. This Sunday, the Sunday after Easter, was designated Low Sunday. The most likely reason for it being called this was that it came immediately after the excitement and exhilaration of the Easter celebration. Paul and many of his fellow clergy were convinced that there was a far simpler explanation. After the large congregations on Easter Day it was back to normal with a vengeance. The worshippers who attended every other Sunday, once a month or twice a year (Christmas and Easter) were all absent on Low Sunday. Even some of the very regular attenders appeared to take a day off. It was not just Low Sunday, it could well be named Lower, or even Lowest, Sunday.

Paul would usually choose items of praise that continued the triumphant theme of Easter: Christ's victory over death, God's gift of love, the forgiveness of sin, the promise of new life; in short, the good news. Last Sunday he had been careful not to imply that somehow the tragic accident involving the five young parishioners was just one of those things, but he couldn't just say, 'Never mind, God is love and all is well with the world.'. He could think of some believers who took that attitude, but not him. He had to show God's love in such a way that they saw also his concern for them. At Wilma's interment, after much debate with himself, he had omitted the words 'For as much as it hath pleased Almighty God' as he committed her body to the ground and her soul to His keeping. He would do the same at the other funerals.

He had selected the readings and the praise for Low Sunday earlier in the week, and jotted down some pointers for the sermon. The theme would no doubt play in his head before he fell asleep, as it often did, and at some point he would make sense of these thoughts and finalise his script. Well, he hoped he would. At present it was all still a bit of a jumble. He had phoned Harry the organist and given him the list of hymns. Harry commented that it was a good choice, especially as the choir had cancelled their usual Thursday night practice.

'We thought about a run-through on Sunday morning before the service,' he informed Paul, 'but no one was really all that keen. We knew we could trust you to pick the right hymns for the occasion. And ones that we knew backwards,' he added.

Paul was not sure if it was a compliment or a dig that there were times when his choice of hymns was from a very limited list of old favourites. The choir loved them, but Harry always wanted to try new or unfamiliar ones.

Paul did not rise to the bait and the conversation ended with Harry reminding Paul to take care of himself in view of what lay ahead in the coming days. He promised that he would, adding that Ruth was already doing her best to make sure that he kept his promise.

It should have been no surprise to anyone, but the attendance on Low Sunday was greater than at most ordinary Sunday services. It seemed that people wanted to be together, to find comfort in some way. As one of the elders remarked at the end of the service, 'When everything is going well, people forget God, but when the going gets tough they want reassurance that He is still there.'

123

Paul was heartened by the comments from many of the worshippers as they shook hands with him on leaving. He had given them what they had needed to hear. The evening service was also well attended. This time those who said more than simply, 'Good evening' as they left the church, seemed to be more concerned about the task that lay ahead of their minister. 'We'll be thinking of you', 'I'll be remembering you and the families in my prayers tonight and every night' were quite common comments, along with, 'And you remember and take care of yourself.'

Back home, Paul did his best to relax, but it wasn't possible. His mind was all over the place, mentally reviewing what he would say about each of the young ones, wondering how the parents and other family members would react. Ruth did her best to reassure him.

'You managed fine on Friday. The Watsons were very appreciative of all you said. You'll do the same again.'

'Yes, but Wilma was almost our next-door neighbour. I knew her.'

'And you know the Meikles.'

'Up to a point. But I didn't know Sally all that well. And I'd never even spoken to Brian.'

'You've talked to their parents. If you get it wrong it will be because they forgot to tell you something,' Ruth pointed out.

'Maybe I forgot to ask the right questions when I was discussing the funeral.'

'Now you're being silly. Calm down. I have every confidence in you, and so does everyone else.'

'Was that supposed to make me feel better?' Paul asked.

'Do you want tea or a dram?' she asked, ignoring his question.

'Dram first, tea later. And I know you're right. I'll manage. And I'll do my best not to make life impossible for you in the coming days.'

'See that you do.' Ruth rose and made her way to the drinks cabinet.

Paul had arranged to meet with Bob and Jessie Meikle on Monday afternoon. He would have preferred to have had the day at home but there was no other time to talk over the arrangements for Sandy and Kirsty's joint service. Saturday had been out of the question. He had driven out to the farm immediately after lunch, only to discover that most of Bob's farming neighbours had had the same idea. A brief chat with Jessie and Bob was all he had managed before these friends began to arrive. Being surrounded by their friends would help them every bit as much as anything Paul could say.

Paul made notes of the things that mattered to Sandy and Kirsty: their interests, their educational achievements and their hopes for the future. All the time he was listening and writing he was thinking yet again that no one would ever know how much had been lost in this terrible accident. He could not get that thought out of his mind as he drove back to Burnbrae. It was more than the loss of five lives. These young people had had so much to give, to their families and to society. What a waste. If only the cause of the accident could be   ascertained, that might help, but it would not undo what had been done.

Back at the manse Paul made a rough draft of the tribute he would pay to Sandy and Kirsty. He also checked over his notes for Brian and Sally's funerals and tried to work out what he could say about Miss Henderson. She had been a resident in the Eventide Home for many years. Paul remembered her as a rather quiet person. She had appreciated his visits and the Sunday afternoon services he had conducted when it was his turn on the rota, but she had had little to say for herself and, according to the staff, she kept herself very much to herself. From one of the oldest members of the congregation he learned a little more: her fiancée had been killed in the First World War; she had never really got over that and had very much kept herself to herself. That phrase again. She had also been the only child of wealthy parents. Lachie, the undertaker, had been able to add a little more. Her inheritance had enabled her to donate to many of the local organisations in Burnbrae, something she had done frequently and without any publicity. It would be interesting, Paul thought, to see how many local people turned out at her funeral.

17

Six funerals in seven days was not unheard of, Paul reflected, but in a town the size of Burnbrae it happened very rarely. From time to time an outbreak of flu, or simply very severe winter weather, was the cause, and most, if not all, of those who died, were infirm and elderly. A fatal accident was always a possibility in any community, but one that claimed the lives of so many was perhaps a once in a lifetime occurrence. The death of a young member of the community was always hard to bear, be it an infant, child or young adult. If the death was expected due to illness it was more a sense of sorrow for the relatives that the general public experienced. When it was accidental, many people realised how precious life was, and how easily it could be ended. Of course, life went on as it always did and before long it became part of the local history. For most people the accident was something that had happened to others; the daily routine continued. In days to come, someone would recall this particular tragedy when reminiscing about past events; for a few days vehicle drivers would be more cautious but soon the bad habits would return, and that was how it would be in Burnbrae.

The funerals took place as planned. The words Paul read were the same but there was something different, even unique, at each service, as those present remembered the deceased as they had known her or him.

Doreen and Ed, Doreen's mother and father, a few other family members, some of Brian's classmates and one or two neighbours made up the small congregation at the crematorium for Brian's service. They did their best with the singing of 'The Lord's My Shepherd' though Paul at times felt that he was singing a solo. Doreen was heartbroken; her mother did her best to support her and Ed appeared to be oblivious to what was happening. That might possibly have been a manly attempt to hide his own feelings but it might signify that his love for Doreen was a thing of the past. Paul could not help but wonder what kind of a relationship father and son had had over the years.

Paul made time to go back to Doreen's parents' home where the family, joined by several of the mourners, had gathered for some light refreshments. It was a rather strained atmosphere and did nothing for Paul as he began to clear his mind of Brian and his family in preparation for Sally's service. As soon as he could, he made his excuses and left, promising to call on Doreen the following week. How she would be feeling then he had no idea, but he was convinced that her husband would not be present.

Sally MacCallum's funeral took place in a full to overflowing funeral home. For most funerals the accommodation was adequate, but this afternoon it appeared that, along with the family and friends, many of Tom's customers had turned out to pay their respects, and a coachload of Sally's classmates and school friends were also in attendance. Lachie had anticipated this and had rigged up a loudspeaker system to relay the service to those who were standing in the yard outside.

As the family took their place in the front row of the funeral home, it was obvious that Sally's mother, Nan, was struggling. She was supported on either side by husband Tom and son Gary. Throughout the short service she sat immobile, staring straight ahead. Some of those present were convinced that she had taken some kind of sedative to calm her. Paul saw a mother who had withdrawn from the world rather than face up to what had happened.

Again the 23rd Psalm was sung. This time the large congregation sang the words with real feeling. Tom stood to sing while Gary sat holding his mother. If she heard the words, she showed no emotion. During the service several of Sally's classmates were overcome with grief. One poor girl became hysterical and had to be helped outside by one of the teachers accompanying them. The other teacher did her best to calm the other pupils, and Paul had to wait till everyone had recovered before continuing with his tribute to Sally.

The service ended with 'Abide with Me', a hymn that brought tears to many an eye. Nan was comforted by female relatives while Tom and Gary walked behind the coffin as it was carried out to the waiting hearse. Another group of mourners was waiting at the cemetery gates. The short act of committal was solemnly and reverently carried out. Paul was impressed by how well Gary took his place at the foot of the coffin to help lower his sister into the grave. The male relative standing behind him, just in case it all became too much for Gary to cope with, did not have to assist him.

Those who gathered afterwards at the Two Magpies were as subdued as those who had joined Mary and William Watson at The Rowans. Indeed, many of them were the same people, customers of both the bank and the ironmonger. Paul also noticed that, as usual, the 'freeloaders' were present. He had given this very small group of pensioners the nickname because at every funeral they were always present. To be fair, sometimes they might actually have known the deceased, but often it would be nothing more than a passing acquaintance. They were there for the free food and drink, among the first to arrive and the last to leave. Perhaps it helped to ease the strain on their pension but it was so blatant. Everyone commented on it, but no one had the heart to challenge them. Paul made a mental note that it might be something to be looked into. How many in the parish were suffering from lack of money to provide the essentials that others took for granted, and how many were simply selfish and greedy?

Paul was one of the first to leave the Two Magpies, which like the larger and slightly grander The Rowans had once been the home of a wealthy Dalcairn merchant before becoming a hotel. He had to get back to his study to prepare for Miss Henderson's funeral the following day. Before he left, he managed a quick word with Gary. It was a bit of a one-sided conversation. Gary said little, as did many of his age who were not used to speaking to a member of the clergy. Paul complimented him on how well he had done, decided that he was coping, wished him well and hoped that he might see him when he called at the house sometime the following week. This was a visit that would be top of his priorities; Gary's mother had insisted on going straight home after the service in the funeral home. Paul was becoming more and more concerned about her mental well-being.

Back in his study, Paul had a problem; he still knew very little about Miss Henderson. How could he pay a fitting tribute to someone who, in her own quiet way, had done a great deal to help so many in the community? If he was to make it personal, he had to know the whole person, not simply the old lady who sat quietly in a corner of the lounge at the Eventide Home but most often was to be found sitting alone in her own room. She was polite, well read, generous, had come from a good home where she had wanted for nothing, but that was about it. Had the loss of her young soldier laddie changed her? What would she have been like if life had been kinder to her? It was not much but that was about it, and it would have to do.

Paul was surprised the next day at 11.55 a.m. when the hearse, driven by Lachie, pulled up outside the manse. He opened the front door and stepped out.

'Great timing as always, Minister,' Lachie joked.

'Who, you or me?'

'Both of us I think.' Lachie was grinning.

Paul had not expected Lachie's light-hearted attitude. This was a funeral after all. Not a grief-filled one as the others had been or were to be, but still, it was unusual for Lachie to be quite so cheerful. After everything was over and the mourners were well away, Lachie could laugh as much as anyone else, not before.

'Is everything all right?' Paul asked.

Lachie's mood changed instantly. He was the complete professional again. 'Depends what you mean by all right,' he replied as Paul and he settled into the front of the hearse. 'I have a feeling that this is going to be one of the smallest attendances you've ever had at a burial, so small, indeed, that I may have to ask you to take one of the cords.'

'I'm sure I could manage that but I might have to ask someone to hold my book.'

'That's just it. There won't be anyone else. I sent my lads on ahead so that I could put you in the picture. I don't know what you're intending to say or do, but it may be the cemetery lads, my guys and you and me. '

'I hope you're wrong. Miss Henderson deserves more than that. No offence to your lads,' Paul hurriedly added.

'None taken, but I think I'm right.'

They approached the cemetery gates. Paul could see five men standing waiting. He recognised three of them: a lawyer from Dalcairn and two of his older church members. The other two he did not know. There was no one else.

Paul cut out one of his readings, said a few words about Miss Henderson and read the prayers. It was time to lower the coffin into the grave. The custom in Scotland was that the coffin was lowered into the grave by cords attached to the eight handles. Family members and close friends were allocated a cord and together, guided by the gravediggers, they lowered the coffin into the grave. The five mourners, Paul and Lachie's lads each had a cord. Lachie took care of Paul's book. Slowly they lowered Miss Henderson into her grave. When the coffin was in place the men threw the cords in and stepped away from the grave. Lachie handed the book back to Paul.

After the words of committal Paul thanked everyone. There was no cup of tea, no dram, no nothing. That was it. A very generous contributor to local groups had been laid to rest and it seemed that no one cared. That was not quite true. Paul was told later by several people that had they known how few mourners were to be present they would have been there themselves. They all said more or less the same thing. 'My parents knew her well and I knew she had been very generous to the community, but I didn't know her personally. I just never thought so few would turn up. I could have been there. Sorry.'

Lachie had made a very shrewd comment as he drove Paul back to the manse. 'Never judge a person's character by the number of mourners at their funeral. I've seen crowds at the funeral of a workmate who was not at all liked, not a good worker, but his colleagues were given a half-day holiday to attend. So they attended and went to the social club afterwards. There they enjoyed the free booze and quickly forgot why they were there.'

'Human nature,' said Paul, wondering how long it would be before the accident and its dreadful consequences were forgotten by most of the community, and if the families would ever be able to forget.

Thursday morning was overcast but dry. The forecast was for possible sunny breaks later in the day, but no rain.

'Thank goodness for that,' exclaimed Paul as he opened the bedroom curtains and saw that, so far at least, the forecasters were correct.

The possibility of rain had been factored in when the plans were being drawn up for Sandy and Kirsty's funeral but it would be much better for everyone if the dry spell continued.

Paul had been surprised when he discovered that the Meikles wanted the service to be held at the farm and, if at all possible, in the open. He had assumed that due to the numbers who were likely to be present, the most suitable place would be the church. There would be accommodation for all, and shelter if it was wet. He had conducted a number of funerals for members of the farming community since becoming minister at Burnbrae, but the service had always been held in the house before moving on to the cemetery or crematorium.

'It used to be very common,' Lachie had explained to him. 'The coffin sat outside the front door, the people gathered around and the minister stood on the doorstep.'

'What if it was raining?' Paul asked.

'We're talking about farming folk in the West of Scotland. They're used to the rain. They had the gear, so they just got on with it, or moved into a barn if it was really pouring down. Though, to be fair, it is quite a while since we had an outside service. Even farmers are getting used to warm, dry houses.'

By the time Paul arrived at Fauldshead the farmyard was full to overflowing. Farmers and their families from miles around were present to pay their respects and to give their support to Bob, Jessie, Iain, Alec and Helen. They were joined by many of the townspeople and once again Sally and Kirsty's classmates were in attendance.

Bob and Jessie had insisted that there would be singing at the service. The two items of praise were well known to most churchgoers, but to make sure that everyone could join in, a hymn sheet had been handed out. A local farmer whose singing had entertained the guests at many a farming event led the praise.

Paul was impressed by the singing of the 23rd Psalm. He hoped many would find comfort in the words they sang, and in the Scripture passages he was about to read. The eulogies presented a problem. The family were adamant that whatever he said, he must make sure that Sandy and Kirsty were treated equally. Paul spoke first of the family in general before reminding the congregation of Kirsty and Sandy's achievements, hopes and ambitions and the great sense of loss that was now being felt by so many, but most of all by their parents, brother and grandparents.

The final hymn, 'O Love that wilt not let me go' was sung with feeling, though some were struggling to keep their emotions in check. Bob and Jessie had insisted that George Matheson's great hymn of faith in adversity would be sung; it expressed their faith and it reassured them as they faced up to what had happened. Every verse had something that spoke to them, but none more so than the final one.

'O Cross that liftest up my head,

I dare not ask to fly from thee:

I lay in dust life's glory dead,

And from the ground there blossoms red

Life that shall endless be.'

With so many cars to manoeuvre out of the field where they had been parked it took much longer than expected before everyone arrived at the cemetery. When they did arrive there wasn't room for all the cars inside the grounds, so there was another delay while those parked outside made their way to the grave. Paul found himself talking to Jessie and Helen while their husbands spoke to other relatives and friends. It was clear that Jessie and Helen simply felt that they had to be at the graveside. It was not something they had done before, but this was different: the final farewell.

'I don't know why women aren't present,' Jessie said at one point. 'It's part of the service after all.'

'I think it might be a custom that goes back to the days when the menfolk walked behind the coffin, or in some country areas actually carried it to the burial ground. The women stayed at home and prepared something for them when they returned,' Helen suggested.

'I think you may well be right, Helen,' Paul agreed. 'Times change, but some customs last even when people forget why they're doing it.'

Once everyone was in place the committal began. There was no way to make it easier on the family. Each coffin had to be lowered into the grave separately. Paul quoted several Scripture sentences. Sandy's coffin was carried from the hearse and placed on the batons over the open grave. The cord holders were called forward and reverently they lowered Sandy to his final resting place. Paul spoke the words of committal. In the silence that followed, Kirsty's coffin was brought forward. The emotion was almost palpable. Slowly Kirsty was lowered in, the words were repeated and the service brought to a close.

Paul stepped away from the grave after thanking all those present and reminding them of the invitation to join the family at the community centre.

The crowd took their time dispersing. Some of those who were not able to go on to the community centre came forward to shake hands with the family. Lachie did his best to keep them moving but no matter how polite but insistent he was, it made little difference. It was with some relief that Paul eventually escorted the Meikle family to their car.

Bob and Helen were well known at The Rowans. The hotel would have been happy to provide hospitality to the funeral party but it simply could not handle the numbers involved, neither at the hotel nor at the community centre. Fortunately the outside catering company who serviced the local agricultural shows was more than willing to help. Paul had no idea how many were present but it seemed that everyone had found either a seat, or at least a corner to stand in.

Making his way back to the manse after what had been a long, trying day, Paul was thinking that it would take him a bit of time before the events of the past 15 days faded into the background and life and work for him went on as before. And if that is how he felt, how long would it take the families to recover, if they ever did completely get over this traumatic event?

18

After the morning service on the Sunday following the week of the funerals, Paul told Ruth that he wanted to pop in on Doreen and Ed on his way home. Ruth was not amused.

'You have had a busy, stressful week and what do you want to do now? Start the new week with extra work, that's what. Surely a visit to Doreen could wait a few more days?'

'It could, but I'm really worried about her relationship with Ed. I think he could be quite violent if things weren't going his way.'

'What if he resents you poking your nose in? You said he was very angry at times when you were there before. And you told me that he hardly spoke to you at the funeral,' she added.

'I know, but I just feel I have to do this. I don't know why.'

'You and your feelings! I know you'll go, no matter what I say. So, OK, but be careful, and don't be late for your lunch.' Ruth shook her head in despair.

'Don't worry,' Paul assured her. 'Twenty minutes tops, and less if Ed is playing the hard man.'

It was Doreen who answered when he rang the doorbell.

'Oh, it's you. I didn't expect to see you today. You have plenty to do without bothering about us.' There was something in Doreen's manner that suggested to Paul that all was not well.

'If it's not convenient, I can come back later. I just want to see how you're getting on. Is Ed still at home?'

The words tumbled out of Paul's mouth. He didn't want to force his way in, but he didn't want to go until he was satisfied that Doreen wasn't in any danger.

'Yes, come in, it's OK. Ed's here. He's packing. He has to go back to work.'

'Right. Just a quick call. Don't want to hold him up.'

Ed wasn't in the living room, but judging by the noise from what was presumably a bedroom, he was having quite a problem with his packing. Doreen apologised and went to ask him to come and meet Paul. It was one angry man who muttered a hello to his visitor. Paul made to shake hands but quickly changed his mind. Ed flung himself into a fireside chair. Doreen indicated to Paul that he should sit in the other one. She remained standing.

Ed was adamant that he was managing and that there was nothing he needed from the minister.

'Anyway, I have to get back to work. I'll get the late train from Glasgow, so I have to get on my way soon.'

'Could you not get a few more days' compassionate leave?' Paul asked.

'No way! It was bad enough getting off early for the funeral. The folk at the top can do what they like, but for us, it's work, work, work, They treat us worse than the machinery,' he added angrily.

Ed went on at some length, and the more he said, the more Paul became certain that he was lying. He had to go back to work, there was no doubt about that, but when was he going out to the rig? Paul didn't know too much about the oil industry but he had a feeling if Ed had been allowed off the rig early, he would not be due back until his next regular shift. Doreen was now sitting on the only other chair in the room. She had said nothing, but the look on her face spoke volumes. She was hurt, she was angry, and above all, she looked defeated. Paul decided it was best to leave. He would be back to see her as soon as he could.

He was home in time for his lunch. Just.

A few days later Paul was leaving Nan MacCallum's house after what had seemed to him a very fraught and fruitless visit when he noticed Doreen on the other side of the road. He hurried across the street and caught up with her.

'Hello, I was hoping I might catch up with you. How are you?'

'I'm all right. I've just got back from work.'

'Yes, I realise that. Look, if you would rather I came back at a more convenient time, I will.'

'No, eh, this is OK. Ed's back at work, or wherever. I'm on my own.'

Doreen burst into tears. Paul was embarrassed for her. If only he had waited till they had at least reached the entry to the flat. If he put his arm around her, standing here on the pavement, the local gossips would have a field day.

'I'm sorry. I didn't mean to upset you.'

'No, it's not your fault. I find myself in tears quite often. Come up to the flat. I'll make us both a cup of tea. I'm glad we met. I have to talk to someone. I can't go on like this. Talking to myself just makes everything worse. Effie is a great help but it's not fair to burden her with my troubles.'

'I'm sure she's more than willing to help. Sometimes an older person understands better than anyone else what you're going through.'

Doreen got her key out and Paul followed her into the flat.

'Probably, but I wonder if I'm taking advantage of her.'

'I'm sure she doesn't think that, but I understand what you're saying.'

They stopped in the hallway. Doreen was a little more composed.

'Go through into the living room and make yourself comfortable. I'll put the kettle on and freshen myself up,' she told Paul.

She soon joined him in the living room, handing him a mug of tea before sitting in the chair opposite. Paul watched as she took a sip of the hot tea. She didn't look at him. He drank a mouthful of the sweet tea in his mug. She had forgotten if he took milk and sugar. Milk was fine, but not sugar. Paul tried not to show his dislike of it; she had more than the way he liked his tea to worry about.

'So, I take it Ed got back to Aberdeen safely?'

Not perhaps the most subtle of opening remarks, but he could see no point in discussing the weather and how work at the factory was going. It might have been cruel, but it worked. In no time at all Doreen had forgotten her tea. She was in full flow.

'I suppose he did, not that he thought to let me know. Never does. Whether he's in Aberdeen or out on the rig I have no idea. Could still be in Glasgow. For all I know he might have a fancy woman there as well.'

As she drew breath, Paul managed to get a word in. 'I thought by the look on your face on Sunday that you didn't believe all that he was saying. If it's any consolation, I wasn't too sure it was the truth either.'

'I stopped believing most of what he told me a long time ago,' Doreen replied. 'I had hoped that I was wrong and, to be honest, I have no reason to say these things, no proof. The real problem is that our marriage is in name only, and has been for years. For a moment I hoped that it might not be, that it might be possible to sort things out.'

Doreen seemed embarrassed. Paul wasn't sure what to say. 'Take your time. I'm in no hurry.'

Doreen looked at him, her face becoming red as she blushed. She looked away again.

'Doreen, your relationship with Ed is none of my business, unless you want to ask for my advice on some aspect of it. If Ed is mistreating you then I will do whatever I can to help you sort things out. If you want to talk about how things are, I'll listen and, if I can see how you might be able to make things better between you, I'll advise you, but what you do is up to you and Ed. I can only offer suggestions.'

'I thought before the funeral, when he came home, after he calmed down, that we were back to the early days. He was helpful; he even washed the dishes. He never did that before.' Doreen managed a smile. It vanished as quickly as it had come. 'But by last weekend he was back to his usual, selfish, uncaring self. I think you saw him in full flow.'

'I did. I'm sorry, Doreen. You've had a terrible time these last days. This is never a good time to make big decisions, but I really think you have to be the selfish one now, to put yourself first. Do what is best for you. But be careful. I also saw a man with more than a bit of a temper.'

'He's never hurt me, not physically anyway. I don't think he would ever do that. Anyway, I'm not sure if he'll come back. He took all his personal things with him this time. At the moment I think it would be best if he does stay away.'

Paul ended up being late home for his evening meal. Ruth wasn't too pleased but when she heard why she realised yet again what a caring and kind man she had married. Fortunately the meal was none the worse for being kept hot.

19

Winter had given way to spring. The days were longer and the weather was warming up. The snowdrops and crocuses had been the first sign that nature was coming back to life. Now the daffodils in all their glory were being replaced by tulips. Primroses had appeared in road verges and on the riverbanks. Trees were in bud and the birds were busy preparing their nests.

In Burnbrae the winter activities were drawing to a close. Indoor five-a-side football was forgotten. It was proper football now on the sports field for the youngsters. Badminton had given way to tennis and golfers had no more excuses for bad shots and missed putts due to waterlogged fairways and greens. The Woman's Guild, the Young Mothers' Group, the Scottish Women's Rural Institute (The Rural) and several other organisations had held their annual general meetings. Soon the committees would be drawing up their plans for the next session. On the farms, the work was dictated by the weather and it had to be done.

The dark cloud that had hung over the town and its people was beginning to lift. The first topic of conversation when people met was no longer the accident or the funeral services. It was the everyday things of normal life. People were once again thinking and doing what they usually did. In one way it helped the families who had lost loved ones. They were not continually being asked, 'How are you feeling?' The first topic of conversation was once again the weather.

One question was, however, still being asked from time to time. It had not been answered and it was doubtful now if it ever would be. What had caused the accident? Several theories had been put forward by different people at different times, but it was all conjecture. The car had been mechanically sound therefore Wilma had to have been at fault, but why? There was no evidence to suggest that she had taken ill so that theory was wrong. There was no road defect that could have caused the car to swerve, so that was not the cause. There had to be a reason, but what? And why had she been unable to react to it? Was she simply not paying attention? That was not at all like Wilma. She was meticulous in everything she did. If only someone could come up with an answer.

The subject of the accident came up at the church Bible study group. The group normally met in the Session room at the church, but Paul had insisted that the final meeting before the summer break should be more of a friendly chat than serious study and that it should be at the manse. No one had objected to that. Normally Paul would sum up what they had been studying and complete any unfinished part of the winter's theme before they moved on to the savouries and cakes that Ruth had provided for them. The small group appreciated this and looked forward to it every April.

The group had been looking at the Book of Psalms over the winter. Paul had guided them through the different subjects expressed in the poems: creation and the Creator, history, personal faith and doubts, confession and forgiveness, the whole gamut of human emotion. They had discussed the life of David as they read his writing and considered how many of the psalms were written by others, although most were the words of the shepherd boy who became a great king.

This provoked a strong reaction from Richard, the most vocal member of the group. Richard was a born-again Christian who believed that every word in the Bible was the very word of God. He came down hard on anyone who said otherwise. As far as he was concerned there was only one interpretation, which just happened to be the one he held to. He even believed that the world had been created by God in seven days in the year 4004 BC. No one and nothing would convince him otherwise. From time to time Richard upset someone in the group by informing the person that he or she was not a true believer, even suggesting on one occasion, when he and Paul had had a somewhat heated exchange of views, that Paul was not fit to be a minister.

This evening Paul was determined that there would be no controversial material under discussion. Paul said what he had to say; a few comments were made by some of the group, mainly expressing how much they had enjoyed studying the psalms and how much they had learned. Agnes, one of the older members in the group, rarely contributed anything, preferring to listen to the others, but tonight she spoke up to tell the others how much she felt her prayers had become a constant repetition of the same thoughts.

'I don't know how God felt about it, but I was getting fed up myself hearing the same words night after night. Now I look forward to using David's words, as well as some of my own, of course,' she added.

Paul thanked her and suggested that others, himself included, could do well to follow her example more often. He was about to bring the study part of the evening to a conclusion when, to his dismay, he heard Richard speak out. 'Before we move on, Paul, I would like to raise a matter that has been troubling me.'

Paul almost gave a sigh of dismay. What now? he thought. 'Yes, Richard, if you think it will be of interest to us the floor is yours.'

He really wanted to tell him to keep whatever it was to himself, though to be fair, Richard did have a deep knowledge and not everything that he said was controversial.

'It's something you said at the recent funerals, or rather something you didn't say.'

Paul waited. He had a premonition that he already knew what Richard was going to say.

'Normally at a funeral, you, and every other clergyman I have heard, say the words, "For as much as it hath pleased Almighty God, to take unto Himself the soul of our brother, or sister, here departed", but you didn't say that at the young people's funerals. Why not?'

Paul's guess had been correct. Quietly, but firmly, he gave his answer. 'The simple and truthful answer, Richard, is that I did not believe that God was pleased. I believe that as I commended them to His care and keeping He would receive their souls, but I do not think for one minute that our Heavenly Father was pleased that this accident had happened.'

Richard was getting on to one of his high horses. Paul wanted to tell him to come and see him at another time when the two of them could discuss the matter privately, but there was no stopping him. The others listened, but made no attempt to join in.

Richard's argument was quite simple. 'From the moment we are born God has a plan for each one of us. It is our duty to discover what that plan is and to stick to it. If we depart from it we have to confess, ask to be forgiven through the saving grace of Christ and get back on the right path,' he stated with conviction.

'As Christians we still have the ability to choose,' Paul responded. 'Sometimes the choice is wrong, sometimes it is contrary to the teaching of Jesus and to the advice given in Scripture, but it is our choice. We're all responsible for our own actions. If we make a mistake and confess, we will be forgiven. But we are not puppets. God does not pull our strings. We are free to choose. Whatever happened that night, I am convinced it was not part of God's plan. It was an accident, tragic, but an accident, and I'm still convinced that I had every right to omit that phrase.'

Richard would not give an inch. The argument could have gone on all night until Paul put his foot down.

'Richard, you've had your say. I respect your view, but it's not mine. If I'm wrong, that's my problem, but I'm sure I'm not. The God I serve is a God of love. He loved Sandy, Wilma, Kirsty, Sally and Brian just as much as he loved Miss Henderson. I stand by what I said, and I would do it again. I *will* do it again. I hope no family will ever have to experience what our friends have endured in these last days, but we all make mistakes, and sometimes the price we pay is high, very high. But it is our mistake, not God's plan.'

Before Richard could begin to respond to Paul's outburst there was a knock at the door. Ruth popped her head in and announced that supper was ready.

'Thanks, dear,' Paul replied. 'We'll be with you in a minute. I'll just say grace in here and close our meeting with the Benediction.'

Ruth had done them proud. There was a lovely spread laid out on the large dining table. The members of the group took their seats and soon the acrimonious exchange between Richard and Paul faded into the background as they tucked in. Paul had hoped that would happen. It usually did because once Richard had made his case, often in the strongest possible terms, and not prepared to give any ground to those who argued against him, he calmed down and became his normal pleasant self. Now he was helping his neighbour to a savoury tartlet and calling across to Ruth, 'I'll need to get the recipe for these before I leave. They're delicious.'

Richard was a civil servant. He had lived in Burnbrae since being appointed manager of the employment office in Dalcairn some years earlier and had very quickly become an enthusiastic member of the church. Paul was grateful for all he did, but often found himself having to reassure another member who had been upset by one of his very dogmatic and quite unsympathetic utterances. Paul was at a loss to understand how such an intelligent person could believe some of the things he did. Even more worrying was why Richard had on occasion seen fit to reduce people to tears as he explained how God dealt with unbelievers. At least tonight it had been Paul who had been on the receiving end and he was gracious enough to hope that Richard never had to learn the hard way that accidents can happen to anyone.

'That's that until October,' Paul said to Ruth when the last of their guests had gone. 'Thanks again for the supper, dear. It was delicious as usual. So good that I think it keeps some of them in the group.'

'Do I detect a hint of sarcasm there?'

'Perhaps, but there might be more than a grain of truth as well.'

'Let's get this lot tidied away, then we can chat.'

'I'll get the dishes in the sink and I'll wash them while you deal with the leftovers, not that there is much left over. And I've talked enough for one night.'

'But not to your wife,' Ruth joked, as she gave him a friendly push towards the table.

20

The following morning Paul was glad to get out into the garden. He was not much of a gardener but he did his best. He knew that the vegetable plot should have been turned over in the autumn. Now it was urgent; the first of the vegetables should already be in. According to one of his members who won prizes for his onions in every horticultural show for miles around, the first of January was the date. That may be so, Paul thought, but as long as mine are good enough for Ruth to use over the winter, that's all I can ask. It was good to be out in the fresh air, to get some exercise even if he would suffer for it later. He tried to concentrate on what he was doing, to forget, if only for an hour or two, all that had happened in recent days. It was no use. As he turned over the soil he was reminded of the open graves. That led on to thinking about the parents, the families and even himself. How did you get back to some sort of normality? If he was finding it difficult, how could he be of help to the others?

He had made up his mind that he would not visit the bereaved on a certain day each week. He would gradually increase the time between visits unless he thought that someone needed special attention, and he had to take care of other parishioners who also needed his pastoral support. By lunchtime he had dug half the plot. The rest would have to wait until tomorrow; there were visits to make. That was the plan, but the best-laid plans did not always become reality.

Paul was heading for the back door and his car after lunch, ready to begin his round of visits, when the front doorbell rang. He gave a sigh, turned around and went to answer it.

'Oh, good afternoon, Doctor. Come in.' Paul was surprised. He could not remember if Dr Wilkie had ever called unexpectedly before.

'Afternoon, Minister. I won't take up too much of your time. Were you on your way out?'

'Yes, I was, but there's no rush. Come through in.'

'Then it's perhaps good that I called when I did.'

Despite the seeming formality of the greetings, Paul and Dr Wilkie were on first-name terms, but as most of their patients and parishioners called them by their professional title, they had somehow got into the way of doing the same. Dr Wilkie, Albert to family and friends, apologised for calling without warning.

The two men sat down facing one another in the study. Paul must have looked puzzled as Albert smiled and said, 'Nothing to worry about, I simply want to give you a warning in the hope that you will not require my professional services further down the line.'

Paul was not in the least reassured, having no idea what had prompted the visit, or the comment. 'I'm fine,' he replied. It's been a tough couple of weeks, but I'm OK.'

'Sleeping all right?'

'Yes, most nights. Sometimes takes me a while to drop off. Too much running around in my head. But that's all over now. I'll be fine.'

'I hope so, and you probably will be,' Albert replied. 'But can I give you a bit of advice?'

'Of course, I'm always open to advice from those who know what they're talking about.' He was thinking of Richard and his remarks the previous evening.

'When people have been through what you've been through, their adrenaline levels are increased. It's the body's way of coping. In most cases when the emergency is over, the adrenaline level returns to normal, but sometimes it doesn't. That can cause real problems.'

'If I never knew that the level was high, how do I know if it's back to normal?'

'By how you're reacting. The strange thing is that in the emergency it helps. People have lifted huge weights to free someone trapped under debris, even a small car, that kind of thing. In your case you did what you had to do, and you did it very well.'

Paul nodded his acknowledgment of the compliment.

'If you find that you're restless, your sleep pattern is different, especially if you wake around 4 a.m. and don't get back to sleep, that's often a good indicator. You might also find you spend a great deal of time thinking about work, but don't actually do any.'

'I was on my way out when you arrived,' Paul protested.

'And that's good, provided you don't overdo it.' Albert laughed. 'I know, don't sit about, don't overdo it. Rather contradictory, but it's not an exact science. Not everyone reacts in the same way. And in some instances, some people develop clinical depression.'

Before he could finish what he was saying, Paul interrupted. 'I'm not that kind of person. I don't get depressed. A bit down at times if something goes badly wrong, but I soon bounce back up again.'

'I'm not for a minute saying that you will have problems, but I want you to be aware of the symptoms. Leaving it too late to get help makes the condition worse and takes longer to cure.'

'Sorry, I thought for a minute that you had noticed something about me. Forewarned is forearmed. I'll be on the lookout. Don't worry about me. If I think I need help, I'll be in touch. And there's always Ruth. She's been telling me what to do and what not to do.'

'Good,' replied Albert. 'Just make sure you take her advice. And that leads me on to the other thing I wanted to say.'

Paul had no idea what was coming next as Albert continued. 'I would appreciate your help. I've seen the families and offered medication to those who I thought required something. Whether or not they actually take it is another matter. Patient confidentiality is paramount for both of us, but if you think that someone is struggling, could you let me know?'

'Of course I will. We actually received some training in this at divinity   college.'
Albert looked surprised but said nothing as Paul explained. 'Training is probably not the right word. The hope was that we would be able to tell the difference between someone who needed support, a shoulder to cry on, a bit of encouragement, that sort of thing, and the person who needed professional medical help.'

'Good advice, but sometimes not easy to spot that difference. Even for someone with my training. What I want to try to prevent is someone coming to the surgery after the damage is done. Or worse still, not coming at all.'

Paul could see from the look on Albert's face that he was deadly serious.

'I'll let you know if I think someone needs help, I really will. We've combined our services in the past to the benefit of one or two people. I just hope I don't miss the signs.'

'You won't. Even if it turns out to be a false alarm, that's always better than no action at all. Now, I'll leave you in peace and get on with my own work and let you get on with yours. Thanks for your time.'

'Not at all. And thanks for your concern.'

The two men shook hands. Paul stood at the door after Albert's car had driven out of the crescent, deep in thought. How long would the tragedy affect all concerned? Would everyone involved, himself included, ever get back to normal?

21

Mary and William were relaxing after their evening meal. Mary was watching television and William, true to form, was having a more careful read of his morning paper. At least that was what Mary had assumed. As the credits came up on the screen, William carefully closed and folded the paper before laying it down, just as carefully, on the table by the side of his chair.

'Mary, I was wondering if we could have a chat about a matter that has been much in my thoughts since Wilma died.'

'Of course, dear, but I had no idea you were worried. I thought we were coping remarkably well.'

'We are, of course we are, and you have been wonderful. I have my work to keep me busy, but you have many hours on your own. I'm sure you often think of what might have been. I do, and that's what I want to talk about.'

Glancing at the television, he asked, 'You aren't watching anything important, are you?'

Her anxiety must have shown on her face as William hastily added, 'It's nothing to worry about.'

'No, I was going to ask if you wanted to watch the next programme.'

'No, I don't, but I think it's time to share these thoughts with you. Do you want a drink first? What I have to say might lead to a rather lengthy discussion.'

'Of course, if you want one, then I'll join you.'

Mary was now totally puzzled by her husband's manner. An after-dinner drink was not unheard of, indeed it had become the norm since the accident, but this was not going to be a relaxing drink. William was in a serious mood. His bank manager's face was on. Mary could not guess what was coming next. She watched as William poured the drinks. He was deep in thought, but he remained silent. He handed Mary hers then sat down opposite her with his own.

Mary raised her glass. 'Cheers. I'm all ears.'

'It's not really anything to cause concern, Mary. I want to run a couple of things past you and get your reaction.'

'OK, but if that was meant to reassure me, it's not working.' She took rather a large sip of her gin and tonic and waited.

William cleared his throat, something he often did when he was not sure how his comment or advice would be received.

'As you know, I've been making an investment for Wilma since the day she was born, to help pay for her education and whatever was to follow. There's a considerable amount of money that now comes to us. I've also made sure that we will be well provided for on my retirement. So, what do we do with this investment that was meant for Wilma?'

William stopped abruptly. There was more emotion in his voice than Mary had heard since the evening of their dear daughter's death. She could feel herself welling up. She forced herself to reply.

'I don't really know. I suppose I assumed that you would add it to your pension fund. You're not really one for splashing out just for the sake of it, though I think we would both benefit from a nice holiday in due course. Somewhere warm and relaxing.'

'That's not a problem, but I can well afford that without touching any investments. No, what I had in mind is quite different. I was wondering about a youth centre.'

'A youth centre?' Mary was lost for words. 'I might have thought of a few things, but never a youth centre.'

'I know, it took me by surprise too. Let me explain.'

'Let me get us a refill,' Mary added, moving over to the drinks cabinet. 'This discussion may become quite detailed and involved.'

Drinks refreshed, William explained that at first he had thought of making donations to various charities. Wilma had always been a willing supporter of several good causes during her all too short life. The money would be put to good use, but there would be nothing permanent.

'So, what I've been thinking of recently is a youth centre,' he continued. 'Wilma loved her   time in the Guides and Brownies. She was active in outdoor activities too.'

Mary interrupted William. 'But we already have a community centre. The church hall is used by The Boys' Brigade and the Scouts and Guides have their own premises. Do we really need another building?'

'That was what I thought to begin with, but two of these buildings are for a specific group as you said. The church hall is used by several groups throughout the winter then lies more or less empty the remainder of the year. What I'm thinking of is a place where the young folk can meet in a less formal manner and do whatever they decide to do.'

'What?'

'I know what you're thinking, but there would be a youth leader in charge, someone trained for the job. The good thing is the hall and any other rooms would be entirely at their disposal. Things would not have to be put in cupboards at the end of an activity only to be brought back out the next day. That sort of thing.'

'Fine, but it all sounds rather expensive, and where are you going to find this building?' Mary was struggling to prevent herself from rubbishing the whole idea.

'That's just it. I've found it.'

'You've what?' Mary could not believe what she was hearing. William had been doing more than just thinking about this idea, he had been working on it, and he had kept it all to himself. Until now.

'The former UF church building is available. The congregation are now part of our congregation, and their building is still on the market.'

'You have been busy,' Mary said as she tried to take it all in. 'Have you really thought this through? We don't want to end up owning a building, and certainly not a redundant church of all things.'

'I have. At first I wasn't sure if it was workable. Now I think it is. There's still a great deal to look into, but I want to do just that. What do you think?'

'I think you've already made up your mind, and if you have, and it can work out, I think it might turn out to be a great idea, and a worthy memorial to Wilma. Promise me one thing, though. It seems quite unlike you, this plan I mean, so if you have any doubts about its feasibility, please say you'll drop it.'

'I will, I give you my word.'

'Then here's to the youth centre!' Mary said as she raised her glass in a toast. She put her empty glass down on the side table. 'Were there not two things you wanted to discuss with me?'

William looked puzzled for a moment. His mind seemed to be elsewhere. 'Oh, yes, of course. I am so glad you are prepared to allow me to proceed with the first idea. The other one won't cause you any problems. At least I don't think so.'

'Well, get on with it. I'd like to watch the news.'

'Right, so here it is. I've also been thinking about retiring.' He seemed to realise that Mary was about to say something, so he hurried on. 'I mean, taking early retirement, if I can.'

'But I thought you loved your job?'

'I do, but it's changing. Being a branch manager is becoming more about persuading customers to take on loans rather than think about saving. To think about a loan for a new car rather than saving for it. To think about a bigger house, and a bigger mortgage to pay for it. In fact, to borrow to the limit so that the bank makes more money. That doesn't make sense to me. All right if everything goes to plan, but if it doesn't they can be in real trouble. The bank might make a bit of a loss, but the customer could lose it all.'

'What do you mean, lose it all?'

'Mary, the bank will repossess the car, the house or whatever else if the customer can't keep up the payments. That's not my way of doing things. I know my customers. I know what they can afford, but now someone is looking over my shoulder and encouraging me to advise them to use some of that nest egg they have in a savings account. It's spend today and don't worry about tomorrow. Complete opposite to what I was trained to do. So, if I can get out soon, then I will. We can afford it. What do you think?'

'I think it's a great idea. Have you any plans for when you no longer have to go to the bank every working day?'

'Not really. I have some ideas, but that's something for us to talk over at our leisure, and I've still to find out if I can actually retire early.'

'That might be a problem, dear. You've done a really good job. They might want to keep you on for as long as possible.'

'Thank you for the compliment, but that's exactly why they'll want me out. I'm old school, and they can't teach this old dog new tricks. They'll be glad to see me go.'

'Really?'

'Yes, really, but I'll make sure I don't go cheaply.'

Mary was glad she was not the person who would have to deal with William Watson as he negotiated his departure terms. He was a very fair man, but also a very determined one when he had to be.

22

Paul had made a couple of calls to the folk at Fauldshead in the days that followed Sandy and Kirsty's funeral. On the first visit he had found the grown-ups unusually quiet, but that was understandable. They spoke about their loss with an acceptance of what had happened that amazed him. Paul found it difficult to imagine what these families were going through. As Jessie and Bob, Helen and Alec were talking he could not stop himself thinking of Malcolm and Jennifer. He wasn't sure that he would be quite so calm if, God forbid, anything was to happen to one or other of them. While he listened he wondered if there was a deep hurt being kept under control. He was remembering Dr Wilkie's advice and vowed that he would return fairly soon.

As always it was not possible to visit a farm without enjoying tea and a delicious spread of home baking. By the time he said his goodbyes it almost felt like any of the other visits he had made before the accident, but not quite; everyone, himself included, knew why he was there. He had a feeling that no matter how many years went by, every time he called, that day and its aftermath would always be present in his mind and no doubt the others would be thinking the same when in his company. The Meikles, the Watsons, the MacCallums, Doreen and Paul were bound by a deeper, different relationship, by the awfulness of what they had in common.

On Paul's next visit to Fauldshead he felt that there was more of an air of normality. Bob and Alec were attending to a newborn calf while Jessie and Helen were getting on with things in their respective homes. Jessie was baking in preparation for some competition at the Rural and Helen was finishing off some knitting for the same event. Iain was back at school and as far as his parents could make out, he was settling down to his studies and giving no cause for concern.

Unfortunately, all was not well in the MacCallum household. Tom was very worried about how Nan was coping, or rather not coping. She remained in a world of her own. He assured Paul that she was taking the medicine Dr Wilkie had prescribed for her, and she was eating, though not as much, perhaps, as before, but she was not saying anything more than she had to. Paul had tried to engage her in conversation, but no matter what he said, all he got in reply was yes or no, a shake or a nod of the head, and more often than not, no response at all. It was obvious that she heard what he was saying, but she simply wasn't interested. She had her own thoughts and she was keeping them to herself.

'I don't know what more I can do to help her,' Tom confessed to Paul. 'I've tried everything I can think of. Dr Wilkie has been very good to us. He has been to see her several times, but the pills don't seem to make any difference. I think they might even be making her worse.'

'I'm not an expert,' Paul replied, 'but it could be that they're a sedative, giving Nan time to come to terms with what has happened without making her even more worried than she already is.'

'Maybe, but I get the impression Dr Wilkie isn't happy about her. She's not getting any better.'

'But she's no worse. There's no set time for getting over what you've all been through. Has Dr Wilkie given you any idea how long it might be before you see some improvement?'

Tom shook his head. 'Not really. He did suggest that if there's no change soon, Nan might need to see someone else. Surely it won't come to that? She was always the one who coped best in a tight spot.'

Paul thought carefully before he replied. He was no expert in this area. Even the best- intentioned comments could turn out to be the worst possible thing to have said.

'Let's leave it to the experts,' he said. 'I have every faith in Dr Wilkie. He'll do what's best for Nan, for all of you, and should Nan need counselling, he'll know the best person to provide it.'

'Aye, I suppose you're right, Minister, but I still feel I should be doing more.'

The talk continued for a bit about Nan but they were both at a loss as to what else they could do.

'How's Gary? Is he coping?' Paul eventually got around to asking.

'That's a good question. How do you know what goes on in a teenager's head?' Tom replied, with a sigh of resignation. 'He goes to school, he comes home, and when I come up from the shop, he's in his room and the music is blaring out as usual. Nothing seems to have changed there.'

'I remember these days at the manse. Sounds as though he is indeed managing. And what about yourself? An honest answer this time.'

Tom gave a rueful grin before he replied, 'There's no fooling you, is there? I'm OK. I have my moments. Life will never be the same again. How could it be?' Tom stopped suddenly, as if his mind was jumping between what had been and what could have been.

Paul waited. This was not the moment for clichés about time being a great healer or anything similar.

Tom raised his head and looked his visitor in the eye. 'I know I can't change what has happened. I don't know what lies ahead, but I'm determined that Sally will not be forgotten. That Gary will not suffer as a result. That Nan and I will get back to where we were before. I'll do whatever I have to do to see that this family remains a family. I'm not a man of prayer, not a man of faith, but I know you are. You believe, and I know you and your congregation are praying for us. With the help of folk like you, we'll get through this. We will.'

Paul got to his feet. Tom did likewise. In a moment they were holding one another.

'God bless you, Tom. He will give you strength, and you will be able to do what you have to do.'

'Thank you, Minister.'

Paul wiped away a tear as he walked back out onto the street. He had no idea where he was going next. There were a number of non-urgent calls on his list, mostly elderly housebound parishioners. He tried to look in on them fairly regularly despite the time it took. He was never sure if they were glad to see him because he was the minister or simply because he was someone different. From day to day they saw the same few people: a family member, a health visitor or a neighbour. They were the lucky ones. Some people who lived alone saw only one person every day, the same person, and a few he suspected saw no one for days on end. A visit from him meant a welcome change in the daily routine, a change in the conversation, though Paul felt he had heard some of the stories so many times that he now knew them as well as the person telling them.

Paul realised someone was saying hello. He stopped. 'Sorry, I was miles away,' he   explained.

'Obviously,' replied Constable Ranald MacDonald. 'Thank goodness you're walking and not driving. For a moment I thought you were going to collide with me.'

Paul apologised again.

'Is everything OK?' Ranald asked.

'Yes and no. Do you ever think that despite your best efforts you're not really making much difference?'

'Most of the time,' Ranald replied, a wry smile on his face. 'We do our best but people are people. The good ones get on with their lives and the bad ones, it seems, continue to mess up their own lives and the lives of the rest of us.'

'That's a bit cynical,' replied Paul.

'Maybe, and it was a bit of an exaggeration, I suppose, but you can only do your best. What happens is up to the person themselves. They can take your advice and move on or they can ignore it and continue as before.' He looked at Paul. 'From what I hear you're being a great help to the families who lost their loved ones, but you can't mend everything, not immediately anyway. It takes time and it's still early days.'

More clichés, thought Paul before replying. 'You're right. I'm being unrealistic, but I can't help feeling that certain people may suffer more hurt before things get better. I hope I'm wrong, but I don't think I am.'

'Great talking to you, Minister,' Ranald said, looking at his watch, 'but I really must get going. And believe me, you really are helping these poor folk.'

'I hope so, and I hear good reports of you,' Paul replied before they parted.

Paul continued on his way, his thoughts now more focused on what he had done rather than on what he was intending to do. Get a grip, he said to himself. He looked around and realised that he was outside the entrance to Bessie McNaughton's home. Was it accidental, or had his subconscious led him to one of the homes where he found peace and wise words? Bessie was a retired midwife, a long-retired midwife. She was well into her nineties but her mind was as sharp as ever. She lived on her own and as far as Paul knew, she really didn't need much help from others. She was well liked and very much respected by those whom she had helped over the years, having been involved in the births of two generations for many of the local families in Burnbrae. It might have been three generations for some but with the move to births taking place in nursing homes or hospital, Bessie, well over retiring age, had been forced to stop working. That had not stopped her keeping an eye on the young mums of the town. Sometimes they thought she was out of date with her advice, but more than one distraught mother had been very glad of her expert help.

Paul loved the stories she told of the old days. She never mentioned names but he realised she had never forgotten any of the babies she had delivered. She had watched over them, from a distance in most cases, as they grew and matured. Where there were difficulties she was always ready to offer wise advice. Paul had heard some amazing stories from her lips. Had someone else told them he might have thought that the truth had been much embellished but with Bessie he soon came to realise that she was simply recounting what had actually taken place. Some of the tales were incredibly sad.

Bessie, like many of the older parishioners, insisted on addressing Paul as Mr Johnson. As usual she had made a cup of tea for her visitor. She was nothing if not direct. She watched Paul closely as they spoke and sipped the tea.

'And how are you managing, Mr Johnson?' she asked. 'Are you getting enough rest, a good night's sleep?'

'Yes, things are more or less back to normal now.'

'That's good. You can't help others if you don't look after yourself.'

Paul looked at her. He couldn't resist it. 'And did you always follow your own advice?' he asked.

'Usually,' Bessie replied with a glint in her eye. 'But it isn't always possible, is it?'

'No, it's not, but I think I manage, most of the time.'

'From what I hear you've been a great help.'

'Thank you, that's very kind of you. I just hope I did enough. Am doing enough.'

'Mr Johnson, you can only do so much, and no matter how hard you try, you still feel it is not all that you could have done, but people have to help themselves. I learned that lesson a long time ago. Some will, some won't. Most of them will keep on going, but for some it will be nothing like the life they had before, or wanted for the future, but it's a life. Some will struggle and will need help from time to time, and some, I'm afraid, will just not make it.'

Paul was alarmed. What did that last phrase mean?

'Not make it, you don't mean–'

Bessie interrupted him. 'I realise that that's not perhaps what you had hoped to hear, at least not all of what I said, but that's my experience. The ones who don't make it will find a way of coping. Drink perhaps, or shutting themselves off from other people, and yes, some will decide they can't go on and will try to end it all. And some will succeed.'

'But, there must be some way of preventing that, surely.'

'There are ways to try, but just every so often, no matter how hard you try to prevent it, they find a way. And when that happens, no matter how difficult it is, you mustn't blame yourself. You weren't the only one trying to help. The family, the doctor, friends, they were all doing what they thought was best, but in the end the one who wanted out found a way.'

'Do you think that will happen to someone this time?' Paul was thinking of Nan MacCallum.

Bessie looked Paul full in the eye. 'Mr Johnson, I don't know some of the folk all that well. I don't get out very much nowadays as you know. I'm talking from my days as a midwife. Some of these mums and dads suffered terrible tragedies. Sometimes the ones I was really worried about got over it and carried on, sometimes they didn't. And sometimes, just sometimes, someone who appeared to be coping suddenly gave up without any warning. There's no way to know in any particular situation what the outcome will be.'

Paul sat in silence. Bessie refilled his mug. 'Don't look so worried,' she said as she sat back down. 'Most people are very resilient. They get back up and get on with whatever it is they have to cope with. You must have seen that already in your ministry?'

'Yes, but this accident was so horrendous.'

'It was an accident. Is it the first time you've been involved in a sudden death?'

'No, there have been a few, but nothing like this.'

'In the other cases, did everyone accept it as just one of these things?'

Paul thought for a moment, remembering people who had suffered what he had thought at the time was a terrible loss, but which over time became just a sad part of their lives and of his ministry.

'No, of course not,' he replied. 'There have been one or two infant deaths and sudden deaths of folk in midlife. And while some were expected, they were still difficult for the family members to accept.'

'That's what I am trying to say. This accident was a terrible thing because they were young and because five died. But it was an accident and each family, while mindful of the others, is really only thinking about their loss. Except for Mr and Mrs Watson, of course. They're the ones who carry the whole burden.'

'But they are the ones who seem to be coping better than anyone.'

'And they may well be,' Bessie acknowledged.

'But you're telling me that it's not always possible to spot the person who needs the special attention?'

'No, not always. But don't worry about that. If you spot it you do what you can, and if you don't pick up any signals, well, there was nothing you could have done. You're not a mind reader, are you?'

'No, well, not any more than anyone else.'

'So, there you are, but there is one more thing I would add. When I began my work, death was an everyday event. It was part of life. Babies died, toddlers died, teenagers died, but infant deaths are now quite rare, thank God. And TB and polio are gone. People expect to live well into old age, like me.'

Bessie gave a chuckle as she added the last comment, but Paul realised that she was making a very valid point. Before he could respond, she continued.

'It is good that these diseases have been defeated, that people's living conditions have improved out of all recognition, but the result is that people do not talk about death, not seriously anyway. The result is that they are not prepared for it when it comes, and they take it bad.'

'I never really thought of it like that,' Paul replied, realising yet again how perceptive Bessie's comments were. 'I am not sure that I have spoken much about death either, except to those who have been bereaved, and I certainly did not appreciate exactly what it was like for some people. These last few weeks have given me a new insight. I thought I understood, but I didn't.'

'Maybe there's a subject for a sermon then. Now, I'm not pushing you out, you know you are always welcome, but you get away home to that lovely wife of yours, and leave this auld buddy to her memories, the good ones and the not so good ones.'

Paul rose from the chair and looked thoughtfully at Bessie. 'Before I go, can I just say that I think I was led to your door today. I had quite a few questions going around in my head. I don't know how you did it, but I know that I have found some of the answers.'

Paul took Bessie's hand in both of his and held it firmly. 'Perhaps you are the mind reader.'

'Aye, perhaps I am,' replied Bessie. The twinkle was back in her eye.

23

Paul was much more relaxed after his chat with Bessie McNaughton but he remained concerned about Nan MacCallum, who showed no signs of improvement over the following weeks and, despite calling several times, he had failed to make any contact with Doreen Thomson. Her next-door neighbour, Effie, assured him that Doreen was managing but she seemed to be staying with her parents in Dalcairn most weeknights. Paul had tried calling on a Saturday morning a couple of times but still he had had no luck. As he put another of his cards through her letterbox, he shook his head and thought that, if she did happen to be staying in her own home, she might be out shopping. He hoped that his brief message on the back of the card enquiring how she was keeping might at least prompt her to give him a phone but he wasn't too hopeful. He was wrong.

'Who can this be on a Saturday afternoon?' Ruth exclaimed as she heard the front doorbell.

'I have no idea until I open the door,' Paul replied as he put the last of the dishes he was rinsing into the dishwasher. 'But we're open for business every day,' he jokingly added. For a moment he thought Ruth was going to hit him with the pan she happened to be holding.

On opening the door he was surprised but pleased to see that the caller was none other than Doreen Thomson.

'Come in, it's great to see you.'

They shook hands as Doreen stepped into the hall. Paul thought she looked well but rather subdued. He would no doubt find out very soon why she had arrived in person rather than simply phoning him. Once settled in the study the conversation between them didn't flow very well. He asked some questions about how she was managing at home and at work. Her replies were brief but didn't tell him very much. Her parents were a great help, she acknowledged, but she didn't like to impose on them.

'And are you keeping well?' he asked.

Doreen looked away, hesitated, then answered so softly that he had to strain to hear her reply. 'I'm pregnant.'

Immediately her whole body was wracked by great, heaving sobs.

Paul moved over to stand at her side. He put a hand on her shoulder and spoke soothingly to her. 'Just take your time, and when you're ready you can tell me whatever it is you want to tell me.' His mind was in a whirl. Was her husband not the father? Had she met someone else? However this had happened, she was anything but pleased. Until she told him more there was nothing he could do but stand there with what he hoped was a comforting touch.

Gradually Doreen's sobbing subsided. She fumbled in her pocket and found a tissue. Wiping her eyes and cheeks, she muttered, 'Sorry.'

'It's all right, best to get it out, and as I've said before, I'm always here to listen to what's troubling you and, I hope, to be of some help.'

'I feel terrible. It was after Brian's funeral. That very night. Ed had been really supportive when we got back to the flat. He got fish suppers for dinner and he only had a couple of cans of beer. It was like it was at the beginning. I thought we might be able to start over again.' Doreen finally looked directly at Paul. 'At least some good might come out of all this, I was beginning to think.'

She wiped away more tears before continuing. 'I know that sounds terrible, but I so much wanted everything to go back to how it had been with me and Ed. Brian would always be in my thoughts, maybe even the inspiration to make sure we got it right this time. To honour his memory in some way. I don't know. It doesn't make sense now when I hear what I'm saying, but that was what I thought. Or hoped,' she added.

'I understand,' Paul replied quietly, hoping that perhaps there was indeed a possibility that Doreen and Ed might get back together, and this time make a go of it.

'It was all a dream,' Doreen suddenly blurted out. 'I should have known better. That night we ended up in bed, making love. There was nothing said. It just seemed the right thing to do. Afterwards, I had the first decent sleep since the accident, but by the time Ed went back to work I knew it was all wishful thinking. He took most of his things with him and I haven't heard from him since. It's over. And I'm pregnant. What will people think?'

'What do you mean?' Paul asked, not sure if Doreen was referring to her broken marriage or to her pregnancy, or perhaps to both. Before he could think of a suitable reply, Doreen answered his question.

'They'll think I'm no better than an animal. Getting pregnant on the night of my son's funeral.' She was now too angry to shed any more tears.

'What you and Ed did that night is what many couples do after a family death. It's a perfectly natural thing to do as you seek comfort from one another.'

Doreen's anger disappeared as she heard these words. Her look was one of astonishment.

'And,' continued Paul, 'there are some experts who think that it's an instinctive reaction. Nature is saying that we must keep the family numbers up. I'm sorry, that doesn't sound right, but you understand what I'm saying?'

'Yes. The only trouble is I don't have a family. I'll be a single mum.'

'And with the continued help of your mum and dad, I'm confident you'll find a way.'

'I'm not so sure. They never liked Ed. and now when I tell them this, I hate to think what they might say.'

'Well, I suppose they might not be too happy at the news, but they love you. They are on your side and once they get used to the idea, I think they will be a great help.' Paul could see the doubt on Doreen's face.

It took some persuasion, but eventually Doreen calmed down and began to see her unplanned pregnancy in a new light. It would be difficult but, with the help of her mother and father, it might be possible. A great deal would depend on how her parents reacted.

They had supported her through the difficult periods in her marriage and since their return from holiday they had been a great help. Paul had persuaded her that what she and Ed had done that night after the funeral was not an act of lust but one of love. But would her parents see it that way?

He was not in a position to speak for her parents but from the contact he had had with them he felt that they would be supportive, but exactly how much help they could offer Doreen he had no idea. From something he had heard from Effie Melville he was aware that they were looking forward to retirement and possibly moving away from Dalcairn. He kept these thoughts to himself as he assured Doreen that she should not be afraid to ask for his opinion as she sorted out her life. He wished her well in the days and months ahead. Doreen promised that she would keep in touch.

'Thanks for listening and for understanding,' she said to Paul as she left the manse. 'And I promise, I'll try not to be a nuisance.'

Paul was glad to see that she was much more composed as she shook his hand. There may not have been a smile, but the worry that had been so obvious on her arrival had gone. It would not be easy for her but he had a feeling that she would manage. He stood on the doorstep and gave a final wave as she turned to walk down the crescent to the main road. That was the last time he saw Doreen Thomson.

24

Towards the end of May it was time for the annual Sunday School picnic. In days gone by, this was a huge day for many. It had only been a journey of a few miles by horse and cart into the countryside but it was so different from every other day that it was great fun and eagerly anticipated. When buses replaced the horse, it was off to the seaside. For the children of today even that was no longer as exciting as it had once been. Paddling in the sea and building sandcastles on the beach had become something that happened on many a fine summer weekend, thanks to the family car and the five-day week for so many workers. Most families now went to a coastal resort for the annual two-week summer holiday; some even ventured abroad.

The excitement now was in the journey, surrounded by friends, telling silly jokes, and no parents or schoolteacher to look disapprovingly, though if it got a bit rowdy, and it often did, the Sunday School teachers accompanying them did their best to make sure things didn't get too wild. And there were the races with prizes for the winners, not that the prizes were anything special, but to be a prizewinner gave one certain bragging rights on the journey home.

This year the trip fell on a warm, sunny day, and after the races, most, teachers included, braved the cold water and paddled about in the shallows. There was some splashing and some of the older boys had rather damp trouser legs when they sat down for the picnic. Before it was time for the return journey there were games for the younger children, skipping for the older girls and football for the boys. Some of the older boys thought the nearby amusement arcade might be a better option but an alert teacher intercepted their escape before they got very far. If anything, the singing on the buses was more raucous on the homeward journey.

It was a tired but happy band of children who alighted from the buses, some thanking the teachers and all promising to be at the prize-giving the following morning. Most of them kept the promise, but then they all knew that they would be awarded a prize, even if for some their regular attendance prize was simply an acknowledgement that they were on the roll.

The prize-giving was always a more or less informal occasion. The children were excited, it was noisy at times and Paul kept his message short and simple. He was certain that some of the regular worshippers thought it was a style he could use more often. The service was soon over and brought to a conclusion the busy life of the congregation for another session before it would begin all over again in September.

June was the month for weddings. Paul had never found out why May was so unpopular. Could the rhyme 'Marry in May and rue the day' influence people to such an extent that he very seldom had a May wedding? There had been one or two and the couples had explained that one reason for choosing the unpopular month was because they had the pick of the hotels for the reception and the weather was normally dry and sunny. June was always busy, as were March and September. Until recently couples who married in March and September had been the recipients of a nice rebate from the taxman as the married allowance was applied to the months in the tax year prior to the wedding. That was no longer the case but March and September continued to be very popular.

One of the June weddings this year was that of a young couple who were both from the local farming community. It seemed to Paul as he looked around the large company that the guests represented more or less every farm in the parish and beyond. At the hotel there was a great deal of merriment as the reception got under way. The Meikles, Jessie and Bob, Alec and Helen were guests. Paul spoke to them after the speeches and had to admire their attitude. It was, they told him, the bride and groom's day, and although Sandy and Wilma, and what might have been, and Kirsty, were very much in their minds, they were going to join in the celebration as best they could. How many of those present were thinking the same Paul had no way of knowing, but he knew that for most people in the parish the tragedy was no longer remembered every day. It was now part of the story of the community, but that was all; it had happened, it was over, there would be other tragedies, but so long as they happened to other people, that was all that really mattered.

The population of Burnbrae was such that the wedding ceremonies were spread out, partly he suspected because most of the receptions were held locally and it was a case of first come, first served at the venues. The news of an engagement quickly

169

spread around the town and the date of the wedding became public knowledge too. On the day of the wedding it was interesting to see the usual group of local women standing outside the church watching the guests arrive and commenting on the outfits of the ladies as they entered the church. When the bride and her attendants arrived there were oohs and aahs as they posed for their photos. During the ceremony some of these spectators would make their way up to the gallery to watch the proceedings inside while the others stood outside and gave a more critical assessment of the styles they had seen.

Paul was no longer visiting the families bereaved by the accident on a regular basis. The Meikles were in church most Sundays, he saw Tom in the shop and Mrs Melville, he was sure, would let him know if Doreen needed a visit. He was, however, concerned about Nan MacCallum despite her husband saying that she was coping 'in her own way' as he put it. That might mean any number of things, Paul thought, especially as Tom had not suggested that he should pop in and see her. Paul left it at that, but made a mental note to call at the house before he and Ruth went off on their summer holiday.

The last day of June was a Monday, the minister's day off, so Paul had promised Ruth that as soon as the Sunday morning service was over, he would be back home and on holiday. Wishful thinking.

One of his last pastoral visits before the holiday was to Nan MacCallum. She was at home, sitting by the window, staring out yet again and not saying very much. The same could not be said for her visitor. Paul did not know Babs, Nan's older sister, very well, but he soon realised that she was nothing like Nan. For a start, Babs was tall, rather thin, dark-haired, had sharp features and talked non-stop. Despite his best efforts to include Nan in the conversation, Paul eventually gave up. Perhaps Babs would leave before he did and give him some time with Nan on her own. The visit dragged on. Paul heard all about Babs's family and the problems she was having with her children despite the fact that one of them was married and the other two were working. Her husband did not seem to be any help. Paul suggested that it was all just part of being a parent.

'That's easy for you to say. Your two are away most of the time. If they're behaving badly you know nothing about it. I have it in my face day in and day out.' Babs was getting more and more agitated as she spoke.

Nan turned from gazing out the window. In a very quiet, yet firm tone, she said. 'At least you have them all. I don't.' She glowered at Babs before turning again and staring out onto the street below.

Babs was about to say something, but Paul got in first. 'And we are both very sorry for what has happened, Nan. There's really nothing we can say. We can only imagine how you feel, and even then, it will be nothing like what you're suffering. But it is still early days, just take your time, and remember you are surrounded by those who love you.'

Nan shook her head.

Babs stood up. 'I'll have to get home and make the meal for my lot. Even the son-in-law comes to me for his meals. His wife is hopeless in the kitchen. In fact they're all hopeless, full stop.'

She gave Nan a peck on the cheek, gathered up her things and, as she made her exit, made sure that the impression she left was that she was the one with the real problems.

After Babs had left Nan apologised for her sister's behaviour. 'She's always been a troublemaker,' she added.

Her comment, and the matter-of-fact way she made it, surprised Paul. He hoped that now he might have a meaningful conversation with her, but no, Nan gave her usual abrupt answers to all his questions, his enquiries about how she and the family were coping. Much of the time he wondered if she was even listening to him.

On leaving the house, Paul popped into the shop. Tom was concluding a sale. His two assistants were busy rearranging the display of goods on one of the shelves.

'What can I do for you today, Mr Johnson?' Tom asked Paul as the other customer turned to leave.

'I'm afraid I'm not buying. I popped up to see how Nan was,' Paul replied.

'Oh, right. And how was she? I don't suppose there was much change since your last visit?'

'Well, that's part of the reason I wanted to talk to you.' Paul looked around. He was speaking quietly and somewhat hesitantly.

Tom clearly got the message. 'Come through to the office, I could do with a coffee. Need a boost. The girls will look after the shop.' As they entered the rather cramped office Paul explained that he had had a cup of tea upstairs.

'Oh, that's unusual,' Tom exclaimed. 'She never makes me one.'

'Babs was there, she made it.'

Tom shook his head and sighed. 'Oh, she was there, was she? That would make it awkward. Did you get a word in at all?'

Paul tried to make light of how difficult it had been before telling Tom about Nan's very pointed comment to Babs, and the apology she gave Paul.

Tom looked surprised. 'It's been a long time since she showed any feeling about anything. Do you think it could be a turning point?'

'I was hoping it was, but I'm afraid that almost immediately she was back to staring out the window again.'

'Still, it might be the beginning of Nan getting back to normal. Normal for her, I mean.'

Now it was Paul who was puzzled. 'What do you mean "normal for her"? I don't know her very well, but I never thought she had a problem. A bit on the quiet side, perhaps.'

'And that's the problem. And Babs is the cause of it. At least as far as I'm concerned, she is. Let me make that coffee before I explain. Just instant, I'm afraid.'

'That's fine,' Paul replied as he sat down on the small chair crammed into a corner of the tiny room.

'Take the seat behind the desk,' Tom called over his shoulder.

'No, I'm fine here.' Paul was hoping whatever Tom had to say he would say it quickly. The chair was anything but comfortable.

Tom handed him a mug of coffee and placed his own mug on a corner of the surprisingly neat and tidy desk before sitting down on the office chair. He turned the chair to face his visitor.

'There's not really much to say. Nan and Babs are completely different in appearance and in character. Babs is loud, opinionated and, quite honestly, a bit of a bully. Nan had a terrible time of it growing up. Babs had to have her own way in everything. Their parents seemed unable to make her change her ways. In the end, Nan simply did whatever her big sister said. I thought once we got married I would be able to change things, but I was wrong. She hardly ever argues with me, seldom even disagrees. That outburst over Sally's death was probably one of the few times I've ever heard her say what she was really feeling. It was embarrassing to listen to her, and she has never repeated it, but I'm sure she does have feelings, opinions, like the rest of us. Hers, unfortunately, are kept well bottled up.'

There was a long silence before Paul replied. 'Tom, I don't want you to take this the wrong way, but after listening to your understanding of Nan's childhood and how it has affected her, I really do think you should encourage her to seek professional help.'

'You mean a shrink?'

'Well, yes, but I'm sure he or she would rather be called a psychiatrist or psychologist.'

'Sorry. It's just that Dr Wilkie has suggested that a couple of times but Nan didn't seem too keen, and I thought that she might just be needing a bit longer than most people to come to terms with what has happened to us. Not that I have come to terms with it myself. Don't think I ever will. Not totally anyway.' Tom was looking quite upset.

'It's early days,' Paul agreed. 'With any death it takes time for the loved ones to adjust to the new situation they find themselves in. With the tragedy you've suffered it would be very strange if you simply accepted it and life continued as it always had done.'

'Some days are better than others, but every now and again there's a really bad one. At least the customers have now stopped asking how I am as soon as they come in the shop door.'

Gradually the talk became less fraught and Paul managed to get Tom to see the sense in getting some specialist help for Nan, if Dr Wilkie broached the subject again.

'And what about you, Minister?' Tom suddenly asked. 'Are you getting back to normal?'

'I wouldn't call it normal, not quite yet, but everything has calmed down. And Ruth and I are planning a couple of weeks away next month.'

'Going anywhere nice?'

'I hope so. We plan to do a bit of touring around the North East. Never been up that way yet, but from what we've heard it should be lovely.'

There was a knock at the door. 'Come in,' Tom called.

The head of one of the assistants peeped round the door and spoke softly. 'Excuse me, but there's a customer who insists on asking you some questions about something he's thinking of buying.'

'Right, tell him I'll be out in a minute or two.'

Paul was already on his feet. 'I'll get on my way. I'll keep in touch, and as always, don't hesitate if you think I can be of some help.'

'Don't worry. I don't know how I would have managed to get to this point if it hadn't been for you and a few like-minded friends.'

25

Paul stepped out of the ironmonger's and looked up at Doreen Thomson's window opposite. His visit to the MacCallums had taken longer than expected. It had also been very stressful. He was about to make his way home but suddenly changed his mind. Doreen would probably now be home from work. It wasn't perhaps the most suitable time to call on her, but if she had begun to accept all that had happened to her, it would not need to be a long visit; a simple courtesy call to let her know she was not forgotten. His mind made up, he crossed the street and climbed the stairs to her door.

As he reached out to ring the bell, his eye caught the shiny new nameplate underneath the bell. The name wasn't Thomson. Doreen must have moved away. Neither she nor Effie across the landing had thought to let him know. He was annoyed and disappointed in equal measure. He would have a word with Effie.

He hesitated. As soon as he entered Effie's house he would be offered a cup of tea. He could not leave immediately after drinking it. And he had just had a mug of coffee with Tom. His decision was made. He felt bad as he turned towards the stairs. At that moment Effie's door opened. Too late.

'Aye, it is you! I just happened to be looking out the window and saw you crossing the road. I thought you might be coming up here. Come away in. You'll be needin' a cuppa. The kettle's on. It's always on.'

The last thing I need is another cuppa, Paul said to himself. To Effie he replied, 'That would be lovely, Mrs Melville. Thank you.'

As Effie led the way along the hallway, she asked Paul, 'Did you not know Doreen had moved?'

'No, I haven't heard from her for some time now,' Paul replied. 'Last time we spoke I thought we'd agreed that she would get in touch if she thought I could be of any help to her.'

'The wee minx! She said she would let you know,' Effie exclaimed. 'Seems she didn't need advice. She had made up her mind. She has gone to stay with her parents. Did she tell you she was pregnant?'

Paul was not sure if there was a tone of disapproval in Effie's voice, but he let it pass. 'Yes, she came to the manse and told me. We had quite a long talk about things.'

'Even more reason for her to tell you she was moving. Now, let me get that cuppa, then we can chat. Go ben the room. You know the way. I'll only be a minute.'

Paul did as he was told. Over the cup of tea Effie provided more information about Doreen, her marriage and her life in general. Apart from the decision to move in with her parents, who were now living somewhere in Lanarkshire, Paul had already heard the details from Doreen herself, and probably in more detail than Effie had been given.

As soon as he could, Paul made his excuses, thanked Effie for the tea and chat and made his way back to the manse. If he managed to make the short walk without anyone else stopping him for a chat or to pass on some information that they thought he needed to know, he would   be just in time for his evening meal. He was closing the front door as Ruth appeared out of the kitchen.

'That was quite an afternoon as it turned out,' he said with a sigh. They kissed as they always did. Ruth stepped back. 'And it's not over yet,' she announced. 'Lachie the undertaker phoned. Bessie McNaughton, the old midwife, has died.'

'What? I saw her the other week. She was her usual self. No complaints, looking great for her age.'

'Well, you can phone Lachie later and find out what's what. He said there's no hurry. And your dinner's ready, so before you even start to tell me about your afternoon, in great detail no doubt, we'll eat.'

As always, Paul knew better than to disagree.

In due course he made the call to Lachie. It seemed that Bessie McNaughton had simply gone to bed the previous evening as usual. One of the district nurses had called mid-morning but could get no answer. A neighbour who had a key to Bessie's house had opened the door for her. The nurse found Bessie lying in her bed.

She knew as soon as she saw her that the old midwife had passed away in her sleep.

'A nice way to go,' Paul commented, 'but I can't really believe she has gone. In all the time I've been visiting her, she has never changed. Somehow I thought she would go on forever.'

'Well, she didn't. Her nephew, who's a fair age himself, has been in contact. He would like the funeral next Monday.'

'I suppose that will be all right,' Paul said, hesitating as he spoke.

'You don't seem too sure. Have you something else on that day? I know it's meant to be your day off.'

'It's not so much my day off, it's more the start of my summer break. I was hoping to get away on Sunday evening. Because Monday is my day off.' He added rather cynically, 'At least that's what it should be, but so often isn't.'

'Look, don't worry about it,' Lachie replied. 'Who's covering for you? I'll get in touch with him. It won't be a big funeral anyway, I shouldn't think. Never is when folk get to that age.'

'No, you won't ask someone else. I'll do it. She was a good friend and a wise woman who understood people. She was often an inspiration to me.'

'If you insist, Minister. If you change your mind, just get in touch.'

'I won't. What time were you thinking of?'

Soon the arrangements were made and if Ruth was disappointed at not getting away on holiday the day they had planned, she said nothing. She had married him knowing that he wouldn't put himself or his family before his parishioners in their hour of need. She understood and respected him for that, and she had known before they married that that was how it would always be. She also understood how much sensible advice Bessie had given to Paul, advice that had often calmed him down when his workload was getting him down.

The funeral was attended by a surprisingly large number of local people, most of whom hadn't seen Bessie for many years, but they had not forgotten the very important part she had played in the lives of their family.

In a strange and unexpected way, the wedding and the funeral were the perfect preparation for the holiday. After all the turmoil, heartache, grief and trauma of the accident, these two events were normal. They were, of course, special for the people involved: the young couple starting out on life together, the old lady laid to rest at the end of a very long life of service to her community and a passing that was so peaceful. These two events also highlighted what the Watsons, the Meikles, the MacCallums and the Thomsons had lost and would never get back. What they had experienced was exceptional, but unfortunately not unknown.

The bereaved, apart from Nan MacCallum, were coming to terms with what had happened to them, and each one, in his or her own way, appeared to be settling down to their new situation. They still had moments, hours and even days when it all came back, but they helped one another. Paul had made a short visit to them all in the week before his break. They thanked him for all he had done and wished him a happy holiday and a good, restful two weeks. Bob Meikle summed it up. 'Off you go, Minister, forget about us, forget about the parish. You and the good lady deserve some time to yourselves. Away you go and enjoy your time together.'

When Paul repeated Bob's words to Ruth, her reply was brief and to the point. 'Well, that is exactly what I intend to do. You make sure you do the same.'

And they did: exploring new places, spending time together and above all, appreciating being free to take it easy and relax.

26

William Watson had spent a considerable amount of time since Wilma's death exploring how he could use the money set aside for her to help the young people of Burnbrae in some way; it was one way of coping with the loss of his beloved daughter. As Wilma was growing up, her parents had soon realised that she was a girl who got on well with her peers, who loved helping others and who seemed almost certain to choose a career where she would make good use of these attributes. It was no surprise to Mary and William when, even before she had left primary school, Wilma announced that she wanted to be a teacher.

As a teacher she would have helped all the children she taught and William was convinced that the best way to spend the money in her trust fund was indeed to establish the youth centre. It soon became apparent that this might be easier said than done. First there was the problem of premises. Once the disused church was altered, it should be a great place for the local youth. Ensuring that there would always be sufficient funding to maintain and run the centre was more problematic, but William was fairly certain that when it was operational, the local council would see the benefits it brought and make some funds available. The question of a leader, or leaders, would be sorted out in due course, but trustees would have to be appointed by William and Mary, guided by their lawyer, to administer the fund. Normally this would involve people such as the doctor, the minister and the bank manager.

William worked away quietly, talking over his thoughts with Mary. She was fully in favour of what he was hoping to achieve and raised some very helpful points in the early stages. One thing they could do without any difficulty was to present a special trophy to the local tennis club where Wilma had been an enthusiastic member and talented player. Mary and William were guests of the club when the final match was played, and Mary presented the Wilma Watson Memorial Trophy, Girls Singles, to Avril Wilson, winner of a close-fought match.

Over the summer, plans for the youth centre began to take shape and William was ready to make his dream a reality, providing, of course, that others agreed that the youth centre was not only needed, but that it would work. The few people to whom William had already spoken had encouraged him in his venture. Finding others willing to be involved was the next problem.

They were sitting in the garden enjoying the cool of a summer's evening. William turned to Mary. 'By the way,' he said, 'Dr Wilkie was in the bank this afternoon. I got a chance to speak to him about the youth centre. He's very enthusiastic about it.'

'I thought he would be. Will he be a trustee?'

'Yes, but there's a problem. He's getting towards retiring age and as he will be moving away from Burnbrae, his involvement might not be for very long.'

'Still, every little helps, and his successor may be willing to take his place. And he, or she, would likely be nearer the age of the youth centre members,' Mary added. 'Speaking of which, I wonder if you should ask Ruth to be a trustee, rather than Paul. Paul has plenty on his hands already.'

'The trustees don't actually do all that much. Their job is to make sure that the centre is being run according to the conditions of the trust deed. If all is well they may meet only once a year. I was thinking that Ruth may very well be a suitable leader.'

'That's a great idea. She would be excellent. Have you mentioned any of this to her or to Paul?'

'No, not yet, and I don't want to get ahead of myself. Once the idea begins to become a possibility, then I hope people will be less able to find an excuse for not becoming a part of it.'

'William Watson, you can be quite a sly old fox when you put your mind to it.'

William's face fell.

Mary laughed. 'You are, you know.'

'I would prefer to say I'm pragmatic.'

Mary shook her head. This was no joking matter. The youth centre he hoped would be a place of enjoyment for those who frequented it, and for him it was a very serious matter. He would make sure it was a fitting memorial to Wilma.

William failed to hide the hurt Mary's remark had caused as he wiped a tear from his eye. She reached over and took his hand in hers. 'I'm sorry, dear, I didn't mean to cause offence. I know how much this means to you, and to me. With your careful planning, I'm sure it will be a welcome addition to the community, and be of great benefit to those who use it.'

Summer at Fauldshead followed the usual pattern. It had to, as they worked with nature, but this summer, without Sandy, there was more work for Bob and Alec. Iain spent almost all his school holiday doing as much as he could, and it was a great deal, but he didn't yet have the experience to be left on his own with some of the tasks. Bob was worried that his dad was doing more than he should. Alec was fit, but it was time that he slowed down and enjoyed life with Helen away from the farm. Even Helen was getting involved with jobs that she had not done in a long time. It helped her feel that she was doing her bit and making life slightly easier for her menfolk. No matter how hard they worked, all of them were very much aware that Sandy and Kirsty were no longer with them. On several occasions Bob had caught Jessie still setting their places at the table and shedding a quiet tear or two when she realised what she was doing.

The DIY side of Tom MacCallum's business changed from inside to outside tasks for many of his customers as gardens needed attention and the better weather and longer daylight meant that work on the exterior of buildings could be undertaken. One thing that did not change, however, was Nan's health. Since the outburst Paul had witnessed between her and Babs, Nan was talking a little more, but there were still long periods of silence when she withdrew into her own private world. What she was thinking was impossible to know.

She seldom spoke about Sally, and Tom had discovered, quite by accident, that she had several photos of their beloved daughter in one of her handbags. He had never come in and found Nan looking at the photos, but he was sure that that was what she did when she thought no one would be about, and when she did go out, the handbag was always with her.

Soon it was autumn and time for the start of the winter cycle of activities in church and community. The children were back at school, the youth groups were already meeting and the adult activities would not be far behind. Tennis and bowls once again gave way to football and badminton as the days grew shorter. On the farms there was no let-up. Less daylight meant less time to do what had to be done outside.

At the Meikles' farm Sandy was missed more than ever and Bob had on more than one occasion to remind his father that he was not as young as he thought he was.

'Age is just a number,' Alec retorted after yet another warning. 'My father was a good bit older than me before he gave up working on the land altogether.'

'I'm not asking you to give it up, I'm telling you to slow down. I saw you the other day. You were leaning on a gate, trying to get your breath back. Take your time, there's no rush.'

That last remark was not quite true. There had been times when Bob wished that he had done some jobs himself. He would have had it done and been well into the next one before his dad finished what he had been working on but, to be fair, without Alec helping him, he would be working all day and a good part of the evening. Iain had his schoolwork to concentrate on, though he too did what he could, especially at weekends.

Alec had popped into the bungalow for a mid-afternoon cup of tea. He seemed to do it more and more often these days and Helen was more than a little concerned that he was overdoing things. She had said as much on a number of occasions but her words had fallen on deaf ears, and even provoked a rather heated response from Alec the last time she had mentioned it. Now she kept her opinion to herself.

'Just what I needed. Thanks, love,' Alec said, as he placed his empty mug on the table. 'I'm off to the low field. Bob mentioned something about a fence that needs looking at. I'll go and check it out.'

'Just be careful then. It might need two of you.'

'Aye, it might, and if it does, I'll have had a lovely walk on this beautiful autumn day. Think this might be an Indian summer.'

'It might, but it's not much of a forecast for later in the week.'

'All the more reason to be mending that fence today then. Cheerio. I'll be back before you know it.'

The fence took a bit longer to repair than Alec had anticipated, but he got there in the end. He was quite out of breath as he leaned on a post. He had to admit that perhaps Helen and Bob were right; he was finding the work, or at least the amount he was doing, not as easy as it had been. If only Sandy were still around, but he wasn't. He had to do his bit. He gave a sigh, for the loss of Sandy and for his own advancing years, then made his way home.

'You made it.' He was sure there was a sense of relief in Helen's voice as she added, 'Dinner will be in half an hour.'

'I think I'll have my dram before my dinner today. That fence was a bugger.'

Helen turned from what she was doing. 'I was beginning to get worried. You sit down and relax. I'll get your drink.'

'Thanks, lass.'

In no time at all, Helen was back with Alec's whisky. He was slumped in his chair.

'Alec,' she gasped, then dropped the glass and rushed towards him.

27

Bob was refuelling the tractor when Jessie came rushing out of the farmhouse.

'Bob, where are you? Your dad! You need to get over there now!'

Bob didn't wait to ask what had happened. He stopped what he was doing, ran to the pickup and jumped in. The keys were in the ignition as usual. Moments later he was parked outside the bungalow. He hurried inside to find his mum cradling his dad's body in her arms. It didn't look good.

'Have you phoned the doctor?'

'No. It's too late, Bob. He's gone.'

'There must be something we can do! Mouth to mouth, I'll try that. You phone Dr Wilkie.'

Bob had only a sketchy idea of how mouth-to-mouth resuscitation was done, but he had to try. Anything was better than doing nothing. Did he put his dad on the floor? He had to. When he had seen it done on TV the patient was always lying down. It wasn't easy but he managed it just as his mum re-entered the room.

'Dr Wilkie is on his way.' Helen watched as Bob did his best, but there was no sign of life returning. Helen put her hand on his shoulder. 'Leave it, Bob. You've tried. I think you should stop now. The signs were there, but he was stubborn. He just wouldn't listen to me. I knew he was doing too much. It's all my fault.' The dam broke as sobs wracked her body. Bob got up and held her tight. He was still holding her when Jessie arrived. Dr Wilkie was close behind.

There was nothing he could do. Gently and calmly he explained that Alec had had a massive heart attack. 'Sometimes there are no warning signs,' he concluded.

Helen appeared to disagree. 'But I told him he was overdoing things, ever since Sandy died. He wouldn't listen. He was trying to help Bob, but he wasn't up to it.'

'And I told him, more than once, he didn't need to do all that he was doing. But he always said he was fine,' Bob replied.

'None of us could have stopped him,' Helen added. 'He was his own worst enemy at times.' As soon as she uttered these words the floodgates opened again. Jessie tried to comfort her.

'You mustn't blame yourselves,' Dr Wilkie explained. 'Even if I had examined Alec yesterday, I doubt if I could have predicted this. I too might have suggested that he should slow down, do no more strenuous work, but I don't think he would have paid any attention to me either. It's little comfort, I know, but he died peacefully at home, having done the job he loved.

'I will have no problem issuing the death certificate. It was natural causes, and it happened within the home. I am just sorry that you had no warning, and after all that has already happened. Look after one another, and don't be afraid to ask for help if you are struggling.'

On the drive home from the farm, Dr Wilkie wondered what more he could have said. There was only so much people could take. The loss of the young ones, the guilt that they might feel over Alec's sudden death, it could all build up. He made a promise to himself that he would keep a close eye on them.

What had happened to Alec could have been so much worse. He might have been driving on the public roads when he had that sudden, fatal heart attack. There might have been an accident involving other people, serious injuries, even fatalities. Thank goodness it had happened at home, sitting in his favourite armchair.

Word of Alec's sudden death soon got out and it spread like wildfire around the farming community. Fauldshead was inundated by a constant stream of visitors, so much so that there were times when some visitors had to wait outside in the yard, talking to one another until some of those inside departed, or more often than not, joined in conversation with friends outside. In Burnbrae itself, Alec's death was also a talking point. As Paul went about the parish, friends of the Meikles and even people who had never met them expressed concern for the family. Inevitably the conversation ended when they stated that they wondered how they would manage if a similar sequence of events were to occur within their own family circle.

The evening before Alec's funeral, Helen, Jessie, Iain and Bob were alone. The constant stream of visitors had finally dried up. They were seated in the lounge of the farmhouse. Bob broke the silence.

'Tomorrow won't be easy for any of us. Don't be afraid to let your feelings show. We will all be there for each other.'

'Do you think we are being punished?' Helen suddenly asked.

Bob was surprised at his mum's question. She was the most level-headed of them all. 'It does make you wonder, but I don't think so, Mum. We've lived decent lives, tried to do our best. What would we be being punished for? It's just the way it goes sometimes.'

'But why us?' Jessie asked. 'I've often found myself thinking the same, and that was before Alec died. Bob and I have tried several times to find a reason to explain why Sandy and Kirsty, and the others, were taken so young, but there is no answer. Even if it had been through illness, there would still have been no answer. Why them? Why now? Why us?'

'I think this is a bit heavy at this time of the evening, and this night of all nights. Maybe Paul will give us an answer, and if he doesn't, I'm sure his words will at least give us comfort.' Bob looked at his loved ones. 'I'm going to make a cup of tea. Anyone want one?'

Most funerals in the farming community were well attended, and Alec's was no exception. Farmers met at market on a regular basis, they knew their neighbours and helped one another out when needed. Close friendships were formed over several generations as the farms were handed down from father to son, and many a farmer's son married a farmer's daughter. Of course there were disagreements, sometimes quite heated ones, but after those involved had had their say, the normal order was usually restored over a dram or two in the market bar or the farmhouse kitchen. Every farm in the area was represented at the funeral and there were a goodly number of people from the town and further afield.

Many townsfolk who hardly knew Alec had felt obliged to be present out of respect. For most people in Burnbrae the terrible tragedy had been pushed well to the back of their minds over the weeks and months that had passed, but once again it was foremost in their thoughts. How much more would the Meikles have to endure? How much more could they take? Paul heard these kind of comments from the people he met. Some had added, and he hoped it was only a few, 'rather them than me'. Many, he suspected, had yet again been made aware of the unpredictable nature of life.

On this occasion the service was held in the church, partly because of the numbers expected and also because the weather forecast was not good. On the day, it was dull but the rain held off until later in the afternoon. The invitation to meet with the family at The Rowans after the service was accepted by almost 200 people. At first the conversation was muted, but by the time the company had been fed, there was animated chat and from time to time a burst of laughter. Life was, once more, returning to normal.

The last of the relatives had finally left. Bob, Jessie and Helen could relax. It had been a very emotional day: so many memories, so many thoughts; a mixture of happiness and great sorrow. There was little conversation. Before long Helen announced that she would get back to the bungalow.

'I'll walk you across,' Bob said.

'No, I can manage. You sit here with Jessie.' Iain had gone up to his bedroom some time earlier.

'I'll see you safely home. I have to go out anyway and check that all is well with the beasts.' It was something that had to be done; it would be good to get back into the normal routine as soon as possible.

'I'll just come in and see that everything is OK,' Bob told his mum as she unlocked the door.

'You will do no such thing. I have to get back to normal too. I don't like not having Alec around any more, but that is how it is. You get off and do what you have to do, and get back to Jessie as soon as you can.'

Bob gave her a peck on the cheek before he turned to leave, full of admiration for her strong will and sensible advice.

When Bob returned to the farmhouse, Jessie was still sitting where he had left her.

'Are you sleeping?' he asked softly, not wanting to wake her if she was.

She turned her head. 'No, I'm just thinking, how will I stop you from overdoing it now? You can't possibly do everything on your own.'

'No, I can't. And I won't be on my own.'

She raised her eyebrows in surprise. 'What do you mean? Iain can't leave school yet, and even when he does, he'll be going to college for three years before he works full-time on the farm.'

'Of course he will.'

'So, what's your wonderful plan then?'

'Jack Jackson had a word with me at the hotel.'

'I saw you speaking to him. It was more than a word. I never knew he was one of your close friends.'

'He's not, but he might be now.' Bob knew that he had to get to the point quickly, so he pressed on. 'His son finished college at the start of the summer. He can't afford to keep paying someone else so Malkie Oliver, who worked for him, is looking for a place. Jack says he's a great worker. I knew that already from seeing him at the market from time to time.'

'Good, but we don't have accommodation here. Where will he stay?'

'And that's not a problem either. He has already moved into a council house in Burnbrae. Jack made it clear to the housing department that he couldn't let him stay on at his place so he would be homeless. There was a house available, and he got it.'

'And will he want to come and work here?'

'That we will discover tomorrow when he comes to see the farm.'

'The farm's fine,' Jessie joked. 'It's his new boss that might be the problem.'

'Very funny. What about a nightcap and an early night? It's been a long day.'

'It has indeed. I'll have tea. You get your dram while I boil the kettle.'

As Jessie stood up, Bob moved towards her, his arms outstretched. Neither seemed to want the embrace to end. They would get through all this. They had to, and together they would, Bob vowed.

28

Planning the youth centre continued. In strictest confidence, William had first sought the opinions of a few very carefully chosen people. They had been supportive, but cautioned William to make sure that the venture would be supported by the community. Eventually he had had to widen the group who knew about his proposal. Still there was support, but of course, the word got out into the wider community. The young people were enthusiastic, as were their parents, but there were also the critics.

Some of those who had worshipped in the building now no longer in use were very annoyed. After all the hard work to build and maintain the church through the years it would be sacrilege to hand it over to young people, teenagers who would be up to all sorts of things within its hallowed walls. This was a tiny, but very vocal minority. There were also quite a number who simply wanted the building to remain as it was, a memorial to generations past.

'Now we really have a problem,' William announced to Mary as he returned from the bank at the end of another day's work.

'Is that the "we" at the bank, the "we" at the church, or the "we" who reside here?'

'Very good, Mary,' William replied with a smile. 'I'll start again.' He gave her a peck on the cheek, his normal greeting. 'How was your day? Everything all right?'

'Everything is just fine. Well, it was, but clearly it isn't now. Do you want to eat before you tell me what your problem is, or would it be better to tell me first?'

'It won't take long to tell you the problem, but it might be months before the problem is solved, and the outcome might well not be the one that we want.'

'OK, dinner will be ready at the usual time, so that gives us half an hour. You get out of your suit while I pour the wine and make sure all is well in the kitchen.'

Seated in the family room, glass in hand, William, as was his norm, got straight to the point. 'There's someone else interested in buying the old church,' he said.

'You're joking?' Mary gasped.

'No, I'm not. He is a builder in Dalcairn and he has got his eye on the building. He wants to convert it into a house.'

'A house! Surely no one would want to live in an old church?' Mary shook her head in disbelief.

'You'd be surprised. I'm not sure if he intends to make it a large house for one family or convert it into a number of flats, but the worry is that he has indicated that whatever I offer, he will top it by at least ten per cent.'

'Can he do that? I thought you made your offer and the seller decided which one to accept.'

'That's the way it should work, but now that the church trustees, who will make the decision, know of his offer, at least one of them has put it about that he wants to get as much as possible for the building. And if someone who just happens to be treasurer of the other congregation, meaning me, doesn't get it, so much the better.'

'Not a very Christian attitude,' remarked Mary.

'Maybe not, but the money they get will be put to charitable causes. If that's what happens, the plans I had for Wilma's memorial will have to be changed.' William gave a sigh. 'Still, it's early days yet. And dinner smells great. Let's enjoy our dinner. Perhaps his plans will come to nothing.'

Over the next few weeks Mary sensed that William was not his usual self. Never one to show a great deal of emotion at the best of times, he became even more withdrawn. As far as she could tell, his work did not suffer, but there was a tension in the home. She tried once or twice to persuade him to talk about the problem but his answer was always the same. 'There's nothing I can do. I know exactly how much money we'll have available. The other interested party will pay more. That's it.'

There had to be something she could do to help, but what?

The help came about quite by chance. Mary was setting out for the shops when Ruth happened to be leaving the manse. She too was carrying a shopping bag. The two neighbours set off together. Their conversation began with the usual comments about the weather, how they were keeping and eventually got around to what they were planning in the near future.

At this point, Mary inadvertently gave a sigh. Ruth turned her head and looked more closely at Mary.

'I don't mean to pry, but if there's something bothering you, and you want to talk about it, please do.'

Very briefly Mary explained about the problem hanging over the proposed youth centre. 'So there you have it. We just have to wait and see what happens.' Mary gave another sigh.

'I wonder if Paul could be of some help,' Ruth replied, much to Mary's surprise.

'I don't mean in any practical way,' Ruth hastened to add, 'but he's very friendly with the minister in the parish church at Dalcairn. He might know something about the other possible purchaser. Is he likely to actually make an offer? Are his ideas practical? That sort of thing. I know it's not much, but it might just help.'

Mary was ready to clutch at any straw if it would help to lift the cloud that was hanging over William.

'Thanks, Ruth. It may not change anything, but if Paul doesn't mind, at least I'll feel that I've tried to help.'

Mary did not tell William about her meeting with Ruth. It was very likely that he would not have approved of her passing on the information regarding the sale of the old church.

When William opened the door a few days later to find Ruth and Paul on his doorstep he was quite surprised. His first assumption was that they had something personal to discuss, but what? He invited them in.

The information that had come back to Paul was very helpful. He and Ruth had decided to give the news to their neighbour face to face. After the usual pleasantries were exchanged, William was taken aback when Paul, without any words by way of introduction, announced, 'Well, William, you'll be pleased to know that I have good news for you. At least, I think it's good news.'

William looked mystified, Mary looked embarrassed and Ruth and Paul looked to one another.

'After Ruth suggested to Mary that I might be able to get some info on the builder in Dalcairn, the one who wants to convert the old church into a house, I got in touch with my colleague over there.'

William was now somewhat annoyed.

'It's OK, he can be relied on to keep it to himself. And me too, of course,' Paul added with a grin.

'That's not what's troubling me. It's the fact that Mary went behind my back. I never knew anything about this till now. I thought you were here to ask me for some advice, or tell me something regarding your own plans for the future.'

Before Mary could respond to William's rebuke, Ruth said, 'It was me, I suggested that Paul could make some enquiries. Mary was concerned that you were really worried that your plans for the youth centre might come to nothing.'

William wasn't too happy but what was done was done. There was nothing he could do about it now, and he had to admit that he had not been the best of company and Mary was the one who had suffered most. He apologised to both Ruth and Mary, his normal calm manner returning.

He looked at Paul. 'You said you had good news?'

'Yes. The builder is a good one, and he's ambitious. He seems to have thought that doing something with the church might show people that he was not your ordinary sort of builder.'

'And that's good news, is it?' William commented sharply.

'Sorry, William. I'm not making a very good job of this,' Paul responded. 'The good news is that he almost certainly will not be converting the church into anything. He will probably not be able to buy it. The national financial situation might improve eventually, but he has realised that this is not the time to be borrowing money that may take some time to repay. Instead of making a name for himself, it's more likely to make him a bankrupt.'

After some further talk on the matter, William rose from his chair, thanked Paul and Ruth with a warm handshake and gave Mary a peck on the cheek. 'I'm sorry, I should have known that none of you, and especially you, Mary, would do anything to hinder my plans for the old church. What you've discovered calls for a celebration. What will you have?'

It was not too long after Ruth and Paul's visit that William heard officially from the trustees of the old church that they were happy to accept his offer to buy the church, wishing him well in his venture and promising him their full support.

While William and Mary were pushing ahead with plans for the youth centre, there was a different mood at Fauldshead. Jessie had noticed a change in Bob since his father's sudden death. Bob took most things in his stride. When something caused a problem: a mechanical breakdown, complications with a calving or a lambing, things of that nature, he would utter some curses then get on with fixing the machine or helping the mother in distress. But this was different. He was getting on with the work on the farm and Malkie Oliver had settled in very well. Jessie knew that Bob was grieving, but he was keeping his thoughts to himself. No matter how many hints she had dropped, he would not open up to her. Matters came to a head one evening as they watched television.

The drama was like many others they had watched. Jessie had a feeling that Bob was not as interested in the story or the outcome as she was, but at least he was relaxing, or so she thought. One of the characters in the story had had a run of bad luck. He was talking to a mate about what had happened. He shrugged his shoulders and said, 'Well, that's life. You just have to grin and bear it.'

Bob thumped the arm of his chair, spilling his whisky in the process. 'What the hell does he know? Grin and bear it? It's no laughing matter.'

'Bob, calm down. It's only a play.'

'Aye, and it's nothing like real life. Written by someone sitting at a desk, typing away. Looking out the window every so often, thinking he knows what real life is about. Real life is about losing your son, your daughter and your father. All in six months! That's real life!'

Bob's tirade stopped as suddenly as it had begun and his body was wracked by great, heaving sobs. Jessie rushed to his side and held him until he calmed down. He looked embarrassed. What had just happened was so out of character. Her husband liked to think of himself as someone who could face up to whatever life threw at him. 'I'm sorry, Jessie. I'm being silly.'

'No, you're not. You've been holding back, trying to be strong for the rest of us. You needed to get it out. Now, just you sit there and try to relax. I'll wipe up the whisky, refill your glass and then we can talk this over.'

Spilled drink wiped up and refilled glass returned to Bob, Jessie sat back down in her chair and as she switched off the TV she said, 'Now, take a drink and when you're ready, start talking. Whatever you say, I'll listen. No interruptions, I promise.'

'What happened to Sandy and Kirsty was an accident. A terrible accident.' Bob shook his head as he repeated the words. 'The fact that Wilma and the other two youngsters were there just made it worse. But it was an accident. Accidents happen. They happen all the time. But they happen to others. Usually.'

He stopped as if to catch his breath. He made to lift his glass, but held back. Perhaps he had realised that drink wouldn't help. He looked at Jessie, resignation written all over his face.

'I will never get over losing our two lovely children, and probably a lovely daughter-in-law.' His voice was breaking but he forced himself to continue. 'Sandy and Wilma had a meeting, the others had a school dance. It was going to be a good night for them all. Whatever happened, happened. All right, that's life. The chap on the TV was right. But my dad's death was not all right. I shouldn't have allowed it to happen.'

Jessie was puzzled. She couldn't understand what he meant, but she said nothing. Bob seemed to be thinking about what he had just said.

'I should have stopped him working all the hours he was putting in,' Bob continued. 'It was too much, and some of what he was doing wasn't work for a man his age, and certainly not on his own. But I thought it was helping him. He was a man of action, like me. He couldn't sit still when there was a job to be done. He died because I didn't stop him,' he repeated.

This time Jessie did speak. 'And if you had forced him to stop, he would have been miserable. He might even have died of boredom. At least he died doing what he loved. And he had been hiding his symptoms from all of us. That breathlessness, that should have been a clue, but we just thought it was from exertion. But it wasn't. It was his time. I know the accident may have had some part to play in his death, it has affected all of us in ways we never thought possible, but even without that your dad may not have lived much longer.'

Bob didn't seem convinced. 'You may be right. And we will never know for certain. I suppose all of us want to have a long, happy, healthy retirement, but not everyone does. Let's leave it there, and thanks for listening. I had to get it out. It was becoming all I could think about.'

'Well,' replied Jessie, 'it's out now, and you're right. Let's just leave it there. We have many happy memories. Think on them instead. Cup of tea, or another whisky?'

'I think it's time for bed. I have a feeling I might sleep a bit better tonight.'

29

The following Sunday, Paul was surprised to see Jessie lingering as the congregation made their way out from the church. A few weeks after the accident she had apologised for slipping out a side door, a practice that had continued, until now.

Paul had called at the farm to see how everyone was coping shortly after Jessie had begun to use that particular exit from the church.

'I'm not avoiding you,' she had explained during the visit. 'I will never forget the great help you have been to us these last weeks, and to all the others. It's just that so many people seem to feel that they have to talk to me after the service, to ask how I am. I know I shouldn't complain, it's kind of them, well, most of them anyway.'

Paul was surprised.

Jessie gave a wry smile. 'You would be amazed at how many people now seem to think they're my best friend. Before, the most I ever got was a curt hello, if that, as we passed one another in the street, at church or wherever. I'd like to think they were sincere, but some, I'm sure, are just downright nosey. So I try to avoid them if I can.'

Paul had to admit that there were quite a few people, men and women, he too was quite happy to avoid if he could, and for much the same reason as Jessie had given. Unlike Jessie, he could not use the side door; he had to stand and shake hands with everyone as they left through the main door.

As the last of those waiting to have a word with the minister took their leave, Jessie stepped forward.

'I won't keep you long,' she said before Paul got a chance to greet her. 'I want to apologise for Bob's absence this morning. He told me he had something that needed doing urgently.'

'That's all right,' Paul responded. 'There's no need to apologise. Life on the farm is very demanding and some things can't be left unattended.'

'Yes, but that was just an excuse. He hasn't been himself since his dad died. It has affected us all, but Bob is taking it very badly.'

Paul was aware that some of the office-bearers who were clearing up could probably hear much of what was being said.

'Look, Jessie, would it not be better to move round to the vestry where we can have a bit of privacy?'

'No, that's not necessary. It's just that he blames himself for not stopping his dad from working so hard in the weeks before his death. He opened up to me the other night and he said he felt better afterwards, but I don't think he'll ever be able to forgive himself.'

'I suppose that's only natural. Whether he's correct, of course, is quite another matter, and I'm not so sure he is.'

'That's what I said, and he kind of agreed but...' Jessie's voice fell away.

'Look, I'll pop round and see if I can help. It's no trouble. Some morning later in the week, perhaps.'

'No! It's very good of you, I mean, but if he thinks I've been telling tales that will only make it worse. I just want you to be aware of how he feels. He's not yet back to his old self and I don't want you to think that you've somehow failed to help him. And the moment I think he does need help, you'll be the first to know. Well, you and Dr Wilkie.'

'Is that a promise?'

'It is, but I hope we'll get over it without bothering either of you.'

After Paul had asked how Helen and Iain were getting on, Jessie left and Paul made his way back to the vestry to change out of his vestments. He was fairly confident that Bob would sort things out. He was a very sensible, rational person. If only he could say the same of Nan MacCallum. Poor Nan seemed to be resisting all attempts to help her.

During several visits to the MacCallums in the immediate aftermath of the accident, Paul felt that his words of comfort had fallen on deaf ears with regard to Nan. She appeared to be in another place most of the time during his chats with her. She very seldom looked at him and only occasionally replied to a direct question with anything other than yes or no. The answer suggested that she had heard, but what she was thinking was known only to her. It was early days and Paul expected that, given time, Nan would come to terms with what had happened.

He and Tom discussed how Paul could best help after yet another frustrating visit from his point of view. He made it clear that he had no intention of giving up on Nan and Tom assured him that while he appreciated his concern there were other people who also needed his care.

It seemed that neither of them was willing to accept the other's position. 'As soon as Nan becomes more like her old self, you'll be the first to know,' Tom insisted. 'Until then, if you don't hear from me, you don't need to worry. It means Nan is no worse. And I'm managing,' he added.

Paul was not happy with that suggestion.

'Some people are not very good at asking for help because they don't want to be a nuisance. In your situation, Tom, I would rather keep in touch. The way things are at present, I would never regard you as a nuisance.'

Tom was about to protest. Paul stopped him. 'How about this? I'll drop in to the shop for a blether every so often, and I don't mean every Tuesday at half past two, I mean from time to time. In between, if I haven't heard anything from you I'll know there's no change, or, I hope, some improvement.'

'Who am I to tell you how to do your job?' Tom replied. 'And I am grateful that you are prepared to do that. Now I feel even more guilty that I never pop into the church.'

'You know the door is always open, at least on a Sunday,' Paul added with a brief smile, 'but looking after Nan is more important at present.'

The arrangement worked well, so well in fact that sometimes when Paul called in at the shop Tom said, to the amazement of his two assistants, 'Here he is. Our minister thinks this is a café, not an ironmonger's!'

Eventually Paul had to admit to Tom that the chat and the cup of tea or coffee was sometimes a welcome break from some of the other necessary but routine visits that seemed to achieve no obvious results.

Once or twice on these visits Tom had taken Paul upstairs to chat with Nan. She did appear to be making some progress now, but it was slow. Tom was worried that he was not doing enough to help her and Paul was becoming more and more certain that she needed some kind of psychiatric intervention. He had broached the subject with Tom on one of his visits.

'Has Dr Wilkie made any suggestions as to how you can help Nan get back to how she was before you lost Sally?'

'He prescribed tablets for Nan, almost from the start,' Tom replied. 'At first, she refused to have anything to do with them. Eventually she was persuaded to give them a try. She did, but very reluctantly. They were fairly mild and I couldn't see much difference. It was then suggested that something stronger might be needed. Nan would have nothing to do with that. In a way I was pleased that she was getting quite worked up about it all. I thought maybe that was a turning point. Dr Wilkie gave her a new prescription in the hope that I could persuade her to give these pills a try. I couldn't.'

'Why did you not tell me? I might have been able to help.'

'No offence, Paul, but the way she was, I doubt if the Good Lord himself would have managed.'

'So, if she won't take the pills, she certainly won't see a psychiatrist.'

'Exactly, and that's where we are now. She's no worse, but not much better. She does what she has to do in the house, but her heart's not in it. Don't get me wrong, she looks after Gary and me, but as soon as she has done what needs to be done, she just sits there, saying nothing.'

Paul was concerned for Tom, but what could he do to ease his burden?'Does she talk about what happened, how she feels? I know she has kept her thoughts very much to herself when I've managed to get some response from her, but I thought maybe she would open up to you.'

Tom sighed. 'Not really. I tried more or less forcing her to speak one evening, but it only made matters worse. She ended up shouting at me.'

'At least you got a reaction,' Paul remarked.

'Aye, I got a reaction all right. She told me it was all right for me, I wasn't Sally's mother. I hadn't given birth to her. That made me very angry and I shouted back.' There was a long pause before Tom added, shaking his head as he spoke. 'She hardly even looked at me for several days, never mind spoke to me. I learned my lesson. I don't tell Nan what to do.'

'How awful for you, Tom but–' Paul paused, choosing his words very carefully before continuing '–at any time you need to speak to someone, to unburden yourself, remember, I'm only a phone call or a short walk away. Please, I mean it, don't think twice. Just get in touch. I'll still call into the shop as before, but you don't have to wait for my next visit if it all gets too much for you. Get in touch.'

'Thanks, Paul, that means so much, but quite honestly that night was the worst we've had since the funeral. I'm hoping that one of these days, and I hope it's sooner rather than later, the old Nan will be back. Until then I'll do my best to support her. But I won't push her.'

30

It was the evening of the traditional Harvest Thanksgiving social evening in the church hall. Bob was one of the main organisers and to Paul's surprise and relief he had made it clear that he would be doing what he had always done. And he had, up to a point. Bob was often involved in rather silly little performances by a few of the farming members of the congregation, performances that poked fun more at the performers than at the audience. This year he had opted out of that part in the evening's programme. As he explained beforehand to Paul, he was afraid that his emotions might get out of control and ruin everything. Paul understood, but never let on to him about his conversation with Jessie. From time to time during the evening Paul found himself having what he hoped was a discreet look in Bob's direction. As far as he could tell, Bob was his usual self. Perhaps Jessie had been worried unnecessarily; either that or Bob was very good at hiding his true feelings.

The event went rather better than some present had expected. The meal was excellent as always and the conversation was flowing. If people were thinking of the Meikles, and many were, they gave no outward indication. Indeed, it almost appeared as though everyone was determined to make sure that this Harvest Thanksgiving would be better than ever, not to block out what had happened to the folks at Fauldshead, but to show them their love and support.

The entertainment revealed yet again how much talent there was in the area: singers, musicians and comedians, both young and not so young. There were also a few dances: the traditional country dances, a couple of ballroom ones and even "the Slosh", the latest craze to hit the dance floors around the country. At some point in the past, one of the elders had given a rather good impersonation of Sir Harry Lauder, singing a few of his well-known songs and telling a couple of his stories. Of course he had ended the performance with a rendition of 'Keep Right on to the End of the Road'. As he sang, the audience joined in heartily. Ever since that night there had to be community singing before the final dance, and the last song had to be the Harry Lauder classic. And so it was on this occasion. The songs were well-known Scottish songs with a couple of pop songs thrown in for good measure. Everyone joined in but as the company got to the end of 'Keep Right On' many found that the final words were almost too much to bear. The sentiment was inspiring, but the words were just too close to home. The mood changed, the merriment gone. The song finished. There was a moment of silence.

Paul felt he would have to say something, but what? He got to his feet, but he was not the only one. Bob Meikle was also standing, and he began to speak, quietly but firmly. 'Friends, this is a night of thanksgiving, thanksgiving for the harvest from the fields, for the work done to secure another harvest and to gather it safely in. We have enjoyed a lovely meal, good entertainment, good company. Suddenly we have been reminded that not everything works out as planned and hoped for, but we have to keep on going, and the support of our friends is what keeps us going. Thank you, my friends, for your support. Now, let's sing the song again, and sing it right through. No giving up before the end.'

And they did. Paul felt certain that he was not the only one who left the hall that night feeling that no matter what they met on life's journey, they would have the strength they needed to keep going along life's road.

Autumn was now giving way to winter and the nights were drawing in. Halloween and Bonfire Night were celebrated in the traditional ways. Soon it would be Christmas and New Year, a busy time for many, a lonely time for some.

The older members of the community were invited to a Christmas lunch the week before Christmas. There were parties for the children: several parties for many of them. The Sunday School and Bible class had a party, the uniformed organisations had a party, the school had a special Christmas lunch and the children presented a Nativity play. Adult organisations also had lunches or dinners or dinner dances. As always it was a hectic time for many.

Paul found that he was becoming more and more aware that despite all that was being organised, there were some people who would always be on their own on Christmas Day and again on New Year's Day. Was there more that should be done, and if so, what? Was he being realistic, or selfish, when he decided that as people were busy preparing for the big day and looking forward to spending time with their families, it was better if he did not get in their way? If he was honest, he too was very much looking forward to being with Ruth, Jennifer and Malcolm, although Jennifer would be working over New Year. It was not only those on their own who missed out. People in the medical and emergency services had no option but to remain on duty. As far as the lonely in the congregation were concerned, they would be visited as soon as possible in the New Year. Not ideal, but what else could he do?

The family at the manse made the most of their time together over Christmas. With Christmas being midweek, Paul was able to relax after the now traditional Christmas Eve service. The church had been almost full, the singing of the familiar carols was uplifting and everyone was in festive mood. Some had clearly been celebrating in the hours leading up to midnight but apart from one interruption from a young man who had failed to realise at one point that Paul's question had been rhetorical, nothing untoward happened. He was about to emphasise the humble birth of God's son. 'Why was Jesus born in a stable?' he asked, and before he could continue, a voice rang out. 'Because Joseph forgot to book in advance!'

Paul had not expected to get an answer, and especially not that one. He waited till the laughter died down before going on to explain that Jesus did not come among us in power and majesty, but in humility, to share and to understand our lives. The interjection meant that many present would remember the point Paul had been making long after the service was over.

Christmas Day was a leisurely day at the manse, everyone doing their bit to help. Presents had been opened after a light breakfast then Jennifer helped her mum in the kitchen. Paul and Malcom attended to the fire in the lounge and set the table for the meal. The meal, as always, was enjoyed by all four and for a time afterwards there was little chat. When Ruth suggested later in the evening that it was time to play charades the rest of them groaned, but it was a tradition and it had to be done, Ruth insisted. Once they got going the laughter was almost hysterical at times. There were accusations of misleading clues, arguments of whether a title was a book or a film, or both, but it was good fun, and brought back memories of Christmas in the past. Happy Days. It was well into Boxing Day before Paul's thoughts returned to the lonely in the parish and in the world. He felt ashamed and realised that if something was to be done it would have to be organised well in advance. He had no practical solution in mind and doubted if he ever would have. Perhaps if he put it out there, someone else would find the answer.

Mary and William Watson were having a very quiet Christmas, almost too quiet. They had agreed, many weeks previously, that they did not want to be away from home. They would spend the day quietly and remember. In any case, William's parents had died some years earlier and his only brother lived too far away for them to even consider being with him and his family in the middle of the working week. For the same reason, a visit to Mary's parents was also out of the question, but New Year would be different this year: the bank would be closed for four days. The first and second of January were official bank holidays and this year they fell on the Thursday and Friday. As soon as the bank closed they would be off, returning on the Saturday.

William had tried to get out of the journey altogether. At the beginning of December he had informed Mary that they might have to change their plans for New Year.

'We can't do that. Mum and Dad are looking forward to having us. They think they are helping us,' a rather shocked Mary answered, although she too had had her reservations about going away.

'Something has come up,' William announced.

'What can possibly have come up? It's a holiday. The bank is closed.'

'Yes, but if everything goes to plan, I may get the keys to the old church on Hogmanay.'

'So what? Are you going to sit in a cold, damp, empty building to welcome in the New Year? Don't be stupid.'

'No, no, of course not. I just mean we may be delayed in getting away and if the weather is bad, well…'

'If the weather's bad, I'll drive,' Mary exclaimed.

William smiled. 'It was worth a try. I didn't think you would agree, but we did both have doubts about going away. Of course we'll go. If I get the key we can camp out in the old church on our return.'

'Really, William, you are unbelievable. If I told the folk at the bank what you're like at home, they would never believe me.'

Throughout their weekend away, they shared memories of happier times. Of course there were tears, but there were also smiles and some laughter as she and William shared memories of Wilma with her parents. It might not have been the most happy of occasions but once back home, she and William agreed that it had done them good to get away, and her mum and dad had been very considerate hosts. It was more a time to relax, sometimes to talk, to watch a special programme on TV, but often just to sit quietly, to think one's own thoughts in the knowledge that you were in the presence of loved ones who felt as you did: heartbroken but determined to keep going in honour of the ones they had loved and lost. Lost, but never forgotten.

There was one family involved in the accident whom most people in Burnbrae had now forgotten. Few had met Doreen Thomson in the short time she had been a resident in the town. Brian had settled in well enough at the school, but Gary MacCallum had told Paul that according to Sally, Brian's mum and dad were having big problems and he was never quite sure what might happen next. He did his best to help his mum in any way he could, but most of the time he stayed in his room listening to music especially if his dad was at home.

It was the longest conversation Paul had had with Gary.

Paul was hoping that in the early days of 1976 he would hear from Doreen by letter or perhaps a phone call. He had never forgotten the emotional visit she had made to the manse. The baby should have been born around New Year. The days went by, but no news came. Eventually he called in on Effie. Of all the people in the town, she was the one who would get word. He was wrong.

Effie was pleased to see him. They wished each other a Happy New Year.

'Did you have a nice time over the holiday period?' Effie asked.

'Yes, we did. It was good to have some time to relax and catch up with the family.' Paul told her about Jennifer and Malcolm, how they were and how their studies were going.

'My Christmas was quiet. It always is now,' Effie said. Paul saw the distant look in her eyes. She gave a sigh before adding, 'But I have happy memories to look back on. She sat up straighter in her chair. 'And did you hear anything from Doreen? Has she had the baby? Did everything go well?'

Paul couldn't hide his surprise. 'I was hoping you would be able to tell me. I've heard nothing since she left the town. I thought you were sure to have heard. You were so good to her when she needed someone to help her.'

'Aye, well, I'm not wanting thanks, though she did say thanks before she left. She even gave me a wee present. That vase over there on the table. I often look at it and wonder how she is. And how she is coping with the baby.'

'And have you been in touch with her since she left?'

'Aye, she gave me a call to say she was hoping to get some place for herself. It was OK at her parents' house to begin with, but she wanted a place of her own. Between you and me I think her mother was keeping a very close watch on her. Too close for comfort. She said she would let me know her address in due course. She never did. I hope they're all right.' Effie was close to tears.

'I hope so too. Could you not phone her parents? Perhaps they would be prepared to tell you what's what.'

'I would, but I can't. I never asked for their address or telephone number. I thought Doreen would let me know her new address when she got settled, but so far, nothing.'

'Maybe you'll get word soon. The new baby will take up a lot of her time, and moving in to a new house wouldn't be easy in her situation. And after everything she had gone through before that.'

'That's what I thought, and I still hope I'll hear from her. Let's hope so. You'll be as anxious as me.'

'Yes, indeed,' Paul replied. 'And as soon as I hear anything, you'll be the first to know. Now, how about a cup of tea?'

31

If Christmas had been quiet at Fauldshead, New Year certainly wasn't. In a way it was Bob to blame, but what happened took him completely by surprise, and Jessie was not amused, to put it mildly. At the last market before Christmas, a number of Bob's friends and acquaintances asked him what his plans for Christmas and the New Year were. Each time his answer had been, 'Not much. Think it will be quiet this year. Just the family.'

That was what had happened at Christmas, but New Year was rather different. Helen had joined Jessie, Bob and Iain for dinner on Hogmanay and stayed with them to see in the New Year. After the bells, it was her intention to go back to the bungalow. The others would go to bed soon after. The customary New Year wishes were exchanged. In the silence that followed, Bob said quietly, his voice trembling as he spoke, 'I still can't believe it's just the four of us.' The others nodded in agreement. Even Iain wiped a tear away.

Jessie suggested a cup of tea before Bob escorted his mum home to the bungalow.

'You could always stay here, Mum,' Bob suggested. 'I'll put the heating on in the spare room. It will soon warm up.'

'That's kind of you, Bob, but I have to go home. I am getting used to being on my own now. I am not saying it's easy and tonight has brought back many memories. I could be tempted to stay here, but one night might become two. Christmas was the same. I'll have that cup of tea, but once I've drunk it, I'll go home to my own bed.' Her voice faltered a bit but she insisted.

Bob knew it would be best in the long run to let her go home. He had another dram before going to fetch his mum's coat. That was when he heard a car drive into the yard.

'Who can that be?' he muttered to himself. He put the coat back on the peg. 'We've got visitors,' he announced as he re-entered the room.

'Did you invite anyone to come round?' Jessie asked.

'Of course not. We agreed that we wanted to be on our own this year. And I told my pals that was what we were doing.'

'Well, someone is here. You better answer the door.'

'Happy New Year, Bob,' called out John, his next-door neighbour, as soon as the door was opened. John was stretching out his right hand in greeting and clasping a bottle of whisky in his left. Close behind him was his wife, Janet. She was holding a basket covered with a dish towel.

'And the same to you,' Bob replied, shaking the proffered hand.

'Are you on your own?' John asked.

'Yes, it's just the family. Come in. We weren't really expecting anyone. In fact, Mum's just about to go back over to the bungalow.'

Bob led the way through to the lounge. Once everyone had greeted everyone else, John took a packet of shortbread from Janet's basket and handed it to Jessie. 'I think I must be your first foot, so, a wee gift.'

'Thank you,' Jessie replied. Bob hoped he was the only one who had noticed the rather formal tone in her voice. He also wondered what was in the large covered basket Janet was carrying.

'What would everyone like to toast in 1976 with? The usual?' Bob asked. The usual it was. Bob made his way over to the sideboard where the drinks were kept.

'Is it all right if I take this through to the kitchen, Jessie?' Janet asked. 'It's just a wee something in case anyone is hungry,' she explained, holding out the covered basket as she spoke.

Before Bob had organised the drinks, another carload of neighbours arrived. With several more arriving in quick succession, Iain found himself acting as doorman, Bob was busy being the barman and Jessie was in and out of the kitchen as all the wives had brought food. To begin with things were more sedate than usual but as more and more neighbours arrived all that changed. It was almost like old times, but not quite.

Hours later when the last of the visitors had departed, little was said as Jessie and Bob finished off the clearing up. It was more a matter of putting things back in their proper place; some of the other wives had washed up and any leftovers had been wrapped up and taken by whoever wanted them, leaving some for Jessie to use.

'Bob, you get off to your bed. You're out on your feet and you're just getting in my way. With a bit of luck you'll get a few hours' sleep before you need to be up again.'

Bob protested but Jessie was right, he was more of a hindrance than a help. Exhausted, he didn't hear Jessie coming to bed.

Bob was up at more or less his usual time. He was most definitely not raring to go and getting washed and dressed took a bit of an effort. He managed to do it without waking Jessie. As he carried out the essential work on the farm he had a feeling that when she did wake, she might have something to say about their guests and what had certainly not been how they had planned to see in the New Year. His neighbours had meant well, and he appreciated that. Perhaps it had actually helped to be surrounded by friends, he thought as he made his way outside.

Jessie was still asleep on his return. He made himself some breakfast. He wondered about taking a cup of tea up to her, then thought better of it. He hoped that Iain would appear to give him a hand with one or two jobs that still had to be done, but he too was sound asleep. A couple of Iain's pals had been among the visitors and they had had their own celebration in Iain's bedroom, leaving the grown-ups to get on with theirs.

When Bob returned from doing the rest of his chores he found Jessie in the kitchen organising the traditional New Year's dinner. The butcher had made the steak pie. Jessie was preparing the vegetables to go with it. The soup and trifle had been made earlier. She did, however, have some questions for him.

'Good sleep, dear?' he asked as he made to kiss her. She returned the kiss, but there was a coldness in the way she did it. Bob sat down. He waited, not sure what was coming, but feeling that it would not be good.

Jessie did not mince her words. 'Did you invite those people?' she asked.

'No, I didn't. I was as surprised as you when they turned up.'

'Well, if you didn't invite them, how come they not only came, but brought all that food with them? The Ne'erday bottle is one thing, but that was ridiculous. And as for Hamish and his accordion…'

'Honest, I had nothing to do with it.'

'Well, someone organised it. Are you sure you didn't say something to someone?'

'I didn't. Some of the lads asked what we were doing at Hogmanay, and I said we weren't doing anything. We would just be sitting at home.'

'So, it was you. I might have known.'

'No, it wasn't me. I never invited anyone. We agreed it would just be the family. No celebration.'

'And you said it as though you weren't looking forward to it.'

'Well, I wasn't,' Bob replied.

'And as you said it, you looked miserable, and they thought they would come and cheer us up!'

'I suppose so. I just never thought.'

'Never mind, it's over. Let's forget it. Today it will just be the four of us.'

'And the steak pie,' added Bob.

Jessie's mood changed. 'Come here,' she said, drying her hands and moving towards him. She put her arms round him and held him tight. 'I'm sorry,' she whispered. 'I know they thought they were doing the right thing, and you do love a ceilidh, but they were wrong, very wrong. Last night was a time for remembering, not trying to forget.'

Bob kept his earlier thought that perhaps it had helped to himself.

Mary and William had enjoyed a quiet, relaxed time with Mary's parents. From time to time something about Wilma would come up as they chatted, but they were happy, often amusing memories. The worst of their grief was receding, but that sense of loss would never be very far away and every so often it would blot out whatever else was happening at that particular moment. Mary and William had talked about it and agreed that no matter how painful a memory was, they would rather have that than discover that they had forgotten all about Wilma. That would never be allowed to happen.

Mary sensed that from time to time William had dropped out of the conversation. He clearly had something else on his mind, and she thought she knew what it was. Back home and getting ready for church on the Sunday morning, William announced that he had somewhere he wanted to go on the way home, and he would like Mary to accompany him.

'Your lunch might be a bit later than usual if I don't come straight home. Unless, of course, you're taking me out for lunch,' she teased him.

'No, that will be all right. What I have in mind will not take long. A few minutes, in fact. Attending to the offering will take longer.'

Mary was certain she knew exactly where they would go and the fact that William never commented on her remark about lunch convinced her the assumption was correct. As she took William's arm on leaving the church, Mary asked him, 'Did you bring the keys?'

'What keys?'

'Do you really think I don't know where we're going? Even at Mum and Dad's your mind was elsewhere from time to time, and judging from the direction we are heading, this is where it was.'

'OK, you win. I can't wait until tomorrow. I have to open that door and step inside. I still find it hard to believe that I've done this.'

'And here we are,' Mary said as they crossed the road to the empty church. The FOR SALE sign now displayed the word SOLD across it.

William had the keys in his hand before they reached the door. With a bit of difficulty he got the key in the lock, turned it and pushed the door open. There was a musty smell in the cold vestibule. Inside the church itself it was even colder. The electricity had been switched off. It was dark and gloomy.

William's excitement was short-lived. 'Do you think I'm doing the right thing?' he asked Mary.

'Bit late for that,' she replied. She turned to face her husband, smiled and gave his arm a friendly dig. 'Come on, this will be all that you want it to be. And much more, I expect. What you are seeing is an abandoned church. It looks rather forlorn, but once the builder gets going and the young folk flood in, it will be a place of fun and hope.'

William gave a long sigh. 'I know you're right. It just seems quite a task to turn it around. And it still surprises me that I'm doing this.'

'Surprises me too, Mr Bank Manager. But I have every confidence in you. Have a look about and then let's get home where it's warm and lunch awaits. Or at least it will do, once I get it made.'

32

On the Monday evening following the extended New Year holiday, the trustees of the youth centre met with two local builders and discussed what needed to be done to convert the church into a building suitable for the needs of the young people. There was plenty space; it was a question of making the best use of it. Also present was a youth development officer from the local council acting in an advisory capacity. Ideas were put forward, discussed, notes taken and sketches made. By the time he arrived home, William was convinced that his dream would indeed become a reality. How soon he didn't know, but it would happen.

It was well into February before the trustees were able to meet to discuss the estimates submitted by the builders. There was little between them as far as costs were concerned. One of the builders couldn't start the job before April. The other, however, was able to start almost immediately. He was awarded the contract.

Paul had been at both meetings. When he returned home after the second one Ruth informed him that a rather worried young man had phoned to speak to him. He had not given any reasons for his call, but due to the agitation Ruth heard in his voice, she had assured him that Paul would phone back as soon as he could.

'That name is familiar,' Paul said as he tried to remember why. 'I'm sure it was a wedding. Yes, got it. It must have been a couple of years ago. Doesn't sound like a baptism. Wonder what his problem is.'

'Standing there thinking about it won't help. I said you would call him, so…'

'Right. Can I get my coat off first?'

'Maybe you should keep it on if things are that bad,' Ruth commented.

Paul was not quite sure she was being serious, but he made the call, still wearing his coat.

The young man he had thought it might be answered the phone almost as soon as it rang. Without wasting any time he quickly revealed his problem. He and his wife were struggling to pay the financial commitments they had taken on since becoming husband and wife. Paul spoke to him and tried to calm him down. It took a while, but eventually he was able to convince him that although the situation was not good, the bailiffs would not be knocking on their door the next day. Paul, however, would call round the following evening and give him and his wife some practical advice.

'It's not good,' he said, as he ended the call, 'but there's always an answer. Just make sure you know exactly what you owe, how much you earn and how much you have to spare each month. I may not know the best way forward, but I can put you in touch with people who will.'

When Paul arrived the next evening as promised, he found the young couple, Shona and Nicol, were beside themselves with worry. Shona was also very pregnant. The room Paul was ushered into was nicely furnished. He declined tea or coffee.

'Perhaps something stronger,' Nicol suggested.

'Perhaps a coffee, but later. I can see how worried you are. Let's discuss your problem right away and see if we can find a solution.' Shona clearly was close to tears.

'Right, I did as you asked,' Nicol answered, as he walked over to a small table and picked up a couple of sheets of paper lying on it. 'I'm afraid it doesn't make very pretty reading.'

Paul took the papers and cast his eye over them. It did indeed look bad: an overdraft at the bank, a credit card bill and the usual household bills. He suspected that the total for food each month might be somewhat less than the actual cost.

'Yes, it doesn't look too good, but there's a little left over.'

'But some months there are extras. Then there's nothing left. And Shona will have to stop work before much longer,' Nicol added, his voice quivering.

'I realised that. Congratulations, by the way.'

'Thanks, Mr Johnson, but it may not have been our cleverest move.'

'Well, maybe not, but on the other hand, it might motivate you to do what you have to do to get these finances sorted out. Oh, and Paul will be fine. I'm here as a friend.'

'I hope it does,' replied Nicol.

'Right, let's discuss your options, but please remember that what I say will simply be how I see things. You'll have to talk things over with your creditors if you need to spread the payments over a longer period. And I think that might be the solution.'

Nicol did most of the talking, Shona said almost nothing, leaving her husband to answer the questions Paul asked as he teased out the full details behind the figures. He was not surprised to learn that in order to furnish their home the way they wanted it to look, with all the fittings they had chosen, they had had to borrow. At first they had had no problem making their monthly repayments on the credit card and to the hire purchase companies. That was until an unexpected repair was needed on the car. Paying that bill had put the credit card at its limit. They missed a couple of repayments. That had been rectified, but all they were doing was making the minimum repayment each month. The bank overdraft had increased and it was very unlikely that it would be increased further. Indeed, with the baby on the way, even if more credit was available, taking it on would only make matters worse.

'So,' Paul said, 'where do you go from here? Don't look so terrified, there are answers, but it will take a great deal of determination, and perhaps a bit of sacrifice on your part. And, the sooner you start, the sooner it will be sorted out.'

Paul advised them to make a budget and to stick to it. If there was extra money any month it should be used to pay down the debt, not to make unnecessary purchases. They would have to arrange a meeting with their bank manager and be honest with him. It might not be pleasant, but it might surprise them. The bank wanted their money back, but they also wanted to keep them as customers. The credit card was a bit more problematic and a visit to the Citizens' Advice Bureau in Dalcairn could provide some very practical advice.

'I know this is hard,' Paul concluded, 'but you've taken the first step. Now that it is out in the open you know you're not on your own. Whether or not you tell your parents is up to you, but asking them to pay off your debts is not really the answer.'

'We've already decided that we don't want to do that,' Shona said. 'They've been good to us in many ways, but this is our mess. We have to deal with it.'

'And we will,' added Nicol.

'Good,' replied Paul. 'Now, how about that coffee?'

Paul returned home and he and Ruth began discussing how married life was changing. More and more young women were continuing to work full-time. Young children were being put into nursery care, allowing their mothers to continue with their careers.

'Is it really a step in the right direction?' Paul asked.

'Well, if they wait until the last child leaves school, they have no prospect of a job at the top, whatever the job is.'

'No, fair point, but how much does it cost to put the children into nursery school?'

'Probably takes most of the second income.'

'Exactly,' exclaimed Paul. 'So, no financial gain.'

'As usual, you manage to miss the bigger picture,' replied Ruth. 'The gain comes when the children leave school. The mother has a top job, more money for Mum and Dad to do what they want with after having put the children first for so long.'

'OK, I get that, but is it any better for family life?'

'Time will tell. I just hope Shona and Nicol get their problems sorted out as soon as possible. Babies are expensive,' Ruth said. 'Remember how much it cost when we had Malcolm and Jennifer? There will be the usual presents from relatives and friends, but babies have a habit of growing out of things very quickly. If it's not one thing it's another. But we managed and so will they, I'm sure. Now, time for the news, tea and the end of another day.'

'Will be interesting to see how it all goes,' Paul replied. 'I made sure they could always get back to me if things weren't working out, but I hope they do. They seemed relieved after hearing my advice and determined to follow it. Oh, by the way, I saw Nan MacCallum out walking this afternoon. Hope that's a good sign. She looked as if she was heading towards the cemetery.'

'Better than sitting at home brooding, but how often does she go?' Ruth queried. 'Too often might not be much of an improvement. In fact, it could be a sign that she's worse.'

'Worse? Surely not. At least she is getting out. And she looked as though she was walking with a purpose. That must be good.'

'But not if the purpose is to feel nearer to her dead daughter. That's certainly not how I would see it,' Ruth replied.

After discussing the situation for several more minutes, Paul decided that until he had a chance to speak with Nan, face to face, there was no point in continuing to speculate, but on hearing Ruth's comments, he wasn't sure that his first thought on seeing Nan outside was correct.

Despite his change of mind, it was another week and a bit before Paul found the time to make that visit. He stood on the doorstep and rang the bell several times. There was no answer. Either there was no one in or Nan was resting. He would have preferred to speak with Nan first in order to form his own opinion regarding her well-being. Then it would be interesting to find out if her husband was of the same opinion. On entering the shop, Mairi informed him that the boss was in the office.

'I'm sure he'll be pleased to see you, just go through,' Sadie added.

The office door was not fully closed. Paul pushed it as he called, 'Hello, is it OK to enter?'

'Of course, Minister. You know you're always welcome.'

Paul stepped inside.

'Good to see you, and a Happy New Year,' Tom said as he got up and held out his hand.

Paul returned the greeting. As he spoke, something in Tom's demeanour changed. The warm, friendly smile had gone.

'Everything all right?' Paul asked.

'Let me make us a coffee first. The kettle has just boiled. I'll only be a couple of seconds,' Tom said as he lifted the kettle.

When the coffee was ready Tom gave Paul one of the mugs, sighed as he placed his own mug on the desk, sat down and, after another sigh, began to speak.

'I would like to say that things are better, but maybe that wouldn't be true. We got through Christmas. It wasn't easy for any of us, but we made it. New Year was just another day as far as we were concerned. No celebration. No hoping 1976 would be better than 1975. That seemed to be disrespectful to Sally. We'll always miss her, and she will always be in our hearts.'

Paul nodded in sympathy as Tom continued.

'On the first Sunday of the year, Nan said she wanted to visit Sally's grave. We had been there on Christmas Day, and on New Year's Day. I said that was fine. And I had hoped that we would be going anyway. Nan never said anything on these visits. She just stood quietly until I gently held her arm and suggested that maybe it was getting a bit cold. Each time she turned and began walking away. What I've since discovered is that most afternoons, when I am here in the shop, she's visiting the grave. She never says she's going and she never tells me she has been. I'm worried that her emotional state is getting worse, not better.'

Paul thought for a moment, choosing his words carefully. 'I would like to say I think it's a sign of improvement as she is getting out the house, but, like you, I fear that may not be the case. Has she seen Dr Wilkie since these visits began?'

'No, and that's another thing, Nan and Dr Wilkie have had quite an argument over her pills. Nan says she doesn't need them. She doesn't want to forget Sally and what has happened. Dr Wilkie insisted the pills were to help her cope, to let her sleep at night, that kind of thing, not to make her forget. She was keen enough to have sleeping pills for the first few nights.'

'And who won the argument?' Paul asked.

'Well, that's the problem. It was a draw, I think.'

'A draw?' Paul was puzzled.

'Yes, a draw. Nan has the pills, anti-depressants this time, and sometime she takes them as prescribed. Then she misses one, or two. I think sometimes it might be for a day or two.'

'And it is meant to be the same number every day until the doctor says otherwise?'

'Of course it is, and Dr Wilkie has emphasised that over and over again, but it makes no difference.'

It was obvious to Paul as he listened to Tom that Nan had become quite cunning, insisting that she had had her medication, even taking her pill as Tom watched, but then, when Tom had checked the remaining pills, he realised that Nan had been deceiving him.

All Paul could do in the end was yet again to say that if he could help, he would do what he could, but experience had taught him that when someone in Nan's situation behaved as she appeared to be doing, the change in her behaviour had to come from her.

Nan clearly had no intention of changing what had become her routine. Her visits to the cemetery continued, sometimes only one a week, but more often two and occasionally three and even four if the weather was good. Tom did his best to dissuade her. Dr Wilkie suggested that a weekly visit to Sally's grave would be sufficient, but walking was good for her so, on the other days, she should walk in the public park, or perhaps Tom could drive her out of town now and then and they could both get some fresh air. Nan would have none of it.

33

Everything was in place. It was time to begin the task of changing the old church into the youth centre. Before anything else could be done, the church fittings had to be removed. The Communion table and font had been sent to a central depository in the hope that another congregation would be able to use them. The organ was in good condition and it was hoped that it could be sold on.

'Would you believe it,' William said to Mary a week later after a hectic Saturday at the old church. 'Even some of the people who complained about how uncomfortable the pews were bought one for a garden seat to remind them of their old church. Hotels and licensed premises wanted them too. Seems they fit in rather nicely round the walls of the pub or the cocktail lounge. Pity we didn't charge a bit more for them.'

'Take your banker's hat off,' Mary joked. 'You wanted rid of them. Just be glad they're going. I presume you're keeping a couple for the youth centre.'

'Of course, that was always the plan.'

The opening date for the new venture would be decided once the alterations were well under way. It would be after the first anniversary of the accident, but the builder had promised that he would make every effort to get the work completed as soon as possible after that. Once the better weather arrived, he had outside jobs booked. William and Mary had some concern about the opening date. The first anniversary would be hard and for several days around it. To add to their concerns, this year Easter fell in April, not March, but Easter and the accident might be linked in the minds of some of those most closely affected by the accident. Would some of the bereaved find that the Easter celebrations brought back the very vivid memories of the trauma they had gone through, causing them to go through it twice every year? It would be better to think of an official opening ceremony in May. That, unfortunately, would remind everyone for the third time. What should he do?

William was also of a mind that the centre would be less active over the summer months, if indeed it functioned at all. It would be rather foolish to have a grand opening followed by three months' closure. There would have to be consultations with everyone involved. Mary seemed amused to find her normally so in control husband unable to make up his mind.

'William, calm down,' she said more than once. 'It will all fall into place. There are too many unknowns at the moment. Nearer the time things will be much clearer.'

'Yes, but I would like to be sure,' William replied.

'I know you would, but remember you're not the youth centre leader, nor one of the young people. Not by a long way,' she added. 'Others will make the final decision.'

William agreed, but he still worried, and he would continue to worry until the centre was open and well and truly functioning.

Bob Meikle had recently taken delivery of a new tractor. He and Sandy had been speaking about purchasing one for some time, but Sandy's tragic death meant nothing had been done. There was little wrong with the old tractor, nothing that could not be repaired if it broke down, but it seemed that every year there were developments to this essential machine that made life easier for the driver and got the work done quicker.

There was excitement and a certain sadness the day the new tractor was delivered. At one point Bob and Iain were even fighting over who was to drive it first. Bob was insistent that it was his responsibility to make sure that everything was working properly. When Iain finally got his chance to climb into the cab, his dad was amazed at how quickly he mastered the controls.

'It's an age thing,' Jessie explained. 'Once he gets to college he'll be telling you how to run   the farm.'

'He's doing that already,' Bob retorted.

'Just as you told your dad.'

Bob had been about to say, 'as Sandy did' but managed to stop himself just in time. He wondered if Jessie had been thinking the same. It was Jessie who broke the short silence that had followed her remark.

'Are we going to keep the old tractor, along with your dad's old grey Fergie?'

'For the time being, but it will be sold eventually. And the old grey Fergie will never be sold. That machine is a piece of history. It changed farming for the better. I know it's lovely to see a Clydesdale horse, and all honour to the few who have kept one of these magnificent beasts, but it takes time and money to keep a horse. The Fergie just needs a bit of care every so often. And Dad loved it.'

Paul was working away one morning in his study, preparing a report for the next presbytery meeting when the phone rang. It was Effie Melville.

Effie got straight to the reason for her call. 'I got a letter from Doreen this morning.'

'She took her time,' Paul commented, 'but at last she has been in touch. Is she well? And the baby?'

'I was wondering if you would be anywhere near my house in the next day or two,' Effie said, completely ignoring Paul's question.

'Yes, I could be. You're not really that far away.'

'Good. And I'm not all that often out, and if I am it's only at one of the local shops. I'll see you soon.' With that she ended the call.

Paul wasn't sure if he should be annoyed or intrigued. Ruth had no such problem when he told her about the call.

'Who does she think she is? She can't demand you drop everything and rush to her.'

'Whoa, steady on. She's a very nice elderly lady, and she was very good to Doreen when she needed someone to support her.'

'So were you. And look at the thanks you got. Never a word since she moved away.'

'Well, I will be passing her house. I can hardly avoid it. It's only round the corner.'

Ruth shook her head. 'Who am I to tell you what to do? Just do what you like.'

Paul was waiting for an 'as you usually do' or something similar, but it never came.

At the end of a round of visits that afternoon he arrived at Effie's door.

'Oh, it's you, Minister. I'm glad you're here. I have a nice surprise for you. Come in.'

Paul was intrigued. What was the surprise? he wondered.

'Away ben the room an' ah'll get you your tea.'

The last thing Paul wanted was another cup of tea, but refusing was hopeless, even if it was almost time for his evening meal. One thing was certain, this would not be a long visit.

'You not having a cup?' Paul asked as he sipped at the scalding liquid.

'No, I just finished one minutes before you arrived,' Effie replied. Paul could have told her that the one he now had was his third of the afternoon, but he didn't.

As she was speaking, Effie lifted an envelope from the top of the sideboard.

'It's the letter from Doreen. I think you should read it.'

She barely gave Paul time to get his cup down safely before she was handing him the envelope. Inside he found a single sheet of notepaper and a couple of baby photos. Paul read the letter. It was brief and to the point. Doreen had given birth on Hogmanay. Everything went well and mother and baby were doing fine. She was living with her mother and father but hoped soon to find a place of her own. She thanked Effie and Paul for all their help and wished them a Happy New Year. She had not given an address or telephone number.

'Well, it's good news,' Paul said, 'and it also looks like goodbye. Not putting her address on the letter is a bit strange.'

'Not what we were taught when I was at school,' answered Effie. 'Don't know what is up with people nowadays. No manners.'

'I think you're being a bit hard on Doreen. She had a really bad time while she lived in Burnbrae. I think she's making a new start, and the baby gives her something to look forward to.'

'Aye, I suppose you might be right,' Effie agreed, 'but that is no excuse for not letting me know where she is. I was really fond of her. She was a nice lassie.'

'And I know she was fond of you, and she appreciated all you did for her. Let's give her the benefit of the doubt and wish her well, and Ryan.' Paul stopped speaking abruptly and looked at Effie. 'What do you think of the baby's name?'

'Bit fancy, if you ask me.'

'I wondered about it myself,' Paul replied. 'Don't think I've ever baptised a Ryan. But that's not what stopped me. As soon as I read "Ryan" I immediately thought of Brian. I think that's lovely.'

Effie thought for a moment before replying. 'You could be right, Minister. Maybe I am being a bit hard on her. I just would have liked to keep in touch with her, know how she was, how she was doing. And the baby. You never know, she might give us a surprise one of these days.'

'She might,' Paul said, but he was not at all convinced that that would happen.

Before he left, Effie insisted that he take one of the photos of baby Ryan.

'I'm sure that was why she put two in the letter. One for you and one for me.'

'And she hasn't forgotten us. But she really does want to move on,' Paul said as he put the photo in his wallet.

34

Work on the youth centre had gone well. William had spent many hours worrying about problems that might have arisen but didn't, or if they did, were eventually solved. It was expected that everything would be completed by the end of April. That first anniversary with all its heartache for the families would be over. Easter would have come and gone. The official opening was fixed for early May, but before that those who were expected to become members of the centre were encouraged to get involved with putting the final touches to the interior.

Those who came along for the opening ceremony could not believe what they discovered on entering the building. From the outside the church looked as it always had, but inside it was completely transformed. It now had an upstairs. A floor had been put in place so that what had been the gallery was now an area that ran the whole length of the building. Light flooded in from the top half of the original windows. It could be used for many things: badminton, a gym, a concert area perhaps, though at present there was no stage. That could always be added later. It was made clear to some of the young boys present that it would not, under any circumstances, be used for football. There was five-a-side football in the community centre during the winter and that would be where it would stay.

On the ground floor there was one large room and two smaller ones, with an office, kitchen and toilets completing the centre. Where possible something of the old church had been left to remind users of its original purpose. The most obvious reminder was the back wall of the large room. Originally the church had had a pipe organ. Over the years it had become more and more expensive to maintain. Not many years before the congregation had joined up with the parish church, they had agreed to purchase a smaller, free-standing organ. The pipes of the old organ had been left in place, and there they were to remain. There had been suggestions from some of those involved in the refurbishment of the interior that perhaps they could be painted in attractive colours; others wanted them left as they were, and that had been agreed, for the time being at least.

It soon became apparent to William and the rest of the trustees that everyone who had visited the new-look building as it neared completion, would-be members, parents and other interested members of the public, all had their own ideas as to what was still required. In the end it was decided that the interior walls would be decorated in neutral colours initially. One decision to be resolved, before any ceremony could take place, was the name of the centre.

William and Mary had spent many hours thinking and talking about this very matter and they had come to a decision, one that they would not change. At first some of the other trustees made it clear that they were of a different opinion. Several times William had to remind them of why he and Mary had made the decision they had.

Finally he stated, quietly but firmly, 'The centre has come about because of a terrible tragedy. It is in memory of all who were killed in that accident, but, more than that, it is a meeting place and activity venue for the young of the community, those living now and for those who will come after them. Mary and I feel that the name should be the obvious one: Burnbrae Youth Centre. In the vestibule we suggest that there be a plaque recording the names of those who died, their age, perhaps, and the date of the accident. That is all. A reminder, we hope, not only of those we lost, but also a reminder to those who read their names that life can sometimes be dangerous, that care has to be taken.'

Still not all the trustees agreed. It was William and Mary who were providing the funding they stated; the name Watson should be prominent.

'There is one other important factor that I have not mentioned, but you leave me no option. My daughter was the driver of the car that night.'

Paul, who was chairing the meeting, seemed to be about to intervene. Perhaps he was afraid that William was going to admit that Wilma was to blame for what had happened. William brushed him aside.

'No, this has to be said. So long as we don't know exactly why the accident happened, we have to assume someone in the car did something to cause it. Wilma is the most obvious candidate. But why? Was there something outside that made her swerve, did someone inside distract her or was she solely responsible? A careless moment, a reckless action? I know some people had plenty to say at the time, and no doubt still do. Her name will be recorded with the others who died that night. For us it will be her memorial, but it will not bear our surname. It is the Burnbrae Youth Centre and that is that.'

The trustees agreed on the name of the centre without further discussion. The design of the plaque would be chosen from the suggestions made by the firm making it. The names of the victims would be recorded in alphabetical order. The final wording on the plaque was soon   settled and a place in the vestibule was found which met with William's approval.

When it became public knowledge that the centre would be handed over to the managing committee on the first Sunday of May, there was some shaking of heads. It was bad enough turning the old church into a youth centre where goodness knows what might take place within its formerly sacred walls in the months and years to come, but to have some kind of social occasion on the Sabbath, that was too much. The trustees explained that it was the one time when the majority of those who would be using the facility would be free to attend, and it would be a quiet, dignified and respectful opening ceremony.

To call it an opening ceremony was probably too grand. Again there was much discussion by the trustees, the leader and interim committee of the centre about what would happen. William and Mary were reluctant to have a prominent place in the proceedings. As chairman of the trustees, Paul would be the Master of Ceremonies, and it was made clear that there would be no long speeches, nor would there be some local dignitary invited to perform the actual act of opening the centre.

A large crowd of young and old had gathered outside the building by the advertised time. Jessie, Bob, Iain and Helen, Tom and Gary, and William and Mary were standing outside the locked door. Some in the crowd were wondering where Nan MacCallum and Doreen Thomson were. Nan had refused point blank to attend, and no one had been able to contact Doreen. Tom had used all his powers of persuasion to get Nan to change her mind, but it had been to no avail. She said Tom and Gary could go if they felt they had to but she would be at the cemetery as she always was on a Sunday afternoon, spending time with her beloved Sally.

It was time to open the youth centre. Paul called for attention and welcomed all those who had gathered for what was a very special occasion. He explained that once the door was open, the members of the families who had lost loved ones in the accident would enter the building first. He asked everyone to remain where they were until the family members had spent a moment of silence in front of the memorial in the vestibule.

Paul called on William and Mary to present the key to the youth leader, Bert Crawford. Bert took the key, turned it in the lock and pushed the door open. William and Mary were first to enter the building, closely followed by Paul, the families of the victims and finally the other trustees. They stood quietly in front of the simple brass plaque. Whether or not they actually read the names and other details, Paul had no way of telling. All were clearly upset, the ladies wiping a tear, the men comforting them and vainly attempting to hide their own emotions. When it seemed appropriate to do so, Paul led the way into the office to give them time to compose themselves while Bert went back out and invited the crowd to come in and view the building and, after walking round the centre, to partake of the buffet provided by the committee.

Paul was trying to keep a very low profile as the visitors wandered around the centre. He might be the first chairman of the trustees and he would do what he could to help, but today was not about him. Of course, every so often someone managed to ask him a question, sometimes relevant, sometimes not, or make a comment, sometimes helpful, sometimes critical, but mostly he just moved from room to room, nodding to folk as he passed by. He did, however, have a troubling conversation with Tom MacCallum.

Before Paul could ask why Nan wasn't present, Tom blurted out, 'Paul, I'm really worried about Nan.'

They were outside the room marked Office. 'Let's go in here,' he suggested to Tom. 'We might get a bit of privacy if we're lucky.' Paul closed the door behind them. 'I wondered if Nan was all right. I had hoped she would be here, but it must be very emotional for all of you. It's bad enough for me and I'm...'

He realised what he was about to say was not going to help.

'Yes, it's another time of very mixed feelings. Happy to see this place open, but well, you know...' Tom choked up.

'And I take it Nan thought it would be too much for her,' Paul said.

Tom shook his head as he sighed before answering. 'That's the problem. I still don't know what she's thinking most of the time. Today she told me she wanted to be with Sally.' Paul must have looked shocked. 'No, not in that way!' Tom hurriedly said. 'She's at the cemetery. Again. She was there yesterday and the day before that. It's becoming an obsession.' Tom was becoming upset and angry at the same time. 'I just don't know how to help. She won't take her medication. She won't go to see Dr Wilkie, or you. No offence.'

'Don't worry about me. But you need help, and so does Nan.'

The door opened and a head poked in. The young man saw Tom and Paul, apologised and disappeared.

'This isn't the best place for a serious talk,' Paul continued. 'I'll pop round tomorrow and see Nan, though I think to begin with Dr Wilkie would be a better bet.'

'Look, I can't expect you to be at my beck and call, and tomorrow's your day off, if you're lucky,' Tom added. 'You've told me before in some of our chats how many folk phone or arrive at your door on a Monday because they expect you to be at home on your day off. But I will see if I can get her to make an appointment with the doctor. I'll keep you informed, and thanks again. I feel better for our chat.'

He looked at his watch. 'I better get home. Nan will be back from her visit to Sally's grave and in a more settled frame of mind, I hope. Gary is playing pool with some of his pals. Not sure if Nan will want to hear about what happened here today, but I will do my best to convince her that Sally is not forgotten.'

They said their goodbyes, Tom again thanking Paul for everything, and Paul hoping Tom would succeed in getting Nan to see Dr Wilkie.

Paul found Ruth in the kitchen washing the dishes. She invited him to join her.

Mary and William were in a corner, keeping out of the way. They had found it difficult in the main hall, embarrassed by the favourable comments that kept coming their way, especially the gratitude expressed by so many, thanking them for their generosity and assuring them that the centre would be a great asset to Burnbrae. If only it had come about some other way. What had Wilma done to cause the accident? they wondered yet again.

35

On Monday morning, the day after the opening of the youth centre, Tom was busy in the shop. Nan had been in a slightly better frame of mind on her return home the previous afternoon. She had even seemed interested in all that Gary had to tell her about the youth centre. Not for the first time, Tom hoped that this was yet another start for her on the road to recovery.

At lunchtime he made his way up to the flat as usual. Lunch was a simple snack most days, so he did not expect to be met with the smell of cooking as he walked in the door, but he did expect to find Nan. There was no sign of her. It was unusual for her to go out in the morning. Perhaps she needed more milk. He looked in the fridge; there was milk and everything else likely to be needed. Maybe it was something personal she had run out of.

He made himself a sandwich and a cup of tea. He finished the sandwich and got himself a biscuit. Still no sign of Nan. Where could she be? Surely she couldn't be back at the cemetery? He remained in the house as long as possible, but when he could wait no longer, he made his way back down to the shop. He informed Mairi and Sadie that he had some business to attend to and that he would be back as soon as possible.

At the cemetery there was no sign of Nan. He returned home. There was no sign of her there either. He phoned Nan's sister, Babs. She was not with her and Babs had no idea where she could be. It was obvious from the tone of her voice that she and Nan were still not really on speaking terms.

Tom had no idea what to do next. He put the car back in the garage. Should he wait in the house, walk around the town, go back to the shop? He was becoming very alarmed. He would have to tell his assistants that he had more business to deal with. They wouldn't believe him, but that couldn't be helped. As he reached the shop one of his regular customers was coming out.

'Hello,' he muttered.

'Good afternoon, Tom. Glad to see Nan looking a bit better this morning.'

Her remark puzzled Tom, but at least someone had seen Nan.

'Yes. Can I ask you where you saw her? She wasn't home at lunchtime.' He could not keep the anxiety out of his voice.

'She was getting on the ten o'clock bus. She looked fine. Maybe she has gone to Dalcairn to get you a surprise. Is it your birthday, perhaps?'

'No, it's not. She must have forgotten to tell me. Did you get what you needed in the shop?'

Tom was now very worried. He did not want to be rude but he had to get back to the house.

'Of course I did. It's not often MacCallum's lets you down.'

'Good, I'm sorry, but…' He was moving towards the shop door as he replied.

'Yes, of course. You have to get to work and I have to meet a friend. Hope you like your surprise.'

Tom was already in the shop by the time Mrs Burns had finished speaking. Quickly he informed Mairi and Sadie that he just had to pop back upstairs. He had no idea what he would do when he got there, but there was no way he wanted to stand behind the counter making small talk with his customers. Worse still would be sitting by himself in the office.

Back in the house, he stood in the hallway gathering his thoughts. If Nan was going shopping in Dalcairn, she would have taken her handbag, he reasoned. He went into their bedroom and found the bag in its usual place. She would need money. Her purse was normally kept in a drawer in the kitchen. It wasn't there. He went back and looked in the handbag in case she had left it there by mistake. There was no purse in the bag, or anywhere else in the house as far as he could see. He stood looking out the front room window.

Where is she? What is she doing? he said to himself over and over again. He had to look for her, but where did he begin? He looked at the clock. It was now 1.25 p.m. The next bus from Dalcairn was due to arrive in Burnbrae in 15 minutes. He calmed down a little. *I'll wait here. She'll be on the bus. I might even go and meet her.*

In the end he decided to remain in the house. Nan might be annoyed if she found him standing waiting for her as she got off the bus. The last thing he wanted to do was to cause an upset.

The bus stop was only a few yards along the road from the shop. Tom was back at the window when the bus passed the house. Soon the passengers who had alighted from it were in view. Two of them were ladies he recognised. He waited for Nan to appear. Five minutes later he knew that she had not been a passenger on the bus. He contacted the ladies as soon as he could. Both of them had been on the 10 o'clock bus. They had seen Nan, but apart from saying good morning and commenting on the weather, there had been no conversation with her. She had sat by herself. One of the ladies thought Nan had wanted to be alone. She had not seen where Nan had gone once she got off the bus. The other passenger had.

'Yes, I did see where she went. She crossed over to the stance for the bus to the coast, to Millside, I think it was.'

'Of course, that would be where she was going. I should have thought of that. Thank you very much. You have been a great help. Goodbye.'

Tom was not as calm as he hoped he had sounded. He was becoming more worried than ever. Millside was a favourite place. It was a small coastal town with a lovely sandy beach. When the children were younger they had spent many happy hours there, but why had Nan chosen to go there now? And what would she do when she got there? And why had she not told him of her intentions? These and some even more worrying questions were going round and round in Tom's head. He tried to dismiss then and think rationally. He failed miserably. He could either go to Millside and hope that he found her or he could contact the police. If she was in danger, perhaps he should call the police first. They would get to Millside quicker than he could. He decided to phone the local police station. He was told that someone would come to the house to find out exactly what had happened.

Within minutes he was telling Sergeant Anderson all that he knew.

'And that's all I can tell you, Donnie. I just don't know what she's up to, but we have to find her, and find her fast. There's no knowing what she might do.'

Donnie Anderson replied quietly and firmly. 'From what you've told me, you've never had any reason to suspect that Nan would harm herself.'

'No, but she might.'

'Yes, she might, but at the moment all the evidence we have suggests that she has gone to a place where you spent many happy times. Yesterday she visited the cemetery as she often does. Gary told her about the youth centre and she was interested and, if anything, she was a bit better than she had been. Today she appears to have gone to another place where she was happy.'

Tom had to agree with the sergeant.

'Nan is an adult,' Donnie continued. 'She has found it difficult to come to terms with Sally's death, but she's coping in her own way. As far as the police are concerned it's too early to regard her as a missing person. If she has not returned by the time the last bus gets in at six forty-five, then, and then only, will we be able to justify searching for her.'

'I'm afraid I can't accept that, Donnie. If you won't go, I will.'

'Tom, I understand, but I need you to stay here. When Nan returns you have to be here, and you have to let us know immediately that she's back home. When I get back to the station I'll try to get in touch with someone at Millside, but I can assure you, if something had happened to Nan we would have heard by now. OK?'

'OK, I'll wait.'

'Tom, I mean it. Someone has to be here. To let us know the moment Nan returns. If we find her before that we will inform you immediately. Do you understand?'

'OK, I'll be here. Just hurry up and find her.'

Driving back to the police station Donnie had to pass both ends of the crescent. 'Worth a try,' he said to himself as he turned in and drove round towards the manse. The manse came into view, and there was Paul, doing something in the front garden.

By the time he had got out of the car, Paul was standing at the garden gate. In as few words as possible he made Paul aware of the concern regarding Nan's whereabouts and the state Tom was in.

'Give me a minute to wash my hands and let Ruth know where I'm going. I'll be with Tom in ten minutes.'

'Do what you have to do and after that I'll get you there in two. I really am worried that Tom will decide to take matters into his own hands, but it's imperative that he remains at home. We have to be informed the moment his wife returns. Safe and sound, I hope,' he added.

'So do I, but without saying too much, I can imagine how anxious Tom will be for her safety,' Paul replied.

36

Before the accident, Nan would normally be first to rise during the working week. She would prepare breakfast for Sally and Gary. Their bus to school left at 8 a.m. By that time, Tom would have appeared and, after a leisurely breakfast while he listened to the news on the radio, he would go downstairs, picking up his morning paper from the newsagent two doors beyond his own shop before opening up for business. Nan then had the house to herself until he returned for lunch.

Now it was Tom who got breakfast for Gary and himself. Nan never appeared until Gary had left to catch his bus. Sometimes Tom had to go into their bedroom to say goodbye as he prepared to go to the shop. He often thought that by acting this way Nan might be keeping the reality of what had happened at bay. She knew, of course she did, but if she didn't see Gary leaving on his own, did she imagine that Sally too was on her way to school?

This particular Monday had followed the new pattern. When Tom was ready to go down to the shop, he popped into the bedroom. Nan appeared to be sleeping. He didn't disturb her. Quietly, he closed the bedroom door and made his way downstairs.

Nan lay where she was until she heard the outside door close. She waited for a few more minutes, just to make sure that Tom was in the shop. On getting out of bed, she threw on her old dressing gown before making tea and toast for her breakfast. When it was time to get dressed she chose her clothes with rather more care than of late. However, she failed to notice that one side of the collar of her blouse was under her cardigan, the other outside. There was something else in her mind as she dressed. She checked her watch. It was almost time to go. She went out into the hallway and looked at the outdoor clothes on the hallstand. She selected a coat rather than her all-weather jacket. She checked that there was money in her purse before putting it in her pocket. She was ready.

Nan let herself out of the house and turned left. The shop door was to the right. She walked down the street for a short distance before crossing the road. There were a few people standing at the bus stop, mostly women. She nodded to two whom she knew slightly but made no attempt to get into a conversation. The bus arrived soon afterwards. She climbed aboard, found an empty double seat and settled down for the journey to Dalcairn.

At Dalcairn bus station she had intended to find a café and have a cup of tea before embarking on the next part of her journey. When she saw the bus for Millside at its stance, she changed her mind and boarded it. She would have the cup of tea when she got to her destination. There were very few passengers on this bus and nobody she recognised. For the duration of the journey to Millside she sat quietly, gazing out the window but not really taking anything in.

There was a lovely looking tearoom close to the promenade. Soon she was sitting at a window table overlooking the beach. The sun was shining and the water was calm. She sipped her tea, took a bite of the lovely scone, memories of happier days filling her mind.

Lunchtime was fast approaching and a few more customers entered the café. Nan decided it was time for her to leave. She settled her bill and left a rather generous tip. She walked slowly along the promenade, stopping every so often to look at the view. Memories were flooding back as she approached the part of the beach where they had often sunbathed when the children were young. There was now a shelter on the promenade, looking out to sea. She sat on the seat in the shelter. The memories still came: the castles Sally and Gary had built, the games they had played, the race to be first in the sea, the splashing and shouting. Happy days, happy family.

The area was quiet at this time of day. Nan must have dozed off. Somewhere a dog barked. Nan awakened with a start. She was confused. Where was she? She looked about her. Now she was fully awake. She was in Millside. She remembered why she had made the journey. She took a deep breath before getting to her feet. She moved out of the shelter and looked around. There were several people walking along the promenade. Nan could see someone running along the hard sand by the water's edge. A couple were walking their dog on the beach.

Nan walked slowly down towards the sea. On the way she passed by the couple with the dog. They wished her good afternoon. The lady also remarked on the pleasant weather. Nan didn't look at them, neither did she reply to their friendly greeting. She walked slowly on.

'Do you think she's all right?' the woman asked her husband.

'Obviously deep in thought, Annabel. If we hadn't moved out of her path I'm sure she would have bumped into us.'

'I hope you're right. Maybe we should keep an eye on her.'

'Don't be silly, dear. She'll be fine.'

Nevertheless, as they continued their walk, throwing the dog's ball in front of them as they went, they did also cast a glance in Nan's direction.

The dog brought his ball back. The man picked it up and prepared to throw it. The dog stood a few yards in front of him, ready to run.

'Oh no!' Annabel shouted. 'She's gone in the water. She's wading out. Tim, you have to stop her.'

She watched as her husband dropped the ball and ran as fast as he was able towards Nan. He was now in the water. He had to slow down in case he tripped and fell. Nan was getting into deeper water and she too was slowing. The water was up to her knees. Tim was gaining on her. He called on her to stop. Nan ignored him. The water suddenly deepened as she walked on. Nan stumbled and fell. She made no effort to stop herself. Her body sank.

Tim was not the greatest of swimmers. Annabel saw him reach the spot where the woman had fallen. The young man who had been running caught up with Tim. He must have heard her shout. He dived in and managed to get hold of the woman in the water. With Tim's help he got her into shallower water and together they managed to lay her on the firm sand. Holding the dog by its lead, Annabel joined Tim, who was breathing deeply.

'Are you all right, Tim?'

'Never mind me. This poor woman needs help.'

The woman was spluttering and coughing. The young man did what he could to help her clear her lungs of the seawater she had swallowed. He helped her to sit up. When she had recovered sufficiently to stand, Tim helped her to her feet. Slowly they made their way up the beach. The woman was shivering. Suddenly she went limp. Tim lowered her onto the dry sand. Someone appeared with a blanket.

'We were parking our car when we noticed what was happening. My husband has gone to the phone box to call for help.' She placed the rug over the woman.

A small crowd had gathered. No one knew who the woman was. She was conscious, but her eyes were not focused and her breathing was shallow.

'Thank goodness, here comes help,' Annabel informed the others as a police car, followed by an ambulance, arrived.

While the ambulance crew attended to the unconscious woman, one of the policemen asked what had happened. Quickly and accurately Annabel told him.

'And do you know the lady?' he asked.

'No, I have never seen her before today.'

The others present said likewise. A search of the purse left by the woman contained only cash and a photo of a young girl. Soon she was on her way to hospital. Until she was able to explain what had happened and why, and who she was, her identity would remain a mystery.

'Do you think she has had an accident?' Tom asked Paul before his visitor had a chance to say anything.

'Tom, if Nan had had an accident, we would have heard something.'

'I suppose so,' Tom muttered.

'I know it won't be easy, but just try to stay calm.'

'Wait a minute,' Tom suddenly said. 'How will they know who she is if she can't speak?'

He saw Paul's puzzled look. 'She only took her purse. What if her name is not on anything in it?'

'Surely she will have something with her name on it?'

Tom was not sure, but he agreed that getting himself even more wound up than he already was, was not going to help find Nan. Finally, it was agreed that he and Paul would meet the next bus and if Nan wasn't on it they would ask the passengers if any of them had seen her in Dalcairn.

'But if she is not on that bus, what will we tell Gary? He will be home from school soon.'

'Let's worry about that if and when we have to,' Paul replied. 'For the moment just hope Nan is home by then.'

'Aye, that might be best,' Tom said, without conviction as he and Paul began to make their way downstairs from the flat.

'Tom, you have to stay in the flat. Donnie insisted on that,' Paul shouted. 'In case they have any news of Nan.'

Tom was already out on the pavement. 'No, you stay, I'll go. The bus is coming.'

There was no time to argue. The bus was already heading towards the stop. Paul made his way upstairs. He stood looking out the window. Before he saw any of the passengers from the bus, the phone rang. It was Sergeant Anderson.

Paul identified himself.

'Is Tom with you?' Donnie asked.

'No, he's gone along to the bus stop in the hope that Nan will be one of the passengers on the bus just pulling up.'

'I don't think she will be. We may have found her.'

'Good news, I hope.'

'Much as I would like to put you in the picture, Paul, I really have to talk to Tom. Tell him I'll be over shortly. A couple of things to sort out first.'

Tom was pacing the floor in the lounge when Sergeant Anderson arrived.

'Is she all right? She hasn't had an accident, has she?'

'Tom, at this point I can't even say that the woman we've found is Nan. It sounds as though it may be, if she did indeed go to Millside. Let's sit down and I'll tell you all I know, then maybe you can give me a few details. That will help.'

Very quickly Donnie explained to Tom and Paul what had happened at Millside. Tom was desperate to interrupt but Donnie stopped him. 'That's it, that's all I know. The woman is conscious, but in a state of shock. So far she hasn't uttered a word. So, Tom, can you tell me what she was wearing when she left home?'

'Not really. She was still in bed when I left for the shop. I haven't seen her since.'

'Could you check and see if something she might be wearing isn't where it normally is, please.'

He went off to have a look. Paul and Donnie remained where they were.

'Don't think I would have a clue what Ruth was wearing most days, even if I saw her before she went out,' Paul remarked.

'Me too, as far as my wife is concerned. And I'm a police officer,' Donnie replied.

Tom soon returned, shaking his head. 'There's a coat missing from the hallstand, but apart from that, I've no idea. I think what she had on yesterday is in the laundry basket.'

'Don't worry. Can you describe the coat? That would be a big help,' Donnie replied.

'It's just a coat. Kind of greyish.' 'OK, Tom, that's fine. I'll get back to the office. As soon as we have confirmation that it is, or perhaps isn't, Nan, I'll be in touch.'

37

Tom paced about the room. He sat down. He stood up. Nothing Paul said had any effect. Given half a chance, Paul thought that Tom would rush out from the house and drive to the hospital at Dalcairn.

'But it hasn't been confirmed that the woman is Nan,' Paul told him yet again.

'She is. Donnie said she matched her description. And it's all my fault. I should have taken better care of her.'

'And that applies to me as well, Tom. Like you I thought I was doing the right thing, but I never realised that Nan would do something like this. I thought she just needed more time.'

The door opened and Gary entered the room. Paul was glad to see him. Perhaps his presence would change the tense atmosphere.

'Where have you been? The bus was in ages ago,' his dad shouted.

'I was talking to my pals, same as usual. Have you got a problem?' Gary asked.

'Well, you should have been here. Your mother has tried to drown herself!'

Paul was aghast. 'That's not true, Gary,' he said, firmly and calmly. 'Your mum may have had an accident, but we're not yet sure what has happened. She went to Dalcairn this morning and may have gone on from there to Millside. At Millside there has been an accident involving a woman falling into the sea, but who she is, is not yet confirmed.'

'Did she drown?' Gary asked. Paul's words had clearly done nothing to allay the fear caused by his dad's angry outburst.

'No, there were people there to help her. They got to her very quickly and pulled her out. She was conscious but so far she hasn't spoken. She's in hospital at Dalcairn.'

'Is that why the police car was outside?' Gary asked.

Before Paul could reply, Tom was off again. 'You saw the police car, and you carried on talking? Did you not think you should have come home to see what was happening?'

'I, I thought they were in the shop to buy something. I'm sorry.' Gary was now very upset.

'It's not your fault, Gary,' Paul stated quietly. 'Your dad is really worried, but we have to try to stay calm. It might not be your mum, and even if it is, she's being looked after.'

'I'm sorry, son, I really am.' All the anger had left Tom as quickly as it had arisen. He looked quite pathetic.

Paul was trying to work out how to keep the situation under control. The wrong word, or even the right word spoken in the wrong way, might set Tom off again, or it might break him completely.

The phone rang, startling all three. Tom looked at Paul. 'Would you answer it?' 'Of course.'

Paul hurried out to the hallway, closing the door behind him. The call didn't last long. Soon he was back in the room, two anxious faces watching him as he returned.

'That was Sergeant Anderson.'

'Is it Nan? Is she all right?' Tom asked, panic rising in his voice once again.

'It looks as though it is Nan. She hasn't spoken yet, but she isn't injured, not physically at any rate.'

'What does that mean?' Tom demanded. 'She is or she isn't?'

'I'm afraid she appears to have had some kind of breakdown. She is being taken to Glenbeg Psychiatric Hospital.'

'What? She's not mental! Why could they not just bring her home? We can look after her, can't we, Gary?'

Gary appeared to be speechless.

'Where she is going is in Nan's best interest, but until they're sure it is Nan, their hands are tied. Sergeant Anderson would like you to go to Glenbeg and make a formal identification,' Paul explained as calmly as he could. 'There's no rush. There will have to be more tests done at Glenbeg and I would think that they will give her something to ensure that she has a good rest before they try to find out why she did what she did. Of course, it could have been an unfortunate accident. She may just have been having a paddle, remembering old, happier times.'

There was little more he could do. Tom was busy making more sandwiches and as soon as he and Gary had eaten them they would be on their way to Glenbeg. Paul found himself offering up a silent prayer for all three of the MacCallums as he left Tom and Gary to their snack.

His dad was always a careful driver. On the journey to Glenbeg he seemed more careful than ever. Gary sat quietly beside him, looking at the road ahead and wondering what awaited them at their destination. Any other time his dad would have made the odd comment as something by the roadside caught his attention. His silence made Gary even more concerned about what had happened to his mother. He knew she had not been the same after Sally's death, but neither had he. There were moments when, for no reason at all, he found himself thinking about Sally. Someone, Dr Wilkie or the minister or maybe his school guidance teacher, had assured him that this was normal. He would never forget Sally, no matter how long he lived, but through time, these flashbacks as they called them, would become fewer and fewer. He had assumed that it was the same for his mum and dad. Maybe it was for his dad, but he had sometimes found himself wondering if his mum would ever be as she had been before Sally's death.

They arrived at Glenbeg without incident. Tom and Gary were taken into a room to wait for the doctor who was looking after Nan. They waited less than 10 minutes.

'I am Dr Patel,' the doctor said as he entered and shook hands with them. 'Please be seated.'

Tom and Gary sat down.

'As I think you are aware, Mr MacCallum, an as yet unidentified woman has been admitted following an incident at Millside. She isn't injured physically, but she seems to be suffering some kind of shock mentally. She hasn't spoken, and until we find out who she is, there's little we can do. We have sedated her in the hope that when she wakens she will not only be rested, but her body and her mind will be better able to cope with whatever caused her to act as she did.'

'I understand,' Tom replied. 'Can my son come too?'

'I would rather he didn't at this stage, but he can wait outside the room, and if it is your wife, then of course he can be allowed in to see her.'

As soon as Tom entered the room he took one look and rushed up to the bed. 'Oh, Nan, what have you done?'

Without waiting, Gary rushed in and held his dad until the sobbing stopped.

'I'm sorry it had to be like this, Mr MacCallum,' Dr Patel said, 'but be assured we will take good care of your wife, and, hopefully, we will have her well enough to go back home soon.

Gary and Tom sat by the bedside. Tom spoke softly to Nan. Gary looked at him.

'I know she can't hear me, but you never know. Maybe the sound of a familiar voice will unlock something.'

'Dad, she's knocked out. You're wasting your breath.'

'So what? I should have spoken to her at home instead of just letting her sit there in silence for weeks, even months. Anyway, it's helping me.'

When Dr Patel returned he filled out a form with Nan's personal details and made some notes about her behaviour since the loss of Sally.

'It has been a very difficult time for you both, and for Mrs MacCallum. I hope she will get back to how she was before today quite quickly. After that it may take some time until she is fully recovered. She's in the right place. We will do our best,' Dr Patel said.

'How long will it take, Doctor?' Tom asked.

'That, I'm afraid, is one question I cannot answer. Every patient is different. Take one day at a time. Visit when you can, but to begin with I would suggest that fewer visits are better for the patient rather than too many.'

'But surely our visits would help her?' Tom said rather loudly.

'I understand your concern, Mr MacCallum. You want everything to be better overnight, but that's not possible. It will take time, and the most important thing for your wife at the moment is to rest. To recover from what happened today. Be guided by the nurses and myself.'

Tom apologised for his outburst.

If the journey to Glenbeg was fraught with worry, so too was the homeward one. Tom understood that Nan was safe, but she was far from well.

Bert was enjoying his time as leader of the youth centre. By June the youth programme of informal activities was up and running. The members, and those who were thinking about becoming members, tried out some activities suggested by other members and by Bert. Badminton had proved popular and that was definitely on the agenda for the first full session beginning in September. There had already been a couple of nights when two of the boys had tried their hand at being DJs. The members had enjoyed these nights. Bert and the other adults roped in to help out had found the noise level rather high, although not as high as the night the band being put together by five other young men had played; his ears had still been ringing after he had gone to bed. Ideas like yoga from some of the girls and martial arts by some of the boys would depend upon finding teachers. In addition, as he had explained, the teachers would have to be paid and funds were limited.

Hearing about the need for funds led to suggestions from the members: a sponsored walk, a sponsored silence, a sponsored car wash, a sponsored sleep-in and even a sponsored read.

That was met with a shout of 'swot' from someone.

'Let's be realistic,' Bert insisted. 'We want to raise money, do something different from what others have done, bring in the public and give them a reason to come. A sponsored walk is OK, but that would be for the members. All the public would do, and it would be your relatives and friends mostly, would put their hands in their pockets. Same with a car wash and anything else sponsored. As for a sponsored silence, that might not bring in very much from you lot! And I hate to think what you might get up to with a sleep-in.'

'What about a sausage sizzle?' suggested a voice from the back when the laughing and one or two crude remarks had died down.

'A what?' asked Bert, glad of the interruption.

Roddy Brown stood up. 'A sausage sizzle. We had one at Scout camp last summer. It's what it says. You grill sausages, outside, or inside in the kitchen if it's wet, stick them in a roll with onions and ketchup or whatever, charge them a fortune and that's it. A sausage sizzle. Easy.'

'That sounds like a great idea, Roddy,' Bert replied. 'Might need some adults to keep an eye on you but no reason why you lot shouldn't do the sizzling.' That brought on more hoots of laughter.

By the time the day arrived, there had been some refinement to the original plan. Adults from the committee supervised the grilling of the sausages in the kitchen. The price was fair and even William, complete with apron, was not just keeping an eye on things but helping to cook the sausages.

'It was either this or having wet sponges thrown at me outside,' William said to a surprised Bert. 'This is much safer.'

'I would have thought that your customers would have done their best to miss you,' Bert joked.

'I doubt that very much,' William replied, turning over a couple of sausages as he spoke.

The event was a great success. The home baking, bottle stall, raffle and ice cream did a roaring trade and the sausages went down a treat. It seemed that everyone present wanted to throw a wet sponge at Bert or Paul, who took turns in the stocks. All in all, it was a most enjoyable and profitable day.

At Fauldshead the work followed the seasons and the weather. Bob and Malkie had settled into a routine that worked well. 'Make sure you leave something for Iain to do during the school holiday,' joked Bob as he watched Malkie clean out a barn.

'Don't worry, I've noticed a few things that I think he would make a good job of. Might not like them, but it will keep him out of mischief.'

'Maybe, but once he goes off to college, who will keep an eye on him then?'

'Changed days, Bob. 'You and I just did what the old man told us to do. Now the young ones tell us.'

Bob was quiet for a moment. He shook his head. 'Hard to believe he will be off to college in another couple of years. How time flies. Still, he knows what he wants. I just hope it all works out, for all of us.'

'Aye! Best get on with what's still to be done,' Malkie replied, picking up a brush.

'Come on,' Tom shouted to Gary towards the end of August. 'You got the day off school to come with me to bring your mum home. Not to laze about here.'

'I'm ready,' Gary replied as he appeared at his bedroom door. 'I'm waiting on you.'

'There were times I thought this day would never come,' Tom said as they got into the car shortly afterwards. 'I really hope that this is the last time we will make this journey to visit your mum. Today she is coming home. It might take her a bit of time to settle in again, but you and I will make sure that she does.'

'She seemed good to me the last time I visited her.'

On the way home Nan was quiet but Tom felt that once she was in the house he did see a difference in her. She joined in the conversation and she did not stare out the window, well, not all the time.

'Any more thoughts about our retirement home, Mary?' William asked as he put down his paper. The glorious summer of 1976 was coming to an end.

'Not again, William. You have asked me that question at least once every week since you first mentioned retiring. And several times some weeks,' she added.

'I know, but I want to make sure that when we do move, we make the right move. I don't want to be selling up and moving on every other year.'

'Now you are being silly. I understand that it is in your nature to plan everything as much as you can, but until we know if you will get early retirement, and when it will be, let's just have fun making suggestions, even daft ones, from time to time. In the end we will know what we want and that is what we will do.'

'As always, Mary, I bow to your superior wisdom.'

'If I thought that was sarcasm, you might find that you would be on your own, even before you retire, but as it is true, I will help you come to the right decision.'

38

In February 1985, Paul and Ruth left Burnbrae. The move to the new parish had gone as well as these things go. The manse was a modern bungalow and Paul and Ruth were the first to move into it. They had loved the Victorian villa at Burnbrae and were sorry to leave it, the congregation and the community. They had been happy there but there came a time when Paul began to think that he had done what was required of him. His work had been largely appreciated, but it was time to move on. His successor, when he was appointed, would find a congregation in good spirits, willing and able to meet whatever challenges they would face. He and Ruth would be nearer to Jennifer and Malcolm. That was not the main reason for accepting the call to a church in the Stirling area, but it had been a factor.

Jennifer was now a staff nurse at the new Ninewells Hospital in Dundee. She was married to Philip, a GP in Broughty Ferry. They had a two-year-old daughter, Rhona, and her brother or sister was due in June.

To Paul and Ruth's surprise and delight, Malcolm had felt the call to follow in his father's footsteps. With his studies at the University of Glasgow successfully completed, he spent his probationary year serving in a parish in one of the city's large social housing areas. Despite the challenges of working in an area of high unemployment with its associated problems for many of the inhabitants, Malcolm had decided that he would like to continue this kind of work. At university, he met Rachel and within a couple of years they were engaged. Their wedding took place shortly after Malcolm began his probationary year. For the past two years he and Rachel had been living and working in Edinburgh in Malcolm's first parish. The parish was similar to the one in Glasgow. Paul had been concerned that Malcolm was perhaps taking on too much.

'I'm young and I'm fit,' Malcolm assured him. 'I've gained some experience during my time in Glasgow, and I have the assistance of a youth worker and a church secretary. It's what I want and it's what God wants me to do.'

Paul could not argue with that. 'Just make sure you don't overdo it.'

'I won't. Rachel will make sure of that, just as Mum made sure that you took time off.'

They both laughed. 'Like father, like son, like mother, like daughter-in-law,' Ruth joked.

Malcolm and Rachel now had a young son and a new baby daughter. Whenever they could, Paul and Ruth liked to visit their grandchildren, but it wasn't easy. Paul's new parish was well established, but like Burnbrae, there were duties that often fell on that Monday day off. Sometimes Ruth would go off for a couple of days when she was needed to give a hand in Broughty Ferry or Edinburgh. They had bought a second car which was a help, though train and bus services were also available, especially in winter. Ruth had not had much experience of driving beyond the area around Burnbrae and much preferred when Paul was in the driving seat for the longer journeys.

Paul would be inducted to his new charge later in the week. Malcolm and Rachel intended to be present for the service and at the welcome social following the formalities, Malcolm was to be one of the speakers. Paul dreaded to think what he might say, especially as at the social to welcome Malcolm to his first parish, he had revealed some family memories that had been embarrassing to the congregation's new minister. Now it would be payback time.

Malcolm and Rachel had to go back home the day after, but Jennifer, Philip and daughter Rhona would arrive on the Saturday for his first Sunday. As he was being 'preached in' by a friend and colleague in the morning, he would deliver his first sermon at the evening service. Philip and Jennifer had managed to arrange their shifts so that they could stay over until Monday morning.

When she had been told of the extended visits Ruth had pretended to be annoyed. 'Only in the house a few days and two lots of visitors. That means changing beds and extra washing before I know where I am.'

'You don't really mean that, do you?' Paul asked, looking up from the pile of books he was sorting out in his study.

'Of course not. The more the merrier, and we get to see the grandchildren as a bonus.'

Two days before the Edinburgh part of the family arrived, Paul was yet again in his study. The books had been arranged in the bookshelves on two walls of the large room. An impressive collection, but Paul was aware that most of them were for show. He had inherited many of them from a former minister of the church where he had been brought up, from another retired minister who was an old friend of his parents, and as if that were not enough to last him a lifetime, he had added more volumes from the books donated to the divinity college by former students when they too retired. The remainder he had bought when a student or during his ministry after reading a review that suggested he would find the subject interesting and informative. At least he had actually read these ones. He was very mindful of a comment he had heard during his student days: that it was possible to tell the date when a minister left college by the publication date of the newest book in his library. Paul had made purchases from time to time, but it was easier to keep abreast of current trends by subscribing to a couple of monthly or quarterly theological publications.

The books in place, it was time to turn his attention to the papers. The pile in the corner seemed huge. Why had he not been more ruthless before leaving Burnbrae? Not everything could have been worth keeping, he thought. This time he would keep only those of some importance, and even then, if he had never looked at an article, photo or whatever since he had carefully put it away, why keep it now? By lunchtime the 'keep' pile had been greatly reduced. The unsorted pile would not take more than an hour after lunch. That was what he thought, until he came across certain newspaper clippings.

Paul knew they were there. They had been put away after the event but, from time to time, he would open the folder, read again the familiar words, as he was doing now and then put them away. He often thought of the young ones who had died, their families and his close connection with them. It was foolish to contemplate what might have been. Sandy, Wilma, Kirsty, Sally and Brian would forever remain in the memory of those who loved them as they had been before, and as they had been on that evening. They would not change, but their deaths had changed the lives of those they left behind.

His thoughts were interrupted as Ruth entered the study, carrying two mugs of coffee.

'Thought you might have made me one,' she remarked as she handed a mug to Paul. 'I've finally finished all I had to do, but look at this, papers everywhere. And I suppose most of them will be kept, just in case.'

Paul looked up. 'Well, yes, some will, but not all. I was just reading over these reports from the local paper in...'

'I can see what you were reading.' Ruth's voice had become softer as she interrupted him. There was more than a touch of compassion in her tone. 'Don't you think now is the time to put all that behind you? You did all you could, more than many others would have done. We've moved away. They're no longer your concern. Neither of us will ever forget what happened. The memories will remain, and every so often we will think of the ones who died, and the ones who had to live with the aftermath of that terrible evening.'

'I know, but I can never forget them. I did what I could, but every so often I find myself wondering if I could have done more.'

Ruth hesitated as if choosing her words carefully. 'You did what you thought was best. No one would have said and done everything exactly as it needed to be done in a situation like that. There is no textbook to guide you. You have to rely on your training and gut instinct at the time. And you did.'

'But what about Nan MacCallum?'

'I thought you might be thinking of Nan. I don't mean to be unkind, but what about her? She needed professional help. Dr Wilkie admitted to you that even he had failed her, if you have to use a word like that.'

'I understand that, and I know he told me that even a psychiatrist or a psychologist would only have been able to do so much until she was admitted to hospital.'

'And even then, it took time, and she's still nothing like her old self. Come on, drink up, your coffee is getting cold. Here's to a new beginning.' Ruth raised her mug in a toast.

'New beginnings,' Paul replied.

39

Paul and Ruth chatted about more immediate matters as they drank their coffees.

'Do you think we have done everything we need to do before the induction?' Ruth asked as she put her empty mug on the floor.

'Now who's doing the worrying?' Paul joked. 'Of course we have. Don't worry, everything will be fine. The young ones will love the house and Mum's cooking, and Mum, like me, will love having the grandchildren around.'

'I suppose so. And make sure you get this place sorted out before then.'

'I will, as soon as you get out of my way.'

Ruth made a face. 'I'll believe it when I see it,' she said as she left the study.

Paul's thoughts were back with the MacCallums as he picked up the cutting on the top of the pile. The summer of 1976 had not been an easy one for them. Paul had continued to drop in to have a chat with Tom, and he visited Nan in the hospital.

Tom was convinced at first that the intense drug regime she was on was not working.

'Dr Patel says it is for her own good,' he had explained to Paul during one of their chats in the back office. 'He says she needs rest and release from the grief that has consumed her. As soon as the dosage is reduced Nan will slowly return to the person she was before the accident.'

'You have to trust him,' Paul had replied. 'He does know what he is doing. I am no expert, but I have known others who did get back to normal.'

'Gary does try his best to help,' Tom said, changing the subject rather abruptly. 'I told him he did not have to come every time I visited his mum. We nearly fell out over it. He told me his mum would be expecting him. I said I sometimes wondered if she knew we were there. That did not do much to reassure him.'

Tom shook his head. 'I blamed the drugs. I am not sure Gary believed me, but he accepted it. I said I would give his love to Nan, tell her he had something else on. Eventually he agreed and that set the pattern for the rest of her time in hospital. Sometimes Gary is with me, sometimes not.'

After Nan was back home, Paul remembered Tom's account of the events that led up to it. It had been a Sunday in August when Tom, accompanied by Gary, saw some progress. It wasn't much, but Nan was sitting in a chair by her bedside. She was dressed in the outdoor clothes that Tom had taken in the previous week, in the hope that Nan would feel like wearing them. There was some conversation, but mostly it was Tom who did the talking. Nan listened, made the occasional short comment in response to what Tom said, but offered nothing about herself and how she was feeling. Gary had mostly kept quiet.

In desperation, Tom suggested that they make their way to the cafeteria for tea or coffee. To his surprise and delight, she agreed. The short walk along the hospital corridor was slow. Nan clung to Tom for support. Her muscles would have to be built up after the weeks of inaction, but it was a beginning. In the cafeteria Tom thought that the change of scenery was doing her some good. Nan was looking around from time to time, glancing at the other patients and their visitors. She appeared to be showing some interest in her surroundings. When Gary told her what he had been doing since his previous visit, Tom was surprised to hear her say, 'Good for you!' Gary raised his eyebrows as though he could not believe what he had just heard.

Tom and Gary were in a better mood on the return journey, but neither was expecting Nan to be back home in Burnbrae within the month, yet only three weeks later Dr Patel informed Tom that Nan was well enough to be discharged. Her medication had been reduced to the point where it could safely be administered at home. She would have to see Dr Patel for many more months to check on her progress, but he was positive that eventually that too would come to an end.

'You will have to make sure that your wife takes the medication exactly as prescribed,' Dr Patel had insisted. Tom assured him that he would, thinking that this time, for as long as it took, he would stand over her and make sure she swallowed every pill, and they would be locked away, and he would keep the key safe at all times.

Most days after her return home, Nan was better than she had been in a long time. Tom had no difficulty getting her to take the pills. It was as though she was grateful for the change they had made in her behaviour. Not all days were as good, but Dr Patel had emphasised that this would happen and the medication would be required for many months, perhaps even longer.

The improvement in Nan gave Tom the opportunity to relax within himself. It did not happen overnight but it did happen. His main concern was more and more about the business. Slowly but surely trade was falling off. Even his most loyal of customers did not buy everything they required from him. A national chain had opened a large store in Dalcairn. Tom couldn't compete with the prices they offered on most items. His business was more and more supplying something in an emergency, or an item the customer had forgotten to purchase in Dalcairn. It was only a matter of time before he would have to diversify or give up. Like his father before him he was an ironmonger. That was the business he knew and loved. Becoming some kind of upmarket gift shop, or worse still, a supplier of cheap end-of-line goods bought in from the companies who were putting him out of business was not for him.

While Tom foresaw the end of his business, he was pleased that Gary had made it clear that he had no intention of being a shopkeeper. He still helped out in the shop from time to time when his schoolwork allowed, but his real interest was the family car. Tom had shown him how to do the basic routine checks and what to do when minor adjustments were required. For as long as Tom could remember, Gary had made it clear that he wanted to work in a garage, and even one day have his own business. Tom had encouraged him although he was sad that the family tradition would not be carried on. Now he was pleased that at least Gary would have a job that would always be needed, provided he got the chance to fulfil his dream.

Paul could remember how proud Tom had been of Gary. By the age of 21 he had achieved the first part of his ambition and was working in the local garage as a fully qualified mechanic. Getting there had been hard work, but he had loved every minute of it, and it seemed that no matter what the problem was, he soon found the fault and before long had everything running smoothly again. His boss had told him that he was a conscientious worker, good at his job and good at customer relations, something he had subconsciously picked up from his dad.

He had also found a girlfriend. There had been others along the way, teenage romances that sometimes lasted for months, sometimes only for weeks, but this time as he and Evelyn got to know one another, he thought it was more than a passing phase in his life. Evelyn was the one who made the first move to take their friendship to the next level. They were sitting in his car outside her house at the end of a Saturday night out in Dalcairn.

'Next Saturday, would you like to come to mine for tea, before we go to Dalcairn?' Evelyn asked.

Gary was taken unawares. Going for a meal, or 'getting your feet under the table' as people called it, was a recognition that the relationship was becoming serious. He was serious about Evelyn and he had found himself wondering if she might be the girl he would marry.

'Yeah, that would be good. Will it be OK with your folks?'

'Yes, I asked Mum and she said it was fine.'

'And your dad?'

'As long as the food is good, he won't object.'

Gary wasn't quite sure what to say. Evelyn laughed. 'I'm joking. He thinks you seem a nice lad, and you being a car mechanic could come in handy. And that's not a joke, he actually said that.'

Gary was a bit uptight the following Saturday. Evelyn's parents' welcome and friendly chat soon put him at his ease. They did ask a few questions but at no time did he think he was being grilled to see if he was suitable husband material for their daughter. The relationship moved on to a new level after that visit.

He was worried about inviting Evelyn to his own home. His mum had shown some interest in his new girlfriend at first but once she knew who she was and a bit about her family, that was that. He told her where they were going, what the film had been about, if the band was good, bad or nothing special but she clearly was not interested in films or his kind of music. He spoke to his dad about Evelyn coming for a meal soon after he became a regular guest at her table.

'It's tricky, son,' his dad replied. 'I'm not the best of cooks, but I could maybe manage something a bit special.'

'That's OK, Dad. Evelyn understands about Mum. But will she be upset? Will she be thinking of Sally?'

'Probably, but there's nothing we can do about that. We just have to do our best to make it as pleasant an occasion for Evelyn as we can.'

Tom told Nan that Gary had invited his girlfriend for tea.

'That's nice,' Nan replied, to Tom's surprise. He was even more surprised when she added, 'And I will make the tea.'

The macaroni cheese she served up was excellent, as it always had been in the past. When Tom realised what she was cooking, he had become more than a little alarmed. This was a typical Saturday teatime dish before the accident. It was Sally's favourite, but if Nan was thinking of Sally as she worked in the kitchen, or sat at the table watching them all tuck into her delicious macaroni cheese, she showed no sign of it. Tom took it as another step in her recovery.

Evelyn became a regular visitor at the MacCallums' home and Gary at Evelyn's. Tom was not surprised when, in the course of time, Gary informed him that he and Evelyn were to become engaged.

'Are you quite sure that this is what you both want?' he asked Gary.

'Of course we do. Is it not obvious?'

Tom laughed and slapped Gary on the back. 'Of course it is. I'm just asking you the same question as your granddad asked me. Think he was as nervous about this conversation as I am now. I'm pleased for you both, and know your mum will be too. Good luck to both of you. Now, how about you go and tell your mum while I get something to toast the happy couple with.'

During the engagement, and especially as the wedding day grew closer, Tom often had a feeling that although Nan was advising and helping Evelyn, it was Sally she was thinking of. He spoke to their new GP about his thoughts. Dr Newlands, Dr Wilkie's replacement in the Dalcairn practice, had agreed that it was possible but advised that as long as it did not become an obsession, there was probably no harm in it.

'At least it's bringing her out of herself. She's taking part,' he concluded.

The day of the wedding was a lovely spring day. Despite the nerves of those in the bridal party there were no unfortunate blunders. Paul had done a good job in making sure everyone knew exactly what they were doing and when. The speeches followed the usual pattern and then it was time for the dancing. Evelyn and Gary were cheered and applauded as they stepped out for the bridal waltz. They did their best as the cheering continued. Tom welled up as he took his place with Evelyn's mother on the floor beside them. Nan had made it clear that she would not be dancing. Her place was taken by the other bridesmaid who danced with Tom.

From time to time, Tom found himself wondering exactly what Nan was thinking. She was not saying much but was watching her son's bride very closely. Every time Evelyn was anywhere near where Nan was sitting she watched her even more closely. Her eyes followed her when she left the room and when she returned. It was not until they were home, tired but happy, or so Tom thought, that Nan confirmed her husband's worst fears. She turned from the wardrobe where she had hung up her dress, and said, 'Sally looked lovely today.'

Tom stepped forward and held her. He could not stop the tears: they were for Nan, for Sally and for himself. It had been Evelyn and Gary's day, but Sally had never been very far from his thoughts either. As Sally had grown and begun to change from a girl to a young woman, he had occasionally found himself imagining how proud he would be as he walked her down the aisle to meet her husband-to-be. Today reminded him once again of what might have been and how tragically his dream had been lost.

Shortly after the wedding Tom received an enquiry regarding the business, and very soon everything changed. The options he had been considering became a reality. The shop and the house were sold to a Chinese restaurateur, Tom and Nan moved to a bungalow in a new development on the outskirts of Burnbrae and Evelyn announced that she was pregnant.

The new home had a positive effect on Nan's mental health. It was as if moving away from the old house with all its memories enabled her to move on. She still visited Sally's grave from time to time, but she also took an interest in what was going on around her. The arrival of Gary and Evelyn's son was greeted with great joy. Evelyn became used to Nan dropping in unannounced to see if there was anything she could do to help, and to get a chance to give baby Neil a cuddle.

Tom had done well from the sale of the shop and house, but he didn't want to retire. He could not see himself pottering about in the garden or taking up golf, so when a vacancy came up for a part-time worker in the DIY store in Dalcairn, he jumped at the chance. At first he was worried about leaving Nan on her own but Evelyn said she would keep an eye on her. The two of them got on great, so much so that from time to time Evelyn's own mother complained that she felt left out when it came to helping with Neil. Life was good again, but Sally was not forgotten. She was part of the family and always would be.

Paul was brought back to the present when Ruth called that lunch was ready. He put down the cutting he had been holding as he reminisced. Joy for sorrow, but in the background a shadow, he thought.

40

After a lovely light lunch, Paul returned to the study, having assured Ruth that he was almost finished putting everything where it should be.

'Really,' exclaimed Ruth. 'Away, perhaps. But where it should be?'

'New beginnings and all that,' Paul muttered. 'That is what I am hoping. I just have the last remaining papers to attend to.' He beat a hasty retreat.

Back in the study his eye caught the photos of Kirsty and Sandy among the clippings and his mind returned to Fauldshead.

He could see Bob admiring the freshly painted farmhouse, the tidy yard and well-maintained outbuildings at the end of a busy day. The sheep and cattle were doing well, the fences were secure and the hedges trimmed. He often wondered what the visitors who drove past the farm on their way up the glen were thinking as they saw it all. *'Another moaning farmer'* they'd be saying. *'Always complaining about something, but he's doing OK by the look of it!'* If only they knew what the Meikles had suffered, Paul thought.

It was a hard life at times, but a rewarding one, though there were occasions when the rewards were not as much as they might have been, but Bob, Jessie and Iain were comfortable. Not all farmers were so fortunate. For those who were on the borderline between making a small profit or a worrying loss, it did not take much to swing the balance the wrong way: bad weather, disease, a wrong choice and then disaster loomed. For some the struggle seemed to be a never-ending one.

Bob and Jessie had their anxious moments like everyone else, and when the good times did come, they had to admit that they were never as good as they should have been. How could they be? They had suffered a loss that no parent should have to suffer, and in their case it had been doubled. In the company of others they managed to hide their true feelings as best they could, but in the quietness and comfort of their home it was not always possible. This particular evening had been especially bad. It was the annual show and sale at the local market. Fauldshead had shown the overall champion in the beef classes and, in the auction that followed, the winning bid had exceeded all expectations, but the beast had been Sandy's. He had seen its potential, looked after it and shown it around the local shows in the year before his death.

Jessie and Bob had joined in the celebrations at the market as best they could. Their thoughts were very much of Sandy and what might have been, and now that they were home, all thought of celebrating had gone.

'It's been a good day, and a bad day,' Bob commented as he took a sip of what should have been a toast to their success at the market.

'And not the first one or the last one,' Jessie added. 'Do you think we will ever get to a point where there is a day when we don't think of Sandy or Kirsty?'

'Do you want to?' Bob replied, surprised.

'That's not really what I meant to say. I mean, will there be days when we go about what needs to be done without everything we do reminding us of Sandy, or Kirsty, or both?'

'I suppose it must happen eventually, but there will still be those special occasions when it will be impossible, but through time, I suppose it will only be birthdays and Christmas and…'

'And seeing Iain doing the things that Sandy would have been doing,' Jessie added.

Bob looked at her. 'Aye, I've already done that a good few times myself, I have to admit.' He sighed. 'We have to be careful there. Iain misses his brother and sister just as much as we do, but we mustn't make him feel that somehow we think he is Sandy's replacement.'

'Stop it, Bob. You're making things worse. I was looking for comfort, reassurance.'

Bob gave an even bigger sigh before replying, 'We'll get there. We are getting there, but nothing will ever be the same again. And we have to make sure we treat Iain as we would have done if the other two were still here.'

'Kirsty and Sandy, not the other two!' Jessie retorted.

Bob couldn't hide his hurt.

'I'm sorry,' Jessie said.

'No, you're right. I deserved that. Kirsty and Sandy will always be special, but no more special than Iain, and Iain will always be himself. I had a talk with him about going to college. I wanted to make sure that was what he wanted to do.'

'Of course he wants to go to college. He's always helping around the farm and has done since he was a toddler. What a stupid thing to say!'

'Maybe it was,' Bob admitted, 'but I had to be sure. Sandy and I worked together and one day Sandy was to take over. We had spoken about what would happen if Iain wanted to join us. The farm is not big enough to support another family.'

Jessie looked horrified. 'You and Sandy were planning all this without asking me what I thought about it? Or Iain?'

'We weren't planning anything, and it only came up as Iain began to think about his future. Yes, he wanted to be a farmer, and we might have been able to enlarge the farm or take over another one. And there were other options for Iain that didn't mean being the owner of the farm, or even working on a farm.' Bob was becoming more and more worked up as he defended himself.

'Stop, before I become really annoyed!' Jessie exclaimed. 'I am beginning to think you and Sandy were planning to move Iain out of the way, to solve the problem in the way that best suited the two of you, regardless of what Iain or I had to say on the matter!'

Bob was beginning to wish he had never mentioned any of this to Jessie, but it was too late. Somehow he had to convince her that it had all been with Iain's best interests at heart.

'I'm sorry. We were concerned about what might happen to Iain if there was no room for him here. We were wondering if he had begun to think about his future, if farming was to be his choice too and what kind of farming he would want to be involved in. That kind of thing. If it was, then Sandy and I would make it happen. Here at Fauldshead if possible, but more likely by buying another farm if and when one came on the market at the right time, and the right price,' he added, rather lamely.

'OK, I believe you, but maybe you should have included me in your discussion. So why did you have to have that talk with Iain?'

'I had to be certain that he was not going to college to please us. To make up for Sandy no longer being here.' Bob shook his head, his voice breaking up. 'I'm sorry, I miss Sandy and Kirsty so much.'

'Of course you do,' Jessie replied softly. 'We all do. I don't agree with how you went about things, but I know you thought you were doing the right thing. We now have to make sure that Iain gets all the support he needs. And next time there is family business to discuss, make sure I'm part of it. I might even make some sensible comments.'

'I will, I promise, and your comments are always sensible. Well, nearly always.'

Jessie gave him a look. 'Don't push it. My glass is empty, by the way.'

As Bob was pouring the drinks, he was remembering that dreadful moment when he had realised that Sandy's death solved the problem of who would inherit the farm. He had been utterly disgusted with himself, and still was, but it had happened. Now it was the shame that would not go away. How could any father have had such a thought? But he had had, and he couldn't forget it. Perhaps if he could talk about it with someone, it would help, but he had vowed never to reveal that thought to anyone.

'Are you all right?' Jessie asked, as she took her refilled glass from him.

'Yes, just thinking of what might have been. Again.'

'You're not the only one, but we just have to soldier on and make sure that whatever happens, we do the best we can for Iain, and for ourselves, never forgetting Sandy and Kirsty.'

Bob was pleased to learn that Iain was doing well at agricultural college, enjoying the company of others doing the same course, and making new friends. Before long there was one special friend, Sheila, a farmer's daughter from Perthshire.

'She seems a nice girl,' Bob remarked to Jessie after Sheila's first visit to Fauldshead. 'Do you think she could be the one?'

'For goodness' sake, Bob. It's far too early to be making comments like that. But you are right, she is a very pleasant young lady,' Jessie added with a smile.

After the friendship deepened, which Bob was pleased about, and when it came, the engagement was welcomed by both families. As the wedding grew ever closer a decision had to be made about where the young couple would live.

When Alec and Helen had built the bungalow, they had moved out of the farmhouse and Bob and Jessie had moved into it. Before that they had been living in one of the farm cottages which, before mechanisation had changed everything, had been home to a farmworker's family. The two former workers' cottages were now holiday homes. As Helen was in excellent health, it might be many years before Bob and Jessie would move from the farmhouse to the bungalow and Iain and Sheila would take over the farmhouse. For the time being, Iain and Sheila would make one of the holiday cottages their first home. They had no objections and began to plan the changes they would make to it.

Six months before their wedding, however, Helen surprised them all. The postman had been and gone when she walked into the farmhouse kitchen, waving a letter and smiling excitedly.

'Good news?' asked Jessie.

'Great news. I've got a house!'

'Of course you have, the bungalow.'

'No, I've got one in the town. The council have allocated me one of the new flats. A ground-floor one, and it's near the shops. I won't be stuck out here and relying on you and Bob for everything when I have to give up my car.'

Once Helen had calmed down, she explained that after Alec died, she had had to admit to herself that the time might come when living at the farm would make her dependent on the others in many ways. She didn't want that, so she had applied to the housing authority, explaining that with the loss of her husband she needed to move into the town. When Bob heard what she had done he was not pleased, but in the end he had to agree that it did make sense. He and Jessie would be sorry to leave the farmhouse with all its memories, but they had always known that would happen one day. It was going to be sooner than they had thought, and with moving house, helping Helen to move into her new home and the wedding to think about, it was going to be a hectic six months.

The time flew by and the big day arrived. It was a wonderful day. The farming families, relatives and friends of the bride and bridegroom were soon chatting away as if they had known one another for many a year. There were moments when it was almost too much for Bob and Jessie, especially as Iain was making his speech. He began well, telling a few jokes, poking fun at himself, and mindful of his mum's warning, nothing too crude, but when he began to speak about the family it looked as though the emotion he was feeling would be too much. He took a deep breath, composed himself and managed to thank his mum and dad for all they had done for him before quickly moving on to thank the bridesmaids in a few brief words. He raised his glass. 'The bridesmaids,' he managed to blurt out before the first tear fell.

Bob's speech was also rather shorter than he had intended, too many memories flashing through his mind as he welcomed Sheila into the Meikle family.

Despite the problems with the speeches, the evening part of the wedding was a great success. The younger guests danced the night away; almost everyone, apart from some of the farmers who were too busy talking, was on the dance floor for The Slosh and The Birdie Song.

When Sheila and Iain returned from honeymoon, they moved into the bungalow, not the farmhouse. As Iain was helping his gran to move into her new home, he realised that it was silly to expect his mum and dad to move out of their home. He and Sheila would be far more comfortable in the smaller house. They hoped that in due course they would have a family and eventually the time would come when the big house would be great, but until then, or until his mum and dad found the farmhouse too much, he and Sheila would enjoy making their home in the bungalow.

Christmas 1984 was an important one for Iain and Sheila. Their baby daughter, Kirsty, was to be baptised at the beginning of Advent. Paul quite liked when he had a baptismal service just before the actual day, even better if it fell on the Sunday, but he quite understood why Iain and Sheila were adamant that if he was to have a Christmas baptism this year, it would not be baby Kirsty's. The end of November would be close enough. No matter what date it was it would be emotional for the family. Jessie had not been happy about the choice of name, but once she had calmed down, she realised that it was a lovely thing that Sheila and Iain had done.

As the day of the baptism drew near, Paul was hoping that the name he was about to announce would not trigger a flashback to the other Kirsty's funeral service. It would be difficult enough to say the name without seeing in his mind's eye the young girl whose name she bore and the uncle she would never see. He also knew by then that this would be his last Christmas in Burnbrae and very soon he would have to inform the congregation that he was about to move on. Despite another day of very mixed emotions for all those concerned, the service went without a hitch and young Kirsty slept through it all until the water landed on her forehead. She gave a loud cry before drifting off to sleep again.

Paul sat looking at the photos of Sandy and Kirsty. Life was going on at Fauldshead, but he could not stop wondering how different it all might have been and how well those who were left had coped despite everything.

41

Paul picked up another cutting: the photo of a confident, smiling young woman. Now he was recalling Wilma, her mum and dad, what they had lost and how they had remembered her. The youth centre was a great success.

Many of the teenagers in the district became members and most of them took part regularly in at least one of the many activities it offered. William looked in at the centre regularly in the early days. Very soon he knew that in choosing Bert Crawford as leader, the trustees had made an excellent choice. William was happy to let Bert and the small team of volunteers get on with the day-to-day running of the centre while he kept an eye on its finances. Mary was actively involved in looking after the badminton section, giving instruction to those who were keen to play but who were hitting a shuttlecock for the first time. Explaining the rules and the scoring system took up much of her time and patience in the early days. However, once they got the hang of it, there were quite a few who became very good players.

As William's sixtieth birthday drew ever closer, he was hoping that it might also be the beginning of his retirement. He had indicated to the bank that he was willing to go around that time and it seemed that it might become a reality. He and Mary had been talking seriously about where they would live when the day came. Much as they loved their present house, and although the cost of running it shouldn't be a problem, they both agreed that a smaller house, a bungalow perhaps, would be much easier to run. The big question remaining to be answered was where should the house be?

'One reason we decided that Wilma should be buried here in Burnbrae was so that we would be able to visit her grave, a special place where we could stand and remember her,' William reminded Mary as they considered the choices of location for their new home.

'Yes, I do remember, and in the first few months we visited her grave more or less every week, taking new flowers and removing the withered ones. Now we visit on her birthday, at Christmas and Easter and on the anniversary of her death if it does not fall in Easter week.'

'Yes, but we still visit. If we move away, that might not be so easy,' William countered.

'I'm not suggesting that we move to the other end of the country, perhaps not even out of the county.'

'And does that mean that you already know where you want to move to?' William replied, thinking that yet again Mary was at least one step ahead of him.

Mary smiled. 'Perhaps I do, but only if you agree. It has to be a joint decision.'

'So, where is this Shangri-La to be found?'

'I don't know where Shangri-La is, but I do know where Millside is, and I do know that they have some very nice bungalows with a sea view.'

'You have been doing your homework, haven't you? Have you checked with your bank manager to see if this move will be financially viable?' William had now put on his best work face.

'I thought that was what I was doing.' Mary laughed. 'You have been so busy thinking about the possibility of retiring that I decided to get on with exploring the options open to us if we decided to move away. You might get a date for your retirement in the near future. Better to have some options to consider, that's all. We'll decide together as we always do.'

Shortly after William retired in June 1979 they had moved to a beautiful bungalow in Millside, and it did have a sea view. They also kept the vow they had made before the removal took place, visiting Wilma's grave at least on the special occasions and at other times when they were back in Burnbrae visiting old friends. To begin with they visited these friends quite frequently, and the friends enjoyed their return visits to Millside, but as so often happens, these visits became less and less frequent and within a couple of years Mary eventually declared, 'If they can't come to Millside to visit us, why should we call in on them when we are in Burnbrae?' However, the manse was one of the three homes where the old friendship remained strong.

Paul and Ruth found their visits to Mary and William's new home relaxing. Simply being out of the parish for a few hours meant that Paul could truly relax. There would be no phone calls, no ring of the doorbell and any message on the answering machine, unless it was urgent, would be attended to the following day.

Paul was concentrating on his driving after another lovely lunch and pleasant conversation with the Watsons.

'What did you make of Mary?' Ruth asked without any preamble.

Paul glanced over, trying to get a clue as to what Ruth was talking about. Ruth's expression suggested that she was onto something, but what?

Paul was looking ahead again. 'I thought she looked well. The new house and everything seem to be agreeing with her.'

'Yes, but was that all you noticed? Have you not felt that she's becoming more assertive?'

'Perhaps, but I just thought she didn't have to act like the bank manager's wife any more. She could be herself.'

'Exactly,' Ruth said. 'That's what I think too. I hope it doesn't cause problems for William.'

'Surely not, they still seem as happy as ever. William has changed too,' Paul added. 'He's still the bank manager, but no longer worrying about his customers and their overdrafts, no longer on his guard in case he fails to spot something not quite right and brings the wrath of head office down on him. And I rather think he likes Mary being like the girl he fell in love with all those years ago.'

They were nearing Dalcairn and Paul had to give all his attention to the traffic around him. After that visit and the conversation in the car, each time they were in the company of their friends they noticed that Mary had definitely changed, or more likely had become the woman she always had been, but had suppressed because of William's position in the town.

Early in 1982 Mary and William were having what for them was now the usual routine. Mary had done some household chores for part of the morning while William had walked to the shops, collected his paper and a few items from the bakery and grocery shops, chatting to a couple of acquaintances who were doing much the same. Together they pottered about in the garden in the afternoon before relaxing on the patio with a pre-dinner drink.

'Are you feeling all right?' Mary asked, as they rose from the table after dinner. 'You seem a bit out of sorts. Is something worrying you?'

'No, just have a bit of a headache coming on. Think I'll take a couple of aspirins. I'll be back to normal in no time.'

'I'll clear up. You go and get your pills and I'll join you when I'm finished.'

Mary tried not to disturb William when she rejoined him. He appeared to be sleeping but she was not entirely convinced. Every so often his face screwed up with pain and his hand went up to his forehead.

She could not sit and watch any longer. 'Is it not getting better?'

William opened his eyes. Even before he spoke she knew the answer.

'The aspirin is not working. The headache is getting worse. I'll go and lie down. Perhaps that will help.'

'Good idea. I'll pop in later and see how you are doing.'

Mary could not remember William ever having had a headache that was so bad that he had had to lie down.

When the programme she was watching on TV ended, Mary crept quietly along the hallway and looked into their bedroom. William was lying on his back. His eyes were shut. Mary didn't think he was sleeping but she didn't want to disturb him. The medication would kick in and falling into a sound sleep would do him the world of good. She made her way back to the family room and the TV. She couldn't settle, but forever looking in to see how William was would not change anything. If he needed anything he would give her a shout.

Mary thought she heard something, a cry of some kind, coming from the bedroom. She rushed along the hall, becoming more and more alarmed as she approached the bedroom. She flung the door open to find William writhing about in agony on the bed. He was holding his head and sobbing with pain.

'It's all right, dear, I'm here.' She leaned over the bed to hold him.

'Get the doctor,' he managed to say. 'Call an ambulance.'

Mary wanted to remain where she was. She couldn't leave him, but that wouldn't help. She rushed to the phone, called the doctor and explained as best she could what was happening to William. He assured her that he would be with her in minutes.

Those few minutes were the longest Mary had ever endured. She was so uptight that she was loath to leave William's side, but assuming that it had to be the doctor who was at the door, she rushed to let him in.

'Quick, quick,' she blurted out as soon as the door began to open. 'You have to help him. Please, please, hurry.'

Dr Campbell was calm and professional as Mary led him to the bedroom.

'I'll give William something to ease his pain,' he said as he opened his doctor's bag.

Mary watched anxiously. William began to relax. The doctor checked his pulse, then using a small, strong light he examined his patient's eyes. Before Mary could say anything, Dr Campbell turned to her. 'I'm afraid your husband is very ill. I thought that might be the case. Before I left home, I called for an ambulance. There is little more I can do here. He will have to go to hospital.'

'But he was fine until a short time ago. What's wrong? What has happened?'

'Mrs Watson, until your husband is examined in hospital, I cannot be absolutely sure. Once we get there we can ascertain exactly what's wrong.'

There was the sound of a vehicle outside.

'That must be the ambulance. I will go and let them in.'

Mary watched as William was gently placed onto a stretcher and taken out to the ambulance. She went with him. She was in no fit state to drive.

William died in the ambulance.

42

When Lachie Mitchell, the undertaker, arrived at the manse two mornings later, Paul was not entirely surprised. Usually Lachie telephoned from his office, his home, or from the home of the deceased. Paul could always tell by the tone of his voice that there was a family member who might hear Paul's reply to anything Lachie said or asked. Coming to the manse suggested that there may be a bit of a problem that needed to be discussed, assuming that his reason for calling was to do with his business.

Paul was not aware of any member of the congregation being seriously ill and Lachie did not give out any clues as to why he had called as Paul ushered him into the study.

'Not good news, I'm afraid,' Lachie said as he sat down.

'Seldom is with you,' Paul joked.

'Aye, maybe.' Lachie was clearly not in the mood for jokes. 'I'm afraid William Watson died suddenly the night before last.'

'What? Never! I don't remember him ever having anything other than a bad cold.'

'That's as maybe, but I'm afraid when he did get something serious, it all happened very quickly.' Lachie went on to explain that William had suffered a brain aneurism, dying shortly afterwards.

The two of them talked for some time, remembering the man and friend they had known for a good number of years. Finally Lachie asked Paul if he would conduct the funeral.

'It's to be here in Burnbrae. Service in the funeral home and interment in the family grave. Who would have thought William would be beside his daughter so soon?'

'Who indeed,' agreed Paul, 'and, of course, I'll conduct the funeral.'

Many of the businesspeople of Burnbrae attended William's funeral. They were joined by customers of the bank who remembered a man who had given good advice, especially when things had not gone to plan, neighbours and friends. Mary was accompanied by members of the family. If it was unusual for ladies to be present at the graveside, it was almost unheard of for one of them to take a cord. Mary had been adamant. She had stood and watched Wilma being lowered into the ground, a memory that would not go away. She was her mother. She should have been holding a cord, the final act. It would not happen this time. She would be at the head of her husband's grave, lowering him to his final resting place.

She was composed throughout both services. She had shed an ocean of tears the night William died, and in the days since. There were no tears left. That was how it felt to her as she sat in the car on the way to The Rowans where she would meet those who gathered there. Her parents were in the car beside her. She loved them, and would do anything for them, but they could never replace William or Wilma.

Back home at the manse, Ruth expressed her concern for Mary.

'Do you think Mary was really in control of her feelings, or was she simply numb?' she asked Paul.

'I thought she was very much in control,' Paul replied. 'It couldn't have been easy for her. Two sudden deaths in such a short time, and both without any warning. If I had a hat I would raise it in her honour.'

'Paul, I am in no mood for flippant remarks. We agreed that we had seen a new Mary in recent months. I wonder if that spark has been extinguished already. And without William, how will she manage?'

'If that is the case, we will have to be vigilant and supportive, but best not to say anything to her at present. Let's wait and see. And be ready to help if she needs it.'

Within a year of William's death, the new Mary began to return much to Ruth and Paul's relief. They had been foolish to worry. Mary was truly a very strong character. She missed her loved ones, but as she had said herself, she just had to get on with it. Life was for the living, not the dead. Ruth and Paul were taken aback by her declaration.

Mary had laughed at their reaction. 'Don't worry, I am not as callous as that sounded. I simply mean that sitting in my cosy corner, feeling sorry for myself, is not what Wilma or William would want me to be doing. I miss them terribly, remember them every day, but I'll honour them by being myself and helping others, as they would have done.'

Six months later Paul was in the study when the phone rang. Ruth was busy in the kitchen. She was working away when suddenly Paul burst in.

'Mary would like a word with you.'

'Could you not just have said you would tell me anything I needed to know?' Ruth replied, holding up her soapy, wet hands. 'I'm busy.'

'I could tell you her news, but she wants to tell you in person.'

Wiping her hands on a towel as she went to the phone, she wondered what all the fuss was about. When Mary told her the news, she was taken aback. She might have speculated about Mary's new male friend, but it was still a shock to hear Mary tell her that she and George were to be married in a matter of weeks. By the time the call ended, Ruth, like Paul before her, had been given more or less the full story.

George and Mary had worked in the same branch of the bank, the one where William had been assistant manager before moving to Burnbrae. They had been friends, but only friends. George was two years older than Mary and not long after they first met he had become engaged to Jill, his girlfriend. Mary and William had announced their engagement around the time of George and Jill's marriage. Over the years they had lost touch until George turned up at William's funeral. He and Mary had been unable to say more than a few words to each other that day, but a few weeks later, George had telephoned to see how Mary was coping. In the course of that conversation he had informed Mary that Jill had died three years earlier, that he had a married daughter who had a young son and another daughter who was engaged.

They kept in touch, and very quickly the old friendship became something much deeper. Mary was a guest at George's younger daughter's wedding. As the wedding celebrations came to an end, Mary and George were dancing the last waltz. George held her close. Mary had no objection. Indeed, she held George close too.

'Will you marry me, Mary?' George whispered in her ear as the dance was ending. Mary eased herself away slightly, looked up into his eyes and replied, so softly that he barely heard the answer, 'Yes.'

The wedding took place in a country hotel close to the home that Mary and George were busily setting up. It was a quiet but happy occasion. Paul conducted the service. The speeches were short. Jill, William and Wilma were remembered with affection and gratitude. They would never be forgotten. For George and Mary this was a new beginning, another road to travel. They hoped for more happiness, but whatever lay ahead, they would meet it together.

43

Paul was now looking at the photo of Brian Thomson. What could he say? He had never known him. A life ended as it was just beginning. Trite, but true. And what of his mother and her baby? Ryan would now be nearing the end of his primary schooling. Were they happy? Were they in good health? Had Doreen formed a new relationship?

He would never know.

Like so many close pastoral ties between parishioner and minister or priest, Paul thought, once the event that brought them together was over, they went their separate ways. The pastor could only hope that he had helped them when it was needed and that enabled them to continue on life's journey, wherever it might lead.

Paul sighed as he gathered up the newspaper cuttings. Carefully he replaced them in the folder. How different life might have been for the Watsons, the Meikles, the MacCallums and Doreen Thomson. As he often did, he found himself wondering if he could have done more to help them to cope with what had happened and with what lay ahead of them as a result of that terrible accident. They had thanked him, even said they did not know how they would have managed without his understanding and support. Were they simply being polite?

These were sentiments Paul often heard as he conducted the special services of his calling. He sometimes wondered afterwards if much of what he said had any lasting effect on many of those who asked him to baptise a child, conduct a marriage or bury their dead. For many it was nothing more than the expected thing, a rite of passage, and once it was over, life would go on as it would have done whether or not Paul had been involved.

Ruth told him not to be so cynical when she heard him talk like this. She would name names and assure him that his ministry had meant a great deal to them. He had helped them over a bad patch, given advice which had been followed, comforted them when they needed reassurance, reinforced their faith when it had faltered; in short, he had done his job, and done it well.

Paul knew Ruth was telling the truth, but the doubts persisted, especially where death was involved. Benjamin Franklin had once said, 'In this world nothing can be said to be certain, except death and taxes', but how many thought about death until it happened? Even in situations where the prognosis was not good, Paul had encountered family members who had no idea what the deceased wanted at his or her funeral, and who were still hoping for a miracle. It was not something that normal, healthy people talked about. Joked about, yes, but that too was another way of avoiding serious discussion.

Paul placed the folder on the bottom shelf of one of the bookcases. Now he was remembering the early days of his ministry. He could see the parishioners in his mind's eye. One had had treatment for cancer prior to his arrival in the parish. The treatment had done so much damage to healthy tissue that he had suffered a great deal of pain for the short time left to him. The other had had no treatment other than pain-relieving drugs. She had seldom complained, but at no time had she mentioned the word cancer. A relative had whispered the word to Paul but neither she nor anyone else had spoken it again in Paul's presence. Paul and the patient had never discussed it either.

During Paul's many visits to the dying woman it had occurred to him that he too was part of the conspiracy to ensure that 'cancer', or any suggestion of death, was not uttered in her presence. He was not actually lying, but neither was he being truthful. This happened from time to time over the years. Looking back to these years at the beginning of his work in the parish ministry he wished he had been more open. A series of incidents in his own extended family was a case in point.

As a youngster he had visited the elderly relations on many occasions. They had a daughter whom he had met once or twice. She had married years later while working in England. The marriage had not worked out and as her mother by then was not at all well, she had returned home to care for her mother and look after her father. The family doctor told her that her mother was terminally ill with cancer, but on no account had she to reveal this to her father. The daughter/father relationship had not been good before and it deteriorated during the mother's illness.

When the mother died her father was livid that he had not been told the truth by either the doctor or his daughter. The relationship between father and daughter hit an all-time low. The daughter had a breakdown and was admitted to a psychiatric hospital. Her condition improved, but every time she thought she might be discharged, she would find some way to be returned to the secure ward: stealing cigarettes, being awkward with the nurses, and the whole process began again. This continued until on one occasion, when she was not in the secure ward, she managed to have an accident in the hospital grounds which resulted in her death. The cousin who had been the only one to visit her during this time was convinced that it was no accident. It was the only way her cousin could find release from the troubles she imagined she had.

Paul looked at his watch. It was almost lunchtime. He had better finish off what he was doing, but this was a subject that would not go away. That unspoken word was now referred to as 'The Big C'. Progress was being made in diagnosing it and treating some forms, but more and more people seemed to be victims to it. TB was no longer the scourge it had once been in the Western world, life expectancy was increasing, but people were still suffering, long, lingering deaths. Cancer was the one that people were most afraid of. Paul had often been asked if he had visited a certain person, a parishioner who was rumoured to be very ill. When he replied that he had, a second question followed immediately. 'Is it true they've got cancer?' Very often even Paul had not been informed of the exact nature of the illness, but from experience he knew that it was indeed cancer. His reply was always the same. 'I'm sorry, I don't know, but please remember them in your prayers.'

'Cheer up,' Ruth exclaimed as Paul joined her in the kitchen for lunch. 'This is meant to be a happy time for you. A new challenge and all that.'

'Sorry,' muttered Paul. 'I was just thinking about the way people handle death, or more accurately, don't handle it.'

Ruth seemed taken aback. 'Well, I hope your new congregation are prepared for this. Never mind the Good News, it might be all doom and gloom from now on.'

Paul knew she was joking. Well, he hoped she was, but Ruth had a point.

'That is what worries me. People either forget the Gospel teaching, or have never really believed it. And that's only the churchgoers I am talking about. What about all the others?'

'You're serious about this,' Ruth commented. 'And yes, I can see where you're coming from, but your soup is getting cold. Can we discuss this later? And, please, promise me that it will not be the subject of your first sermon.'

'Don't worry, it was never going to be my subject, the sermon is about…'

'It's all right, I would rather hear it when you're in the pulpit. Now, get on with your soup.'

The soup was good as he knew it would be, but the thoughts he had shared with Ruth would not go away. What could he do to help people have a better understanding of death, one that would help them to accept the inevitable?

The induction and introduction to his new congregation was a happy occasion, and it was made even better by having Malcom, Jennifer and their families with them for some of the time. Very quickly Paul and Ruth settled into their new home and life in the parish. These first days in any parish were always ones where everyone seemed pleased to see them. Paul knew that the novelty would wear off and people would realise that he and Ruth too had their likes and dislikes, their good points and some opinions that did not please everyone. They were human, and the sooner they were treated normally, the better it would be.

As was the custom, Paul became a member of the local Ministers' Fraternal. It was a name that would have to be revised as the move to recruit women to the ministry of the Church of Scotland gained momentum, but for the time being Fraternal was still in use. One way the members could get to know their new member was to invite him to speak on a subject of his own choosing at their monthly meeting. Paul was invited to lead the discussion at the May meeting. Easter had come and gone, but the memories of Easter 1975 were still as fresh as ever in his mind. He decided that it was as good a time and place to begin his campaign to help folk overcome their unwillingness even to think about death before they were forced to think about it due to a death in the family.

While preparing his talk, Paul realised, and not for the first time, that if the law requiring front seat passengers to wear a seat belt had been in existence in 1975, the outcome of the accident might have been different. Sandy would not have been thrown out and, although the back seat drivers would not have been wearing seat belts, if Wilma had managed to slow the car's speed, they too might have survived. There were a number of possibilities, but it was all simply conjecture. It set Paul off on another train of thought. How often had he heard the bereaved use the phrase 'if only'?

The more he thought about it, the more he realised that in ordinary life, everyone used the phrase. Hindsight was a wonderful thing, but by then it was too late. The event, whatever it was, had happened and we had to make the most of it. There was no going back. If we were fortunate, perhaps we could make amends, apologise, try again, and if not, well, we just had to get on with it. People who knew what had happened might tell us we had been unlucky, or stupid, that they were surprised that we had not seen it coming and taken action to avoid the problem. If everything went well, they would say the opposite, even wish that they had been so lucky.

This train of thought was not helping Paul in the preparation of his talk. It was to be short, an introduction leading on to frank and free discussion. The way it was going the talk might be longer than it was meant to be and the discussion that followed might go on forever. It had, however, brought Paul's thoughts back to where he had started. It was not only those who were suffering bereavement who needed to be prepared for it, their friends and neighbours also had a part to play.

How could we help our friends in their hour of need? It very much depended on how deep the friendship was and the circumstances surrounding the death. A long life, well lived with little suffering at the end and simply but sincerely expressing one's sympathy and remembering the happier times was all that was needed. Or was it? Even then the bereaved had lost a parent, a friend. Life would be different and a few would take it hard. If we used the phrase, 'I know how you feel' it would sometimes be true, but not always.

In situations where the death had been unexpected it was more difficult. There might be someone who had had a similar experience, but that would be the exception. Those who called to pay their respects would be struggling to find the right words and some would unwittingly make matters worse, if that were possible. Some could say a great deal with a handshake, a hug, or just a look, but they were the exception. Others felt they had to speak, to say something to bring comfort, show support, but so often the words they uttered seemed to those who heard them to be just that: words, but words that revealed how little they understood what the bereaved were experiencing.

Paul was thinking of some of the things he had heard from those who had suffered terrible, tragic losses. The support of family and friends was a great help but at times it was almost too much. They also needed time to be alone with each other. Within a few weeks they then wondered if they had been forgotten. The flow of well-meaning visitors stopped. It was as though their friends had held a meeting and agreed that no more visits were required. There were also those who promised that they would return to see how things were, but never did. Paul understood that it was never easy for close family members and good friends at a time of bereavement either. They too were finding it hard to cope. They had also lost a loved one, a close friend.

Paul was remembering Bob Meikle at the Harvest Thanksgiving social in 1975, struggling, but managing to keep going as he joined in the Harry Lauder song. The sentiment expressed was all any of them could do in such circumstances. They had to keep going, for the sake of those they loved and had loved. Grief was not only remembering who they had loved, it was also selfish: what they had lost. If they kept looking back, it followed that they would never move on. Nan MacCallum struggled and could have lost her battle. That she did not was perhaps only because what she did was observed by complete strangers who averted another tragedy in the family. Paul had done his best, as had others, but could they have done more? Paul was convinced that he could have done more and he knew Tom felt the same. Would it have prevented what had happened on the beach at Millside? There was no answer to that question.

Mary Watson, to everyone's surprise, had certainly kept on going. There had been many ready to criticise her remarriage, but she was happy, George was happy, and quite frankly, Paul had to admit, it was no business of anyone else.

Neither Paul nor Effie heard anything from Doreen Thomson after receiving the short letter and the two photos of Baby Ryan. Paul hoped and prayed that she and her son were happy wherever they were. Had he let her down? He had done what he could, and as sometimes happened in his work, he would never know the final outcome.

Childhood memories were happy ones, Paul was thinking. The long, hot summer days, playing in the fields around his first home, the games in the road. Cars were few and far between in those days. The milkman and the coalman with their horse-drawn carts. It must have rained, but he could not remember much about the wet days. Adulthood was different. The happy memories were always uppermost in his mind, but it didn't take much to bring back the bad ones: a date, a comment, an item in the news, and there they were. They were of other people and what had happened to them. He had been involved, but he had walked away; his life continued. Those other people had moved on too, but they always remembered that day, that day when they got the dreadful news, that day when their world fell apart, that terrible moment when it was not happening to other people. It had happened to them. The happy memories of what had been were all that remained, and with them the sadness of what might have been.

Paul's talk at the Fraternal was well received by his new colleagues. The discussion that followed was interesting but inconclusive. The fight against cancer was intensifying and new treatments and drugs were helping, but there was a long way to go. The care of the elderly and the terminally ill was becoming critical. People were living longer, but for many the quality of life had not improved. Concern was expressed that in some cases known to those at the meeting, all that was being achieved was alleviating pain as best as possible, but leaving the patient confined to a bed in a geriatric ward of the hospital. It was unanimously agreed that no one present wanted to end up in that situation; quality of life was as important as, if not more important than, length of life. Finding a cure for any illness was a worthy aim but it should not come at a cost to those who were already suffering.

As Paul left the meeting he had to agree with those who had argued that many would never accept the need to prepare for death: the death of loved ones and their own. So often that discussion was left to another time, a time that never came before it was too late. Throughout the remainder of his ministry and for a number of years after that as he helped out in congregations where there was a vacancy, he still found himself trying to help family members who just could not accept what had happened, and perhaps never would.

Accidents would always happen and some would have devastating consequences for all concerned. For those most affected, victims and relatives, understanding and supportive friends would help, but eventually there would have to be an acceptance of what had happened. Loved ones would never be forgotten, dreams would be unfulfilled, tears would be shed, but life would continue. Paul did his best to help and support those who found the going difficult, but he caught himself wanting to shake the people who insisted that it should never have happened to their family. And those who thought, 'Thank God it happened to them, not us' neither understood the nature of his God nor how selfish they were.

On a happier note he rejoiced that palliative care for the terminally ill was increasing all the time. There was still room for improvement, considerable room, but it was happening and medical research was constantly making new discoveries. If only everyone was prepared for that time, when it came, for come it would, when only memories remain.

THE END

AUTHOR'S NOTE

For fifty years death was very much part of my life; visiting parishioners nearing the end, conducting their funerals and seeking to comfort the bereaved. Average life expectancy was increasing thanks to medical research and improving living conditions for many. People pushed death to the back of their minds. Births and marriages involved planning and preparation for months and the latter in many cases for well over a year and more. Death caught many unprepared, and after the funeral not everyone was able to cope with the different feelings caused as they grieved.

WHEN ONLY MEMORIES REMAIN is not a textbook to give instructions to those who read it. It is fiction. Few of us experience a tragic event within our own family such as the one that takes place in the early pages. It happens to other people. We learn about it through the media, react, then swiftly move on. In the natural order of things people grow old, we mourn their passing, celebrate their lives, and eventually life goes on. Or does it?

Have you had a chat with a family member about what you want if you become terminally ill? Have you made suggestions about the kind of service you would like. I know, you will get round to it eventually, but there is plenty of time for it. That discussion can wait. One more little illustration.

I was standing at the open coffin, looking down at the face of a man I had never met before. There was an open hymn book lying on his chest. I turned to the newly widowed lady at my side and asked if this had been her husband's favourite hymn. She replied that she had no idea. It just seemed the right thing to do.

Think about it, have that chat and just get on with living. And make sure you leave plenty happy memories!

THANKS to:

SUSAN, of Perfect Prose (www.perfectproseservices.com), who did so much more then edit and proofread. She explained where I had gone very badly wrong and patiently explained the intricacies of Point of View and a great deal more. It was all done in a friendly and encouraging manner. Her frequent emails spurred me on and eventually I got there. Well done, Susan.

Son ALISTAIR, who designed the cover. My brief was completely different but his design was so much better. Australia was a long way to go to sit for the author's photo, but a great result, and a lovely holiday. Also for formatting help before publication. Great work, Alistair.

LAUREN, who gave me permission to use her article *The Month That Was But Wasn't.* When you read it I am sure you will understand why I wanted to include it.

ELAINE, who again read the first draft, corrected the typos, made positive comments and used up a box of tissues in the process. You may see a lot more of me now.

And finally a word of thanks to all who encouraged me during the writing of the book. It was a long wait, but you understand why. Thanks for your patience.

ADDENDUM

As I was working on my manuscript, an article written by my sister's granddaughter appeared on Facebook. I was amazed how perceptive the words were and felt that in a few hundred words, Lauren had captured the essence of so much of what I was trying to convey in my novel of over 95,000 words. I am pleased that Lauren has given me permission to share her words with you.

THE MONTH THAT WAS BUT WASN'T

On some days the words come and on some days they don't. I have been writing bits of this post here and there for a few days now, which isn't something I usually do, but writing about my life recently hasn't been the same as it usually is. I toyed a lot with even posting this, because I'm not even sure how effectively I can string together what is happening in my head. I think I am writing it more for myself than for anyone else.

November felt like a month that was but wasn't. The transition from October into the new month happened as it always does, and my weeks and weekends passed as they always do. I went to work, I translated, I answered stupid questions I had already answered at least 34 times, I went home, I watched movies, I spent time with friends, I explored, I did overly expensive food shopping, I had my usual strange dreams, I ate baked potatoes, I made long lists of what I wanted to do at weekends, I wrote. But everything changed with a phone call.

Whether through illness or tragic accident, no one should ever experience the death of a young person.

Everything stopped but didn't. I went to work, I wrote, but it all felt different. Doing my freelance writing, usually my favourite thing in the world, felt less significant with every word I forced myself to type. What was I doing sitting there telling people the top 20 DIY Christmas ornaments they could make? Why would being able to make a reindeer out of wine corks benefit anyone's life in any way? The importance in everything I was doing felt like it was melting away.

It was my sister who actually said to me that one of the most difficult things is watching everyone else move around you when you feel that you can't. That is entirely true. You have to watch people going about their daily lives as if nothing has happened, because to them it hasn't. It takes so much pushing to force yourself to make yourself like you are still moving at the same pace.

Being away from home for these past few weeks has made things an uncomfortable mix of easier and harder. Being cut off from the direct effects of what happened meant that it didn't feel real, which helped when I was alone, but meant that when I went home for just a few days everything hit really hard. I needed to do that though, I needed to go home, afraid that I would have forever been stuck in a phase of limbo had I not, stuck between what I had been told and what I truly accepted.

If you have to search the thick fog for a silver lining it is that, when life throws one of the worst things that it can at you, you realise how many incredible people you are surrounded by. In the past couple of weeks, I have grown to see clearer than ever before the people who will drop everything for me, the ones who will check on me despite us not having spoken for months before that, and the ones who will search M&S in Paris on a Friday night for my favourite things. There is a lot to be said for the people who stick by you through the hard times, because dealing with someone who is grieving is not easy. It is difficult to cope with someone's constantly changing emotions, and difficult to allow them to misdirect anger towards you. Feeling entirely helpless but still being there for someone is incredibly difficult, but it is the most heart-warming thing to know that someone would do that for you.

Life can be shit. As cheesy as it sounds, however, it can also be pretty beautiful, and in times like these you have to think about the beauty that someone has brought into your life, even if they will never do so again. There are memories to be treasured forever and things will change but you will never lose the times you once shared.

You never know what is just around the corner. Don't refrain from resolving an argument because you are too proud, don't forget to tell people how much they mean to you, don't go to bed upset with someone and don't forget that every day you have is one more than some others got.

Lauren Robertson Nov 2017

Printed in Great Britain
by Amazon